The Push & The Pull

The Push & The Pull

a novel

DARRYL WHETTER

Cover photograph by Arkadiusz Stachowski, courtesy istockphoto.com.
Cover and interior design by Kent Fackenthall.
Printed in Canada on 100% PCW paper.
10 9 8 7 6 5 4 3 2 1

Library and Archives Canada Cataloguing in Publication

Whetter, Darryl, 1971-
    The push and the pull / Darryl Whetter.

ISBN 978-0-86492-507-7

    I. Title.
PS8595.H387P88 2008   C813'.6   C2007-907359-X

Goose Lane Editions acknowledges the financial support of the Canada Council for the Arts, the Government of Canada through the Book Publishing Industry Development Program (BPIDP) and the New Brunswick Department of Wellness, Culture and Sport for its publishing activities.

Goose Lane Editions
Suite 330, 500 Beaverbrook Court
Fredericton, New Brunswick
CANADA E3B 5X4
www.gooselane.com

*For Nicole Dixon and the distance
she travelled with a small knapsack one May*

Father said a man is the sum of his misfortunes.
One day you'd think misfortune would get tired,
but then time is your misfortune Father said.
                                        — *William Faulkner*

What! art thou verily striving to stay the swing of the
revolving wheel? Oh, stupidest of mortals, if it takes to
standing still, it ceases to be the wheel of Fortune
                                        — *Boethius*

1

This one's still alive. Another smashed bird tossed onto the roadside gravel. Behind, beside, now past the twitching bird, the spokes of Andrew Day's touring bicycle continue to slice the fat light of sunset. The tall black centaur of his shadow stretches out behind the right rear pannier and spills onto dry gravel, ditch, strokes the circling bird. He stops pedalling and brakes, feels the wounded bird without looking back.

No traffic smirks in front of him or snarls in the little disc mirror dangling off his handlebar so he shoves the cumbrous touring bike into a full two-lane circle. The sharp turn forces one of the plump red front panniers back until it nearly touches his dusty grey shoe. Two days out of Halifax and he still isn't used to the weighted panniers, how they gulp in every turn.

Turning again he re-approaches the grounded bird. Stops, unclips his shoes from the tight grip of the pedals. He climbs off the bike for the first time in hours. Heat, sweat, thirst and ache leap at him as soon as he stands. Tipping back head, shoulders and ribs, he tries to unstring his bowed spine, temporarily reverses the fall of sweat. Nova Scotia valleys dip and run in front and behind, incised by the endless Trans-Canada Highway. His metal cleats crunch on stones as he approaches the bird. It moves but travels nowhere, crawling around and around in a small radius of injury.

The roadkill is constant, much more than you see from a car. Five birds yesterday. Porcupines. A skunk, two coons. Closer to Halifax there'd been cats. Wind, rain and sun, or another fast run of the tires flatten these dark mounds into puddles then finally just bumpy stains, road scabs. The bodies last longer over on the gravel, the rips and smashes almost preserved by the dust.

The side of the road. If not dead animals or fast-food litter then blown truck tires — black, shredded strips strung out for half a kilometre or more. Pedalling steadily in the recurrent backdraft of the trucks, shiny Lycra tight on his skin, Andrew needs to know how high and wide the flak of each blown tire can reach. When the trucks roar past him, he can feel his organ donor card tucked into the compact tool kit beneath his saddle.

He rests the bike's warm top tube against a humming thigh while leaning over the ruined bird. A truck thunders past, and the bird's fine, mottled breast feathers ruffle in the blast. More than a wing hangs broken. Part of the beak and, worse, an eye are so wrongly pulled. In a car he'd let the speed rationalize, anaesthetize, spirit him away. Touring now at one-quarter of that speed, he'd feel the quivering bird tethered to him on the roadside for valley after valley, share every fading tremor. He straddles the top tube without mounting the bike and raises the front forks like the plunger on a blasting box. Aiming the tire between the swollen panniers etches the bird more deeply, sews that tiny bead of an eye forever into his memory. Looking away he shoves the laden front forks down to crush the twitching bird. The bird, at least, he puts out of misery.

2

Stan was driving and Pat was in the passenger seat, both parents together, so Andy could only have been six or seven. Summer in the early 1980s. He and Mitch were in the back seat, cousins fighting over Big Jim, a large plastic action figure. Most of the doll's hard back had been cut out to form a tombstone-shaped button that drove a feeble but televisable karate chop in one arm. Countless times at home Andy had slid off Big Jim's zippered track suit top to run a thumb or fingertip over the narrow gap that surrounded the impressible button on Big Jim's toffee-coloured back. The large button was the shape of a piece of toast and constituted almost all of the action figure's smooth back. Andy half expected the button to fall out into his hands. Mystery aside, Big Jim was currently in contest. Andy and Mitch yanked, pulled and twisted the half-naked plastic man.

They'd been driving in the summer heat for two hours, Andy and Mitch fighting nearly that long. Pat had bribed, reasoned, yelled. She'd already confiscated an India rubber ball and two Micronauts. Her molars churned with the certainty that these two would fight over air so long as they had an audience. Called it. Did not. Her window was already down, so no one saw it coming. In a flash she turned and dug her hand between the boys, wrestling the undressed doll from their surprised grip. Uncoiling back through the car, she hauled Big Jim in front of their startled faces, past Stan's curved shoulder and across her own fuming chest to fling him into the wind.

The two-pitch drone of tires and engine flooded the car. Tinny AM music returned. Stan glanced once at his wife. Each of them knew red splotches were flooding the unseen plain of her chest. Stan could feel them pulse and spread as he braked. The drop of tires onto gravel was the banging of a gavel, the car's halt the verdict of a stern jury. Raising his right hand up for the gearshift, he needed to wedge the top of his left under what remained of his right triceps for extra lift. Finally, he turned his head as far as he could, not past his shoulder like Mitch's father or even Grandpa. Instead, the reach of Stan's head stopped just before his shoulder. Only his eyes could reach past the lock of bone, and they tried to ignore the tight line of his wife's compressed lips.

Even with his seat belt, Andy turned owlishly until both shoulders were parallel to the window. *Diagonal,* he kept thinking, *diagonal.* Stan, Andy and Big Jim in the distance behind him, they were a *diagonal* line. If he just rode the syllables, he could block out the rest. *Diagonal.* He could see each of three unevenly spaced points on this line.

"Where?!" Stan barked, accelerating the reversing car more and more.

"Farther," Andy mumbled, "farther."

3

Nearly two decades later, Andrew and Betty were in Stan's old bedroom, his parents' ex-bedroom. Andrew said, "My father's body went crazy," after Betty's one night in his Kingston house had become two, four, five and growing. But Stan's wasn't a body he could just talk about. He had to show her.

Andrew and Betty, each of them twenty-two years old, students. Their bodies becoming their own. Their minds finally beginning to soar.

Although Betty was okay with Andrew imitating Stan's half-paralyzed arms, she suddenly wished he would slip back into some underwear for this bit of family theatre. For the first time in their heady, intoxicating week, Betty thought this might not be the best moment for Andrew to be naked. She lay in Stan's old room and in his bed as the healthy son tried to show her the body of the sick father.

Andrew stood beside the bed where she lay prone, switching between director and fellow actor. "At times he could barely get the arm off the bed," Andrew clarified. "He only had this little bit of strength on the underside of his shoulder. You try. Use just enough muscle to get your arm above the hip. That's right. I'd say, *No cheating. Think shoulder.* Really he'd be cheating like crazy, throwing it from the hips, twisting the ribs, whatever he could. Pucker up the right hand. Pull the knuckles back toward the forearm. And roll the thumb and pinky toward each other. Feel that little pouch in your palm? *Okay, and up.* I'd have to tow the arm up, and for weeks he couldn't hold it there himself. Stiffen your arm. He had some strength in the shoulder but not much in the biceps. Picture the whole arm in a plastic pipe perpendicular to the shoulder. Forget about your elbow. Yeah, you can hold that. *Okay now, Stanner, give me some disco.*" Andrew held his own arm out stiffly and swept it back and forth from the shoulder. "*C'mon, Daddy-o, cut a circle into heaven. Bigger. Bigger.*" Accelerating her circle one minute then slowing it the next, he asked her, "Feel how my fingers can do support or resistance?" Eventually, with Betty's arm raised, Andrew's hand ceased being that of a physiotherapist. "All those years of exercising him, though, I never realized how much access this gave me to his boobs."

"Hey. Hey!" she said, swatting him.

4

Cycle enough and you will be shouted at, and with heavier ammunition than the irate *Get off the fucking road!* bellows of those jealous or proprietary city drivers whose only experience with kilometres involves a burning engine. (Let's see them piss without leaving the vehicle.) Ride long enough and you will hear *muffle, muffle, ASSHOLE!* or *muffle, muffle, SON OF A BITCH!* or that focal point of eye, if not mind: *muffle, muffle, UP YOUR ASS!* These high-wire wits only strike from a car, always in groups and usually from the rear passenger seat. Some young thug in a strip-mall T-shirt and a pair of yellowing jeans cranes as much of his beefy neck as possible out the window to bellow as the carload of superior intellect races past, somehow cracking the mechanical codes to realize that they are in a car and you, you faggot, are not. Utterly lost to the auto, they cannot see the finer points of challenge, self-propulsion or province-crushing endurance. Nor can they quite master the physics of a projected voice and a moving car. Stepping back to life before Newton, they shout *into* the wind as their fat American cars approach. These drama slaves turn to face you only for the punchline. *Muffle, muffle, FUCKER! Muffle, muffle, GET A CAR!!*

5

If Betty's ass had truly been such a sunflower, what was it doing on the cold, filthy rim of Andrew's toilet bowl?

"I'm sure you've heard some of this before," he had said to her once, walking home from campus. "Something like the science of ubiquity. Sine waves and guitar frets. Tornadoes, whirlpools. In your tub, in a river, a whirlpool is the same shape, and it's made out of moving molecules. So the shape, the form, is, what?, pre-existing in nature. You know, pattern. There's a fixed number of spirals in the face of every sunflower. You can cover up part of the sunflower and see, exactly, where the rest of the spiral will be because it's some kind of number sequence. Pine cones too. I don't just think you have a beautiful ass, the most beautiful ass ever. I look at your ass — hip becoming ass, leg becoming ass — these curves are beautiful in and of themselves, but I swear they also show me a deeper pattern, world beauty. Clearly, Plato was an ass man."

All this talk and yet after three weeks he still left the seat up. She knew as she flushed that he'd still be exactly where she'd left him, glued to the couch one floor down, head lolling as he listened to music. The rage that shot her off the damp toilet rim had time to collect as she walked back through halls, down stairs and across the entranceway, time to sharpen and gleam. The very skirt that had made the drop to the bowl so quick (would she have checked if wearing jeans?) enabled her plan.

"I was wondering," she began, crossing to where he dangled his head off the edge of the couch, "if you'd like some ass." The pleated charcoal skirt was short enough that she simply had to saw a little wool left then right. Perfectly, predictably, he cranked his body around to get under her. She cooed and did ass until his head dropped fully over the edge of the cushion and his heels climbed the couch's back.

"If you want this ass," she said, glancing back for a final check on his cramped arms and legs, "then love it!" She clamped his head between her thighs. "Love it by leaving the seat down. Got it?! Got it?!" She reached down for a few playful pinches at his cheeks. "Easy, Tarzan. Your arms are not as strong as my thighs. Look up here. Relax. Stop fighting and I'll stop squeezing. Okay? Okay? Listen. You've got bad Ass Rhetoric. If we're going to live together, don't think *right* or *wrong*. Don't think *man* or *woman*. Don't dare think *chore*. Think *more* or *less* ass. You want this ass? Keep it happy, and keep the seat down."

6

Although small, the Sunnyvale Clinic still had one long hallway Stan and the late-adolescent Andrew had to walk down, still had the fumigated smell of a hospital, that sharp bullring in the nose. Andrew was grateful when Stan tried to start whatever conversation he could.

"*Clinic* originally meant 'of, or pertaining to, a bed,'" said Stan, ever the teacher.

"Really? . . . Infectious Diseases of a Bed," replied Andrew, all the while calculating distances, worries and threats as they walked. Make the edge of that open door. Inside edge of its window. Outside.

"Advanced Summer Tennis about a Bed," Stan continued.

"Public Speaking about a Bed."

Stan was okay in the hallway, no cane, no walker. Andrew walked his slow shadow walk, certain Stan too must be swinging from guarded hope to dissolving pessimism to simple impatience.

"So," Andrew asked, "what kind of clinic is this?"

"I don't know. You've got the directions."

"I got us here, didn't I? Seriously, what kind of clinic is this? OT? Muscle? Are there muscle clinics?"

"*Kind?* Christ, I don't know."

Like toddlers who close their eyes in hopes of avoiding danger by ignoring it or people in the 1950s who turned their TVs off before undressing or having sex, clinics, doctors' offices and hospitals politely ask us to limit our knowing to seeing. In a hospital, however, a bedpan needs more than a curtain to hide. One hears so much.

Waiting in their curtained cubicle, Andrew and Stan couldn't help but hear the adjacent conversation, and each counted floor tiles to avoid eye contact.

"Cold," a boy said with a crispness either decisive or affected. "Cold. Cold. Warm."

"It was after a bath," a woman added, "and he says, 'Get that cold cloth offah me.' I felt like I'd been bit."

"Yes. Mm-hmm. Keep your eyes closed, Tyler. A few more."

"Warm. Warm. Cold."

"Okay, Tyler, rubber hammer time."

When a human shadow finally advanced across the curtain of their own examination cubicle, Andrew and Stan would've signed up for anything just to get out of there. By injecting stale urine into the muscles.... Derived from boiled rabbit spleens, this serum...

"Mr. Day. Sorry to keep you waiting. Let's get to the gear." This technician or therapist or salesman held out the antithesis of a Walkman. The unit was small and portable and obviously battery-powered, but electrodes dangled instead of earphones. "We'll show you and your — must be your son, looks just like you — we'll show you and your son how simple the Medtronic is to use. If you're satisfied and ready, you can begin building muscle tonight. Funny that a computer runs this little thing, because computers are a good analogy. You know that computers work with a series of ons and offs. So do muscles. When we want to take a bite out of a hamburger, our biceps need to contract on one side and expand on the other to lift the burger. One side's on; the other's off. Stan, you don't need me to tell you that the on and off commands your brain sends aren't always being obeyed. Unstimulated, the muscles atrophy, and there's less of them there the next time the signal does get through. The Medtronic sends a regular signal to fire those muscles all night long. We'll start with sixteen-second intervals. Ask the Chinese track team about the benefits of working out while you sleep."

Fine, but can I still grab my pecker? Andrew knew his father was thinking. Hand splint. Electrodes. The weakening arms.

The clinic had a return policy, and Stan was about to lose his unique teaching job and the generous health plan that went with it. Stan went electric.

An assistant arrived to show Andrew how to gel the electrodes, drawing rectangles and squares on Stan's shoulders and arms in black marker, assuring Andrew that the electrodes would be more pliant if the unit was allowed to run for thirty seconds before they were applied. The ink outlines remained on Stan's body for a week, as father and son absorbed wiring up Stan into their nightly routine, three more minutes after the trache tube and hand splint. By two weeks,

Andrew could usually get it done without waking Stan — Stan surely not noticing the beery breath wafting above him. By then, the square and rectangular outlines had almost worn off Stan's irregularly curved shoulders and his atrophied arms, inspection stamps fading from old meat.

One night, Andrew had sealed most of the charges, one, two, three, but then he stopped to feel the rise of Stan's bony shoulders while he slept. Defiantly arced toward the ceiling even in sleep, this was definitely, indisputably bone, the steel of the body. Andrew pressed, gently at first, trying to ease that crescent down into the untouched mattress, waiting for gravity to do its share. Instead, the remaining electrode he'd stuck to the back of his own hand suddenly spat current. "Fuck," he whisper-screamed, feeling in an instant the electric charges that didn't even register on Stan's benumbed body. Andrew's arm shot out in front of him, whipping a cord across Stan's chest. The shock stopped as abruptly as it had started, leaving Andrew panting and Stan startled awake.

"Didn't that hurt?"

"Didn't what hurt?"

"G'night, Dad."

Andrew pinched a single toe on his way out.

7

Preparing for his bicycle odyssey, Andrew had looked at a map of Canada so often that it became a folding cartoon with frayed edges, each panel of the map a tired animation cell. Eventually, his native city of Kingston, Ontario, became the tail end of a twitching fish.

Read from left to right, Canada's largest lakes depict a bird diving from the northwestern corner down to the southernmost tip, then rising again, weighted with catch. Great Bear Lake is steady in flight, the smooth hunt; Great Slave, a pair of reaching wings, a bid for air to power the dive of Athabasca, Reindeer, Winnipeg. The Huron-Michigan talons pluck Erie from beneath a dark surface to flash silver in the busy Ontario air.

Halfway between Montreal and Toronto, a middle child with starlet siblings, Kingston marks the end of Lake Ontario and the beginning of the long staircase of the St. Lawrence River. Or the end of the river and the beginning of the lake.

Eastern Canada is caught tight in a cold blue fist. The Labrador Sea is a set of straining tendons, the Hudson Strait the first length of finger past the Chidley knuckle. Thick merchant's fingers reach for Hudson Bay, that fat man urinating, draining his plump James Bay pud all the way down to Kingston.

The Gulf of St. Lawrence is a gouging thumb. Quebec and the Maritimes — Europe's first handful.

Halifax to Kingston: Andrew is biking from a thumb to a fish.

8

Syringomyelia: incurable and practically unknown, Stan's degenerative neurological disease spared him and Andrew false hope and too many hospital parking garages. As long-term diseases go, Stan's offered little medical comfort. Or intrusion. Ensnared in warping bone, he was nonetheless exempt from the roulette wheel of meds. Anti-inflammatories didn't grease his joints but corrode his stomach. Nerve stabilizers didn't cloud his thinking or tip his mood. With the exception of the arced silver tracheotomy tube in his throat and a few specialized physiotherapy devices, Stan's body was little better for four hundred years of scientific medicine.

"This is how it works," Stan said more than once. "Children get stronger."

A few weeks after Chris, Nathan and all of Andrew's school friends left Kingston to attend university somewhere else, anywhere other than where they were born, boredom or emotional self-preservation prompted Andrew to start recycling some of the lecture material he met during the day while he exercised Stan at night. Surely now he knew a few things Stan didn't.

"Otherwise, Donne's a smart guy," Andrew began while aiding then resisting one of Stan's mutinous arms. "But for a time he's just wasted with illness. Boils. Perpetual fever. In bed for months. And what does he do? Scours his soul to discover what sin he's committed. In the seventeenth century, everyone, including you, would take one look at this bod and think, *Child-diddling Satanist.* I'd probably be standing over you with boiling oil, not a helping hand."

Stan's arm weakened even more as he warmed to a story. He stopped staring absently at the ceiling and looked at Andrew. "I wouldn't have been scrutinized for very long. I would have been the guest of honour at a mattress party before I was twenty-five."

"*Mattress party?* What is this, death by orgy?"

"Not quite. Pre-industrial revolution, home was a place of work.

Cottage industry. Tenant farming. Granny's food consumption could only outweigh her productivity for so long. Admittedly, it's tough to axe the old bird directly, and everyone was marooned in the same class, same five-mile geographic radius, same, here it is, *prison of illiteracy*," Stan joked, punning on his job teaching for Correctional Services Canada. "We all understand about Gran. Invite the neighbours, unstop the ale and throw a mattress on top of her. Everybody piles on and no one person is guilty of murder. Six months later it was somebody else's house."

"Jesus," Andrew said, rotating Stan's arm with his.

"The Princess might have had a pea," said Stan. "Everybody else got Mom or Dad."

9

After her fourth consecutive night in Andrew's Kingston house, Betty awoke to an empty bed and the sound of a distant foghorn warning her: *rebound, rebound.* He'd already left for campus, so she had the house to herself. Wrapping her hands around a mug of tea, she wandered through the rooms alternately trying to tell herself that she hadn't just leapt from one relationship to another (*again!*) and that, okay, there clearly was a possible relationship here, but it was a good one. Once your pants were off, once he had crippled you with laughter, what could "take things slowly" possibly mean? "Take it slowly" was for self-help books. The heart doesn't have a throttle.

Her mother, Elaine, might say, "Take it slowly," but both of them would know it was the sort of advice she felt she ought to say, not anything she really meant or advice she'd ever followed herself. Hollywood produces enough caricatures of mothers that Betty and even Elaine have been able to laugh at various satirical portraits of a mom keen to be more hip and rebellious than her daughter. Elaine's idea of cutting the apron strings was asking Betty, "Can you come on ecstasy, or do you spend eight hours half an inch from the finish line?"

When your mom tells you she has trouble reaching orgasm if her window blinds are lowered to different heights, when she tells you this at breakfast, you either learn to raise your voice or you discover solitude and discretion. Baby boomers for parents: what a joke. Baby boomers are baby boomerangs — they keep coming back when you try to throw them away, and when they're not crying or soiling themselves, they're trying to put something in their mouths.

Elaine would forget saying "take it slowly" as soon as she'd said it, but she'd call back later to add, "Make sure you have your own key" and "You know you always have a room here."

Betty did indeed know there was a room at her single mom's house in Ottawa reserved for her, and that was one reason why she was doing her Visual Culture degree here in Kingston. Just last night she'd told Andrew her theory that the phrase *dysfunctional family* is redundant. "All families are dysfunctional."

Until her ex-boyfriend Dave and her ex-roommate Sara had suddenly rearranged the emotional furniture of her Kingston apartment, she'd told herself that living away from home she finally had a room of her own. Growing up in eight different bedrooms, each of them hers alone but only for a while, Betty had read Virginia Woolf as a teenager. Maybe Andrew was right; maybe she needed a whole storey of her own, not just one room.

Their first night, surrendering to fatigue near dawn, mouths tired as much from talk as sex, he had asked if she wanted to sleep alone, offered her any bed, any room in his house. No, that was another, more crucial virginity. She'd always found sleeping together literally much more intimate than the half-hearted and often half-assed sleeping together figuratively. Your chest my back's proper blanket. The top of your foot filling the arch of mine. "Not a chance," she had replied to his offer of separate quarters. Separate home offices, yes. Separate beds, never.

Now, alone in the house, she showered but purposely didn't shave her legs. Time for a think. Hair in a towel, a second mug of tea in her hands, she wandered through the rooms of the 1920s four-on-four-style house. Nice house, nicely cut, but neglected. Acres of hardwood floor. Eight-inch baseboards. Five-inch moulding and corner caps around every door. But the bare walls needed fresh paint and some pictures. The fossilized lighting consisted of a combination of perfunctory overheads (with unoriginal shades) or unfashionably aged lamps seemingly designed to illuminate a minimum amount of space while hiding the remainder of a tired old room in shadow or half-light. He had already tried to explain his renovational siege on the ground-floor washroom, had apologized for the half-open wall. Frankly, she didn't care. As her mom's joke went, she was looking for human texture, not architecture.

The walls were tremendously bare. Save for a large reproduction of what looked like an antique prison blueprint on one ground-floor wall, the house lacked paintings or prints. The few framed photographs that hung on the walls were old, black-and-white wedding pictures and childhood photos from half a century ago, probably Andrew's grand-parents. And they were all tucked away on half-walls and behind corners, available if you wanted to see them but never dominating a room. Upstairs she found a black-and-white graduation photo of what must have been the legendary Stan. Some kind of pioneer hair gel sculpted his hair into unmoving waves. Contrary to Andrew's descriptions of his ailing father, this smiling, late-sixties graduate looked like any old dad. Well, maybe the smile was a little lopsided, one lip barely rising. And there was some asymmetry in the eyes. Only by leaning closer to stare at his eyes did Betty see the ghost of another, absent picture frame hanging beneath this one. Moving back and forth in the bright morning sunlight, she was able to see a rectangle of less faded paint suspended on the wall like an uncrooked version of Malevich's painting *White on White*. At some point, a photo had been taken down. Mysteries and minimalism: the beginning of any romance.

In their courageous and carnal first week, she had given and received thorough orifice tours, and yet she didn't know who was (and was not) in these few photos on his walls. Well, maybe we fall in love out of time anyway. Your parents and mine are in this house and they are not. We're together in something; let's let it grow.

His bedroom had a few posters, but room after room, floor after floor, just paint, and almost all of it in need of redoing. No, wait, above his desk was a small rectangular frame. From halfway across the room she recognized the distinct shape of a personal cheque within the frame. Because she didn't recognize the name *Gamlin*, Betty noticed everything else before concluding that Patricia Gamlin was once Pat Day, his mother. Twenty-one hundred dollars on his twenty-first birthday. Given but not accepted. The framed cheque was uncashed.

In the bottom left corner of the cheque, mirroring her elegant signature at bottom right, his mother had written *Hatred is a burden* in the same graceful hand. Betty had to wait all day and well into the night before she found Andrew sitting again at this desk. She walked over, wrapped her arms around his broad shoulders, nodded at the framed cheque and asked, "Anything you want to tell me?"

10

Surrender to the ride's pain. Graft your breath to the pain. Indissoluble from every endurance sport, synonymous with the very word *endurance*, is one fundamental command — breathe pain. Make the pain your breath. Stretch your lungs with pain. Betty, an occasional practitioner of yoga, once gave Andrew a yogic prescription for "nowness." "Your body is the past; your mind is the future. Your breath unites them in the present."

Now, every aching moment of now, his bike trip is a debate of pain. Any desire must now win approval from the legs. To want is to sweat.

Any desire is a weight. A small bag of fine white powder. The well-folded map. A contraband novel, that decadent slab of unnourishing, non-warming mass, squats with its corrupt weight in the front right pannier. A second novel would've been dead weight, fire fuel long ago. Worse, Betty's twenty-seven European postcards may not be able to stow away much longer from the priorities of cycling. Each towering hill asks three questions of everything he carries: Water? Food? Warmth? Only the worst hills make him doubt his jar of Nutella.

And what's this? Irregularity, the ultimate vegetarian affront. After days in the saddle, he resents the gluey oatmeal's cling to the inside of the compact pot-cum-bowl. Easily thirty millilitres unused. Mountain Equipment Co-op's got to offer a little camper's rubber spatula. Wouldn't take much space. Just a few grams. Make it a fin on the back of a fork or knife.

The more he eats, the less he hauls. Magic gut: just add endless climbing and five grams of oatmeal will disappear. Dehydrated soups, vedge chili, peanut butter he transferred to a zip-lock bag. If only he could get decent cheese. And wine. Betty's right; France, it should've been. *Rouge ou blanc chaque jour.* We could have travelled together and stayed together. Maybe.

Behind him in Halifax is an MA he started in part to maintain ownership of the Kingston house that hangs, distantly, in front of him. His father's house. His mother's ex-house. The house his father did not want him to keep. The Andrew-and-Betty house. Study in Halifax to keep a house in Kingston. Betty did notice the twelve hundred kilometres separating house and MA. "Grad school," she said more than once, "snooze button on the alarm clock of life."

Now he hauls one bag on top of another. Jersey pockets, saddlebags, panniers. Bag, bag, bag. Oatmeal in the pannier's top inner pocket, knife in a long jersey pocket, emergency blanket in the bag beneath his saddle. Hydration sack lashed to the rear. Packing and unpacking each night, he's begun to think in three dimensions. The snug grenade of the stove rides behind his right foot. At back left, the mess kit brawls for all space. Clothing — fluid, co-operative, sometimes another wrapped defence against rain — is spread all round, tarped here, wound there. Four condoms, those coins of freedom, entrance tokens to the land of just in case, shuffle around the waterproof matches in a pocket. The things he carries.

Thanks to condoms, he isn't carrying home any surprises to Betty. That is, if he ever sees her again. The Kingston house he's biking to may no longer really be a home, and Betty may not even fly back from her European Grand Tour. They've been apart eight months now, as much his fault as hers, if not more, and yet he still hopes hers hasn't been a Grand Tour of hooded European cock. Dropping E on Ibiza or sunning topless on the Canary Islands, strangers handing her drinks. Please have used a condom.

Sexually transmitted diseases are a contemporary version of the ancient Greek gods, although they cackle and scheme atop a shorter Mount Olympus. Sure-footed Chlamydia wanders on her rocky shore. Lame Gonorrhea stirs in his dark cave. Herpes on winged sandals doth fly. At least it isn't flying to Kingston.

Habitually, Andrew still thinks of the twice-contested Kingston house as their home, his and Betty's, not his and Stan's — certainly not his parents' — even though that house became too constraining for Betty and too heavy for him. The things he carries.

Think of the knife. Clipping in after breakfast, wobbling up to highway speed, he flicks the chrome pig's tail of the corkscrew open and shut, open and shut as he rides, wondering who thought to thread a removable eyeglasses screwdriver here into its centre. Who stared up the empty helix and saw millimetres of unused space? Two nights ago, when he sawed most of the handle off his toothbrush to shed a few grams, he wanted to know who invented dental floss. Who saw that contested space and thought of how to reach it?

Barking flies through the air like a fist. Given time, man on bike will outrun a dog. Given how?

Two o'clock, gaining, as tall as a pony. Black and tan fur streaming back from bared teeth, from chomping bark. Down, down, down on the pedals, Andrew is up, standing, pumping, all but leaping from the cage of the frame. Time must become maximum distance. He must spin out his road more quickly than the dog devours his lawn.

Acceleration is easier on four legs. Sans panniers, transported to the Prairie, Andrew could crank up to fifty-five, fifty-seven kilometres an hour on the flats. But not quickly. And never four-belly pregnant, panniers swollen with gear. Legs, legs up and down past side dog, ditch-in-one-leap dog, just-ahead-of-gravel dog.

The human skeleton is bipedal, allowing us to walk upright, freeing our hands and prompting us to see the world more than we smell it. A bicycle de-evolves the body, collapsing the straight angle of torso and thighs into the acutely angled hips of a quadruped. The multiple vertices of a bicycle frame fold your hips and force you to mime your hunting-gathering ancestors. On a bike, you pedal out of the biped.

Saved by a rare stretch of flat Maritime road, he has time enough to regard the dog as another stamp in his passport, another border in car country. Between cities, Halifax cast off behind him and Truro hanging in the distance, he has biked beyond confined dogs. In rural Nova Scotia, few people expect (or tolerate) a pedestrian, let alone a half-breed, someone on a vehicle not in one, someone earning his own speed. In the country, many dogs are left unchained, too slow for cars but fast enough for anyone who steps onto their property. Several touring sites recommend a canister of pepper spray strung off the handlebars or a length of wooden dowel lashed to the top tube.

Without the first barks he'd have been nabbed, teeth into a bare, stubbly calf. *Canis familiaris.* No wolf, no predator, would bark then charge. *Here I am. Danger on your right.* Dogs bark for people, not themselves. We wanted them to scare from a distance. We wanted loud terror, and we got it.

11

Week after week, Stan would leave a nearly identical version of the same list of errands on the kitchen counter for Andrew. Groceries. The dry cleaners. A utility bill to be paid. Stan's disease itself, his quarterly losses, his trajectory of despair, was recorded on those lists, deprivation and need written out shakily on the backs of used envelopes. Finally, after months of little change, the seismogram of these lists would record new tremors of disease.

Andrew had to track Stan down in the house to clarify an unprecedented request.

"That's right, a leg bag," Stan confirmed.

"We're talking piss luggage here, yes?"

"It's about time."

Andrew didn't need to look at the jaundiced plastic juice pitcher beside Stan's bed or recall the radius of stains on the bathroom tiles he had washed two days ago for this to seem like a good idea.

"And where, pray tell, would I look for such a gem, better Samsonite dealers everywhere? Boutiques for the executive on the go?"

"The White Staff on Bagot."

Driving downtown, Andrew wondered why they had waited so long. Why, he asked the radio, the dashboard and four red lights, had they endured curious, piteous and even disdainful looks in public washrooms as he guided a moaning, horse-eyed Stan. Why, he wanted the sliding pharmacy doors to tell him, had they been damned by stairwells and hastily used car doors for inadequate cover, with no discussion of alternatives? Why? Why?

"Size?" the pharmacy clerk immediately asked.

A condom catheter would roll over the penis to feed a hose that travelled down the leg. A vinyl bag would be secured to the inside of the ankle with elastic straps and plastic clips. Mute packaging and large print assured Andrew that Sur-Way Valves™ and Quick-Clip Clamps™ would allow drainage with or without removal from the ankle. The clerk hovered about while Andrew read, as if he himself couldn't distinguish large or medium from senior. That or perhaps the Clear and Away™ was a known crowd-pleaser on the gag shoplifting circuit. Either way, Andrew didn't like being scrutinized as he contemplated manageable capacities, sterilization options and recommended adhesives. His concentration slipped from the mental image of Stan's tired old scrotum and pole to the clerk's rectangular black shoes, from his *Steven* name tag to the urine assembly line.

"I'll need to borrow a phone," he said. Walking up an aisle, though, he realized this wasn't true. What would calling Stan do? Fling awkward words between them when Andrew already knew the lay of the paternal land. No, sizing up his father was better than asking his father to size himself up. "Wait. Just give me a minute here." He'd probably miss the phone anyway.

A small August wedding was The Bag's baptism of fire. Paul Tucker, Stan's old friend and fellow teacher, and now his boss's boss at Correctional Services Canada, was remarrying in a yacht club. Ever an attraction, Stan and Andrew stood out even more in the small, well-dressed crowd. Andrew bolted his beer quickly at the start of the reception to chase a buzz that wouldn't threaten his chauffeur's duties at its close. He built two plates at the buffet, joked in line with young moms about eating for two. The thick brownie really was managed best if he simply held it up for Stan's periodic chomp. Feeding accomplished, Andrew helped Stan to his walker and guided him to a panoramic corner before nipping off for a pee himself. Three men shared the washroom with Andrew.

"Quite a job," one consoled, vigorously wiping his hands with numerous paper towels. Andrew pressed his toes deeper into his shoes and pictured a long row of bar shots, then saw car keys and Stan's walker chucked into the sloshing lake.

Returning to his dad, to reality, he found Stan grinning like a peashooter champ. "Okay, big boy, ante up."

"You just missed a Samaritan offering his services," Stan said. "Nice guy, stepped out of the crowd to check on me while you were gone, but he'd caught me midstream. I could barely utter a word. My eyelids must have been fluttering." Stan went on to make astronaut jokes and request another beer.

12

The students, their grandparents die. Betty and Andrew hadn't been together for six weeks when her father, Jim, phoned unexpectedly one night, early in the fall term, to say that her grandfather had died. Betty had tried to return the phone to its cradle, had planned on shutting a bedroom door or catching some air in the backyard, but there was Andrew, his arms enshrouding hers. He said something, but she just concentrated on the feel of his voice, the deep buzz of it against her cheek. He was kissing her hairline and temple, kissing beside those small tears. Neither of them could have predicted that, at least temporarily, he'd appreciate the death.

"My dad's all alone out there," she said. "At least, I think he is. Even at the best of times he'll go two weeks without even going in for groceries."

"So let's go," Andrew said, proposing that they drive immediately to her dad's isolated and distant lake house.

Her tears shifted gears, the last few stumbling out with a kind of relief. By the time they had piled into his car with their sweaters and loose pants, with their quiet CDs and their Thermos of heavily milked coffee, death rolled around like an unseen marble, small but hard, knocking in the corners. The smile they traded in the dashboard light stretched for miles, allowed them to share the dark night like a blanket. If they hadn't had to stop for earplugs, he would surely have kept his hands on the wheel.

Thirty minutes into the intended three-hour drive, he'd been thinking that a long night drive was the emotional equivalent of alcohol, fuelling not just lust but love, when some part of the muffler dissolved or tore away and loosed the car's latent snarl. In a stroke, the compact sedan became a pack of Harleys, a laden B-52. Their music was lost to the engine's roar. The singer, not their muffler, seemed to fall off behind them.

Eyebrows shot up and chins dipped in alarm. He had to raise his voice, "I was literally about to say, if only we could drive like this all night."

"Yeah," she yelled back, "me too.... Are we going to explode?"

"Any minute now."

The roar was constant, inescapable, an oil spill. Music was stripped to faint, insectile percussion. "This is what a car really is," he tried to say, meaning *the true machine* or *shouldn't we admit to this*, but his yell carried only data, beat him back into a mute cave. Twenty minutes ago, they'd been a bubble, a speeding island of grin and stroke. Now, each minute in the roar pushed them further apart, raised a Berlin Wall between them, tolled the bell for Grandpa.

"We'll pass Peterborough soon," he announced. "I think we should look for earplugs."

"Yeah. Okay."

"Earplugs and a snack?"

New to death and how reliable the body's hungers can be, Betty replied, "Yes, surprisingly. Yes."

Leaving the highway, hunting out a late-night pharmacy and then an open restaurant, they were almost an hour before they returned to the rebellious car.

"In ways, I don't feel like we're going anywhere," she said, turning to survey the strange dark town around them. "Just driving."

Back in the car, both chins tilted toward the outside shoulder, then the inner, for a shy insertion of the pharmacy's foam plug. As the plugs began their conical expansion, he was hit with a feeling of intrusion that quickly flipped into a palpable bond with her. They were smiling as the engine threw its muffled roar. Foot bottoms, buttocks, backs of thighs and tailbones felt a roar their ears heard only distantly. Half-deaf, they slipped back onto the black highway.

Twenty, thirty minutes into the mute, buzzing drive, darkness wrapped around them, they were raked by vibrations, two spines and all limbs sprouting from the same crossbar of felt sound. The right half of the back of his pelvis was indivisible from the inside of her left knee because of movement, metal and a sound buried in touch. As soon as he reached fingers to her knee, another circuit opened from his shoulder blade to that stretch beneath her ear. This stir possibly his alone, Grandpa Death and his rickety bones still riding in the back seat, Andrew kept his eyes tunnelling into the road as he raised his hand. Betting this brief farm, he planted his fingertips in a crescent around her ear and dipped his thumb to stroke her neck. Down and up again, a fat swimmer doing three-inch laps, kick-turning off her earlobe. When two became five, when thumb became a whole hand clasping the back of her skull, he finally risked a glance, sending his eyes, but not his face, in two shotgun passes. Her eyelids were fully dropped, but there was no disapproving scrunch around the sockets. The visible nostril had sharpened into an arc. So, up went the whole hand, each fingertip a salon wash, the palm a tilting crown. Nearly deaf, he could now feel each hair, swept worlds with a scouring nail. Provinces of her body sent or received fibre-optic flashes of greeting, challenge and need. Did he tend, or light, the fire in her far hip? Was her solar plexus pulsing before, or after, he plucked its central jewel?

Nothing was said as he took a dark exit, finally moved his head in search of an isolated lane. She slid her seat back, lowered it. When he climbed the Pyrenees of the handbrake, she reached first for his ears and thumbed the plugs in deeper while dragging his mouth into neck, chest. After just six weeks, this wordlessness was already strange. Here in the deaf blackness there were no requests or proposals, no worded bait given or chased, not a single joke. Only after, her last kiss cooling on his neck, as the night's chill air reasserted itself along fogged windows, was speech risked. "It's called the euphoria of survival," he said, his mouth to her full ear.

13

In the climb out of one valley there is always a distinct point at which curiosity about the next valley is abandoned. These recurrent, successive Maritime climbs are, and are not, his bike trip. As the burn of a climb lengthens and deepens, he is exiled from his past. He starts each climb as an individual ego with unique memories, specific hopes and a destination. But then, legs aflame, he bikes out of subjectivity and into pure pain. In ways, every onerous half-metre of inclined asphalt is a mirror. He chose this suffering. He wants it. But he can't want this. Eventually, he is only a sweaty binary of more or less pain. The bike is a switch on the wall of the hill, inching its passage from *climbing* to *climbed*.

His switch flicks just before the apex of a hill. The triumph of a climb. Memory and rationality return to him as he surveys the next valley. Already, just three days into this trip, he has developed a habitual gaze for each new valley. First, he checks out the next climb, appraises the next hill from atop the current one to get his pain forecast. Then, his eyes glance along the middle of the valley, not actually looking at what's there, just sweeping through to check for a restaurant. Can I get more water? Time for eggs? What are the odds of a milkshake? Only then does he finally examine the descent he's rolling into, weighs his conqueror's spoils. Descending, he is washed by speed. His eyes avoid lingering on any single point, as if staring too closely at house, farm or derelict store might slow his accelerated speed, might diminish the cleansing wind. Too elated to pay attention as he enters a valley and too consumed to do so as he leaves, he only becomes fully attentive at some point just before the drop levels out. Some valleys are long and invite observation, contemplation, even social reflection. Two different Protestant churches in a single valley, us and them behind nearly identical white clapboard buildings. Other valleys are more fickle. The inviting drop. The spurning climb.

The longer a valley is, the more likely he is to look left and right, to pry his gaze out of the road's grey chute. So only now, inertia slipping from his pace, the next climb beginning to loom, does he notice a bright orange periscope breaking the green wave of the next forested ridge. A fire tower.

Although the fire tower isn't very close to the highway, it is in North America, so there's no doubt it's accessible by car or truck. If they can reach it, so can Andrew.

His pannier zippers begin to jiggle as he forsakes the highway asphalt for a gravel side road. Minutes later, these same zippers beat out a steady percussion as he leaves the side road for the half-overgrown bush trail he hopes runs up to the fire tower. The tower would be useless if it were in a valley, not on the peak of a ridge, so he must now scale the same height as if he were still on the reliably homogenous asphalt but must do so on the wildly varied terrain of a switchback bush trail. Dirt crumbles and coughs beneath his crawling tires. Every skittering rock and each additional turn pose an unavoidable question: why? Because he wants to see the forest, not just the trees. Because a map isn't an adequate image, and he wants to see where he's headed. Because bike and tower are both simple metal exoskeletons, every bone naked. Cars are still audible on the highway below him, racing past with their closed doors and lowered hoods, with their unseen chambers housing unfelt explosions. Metal and sweat send Andrew crawling away from human evolution into ancestral skeletons and non-electronic technology.

A circular saw blade whirrs inside each thigh. Water sloshes down the croaking pipe of his throat. Away from the highway's busy trough, the May air hangs still on the trail and lets the midday sun find its strength. A sharp turn and a steep ascent obscure the once-looming tower. Finally, a scimitar of curve and climb thrusts him toward the tower's multi-legged base.

The uniformly long grass of this small, treeless clearing is infrequently cut. Barely pedalling now, lungs scraped clean, he reaches, touches and finally stops at the tower's warm metal legs. He unclips, drinks again.

Dismounting, he is tackled by the usual pain. The cupboard doors of his trapezoids have sprung their fit. The back of each knee straightens onto a coarse grinding wheel. His shipwrecked pelvis.

Like those of many urban fire escapes, the ladder on the fire tower does not extend all the way to the ground. The deterrent gap of roughly three metres would be enragingly anticlimactic had he slogged here on foot. As is, he's able to roll the bike beneath, climb onto its top tube and debate a tremendously unwise standing vertical jump. He just makes the standing jump from the bike to the ladder's lowest rung. The padding of his cycling gloves, the gloves that he forgot to remove, is palpably soft, so clearly vulnerable, so much like his own skin amid the stronger ribs and tibia of the metal ladder and its surrounding cage. Fists just catching, idiocy barely confessed, he finally rests, hanging, his cramped shoulders easing apart in the still air. Ascending the ladder, he leaves his helmet on despite the sweat gathering within it.

A cylindrical cage of metal ribs surrounds the ladder. His laboured exhalations are almost chuckles, not quite tears, at the comparison between his body crawling up this metal chute and the diseased, syringomyelic swelling that rogue chromosomes caused in his father's spinal cord. Here in the bright spring air, curved metal all around him, Andrew is now the clambering disease, the neurological saboteur, the ugly face of fate. Two-thirds up, he pauses on the ladder in a spot comparable to the fourteen-inch-long surgical scar that transected his father's back. Simultaneously, he can see the struts and beams of the tower and the distant trees of Nova Scotia, or maybe even New Brunswick, and also that unforgettable scar on a now dead body, that pale record of decades-old neurological surgery. He had looked at the scar thousands of times before he learned that the pre-programmed swelling of Stan's spinal cord could have ruined him in other ways, depending on its location along the height of his spinal cord. A stop on this rung of the ladder took most of Stan's sense of touch, his balance and half the mobility of his arms and legs. A swelling lower down could have taken the legs completely, could have folded Stan into a stained wheelchair. Andrew resumes his climb, ascending the rungs and vertebrae of hearing and sight. Stop here and I'll freeze you blind. Stop here and I'll 'tard your brain.

Preoccupied, he's almost surprised to reach the top of the ladder so quickly, to perch beneath the bulbous skull of the tower's observation booth. Bringing up his knees and leaning into the ladder's ribbed back, he's able to wedge himself into a sitting position. A few bolt-heads press uncomfortably into his back, but the legs take the weight without complaint; these thighs know a burn. A breeze washes over him. The dense green forest flows ceaselessly below. Cool, piny air wipes the sweat from his face and limbs. Up here, sunshine brightens the air without cooking it. Weather and light are perfect for his first, perhaps his only, view from a fire tower. A locked fire tower.

The trap door above him rises barely half an inch before snagging on a bolt or hasp snug on the other side. Stupidly, he tries pressing harder with one hand. It's obvious the incomplete base of the ladder and this hidden lock are designed precisely to keep people like him out, but how many people willing to climb one hundred metres to see trees really need to be kept out? Indignantly, he steps down a rung, scrunches his neck to get his helmet under the door, then lifts with both legs. Although the wooden door strains around the central lock, it remains steadfast.

That the caged ladder is a straight tube of such uninterrupted length he could now become his own lethal injection shooting down its syringe should be discouragement enough against an inverted kick. Hands locked on a rung, he draws his knees up to his chest and then rolls his head and shoulders back until he is hanging upside down. Now that he can stare up at his clenched hands and, beyond them, his feet resting against the door, he has several competing thoughts. One, this might just work. Your legs are strong. You'll feel it if you can't hold the strength of the push. Two, this is the second dumbest thing you have ever done. Three, if you get yourself killed, you'll definitely never see Betty again, let alone reconcile or get her pants off or learn anything. Four, this inverted kick is more than the upper- and lower-body contest you discovered on a mountain bike with Mark.

With this tour, he has biked into his fourth distinct mode as a cyclist, progressing from the independent travel of childhood to the high-adrenalin, whole-body workout of mountain biking to the leg and lung work of road riding and here to the least popular: touring. Now he is both road rider and pack horse.

On narrow mountain bike trails in Kingston, he had learned to dip his chest and steer with his oarsman's abs. His shoulders and arms shoved down against the force of calves and thighs. Pinballing down a switchback hill, rear tire practically brushing his ear, he discovered the secret tool of the bike frame: those alloyed angles were designed to split his body in two, to pit north against south in a wrestling match between arms and legs. He learned all of that one muddy spring, riding day after day alone or with his riding friend Mark, who introduced him to new trails and more.

Now, hanging upside down from a fire tower, Andrew can only dwell on the past so long. He is inverted and exerting, head to the distant ground, legs pushing above him. Setting the soles of both shoes onto the hatch door, he makes a light diagnostic push of steady force. To kick or to shove? That is the question. A shove would be far more powerful, both legs, and he could use the glutes and thighs, the body's biggest muscles. But that could also be too much force, a squat and heave strong enough to send him hurtling down. Perhaps a single, knee-to-toe whip would be enough.

He shoves his way into a sweaty epiphany. The curved metal in his hands, and the controlled shove of the legs, this isn't just strength, but new strength — the leg strength of this trip, of its training and daily annihilation. Holding metal and himself, he rediscovers one of the dumbly profound lessons of exercise: the body can be changed.

The door and his shoulders begin to burst. As the door pops open, his back straightens completely and his forgotten jackknife, which had been tenaciously hanging in the lip of a jersey pocket, falls away. Fully inverted, he's able to watch the red knife plummet down the tube of ladder and cage, then finally bounce off a rung and land somewhere beyond his bike.

Uncurling and climbing up into the tower's panoramic brain, he has much to contemplate along with the view of rolling green hills. That he chose to smash his way in to get this view. That the survival knife has always been on his body and never consigned to a pannier; that he has felt it there as he walked into every restaurant, every men's room. That knife, which was once, briefly, Betty's, is now missing. And the search for it will be a self-inflicted delay. Better enjoy the view.

Shelves run down two sides of the panoramic windows. Pennies, paperclips and tiny scraps of paper litter the unclean and graffitied shelves. Only in a dusty corner of the floor does he find half a pencil. The slips of paper are about the size of a cinema ticket. He has just enough space to print *sorry* and draw an arrow beneath it, but stops himself before he lays it on the floor beside the popped door. The useless word. The wordy word.

Up here, as at a campsite, as anywhere, really, there is no garbage can. He tucks the tiny note into a jersey pocket before lowering himself back onto the ladder. Climbing down, *sorry* at his back, he begins looking around, hoping to find the knife without undertaking a full forensic spiral. *Self-inflicted delay* implies there's a rush, a schedule even, as if the remainder of his MA isn't on indefinite hold back in Halifax (and his ownership of the Kingston house along with it), as if he even knows whether Betty is flying back on her original ticket or flying back at all.

14

In high school, Andrew started arriving early to Stan's bedroom to catch the late-night news on television. He'd wind up there to do Stan's trache tube and the hand splint anyway. By his final year, electrodes added to the nightly routine, Andrew had grown to feel both independently and vicariously lazy just lying there on one side of the bed watching the news.

"Do you need to see this or just hear it?" he asked, knowing that on the weekends Stan routinely glanced at a newspaper while the TV news droned.

"I can usually get by with just listening. Why?"

"Gotcha. Get your butt down and your arm up. Nightly reps."

"Whoopee."

Andrew's smooth arm, still bronze from summer, raised a crooked, pallid one. Circles for the shoulders — guide them, stretch them, resist them.

A few weeks later, the news circus found another euthanasia case to salivate over, legal cases, not policy or debate, being the only way North Americans contemplate euthanasia. When a woman's husband and parents spoke through different lawyers at different times into the same microphones from the same networks, Andrew once again stood at the intersection of Stan's slow body and his quick mind.

"Not to sound too eager here," Andrew asked, "but have you thought of a living will?"

"Living will?" Stan replied. "What do you think you are?"

"Seriously. Ol' Hamlet Senior could have spared a heap of bodies if he'd had a better will."

"Hamlet Junior could have spared a heap of bodies if he'd been clear on what he wanted. If *he'd* had a better will."

"Just think about it, okay? A living will."

"I have thought about it," Stan said conclusively. "I'm saving all my fire for my *dead* will."

15

Near Sackville, New Brunswick, bike and body smashed by cross-winds, Andrew tries to keep Betty's postcards from the devil's hand. Here, finally, is the cluster of radio towers that throw CBC Radio around the world. This anticipated landmark, this thrusting metal hand, marks his passage into a second province much more than did the flags and fake lighthouses of the official Nova Scotia – New Brunswick border one valley behind him. Here, at dusk the towers already glow with red lights. A dozen ruby rings flash from this reaching metal hand. What wired analogue technology of expansions and contractions transforms that metal into a radio transmitter while his bike frame rides by mutely? Betty, cock an ear, and I'll crank the miles, spin this buzz into song.

Read, fingered and sniffed as they arrived over the winter at his drafty Halifax apartment, and now read, fingered, shuffled, flipped and rotated at each nightly camp, Betty's European postcards have stowed away in his innermost pockets of memory. Their very inclusion here in the panniers, despite their useless mass, attests to his obsession for them, and yet that obsession makes the artifacts themselves less and less necessary as they become flashcards of memory. Paris: here I go. Turkey: you're an idiot. Amsterdam: something about fucking, either *Let's fuck* or *Why aren't we fucking?* or *I need a fuck* or *Where the fuck are you?* Copenhagen: who am I?

Originally grateful for his one novel's reliable escape, for the flights of nightly fancy off his dull Therm-a-Rest, he is now routinely dumb with fatigue within minutes of leaving the bike, eyes fluttering then not so much shutting as rolling back into his skull. The novel he tries to raise above his prone chest feels as heavy as a tombstone. Fingers, wrists and elbows launch labour grievances against after-hours work, for work beyond job description. Still, he can't understand the people who ride without a novel. There are numerous blogs by riders who tour with video cameras but nothing to read. Enervated daily, he needs to find a story, not try to make one.

Compared to the heavy brick of the novel, the postcards are oblong fleas, little more than air and ink held in a rectangle. The cards have become his gospel, his tarot. This *homme pendu*, hung from the frame or tacked out on the Therm-a-Rest, sorts and resorts the cards each night, as if one spread or another, one new formation of image or text will spell out some message other than *You made the wrong decision*.

Even the address and postmarks are indicting. Dodging Stan's will, he tried to keep the Kingston house by doing a graduate degree, but three provinces away. Betty, and every smug European man she has met, knows that his studying in Halifax is an absurd way to try to maintain ownership of a house three provinces away. Her cards are mailed from every corner of Europe and are addressed to a Halifax apartment he has now vacated. He's carrying them back to Kingston and a house abandoned by everyone he has ever loved.

The briefest of cards, Barcelona, Gaudi's basilica, took no will to memorize, could not, in fact, be unmemorized.

> *We didn't break up.*
> *We broke down.*
> — B.

16

One September Friday, when Betty and Andrew were still only classmates and campus acquaintances, Betty arrived at class in the wrong clothes. The short tweed skirt was both attractive and ironic, simultaneously swish and marm, but the chocolate-coloured tights — delicate and flagrant with every wound — weren't right for the battlefield that had become her apartment. Thin tights weren't armour enough against her roommate Sara or her boyfriend Dave. Her ex-boyfriend Dave. Thankfully, Professor Klonk was even more late than usual, no doubt held up by a late-breaking Beowulf news flash. Somehow Betty sat there, books on desk, nostrils ostensibly pumping air.

Andrew stole regular glances at her from across the mid-sized classroom. It wasn't that he had never seen her tired or irritable before. He knew from staring at her four thousand times that her left eyebrow was frequently a sickle sharpened on the whetstone of contempt. The plump bow of Betty's top lip would regularly flatten with rage as Professor Klonk tried to jump-start her biblically interminable lectures with some inappropriate, half-remembered example before stumbling along to an inconclusive end. From over her shoulder, he had watched her ignore the so-called lecture and read on, public and private life fenced with a turning page. Glancing at her reading in the library, he once saw tired fascination split into a silent chuckle. Pretending to browse the paperbacks and used CDs outside Of Things Past Antiques, where she worked, he had watched her enduring customers behind the counter and had occasionally gone in with a joke. Never, though, had he seen anything like this grey retreat around her eye sockets, this charcoal smudging around eyes that remained sharp and darting.

He switched seats conspicuously to move beside her and leaned in just a little before he spoke, "Betty, you should skip class and let me buy you a coffee."

"Should I now?"

"Yes, right now. Maybe ol' Klonk is late just so we can go. C'mon, Chez Piggy."

She reached for her books.

Walking downtown alongside him, looking at him obliquely in the mid-morning sun, she wondered. This wasn't the first time she had checked him out. In shorts, his tanned legs had a hundred facets of tight muscle. One look at the neat little box of his hips and ass and she could already feel the flatness of his stomach, the smooth line it gave to everything above and below. Forced out of her apartment by Sara and Dave, maybe she could cling to this Andrew for a while, anchor herself to his long back until the next disaster sent her spinning.

Something had mauled her and still her shoulders rolled back as she walked, hung off her spine like sailors high in the rig. She was in mid-fight, not defeat. Clouded eyes and gemstone cheekbones alike were raised to the late September sun.

Only when they finally sat for their cereal bowls of milky coffee did doubt draw a bead on her. Seeing fatigue, or worry, scurry across her face, Andrew leapt into a surprising but accurate British falsetto to superbly imitate the poisonous moth that was Professor Klonk's trademark voice. Aspirating viciously, enunciating perfectly while being dismissively inaudible, he forcibly recalled a chalky voice from a memory lane of now inaccessible British libraries, a youth traded for a trio of dead languages and a Merrie Englande free of the lager louts and footie of today's living isle.

"Bet-TEA, should you FEE-al your ed-jew-KAY-shun in lit-err-a-CHURE in PEAR-el, revisit Don JEWan before finDING me during my pos-TED office hours."

"Thank you." Suddenly she wanted to nibble him. His bottom lip. His cheek. She pushed a biscuit around her plate twice before she brushed a few crumbs into the bowl and erupted. "If you were to stop and ask me if a boyfriend was more or less likely to cheat with my roommate, I'd have to say more. That possibility grows with every shared bottle of wine, every thong hanging in the shower. I came home from a cancelled class and walked right into that . . . possibility, that possible life. I hate that they got to choose, that I got slotted. I knew in the entranceway, that crashing car kind of knowing. Even the question was slow, naive. What's that noise? They're fucking, fucking."

"You're not crying, not even close."

"No. No. Housebreak, not heartbreak. I knew Dave was a dork. He's got more hair products than I do and walks around campus outfitted like he's going trekking for three weeks in Nepal. This degree, what, forty grand over four years? Like most people here, Dave treats it like a very expensive passport stamp. Stand in line. Pay. Welcome to the middle class."

"And your roommate, this —"

"Sara. Friends since late high school. Maybe that's the problem. I don't know. Well, look, fourth year, I do my work, okay. Every day my bag's got enough books to crush a pony. I'm practically on shift at the library. With my degree, the puzzle's finally coming together: what I'm capable of, what I'm still reaching for, even a bit of the why. Somehow, sometime, Sara chose TV, design magazines and drinks instead of homework. I encouraged her a little, pointed a few things out, but hey, it's her life. When I work at home, though, I get this vibe like opening a book somehow criticizes her. I thought only mothers are this egocentric... We had vague plans of going to Europe together this summer. I'm not upset because that's not going to happen or that Fucko's out of my life; I'm upset because neither of these things should have been in my life in the first place. They're right, they really are. They're the ones who should be together."

"Sometimes we change our address to change who we are."

With the miracle of ten dollars and three blocks they turned their coffee into wine, late-morning wine. Café, liquor store and the Wolfe Island ferry landing were just a few negligible blocks apart. On one of the ferry's secluded benches, he pushed the cork into a chilled bottle with a pen.

"When you come to a fork in the road," he said, "take a boat." All around them green land slid into dark blue water. Distant limestone crinkled in the sun.

September air pinkened their cheeks. Chilled rosé cooled each tongue. When they kissed, their lips were cool but their tongues were warm.

"Thanks for reminding me I can always just drink my problems away," she said.

"Glug. Glug."

Peering into the bottle she had half-raised to her lips, she asked, "Once we evict this wine, do you think I could live in here? Remind me to negotiate a Roommate Switch clause into my next lease."

"Stay at my place tonight."

"Ho ho, prowling the water hole." She poked accusingly at his abdomen.

"Seriously."

"No, wait, it gets worse. I'd already agreed to a weekend with my mom. Fucked out of one wrong room and dragged back to another. On Sunday night I step off the train, cross to a cab and say what?"

"149 Collingwood."

"You're either nice or politely cunning, but don't you think I should have a little space right now?"

"Sure. Have two rooms. Have a floor. I have a whole house to myself. Only child, divorced parents, dead dad — lest you think I successfully e-trade in the off hours."

"Oh. How long ago did your dad die?"

"August twelfth. A year ago, August twelfth."

The water of an international lake sloshed along the sides of the ferry while its engine burned. Sounds both quaint and ugly drowned out his fading voice and his three-word lie. What difference did it make if Stan had died a month ago or a year and a month ago? Dead was dead. And Betty was alive. She kept her thigh pressed against his.

"You have a whole house and no roommates?"

"Not 'til Sunday."

They were young and on a boat, travelling just a little on wine, a kiss and a lie.

17

It's so nice to wake up to the sound of *rain*! Closing his eyes to the grey morning light, he tries to burrow deeper into the sleeping bag. Maybe he can pry off the rain's charming patter, drift back to sleep on the rat-tat-tat before stepping into it. Sadly, he can already feel the dampness on his cheeks, recognizes that the sleeping bag rustles less in the damp air. The tent is swollen with greasy light. The novel, Mordecai Richler's *St. Urbain's Horseman*, could ease the pouring time if his stomach weren't vociferously empty.

Most long-distance riders actually favour one rain day. Wet but not cold, you can clip in and clock the kilometres with less risk of dehydration, less strain on the eyes, spare your knee and bottom lip from the frying sun. In your tent you'd be buggy in an hour. (Idle feet make quick work for the devil.) Out in the rain you can let everything drain into your legs, grab 150, 175, 200 k, as many as you can. Haunt the land when the eye of God grows cloudy.

Kneeling inside the tent, he steps into the full set of Lycra and nylon Russian dolls — shorts, tights, long-sleeved jersey, jacket, even the booties — and is sweating by the time he steps out into the drapes of cold rain. The nylon bag designed to keep water out of the rolled tent is fine if the tent goes in dry, but in the sopping here and now, he folds wet fixings into a wet burrito. More useless weight.

On the bike, each spinning tire becomes a centrifuge of rain. Planning for this trip back in Halifax, riding in the early evening, reading cycling blogs at night, he had fused his growing obsession with weight to his budget's dread of yet another new piece of bike gear and wilfully eschewed fenders. He'd come to touring cycling from mountain biking, where fenders, those clanking prophylactics, were unheard of — physically intrusive, easily clogged with wet leaves, and they denied you your sergeant's stripes of flung mud. But touring isn't mountain biking. He now rides on wide asphalt, not narrow mud, and the first sixty seconds of today's soggy ride are enough to show him the simple merit of fenders.

Although his nylon overboots (the cyclist's thinner version of galoshes) wrap each ankle and shoe to protect the top of his feet from falling rain, they are open on the bottom to allow his metal cleats their bite into the pedals. The front tire's spinning blade of rain cuts steadily into the bottom of each shoe. His wet toes know he'd be better off in civilian shoes, free of the cleat's recessed groove. After the first hour, thin puddles have formed beneath the skin of his feet. Cold begins to chew on his wet toes. Up in the pillory of the handlebars, his sweat-breathing gloves saturate slowly but irreversibly.

Feeling the borders between his warm core and his cold extremities, he doesn't think of the concrete highway overpass growing in the distance as an evolutionary milestone until a leaning motorbike becomes visible at two hundred metres, then its reclining rider at one. An idle motorcyclist sits on the concrete embankment, sheltered from the rain and watching Andrew's approach.

Cars are alien. Their gratuitous speed. Their vulgar girth. The blindness. But the motorcyclist is in between, a wealthy cousin with better teeth. Licensed by the same seasons, given and taken by sunned asphalt, they too ride with a bit of fear clamped behind their rear molars. Their tires are also thin sleeves of air. Watch them closely, watch them from the reduced speed of a bicycle, and you'll observe their camaraderie, see them open their hands to trade small waves, or watch one stranger pull off the road to offer tools to another. Only here, beneath the veil of rain, does he see his edge on the biker. The rain that inconveniences me could kill you.

Andrew gulps cold water as hordes of raindrops slip past his collar. The marooned biker leans back on a concrete incline under the overpass, bulbous helmet and duellist's gloves resting beside him. Andrew must be a slow and boring parade as he limps along at twenty-seven kilometres an hour.

Trying not to stare up at the reclining motorcyclist, Andrew looks instead at the motorbike as he slogs one stroke after another. Their bodies mirror their bikes. Andrew's tires are a third of the width and depth, and he rides a single skeleton of metal not the motorcycle's triangulated frame of conjoined metal. Andrew's membranous layers of Lycra are designed for warmth with the minimum thickness, while the other guy's layers of denim, leather and Kevlar pile protective thickness upon thickness. Andrew wears a skullcap helmet to the other's hydrocephalic dome, wears sunglasses to his face shield. And there's the engine — the herbivore of self-propulsion and the carnivore of a burning engine. Fixated on this shifting border of similarity and difference, staring at the motorbike but not at its rider, Andrew is surprised to hear him speak.

"Game of cards?" the idle rider calls out. "Smoke a hooey? You can't like riding in this."

Andrew doesn't pedal two more strokes without admitting that he'd push the bike off a cliff to stop. Stepping from bike to concrete incline, shaking Richard's thick hand, he stretches out his sopping back on the filthy concrete. The bridge above protects them from rain but not dampness.

"What are we doing?" Andrew asks.

"Me, I understand. You guys are crazy," Richard replies.

Andrew can smell his accumulated sweat. Can Richard?

"I may be slow," Andrew replies, "but I'll finish with all my limbs."

Then, with the flick of a lighter, they add another layer to the fug under the overpass and get high on pungent grass. They play cribbage on a little travel board Richard keeps in his bike's toolbox. *Skunk line,* Andrew thinks when another motorcyclist approaches, then passes in the pouring rain. If he ever steps onto the bike again, he'll ride from cribbage in the Maritimes to euchre in Ontario, jacks and queens and kings fluttering in his spokes.

Richard shakes his head at the other motorcyclist content to press on unsafely in the pouring rain. The passing whine of the other engine is still fading when he says, "There are only two types of riders: those who have been down, and those who are going down."

With the marijuana loosening the vise of his trapezoids and relaxing his hamstrings, Andrew has his first moment of nostalgia for this trip. Thirsty for more than just water, thinking that a puff is great but that a puff and a pint would be heavenly, he thinks back four days ago to his private send-off in Halifax. After friends had wished him well the night before his departure, after the last of his apartment things had been mailed on ahead to Kingston, he shed his civilian clothes, stepped into his shorts and jersey and began his trip across half a country by first crossing the city for a beer. Parking the loaded bike outside a brew pub, he tried not to be too self-conscious with his shaved legs, his bright jersey and the scrotum tray that is a pair of snug cycling shorts.

Once, in Kingston when Andrew was chauffeuring Stan, his father the English teacher taught him the difference between a traditional pint drawn off a hand-powered beer engine, and "the kind of machine piss you're drinking at student bars." Stan had directed them to what he said "used to be a proper old fart's pub before it got trendy." Andrew hauled Stan out of the car's passenger seat and guided him into a pub dimmed by stained glass and a contagion of dark wood running from the bar through the floorboards and into the tables and chairs.

Stan surprised him by saying, "The books I've read in here," then directed them to a corner table to start his disquisition on hand-drawn beer.

"*Draft* means pull. Most of the so-called draft beer in this city, on this continent, is dispensed with compressed gas. Tell me, you little scholar, how can a gas pull?"

Around this same time, Andrew was learning to bike, to really bike, single track off-road trails, or twenty-five-kilometre road circuits out of the city. Mark, his unofficial cycling mentor, once slowed his pace on a road ride and deigned to go behind Andrew. "I'll ride in your draft for a change." Andrew didn't tell his dad about all of Mark's lessons.

In the pub, Stan had ordered for the pair of them, then invited Andrew to watch as the waiter returned behind the bar to work the tall porcelain handle of a beer engine, filling their glasses with slow, even squirts of beer.

"See that? No gas, no electric regulators, just an arm and an ale."

So that's exactly how Andrew began this bicycle odyssey, with a hand-pulled beer and the start of a question that had taken the four days since to crystallize. High, dirty and exhausted, staring from his self-propelled bike to the dozing motorbike, Andrew wonders if memory is pushed or pulled. Pushed at us unconsciously by forces and emotions we can't quite name, or pulled up consciously — obsessions, worries and excuses ordered up from our private archives? Still more than a thousand kilometres from Kingston, Andrew recalls again that the English word *nostalgia* is derived from two Greek words: one for *homecoming* and one for *pain*.

Another time with a bike, when Andrew was a boy and being ungrateful as his mother attempted to teach him to ride, Stan tried to coach Andy verbally in the skill that Pat had spent a precious hour trying to do physically.

"Take it from me," Stan had said, "on a bike, in life in general, you either push or get pulled." Stan had been standing crookedly in an upstairs hallway of the family home, both his wife and his son sulking behind two different closed doors.

18

After his eventful September ferry ride with Betty, Andrew's clock was bent. Yes, it was Friday, but he'd been drunk, fooled around and then napped, all by four p.m. By nine, when he returned from the public library, the beer store and three trips to the hardware store, it already felt like Saturday morning. Saturday morning wasn't too early for the first email.

From: riderback@fmail.com
To: placeyourbets@fmail.com
Subject: post

(1) do you mind if I call you Bet?
(2) are you checking email at mumsie's?

andrew

Thankfully, he had a long list of renovations to keep him distracted while he waited for a reply. Speed the time with busywork. The undoing (fill, sand, paint) was dusty, tedious and entirely within Andrew's acquired skills. As for the pantry-cum-bathroom, beer and Zeppelin might get a wall down, but how would he make a new doorway?

His mother had called the main-floor washroom the straw that broke the camel's back, but Andrew had long ago decided a camel was far too large and stubborn an animal to symbolize his parents' marriage. More like the rotting acorn the chipmunk couldn't be bothered with, or the new litter unappealing to Mr. Meow-Mow. Still, at times he did agree with Pat's description of the ground floor's two pairs of adjacent rooms as "the shunting yard." The kitchen and underused dining room sat opposite the living room and a perpetually dark entranceway incised by a wide staircase. For a few years he had heard his mother refer to the ground-floor rooms as twinned or symmetrical. The finite grid of rooms was originally overlooked by a Pat enchanted with the house's coved ceilings, tall baseboards, endless hardwood and especially "that darling pantry." Then both her voice and her diction soured. The paired ground-floor rooms became locked or constricted or, there it was, repressive.

From: placeyourbets@fmail.com
To: riderback@fmail.com
Subject: In Cephalonia

Perhaps we should see each other exclusively on ferries. Greece would be a breeze.

Yes, Bet's fine.

Ciao

From: riderback@fmail.com
To: placeyourbets@fmail.com

Meet me on the highest passenger deck facing the sun. Travel lightly.

What do you do chez Mom? Flop? Scratch aging pets? Resume biathlon training?

— Andrude

Work, Andrew, work. Fill one door, cut another. Simple. But how do I know I'm not cutting into wires? By the time he had found and disengaged the appropriate circuit and dug out an extension cord to wire Stan's aging circular saw from another room, he'd rechecked his library books enough to realize he needed to open up most of the living-room wall just to make a single doorway into the bathroom. *Rough-stud opening.* Is that architecture or a job ad?

From: placeyourbets@fmail.com
To: riderback@fmail.com
Subject: Lesbos

Scratch old friends. No, sadly I made the mistake of telling Mom I've left Dave. She must have taken the cordless with her when searching out "that special white," because she returned to the table with a whole Ottawa Valley Social Tour. Pumpkin Soup at Doug and Irene's. Tea at Cheryl's. A Drink at Rachel's. (Thanks to Martha Stewart, a dish is now an event). I might just have to schedule a private Pound Vodka in the Kitchen.

Remind me to tell you about the Chardonnay Mafia. (Burn this letter.)

Placing my bets,

He added *one sheet drywall* to the list for tomorrow morning's trip to the hardware store, not quite admitting that this would mean digging out the ski rack and bungee cords and not yet knowing that he would drive home unsafely at sixteen kilometres an hour.

Pantry. Where does that come from? Panty re-entry? (No more beer until you're done with the saw. Yes, Dad.)

When stairs became more and more mountainous to Stan, and his fading sense of touch numbed his bladder, he coveted his wife's neighbouring space and proposed converting the pantry into a downstairs bathroom.

"Stan, it's a kitchen! Even animals know not to shit where they eat."

It was Andy who said "most animals," but he was talking alone in his bedroom, his door almost closed. Architecturally, Stan was right. The pantry was the only non-invasive, unobtrusive place for a downstairs washroom. But atmospherically, Pat was also right. The stove was now just a metre from the bathroom door. When the door was left open, one cooked in sight of a toilet. The toilet was so close to the stove that, a decade after it was installed, Stan and the teenaged Andrew referred to it as "the spittoon."

One more email to Betty.

From: riderback@fmail.com

If you were in a fairy tale, not your mom's house, what colour would the magic door be that transported you out of the Nine Circles of Mom/Martha?

Tap. Tap. Andrew sank a new pry bar, its sticker still shiny and un-wrinkled, into the moulding around the bathroom door frame, sharp metal biting easily into the soft old wood. He couldn't have seen many meals with Pat and this bathroom, but he does remember once stand-ing behind her while she worked at the stove. He couldn't see her face, but he could see Stan's as he walked out of the bathroom, and that had been enough. Stan wore his usual mask of resignation, his getting-by face. Then Pat sent him back a look Andy couldn't see, some jab or lash that immediately swamped Stan's face with a mix of confusion, helplessness and rage.

"What, Pat? What do you expect?"

Andy continued to see his mother from behind. He saw the hand she calmly reached out to turn off the stove burner and then the oven mitt she wrapped around a pot handle. She removed the pot from the heat and then herself from the kitchen.

"What is it *you* would do?" Stan called after her. "What is the solu-tion you can see that I can't?" Stan had been yelling after Pat, but only Andy was in the room.

Now Andrew stood at the same kitchen/bathroom doorway, ham-mer and pry bar in hand. Wham. Wham. The bar bit deeper and deeper with each tap of the hammer. A black seam opened between wall and wood. He had spent years strolling past this cream-coloured wall and its wide moulding and never once thought of them as separable pieces, let alone of the moulding as two strips of wood, not just one. He leaned a shoulder into the sunken bar. The first strip backed away from the wall in two-foot sections, nails hanging like bared teeth. In seconds the entire length of moulding was free, and its straight, sharp nails rode snugly in the dusty air. Looked at individually, each nail appeared efficiently vicious. Secure in the moulding, though, each nail was but a tiny splinter compared with the hard, tooled bar in his hand.

From: placeyourbets@fmail.com

Definitely an orange door. Drunken orange. Burnt orange. No, no — scorched orange.

When the door frame finally released into his hands, he danced it across the room.

From: riderback@fmail.com

149 Collingwood. $10 cab. I've planned a small Ice Cream Straight From the Carton With Two Spoons. (The fuck-me caramel in Dulce de Leche is decidedly orange.)

This was more than just a binge clean before a date, more than just shaving the toilet and sandblasting the stovetop. *To Undo:* The giant handles on each side of every door frame. *Wood-filler.* Railings beside the toilets. *More drywall mud.* The shower rails are fine. Do the taps look like handicapped taps? Where do I shut off the water for new taps? Hacksaw for the old pipes? How do I rejoin?

More than a decade after Andy had watched that half-wordless exchange between his parents in the kitchen, when he had seen Stan's face but not Pat's, he finally asked Stan if he remembered that day. What kind of look had she given him that had angered him so much?

"Pity," Stan answered. "Pity and fear."

19

In the damp air under the overpass, Richard the motorcyclist shakes his head in exasperation and asks Andrew, "How do you stand going so slowly?" Biker and cyclist are wet and dirty and pleasantly high.

"Any faster hurts too much," Andrew replies. "And it doesn't feel slow when it's yours. You see more."

"Trees, trees and trees. How much more is there to see?"

"My dad had two big jokes," Andrew says by way of explanation. "Two bulls — one older, one younger — crest a hill. Below them is a green valley full of grazing cattle. Sweet, the young bull says, let's run down and fuck some of the cows. No, the old bull says, let's walk down and fuck them all."

Staring down the concrete slope to a bike he'd have abandoned an hour ago, Andrew sees through a pannier to his one book from the family library and thinks of another. On his eighteenth birthday, the most tender of Stan's gifts had been a copy of Patrick Leigh Fermor's *A Time of Gifts*, the memoir of an impecunious collegiate youth whose attempted walk across Europe was cut short by World War Two. *Which is the time of gifts, travel or youth?* Stan's spidery inscription still asks inside a box inside a stuffed storage room in the Kingston house.

"It's loaded with recurring questions," Stan had continued over the birthday dinner. "These gifts, are they given or received? Are they exchanged during the trip or because he's young? If there is a time of gifts, when does it stop? Why?"

Now, wet, dirty and hungry under an overpass, Andrew asks Richard, "So, what do you have to eat?"

"Pepperoni sticks," comes the dreaded reply.

Stomach growling, head adrift on multiple breezes, he contemplates asking Richard whether motorbikes still have tuned exhaust. One of his later undergraduate essays, those private dances, compared someone's evolutionary, revisionist poetics to the harmonically tuned exhaust systems of older motorcycles. Grossly inefficient port-engines, such as those on motorcycles or snowmobiles, routinely lose as much as one-third of their fuel as uncombusted exhaust. Knowing that the belched gas exits the exhaust pipes in a series of waves, motorcycle engineers replaced cylindrical exhaust pipes with conical ones to create an internal vacuum. Waves of unignited gas would then leave the combustion ports like swimmers, and some kick-turned off an inverted centre-point to swim back up the pipe and return for one more chance at explosion. Instead of asking, though, he simply stares down at the still cough pipe, the cold gun barrel, the exposed bone.

High, he also sees through the grey air and his damp panniers to one of Betty's Turkish postcards.

> *Dalyan, Turkey*
> *Christian/Islam. Greece/Turkey. Fresh water/salt.*
> *Arrived from Greece and am so glad to leave the sandy*
> *nipple tourism behind. Much more polite here. On the little*
> *van-buses whipping around a city, you board and the driver*
> *takes off, entirely confident that you'll hand up your fare*
> *and others will hand back the change.*
>
> *Went to an island's turtle beach today. Not the right*
> *time to see them, but the island's their breeding ground.*
> *Darwin started with turtles on islands. You?*
>
> *Not in a shell,*
> *You fucking bet.*

20

If Betty arrived at all that Sunday, after their Friday kiss and weekend emails, she would be arriving with one knapsack, not a moving van, and he wanted her to have the (promised) option of her own bed. He'd give her his room, as it was the cleanest, the most recently painted and the only room that didn't, he suddenly saw, look like part of a 1970s museum exhibit. Okay, yes, she'd get his room, but which bed? His own mattress was fine, but Stan's was speckled with pee stains. Another motive to give her his room was seduction by immersion, as if her spending time in a room thick with layers of Andrewness would make her more likely to cross the hall and seek him out. And then what? If she crossed the hall to find him in Stan's old room, the sheets of that bed would be more likely to get pulled off. He'd have to double-sheet Stan's bed.

Breaking down Stan's bed for this long night's shell and pee game of beds and rooms, he suddenly saw the dinginess of Stan's room. Stains ran through the worn carpet in broad channels and bore down in concentrated circles. A thick vinyl blind sat slack-jawed in a dirty window. The paint appeared to be quilted with dull patches.

His list for yet another trip to the hardware store kept growing. *Paint, 2 gal.* Turquoise? A wheaty green? *Flooring: laminate? laminating? Curtains. Curtain rod.* Normally he was aware of the cost of buying drinks for women, yet here he was dropping hundreds on reno supplies he'd be hard-pressed to find time to use. T minus thirty-two hours until her possible arrival.

Through his roles as both ex-nurse and a student who grew up in a university town, he already knew that no drug creates energy. Drugs simply spend energy the body has tried to keep in savings. Caffeine unlocks banked sugars. Pot, for him, for now, retreats from his body with an insomnious flame. But to really keep the home fires burning, to borrow time, he needed to climb a toadstool. None of the renovation books he had taken out of the library, and none of the DIY websites recommended taking hallucinogenic mushrooms to accelerate a home makeover project.

By 4:17 on Saturday morning, he was convinced he wasn't simply painting the walls; he was a tanner, stretching skins. The superfine plaster dust coating every single hair on his head, as well as those on his arms and legs, and even his eyelids, made him feel like a powdered doughnut filled with he-didn't-know-what. While these preoccupations came and went, the reach and claw of other rooms, other floors, was constant. One floor down, the pantry/bathroom lay cut open but unsutured, moaning in its post-op corner. Down the hall, a long plaster gash threatened to slip off the wall then fly through the dusty air and garrotte him. High on shrooms, he suffered no risk of falling asleep on the job, not that he really understood what the job was any more. Peeling up the carpet in Stan's room felt like he was skinning an animal, a long-dead and very aged animal. Ripped from jaws of small black teeth, pried and scraped from patches of mysterious tenacity in the middle of the room, the rough carpet and its clammy underpad were shockingly heavy. Pushing from one end did nothing. Pulling from the other moved the top layer but not the entire roll. Only by bowing his chest completely and wrapping the carpet in a bear hug, a hug that sealed his averted cheek to the pasty underpad, could he waddle it out, inch by infectious inch.

He saw individual rooms, or even single surfaces — a wall, a floor — when he should have been thinking of the whole house. He had painted one room a dark, autumnal orange for her without knowing if she would stay, if there were more kisses to come, or even if she'd arrive at all. He flitted from room to room, painting here, dismantling there, to make the house seem healthy, not sick, the house of a bright future, not a near-invalid past. All the while he did this, he ignored the fact that not two days ago, on the ferry, he'd given everything — this house, their kiss and his own future — a rotten foundation. He'd lied about how long Stan had been dead, giving himself thirteen months of mourning in fiction when life had only given him one. Worse, and unbeknownst to him, his was not the first significant house in Betty's life that had been built on a contentious foundation. He tried to see ahead to her in these rooms but could not see ahead to the other rooms, a restaurant dining room and a lawyer's office, that would send her packing again.

Enough. Enough. The house already had all the doubt it needed. It was time to sand some of the spackling compound. He'd be thirsty with all that sanding. When you're up all night, a beer at six a.m. isn't really beer for breakfast.

21

The exploding car, the croaking bicycle. When you drive, how often do you think of explosions? We pump liquid fuel into cars but don't see the four mechanical strokes that turn that liquid into a vapour and then explode it to roll the beast forward. Tens of thousands of tiny explosions race past Andrew's left elbow and side, fierce combustion tucked beneath a leering hood. Suck, squeeze, bang, blow the cannons again. Fire on past your need for water. At least a hundred kilometres between gas stations out here. An hour's drive. A day's ride.

His passage from Nova Scotia into New Brunswick moves him from ocean to rivers. *Nova* and *New* — new lands to pollute. If his map and memory are correct, rivers should soon begin to snake through these valleys. For the vast majority of this country's history, rivers fed industry and body both, floated all appetites. Choked now with the runoff of agricultural fertilizers, these Maritime rivers are hardly suitable for bathing, let alone slaking endless thirst.

So what *is* floating on by? Back at the University of Nova Scotia, he'd read that the Nobel Prize–winning German chemist Fritz Haber is remembered for two major discoveries: mustard gas and synthetic agricultural fertilizers. The Haber-Bosch synthetic production of ammonia for fertilizer changed the planet. For the first time in the history of farming, fertilizer was cooked, was made with fossil fuels. Few people alive have ever eaten bread that doesn't arrive on a trickle of oil. Terrorists understand sowing and reaping: their bombs are made with agricultural fertilizer. The lawns Andrew has left behind or glimpses infrequently from the highway are sprayed to an artificial, monospecial green with pesticides that cause breast cancer, demanding single breasts, the most valuable of coins, for their toll. The major ingredient used to make the asphalt beneath him is oil.

Water, water everywhere and not a drop to drink. Hydration is as important a balance as the rolling tires. Blood, muscle and all of their messengers are mostly water, and Andrew tugs a steady contrail of perspiration. The push of muscle. The pull of thirst.

When he was still checking his face in the disc mirror, he was amazed at the pair of white lines crawling nightly into the thickening caramel of his beard. Beneath these scrawls of dried sweat and his curved yellow glasses hangs the plastic toggle for his water bag. Swatting the salty nub into his mouth, he draws a mouthful of warm water. He has read that metal hand pumps await him on Quebec's converted rail-to-trail Le Petit Témis, that the water, though drinkable, tastes of iron there beneath small cliffs of auburn rock. Again and again he imagines the unseen pump's curved handle, draws a slosh of water into the plastic hydration sack he's suspended over his rear pannier rack, pumps a *goût du terroir* into this latest evolutionary advancement for the cyclist.

Three major mutations fused the body to today's bike — clipless pedals, shocks and the water bag. Pedals you can snap a shoe into, not set one on, held more of the body's force, burned the waste, tightened the circle. Shocks eased the slide and returned a little vertical action, gave the mammal back its leap. And long, narrow knapsacks were needed to hold litres of the life juice. The water bag, that tall, slender piece of cycling luggage, has itself migrated onto other bodies, impressing gardeners and park rangers with its roaming efficiency, its freedom from the leash of thirst. Not wanting the weight or heat of the swollen, black hump on his back, Andrew has added enough hose to park it in the rear atop his back panniers, above tent and sleeping bag.

It'll easily be another five days in the Maritimes before he rounds Rivière-du-Loup and slips into the busy concrete chute for a straight run at Kingston. Amid the noise and the increasing flak of truck tires, there'll at least be the *Prochaine Stationette/Next Service Centre* signs to regulate his thirst. That is, if he remains on the increasingly busy Trans-Can. For now, he's still riding crapshoot. Every time a distant gas station swells into view, he clamps his molars around the dusty toggle and sucks his fill.

During the coursework of his MA on bicycle culture, he'd read of the multi-century quest to invent a "feedless horse" and eventually came across a description of the horse as the "most naked of animals."

Yes, and surely the bicycle is the most naked of machines, an X-ray of itself. Or a living skeleton, all exposed bones and bared teeth. Teeth. In Kingston, when he'd begun riding trails five or even six days a week with Mark, Mark the quietly proselytizing vegetarian once gave him the dental argument for vegetarianism.

"Look at a dog's mouth. Those are meat-eating teeth. Every tooth's designed to rip and shear. What do we have? Grinders." As they'd finished their break and remounted their bikes, Mark displayed a rare poetic streak as his cleats snapped audibly into the pedals. "On a bike, we've just got these two big fangs," he said, referring to the tough, sharp metal cleats mounted into the bottoms of their shoes.

Biking now, roughly one-third of the distance back to Kingston, these memories rise on one knee and are taken away by the other. Bikes with two fangs. Bi-cycle. Bi-cuspid. Some would say he should add *bi-sexual* to the list.

22

Blinking awake, alone in the Kingston house, Andrew could feel plaster dust on his face. The pounding in his head was actually audible. After two and a half days of renovations and narcotic ups and downs, he wasn't expecting human speech. He thought the distant "Hello? Hello?" he heard was sobriety or rational thought knocking at his door. That sobriety called with a woman's voice didn't surprise him. Wait, shit, it was Betty.

He tried to scramble out of bed, not recalling that "bed" was just a mattress he'd thrown here on the floor of the freshly painted orange bedroom. Losing his balance before he ever found it, he stumbled into a pile of empty beer bottles. His only possible recovery was a kind of jackknife dive for the stairwell. When the clatter of beer bottles finally subsided above, so, too, did the knocking below. With some noises unwelcome and others fading, and mental and physical balance so precarious, he was halfway down the stairs before he saw and felt that he wasn't wearing any pants.

Someone was visible through the front door's stained-glass window, and she was turning away.

"Betty. Betty." His black boxer briefs weren't that revealing. He wouldn't make her wait any longer. "I'm here." From now on, he'd be honest.

The leaded window was divided into panels of stained glass of varied opacity. Half a dozen panels showed the halt, return and pause of her shoulders. Translucent red, yellow and green brought him clarity and relief. He had fallen asleep during the boozy-druggy renos. She had indeed arrived on the Sunday evening train. His lateral move for the lock carried him past a clear column of window glass. The multiple panels of glass simultaneously revealed her climbing eyebrows and a reflection of drool hanging off his chin.

She was wearing a V-neck sweater, a skirt, tights and boots, was incredibly clean. She was also laughing. "You're drooling and have no pants on. Should I take this as a compliment?"

Fortunately, the arm he raised to his chin wore a long gash of orange paint.

She touched it. "Hey. Do tell."

"Come in. Will show." He gestured to the stairs. "First room on your right."

On the climb up, her ass swept everything from his mind. Finally awake and rational again, he prepared a disclaimer, rolled "I needed to paint anyway, so don't feel obligated to stay" to the tip of his tongue, when he saw a charge surge up from the base of her spine. She turned one way then another in the orange room, checking light and layout, appraising the colours first with her eyes wide open then with them half-shut. Looking at the floor, which he had painted a milky blue, she had every excuse to stare at his legs and the collar of black cotton stretched around each of his muscular thighs.

Ostensibly he was lifting a lamp off the floor to shed more light when she turned back and made his brightly lit forearm the longest erogenous zone on his body. She scraped two fingers down the outside of his arm so lightly that mostly the fine hairs were touched, not the skin. A small sheet of plaster dust slipped from his arm to hang briefly in the air between them.

"Divorce dust, people call it," she said, cutting one finger through the dispersing white cloud.

"*Divorce*? Already? Aren't we doing things a little backwards?"

"Yeah," she said, lowering to the mattress and turning, "we can do backwards."

23

On the bike, any desire is a weight. Twenty-seven postcards. The well-folded map. Even a tiny bag of fine white powder.

Andrew has never done anything close to cycling one hundred kilometres a day, day after day, so he can't say whether it's the drain of constant exertion or the prison camp of cycling shorts and saddle that has suddenly plucked sex from his thoughts. Six, seven, eight hours with nothing to think about, and for the first time since he was twelve, sex is not the steady hum beneath each thought, not the rising crescendo of every half-hour. He's worried, absolutely. Before setting out, he considered, but did not buy, an expensive anti-impotency saddle with an accommodating trough running up its middle. If Betty's flying back, and if he makes it home on schedule, he should still have a week or two to heal. Heal for what, he doesn't know.

Alongside the worry, though, there's also novelty. Is this what life is like at fifty-nine, just three flaccid inches? Without his semi-hourly half-erection he realizes he can barely feel the thing. More than once he has reached down to his damp, warm crotch for a confirming probe.

At night — bone-ratchet, carbo-loading night — he peels off the snug Lycra shorts as soon as he can. If he camps near the road, he'll slip into hiking shorts or, in a chill, the rain pants. But if his campsite is secluded, he delights in a southern jailbreak, working pantless as he sets up the tent, his pouch swaying as he stoops to stir dinner or tend the fire. His isolation is measured here not just by his naked crotch but also by the socks, fleece jacket and toque he keeps on. Pantless but wearing socks — here is the official uniform of isolation.

Originally, the chilly May air may have prompted the mild slapping and whacking that now marks the end of supper. Whatever took his large, open hands to the crate of his hips and pike soldier quads, they return largely out of amazement at the perpetual hardening of glute, quad and calf. Whose body is this?

The bike frame usurps bone. All naked tubes and gracile strength, it is a second skeleton, and it stirs a sexual revolution in his. For seven, eight, sometimes nine hours, his nose rides closer to the ground as he de-evolves into a prowling mammal. The crotch is the fulcrum of this transforming body.

With the legs constantly pumping under the rock overhang of stomach, the forest of pubic hair has quickly eroded into a saltwater marsh. Each night, he attempts to undo the day's swampy erosion with a dose of soothing, arid powder.

Obviously he didn't buy baby powder. That's the last thing this youth wants on his crotch. Just add water and... He stood in a brightly lit pharmacy, perfectly dry down south but thinking forward to the Petri dish that would soon be his crotch. There it was: Gold Bond Triple Action Medicated Body Powder. He had no idea that killing bacteria could feel so good.

Of course, in the crucible of weight and space that is the bike, he didn't pack the whole Gold Bond canister. Pouring the medicated powder into three tiny sealable bags, he thought equally of cocaine and of seventeenth-century flour, explorers with their precious burlap sacks of flour threatened by every river-crossing and storm. Out here on the road, he wonders if Cabot, Cartier or Champlain also became addicted to dusting his pole.

Slapping his wide hands into his pillared thighs or the cliff of a buttock, hefting, whacking, Andrew climbs into the tent and stretches out in the narrow sleeping bag. Unable to spread his legs significantly in the sleeping bag, he rolls his heels together and apart. Each long leg rolls in then out, folding and unfolding the raccoon mask of his pelvis. His right hand, the more eager of two brothers, sweeps down stomach to thigh, while the calculating left reaches for the bag of magic powder.

Refining this new, dry sensation, he has taken to sprinkling the powder onto the top of each thigh then driving inward. Starting from the stomach loses too much to the tree line. Approaching from each side he's quickly at sack and pole with the slick chalk. It is the sack that prompted this conversion from wet to dry. Ploughing the smooth snow, he dusts this incomparable scoop of anatomy, this island fruit, this slack-furred butt of a tailless rodent. Plucking one testicle with a jeweller's care, he strokes the seam of his scrotum with a single fingertip, amazed again at the mobility of dry lubrication. The oils of the past now seem dulling and interfering, thick intrusions into these minute fissures of skin unzipped by the thin powder. Where oil dulls, powder intensifies, unravelling his skin into long scarves, fluttering prayers. Each ashen stroke removes him from years of wet. Porn is built on wet, anatomy glistening from hot tub to lagoon. Lipstick and nail polish are all about wet, whereas Andrew has found nirvana, and it's bone dry.

Just as his own heat rises, the nimble hoop of his chalky fist begins to constrict with the powder's medicinal burn. Sack, too, goes up in antibacterial flame, steadily nibbled by heat. A gossamer hood falls on and off his end. Inner and outer heat stabilize on his final approach until the orgasm — looser, almost vaporous — slips out of him, a wiry leap that eases into the still air then splatters onto his papery stomach.

24

When Paul Tucker's hair was still red and plentiful, he was as slim as a cedar plank and Andy called him Uncle. At least twice a summer, Pat, Stan and Andy would drive to Paul's cottage on the Canadian Shield. The small wooden cottage, thoughtlessly painted brown, roasted in a pan of hot, pink rock. The cottage sat on cement blocks directly on top of the sloping bedrock. Andy found this naked foundation amazing. Back in the city, houses had submerged basements and lawns you could dig into. Here, the worn old rock sloped and rolled. A few patches of soil collected here and there, like dust in the corners of a room. Unbelievably, cedar bushes or blueberry plants rooted and anchored in these thin patches. Still, almost nothing but a wooden dock and a small rock face separated the cottage from the dark, lapping lake. Paul referred to the expanse of bedrock as his "rock garden" and teased Andy, saying if he wasn't good he'd have to weed the garden before he'd be allowed to go swimming.

There were bright, cottagey moments when seeing exploded into understanding. Swimming near the shoreline, holding on to the rock ledge while kicking his legs in the deeper water behind him, Andy felt and saw that the rock beneath his hands was part of the same sloping rock that held up the cottage there in the distance, the same rock they drove past, through, or over to get here. The denuded rock and naked architecture of the small cottage he could see and understand. His parents were the dark, unfathomable water that summer.

Standing alone at the dock one evening, Andy turned from the dozing lake and finally noticed a tiny wooden shelf high in the rock face of one of the giant boulders that sat near the shore. No larger than a shoebox lid, the shelf sat seven or eight feet above the inside edge of the dock. Such was his excitement at the mystery of this tiny shelf hanging above the dock's own floating shelf that when he ran back to the cottage, he didn't really process the nervous, doubting conversation he interrupted between Paul and Stan, didn't quite hear his dad's "What choice do I have?" or notice that his mom was off on another of her walks. Fixated on the enigma of that tiny wooden shelf, he concentrated only on Paul's offer of a demonstration, on his obliging stroll back down to the dock, the peeling off of his shirt. How could Andy remember words, mere words, when Paul was climbing the rock to stand on that tiny, tiny shelf, then flying through air and sunshine to clear the dock and dive into the deep lake?

Paul silently absorbed Andy's fascination with these quick dives. As they arrived to subsequent visits, perhaps just one more with Pat, Paul would take an armful of bags out of their car, offer Andy's parents a drink, and then shed clothes as he and Andy headed for the water.

"Can I stand beneath you as you dive?"

"Sure. Just keep your arms down."

The summer before his parents' divorce, that indelible date stamp in a childhood, Andy had perfected his dive off the dock. That summer also saw Paul leaving the traditional classroom for Correctional Services work, but he still made time to show Andy how to curl his toes over the edge of the dock and then sink his butt toward his ankles to load the spring (a light spring, through the knees). When Stan and Andy made their first trip to the cottage without Pat, Paul took Andy down to hammer in a lower shelf. Andy flew long through sun to water, and Stan could still walk himself to the dock.

25

That September, Betty stayed in her orange room, and in no time Andrew was another idiot with shit in his teeth.

As first she, then they, went on clothing and book raids to her old apartment.

She caught them both one night with a joke: "What does a dyke bring to the second date? . . . A moving van." (Betty who couldn't keep her pants up or her skirt down. Betty already on the pill.)

Almost no one recommends living together on the second date. If either of them had told their mothers, the phone would have been ringing off the hook with shrill disapproval and blustery commands. A crew of romantic intervention workers would have been dispatched by helicopter to rappel down and storm the house. Skywriting planes would have written *THINK!* in the Kingston sky. But they both knew that their mothers were experts in ending relationships, not starting them. When they each worshipped at the altar of stimulation, why not live together? Here, finally, was a surrogate education with a lovely mouth. They read to each other. They traded keyboard shortcuts and essay tips. Late at night they proofread each other's work and then made the bed. If romance goes from zero to one hundred, why dally at thirty-five?

On their final trip to clear out her old apartment, Andrew had to carry a heavy box around a young couple who had stopped in the middle of the sidewalk so the woman could scrape something from the guy's front teeth. Arranging his load in the trunk, Andrew clearly thought, *No, never, a line I will not cross.* Not ten days later when they were out for spinach pizza, Betty announced, "You've got shit in your teeth" as cheerfully as reporting a positive change in the weather.

"Oh, thanks."

Between gallery openings, public readings and the city's collegiate café culture, they often dined out before or after some public event. Unintentionally and unequivocally, they created the coded acronym

SIYT: Shit In Your Teeth. Sadly, the same homonymous adaptability and pervasiveness of the word that made it so easy to use surreptitiously in mixed company (*website, insight, sight for sore eyes*), quickly had each of them unnecessarily deforming their attractive smiles or hobbling their growing eloquence when out in public. At the opening of a new art installation consisting of remote-control toy birds dropping family photographs into a paper shredder, he heard Betty's comment about the "site being too passive" and raised a knuckle to his mouth. At a reading of so-called poetry (more undigested journal entries cut by arbitrary line breaks), when Andrew said of the poet, "If he had a single insight it would have died of loneliness," Betty raised a napkin. Misunderstood, the inciting party offered compensatory shakes of the head or darts of the eye, but too often these were taken to mean that the offending crumb or dab was on the other side of the mouth, the lower teeth, the upper, still there. *Site-specific installation. Sites of resistance. Citation.* This gallery- or foyer-Tourette's seemed far worse than consenting to a quick scrape from her fingernail. Thanks.

Her education in visual culture and his in literature threw them into more than a few shared classes. University regulations spoke of major and minor degree requirements, yet there were no official transfer credits for adoration and amazement. *Major, minor, lover,* the transcripts should read.

Settling into a home date one night (*You've never had nutritional yeast on popcorn?*) with Lars Van Trier's *The Idiots*, a film of emotional catch and release taken to extremes, they were a half-naked, half-drunk symposium. The film's bracing story involved bright young people, lifestyle artists (or those unwilling to trade their souls for a pension and a tolerable marriage, or maybe just the cleverly lazy), who would pretend to be mentally challenged in restaurants, public swimming pools. Anywhere they had an audience, including each other. Spazzing, they call it.

"Of course they'd spaz fuck," Betty said as the story reached one of its inevitable conclusions.

Half an hour later, when she said, "Use the third person," lust's keen radar correctly led him to interpret this as "state your wants and/or commands and/or requests" as *he* not *I, hers* not *yours. Drop her tit in his mouth. Use another finger. Ride his tail. Get her hair in your fist.*

Every love is a dialect of love, a local variation of the universal language. My mind and yours. Your body and mine. Our private language of love. As their months together grew, Andrew realized that the house had acquired its third private language. These walls remained conversant with the ancient dialect of Pat and Stan and the Middle English of Stan and Andrew but preferred the flowering argot of Betty and Andrew. Yet only one of these languages started with a lie.

26

He shaves his legs and look what happens. On the bike, he no longer even thinks of them as his legs. He can still think of his calves, those drumsticks of muscle he must gnaw to make each climb. And he still has knees, those wind-scrubbed turnips fried under a merciless sun. Beyond those details, the legs have become more generalized. They are now two loops of pain, and their orbit doesn't stop neatly at his hips. On some climbs he has honestly begun to wonder if his legs don't stretch all the way up into his lungs, if, in fact, his legs and his lungs aren't connected now, beaten together on the anvil of the frame.

A curved profile-bar extends off his handlebars like the bowsprit on a tall ship and allows him to stretch out his forearms and change the angle of his hips, the pitch of his torso. In this, his flattest posture, when the topography is right and he isn't staring absently into the trees or the spinning road, there is sometimes, just briefly, a moment when his two hands and the bar they hold seem to block out the next valley. There is a forest beyond his hands, but, for a moment, the valley is invisible, lost, is not what he must push himself through next. Ride long enough and in some moments denial is as refreshing as water.

Then reality looms. At the nadir of this New Brunswick valley, two bridges leap a wide river. A contemporary bridge, a bridge built with Ottawa dollars, with its computer-modelled arc and expandable grooves, its lack of a cycling lane, leaps the near distance while the stretched house of an old covered bridge hangs another kilometre downriver in a small New Brunswick village. Local roads parallel to each riverbank complete a rectangle between the two bridges, a rectangle only Andrew fills.

A driver would need just a quarter of the time and none of the pain it takes Andrew to get inside the covered bridge. Who doesn't want to see the inside of that bridge? Drive through a house? The density of air lightens as he bikes away from the highway's baying trucks.

In less than two minutes, the enclosed wooden bridge in front of him emerges from quaint oddity into comprehensibility then obviousness. This stretched house of untreated wood is a proud reach over water once brimming with logs. The same templates for the trusses of these homes were obviously transferred over to this gabled bridge. (In her advocacy for bringing down walls, Betty's architect mother, Elaine, once assured Andrew that houses stand upright almost exclusively because of the gabled roof trusses.) Rounding the corner and slipping into the dark, roofed chute, Andrew also knows this is shelter from the valley wind. Step in, brother. There can be respite in movement.

Anticipating a radical shift in light as he moves inside the boxed bridge, Andrew reels in his gaze. At first, bike, panniers and knees shift entirely into grey-scale. Details are lost to shadow. The stubble on his legs, that lengthening Velcro, appears to vanish.

When he had shaved his legs in Halifax, luxuriating in the tub the night before his departure, he knew he wasn't really making himself more aerodynamic so much as he was preparing a record, opening a ledger. His cleanly shaven face and calves, the smooth top and bottom of a cyclist's body, would be the blank sheets upon which this trip would write its daily record. That was only the fourth time he had shaved his legs. He'd dipped his razor into the androgyny of cycling once, alone, meeting the always shaved Mark on the Kingston trails the next day with glistening calves and a knick on his knee. And then twice later, with Betty. Betty shaved him before his last few rides with Mark. One trail in the morning and another by night.

Now, eyes acclimatizing to the shadows inside this covered wooden bridge, he just begins to make out the iron filings of his leg stubble when a car horn blasts beside him. At first glance, the driver is simply an older woman. He assumes she's alerting him to her presence, and he gives her the Stan-nod in greeting, dipping one eyebrow as if stamping the air, then glances back to his ride. Nothing beyond the front tire, save for planked wood and a distant square of light. He's about to check his speedometer when she honks again. Perhaps she's trying to alert him to a loose pannier. The horn blasts again just as he glances down and back but before his eyes can make the mirror, so his second view of this middle-aged woman leering explicitly from her sedan is from a full turn, not cropped in his small mirror. This second look entirely rewrites the first. *Older woman* is actually some version of fifty — brassy hair, a thick grip of flesh around the jaw. The most youthful aspect of her face is a leer made unmistakable by the lean necessary to put it into his view. She trails six inches from his left heel, but his spinning legs and tires maintain their demands on his gaze, pull him from his direct, uncomprehending stare at her to his mirror then back to the road. Again with the horn.

Her smirk has grown. Exaggeration extends smooching lips, slants her eyebrows and adds a coy tilt to the jaw. Her right hand comes off the steering wheel to buff a stretch of air. Horn, leer and gesture translate this mimed arc. *Your ass. Your ass.*

Here is the wolf whistle crammed into a hard, boxy tunnel. Here is *Show me your tits.* Until now, he had regarded these male whistles and calls as poor or desperate rhetoric, ludicrous, self-defeating ad campaigns or sneering admissions of failure. No, the rhetoric is clear. This is oppression, not seduction. Honk. Honk. She's kissing the air now and buffing ass with short, rapid strokes. Because she can.

Her mime is annoying, offensive and tremendously unattractive. He doesn't for a second think it's also prophetic.

27

Pat was grateful that Stan didn't have cancer. Divorce was already cancerous enough, dark knowledge spreading through the house, a drain on all energy, every resource. Stan didn't have cancer. He wasn't in pain. And he wasn't dying. She admired him. She respected him. And yet, and yet.

In ways, you divorce everything. The house, fine. A cost of doing business. She'd even be divorcing the car she was about to use to drive Andy to tell him the news. Gordon, holding her close, had told her that, etymologically, *divorce* came from *a different road*. She let herself be hugged and didn't correct him. *Divorce* actually came from a verb meaning *to turn*. Stan had taught her that years ago. Your road didn't change; you did.

Andy was seven. He'd survive. He might even need this. He'd agreed to spend some time together this Saturday, just the two of them, and he hadn't posed any awkward questions. Aside from vetoing the arcade, she'd agreed to let him choose where they would go. Driving through the city, she didn't care where they were going so long as they were going.

"Okay, left here," Andy told her. "We're close now. There, on your right."

Oh God. The Humane Society.

"They have a little trail where you can walk any dog you want."

"Andy —"

"I know. I know. No dog. That doesn't mean we can't walk one. It doesn't even cost any money."

Parking the car at the animal shelter, she could see clearly how Stan had to lean his curved chest to raise this very gearshift into park.

The twin smells of urine and disinfectant filled her nostrils as they stepped into the animal shelter's cacophony of yelping, whining and barking. Andy's back, no longer tiny, advanced into the room, untouched by her desperate hand. *If dogs can smell fear, what do they smell off me?*

The phrase *your father and I* sat in her mouth like an inflamed tooth while she stood in the reception area listening to her articulate, attentive son chat with the patient staff as two adjacent doors opened and closed, flooding the room with smells and whines, smells and whines.

"Should I try to keep the dog at my left as I walk?"

"These guys are a little out of practice with that kind of walking. Keep both hands on the leash and you'll be fine."

It was shockingly but fittingly easy to fall in behind Andy as he passed through a heavily scratched brown door into bedlam. Grilled troughs ran through the cement floor beneath their feet. A garden hose hung coiled on a dull cinder-block wall. Walking the aisle between cages was like switching on a food processor of fur. Brown, black and golden shapes stirred in their grey cages. Despite the movement and the bars, Pat saw their dark eyes quite clearly, saw, even as they spun or scratched, the sphere of each eye, saw those little bubbles of oil surrounded by unkempt fur.

"Look at this one," Andy called, crossing to a gawky, elongated stretch of fluff and haunch. "I'd like to take them all out, but..." Ten minutes later, shopping bags stuffed into his pocket, Andy guided his mother and a nearly grown collie-something out into the play area.

"I like that she's quiet. I don't think she's scared, just patient."

Pat marched on, holding her speech like a revolver in her pocket. The dog trotted left and right uncertainly, never fully straining the leash but always looking to the rest of the enclosed yard.

"Do you want to run? Hmm?" Andy tore ahead then back.

Catching him on a return sprint, Pat cautioned, "Maybe the puppy isn't used to running."

"Mom, she's a puppy." He slowed purposefully on his next pass. "I could do my next science fair project on dog training."

"That's a good idea."

"So I'd train her —"

"Andy, think of your father." Pat finally jumped for the light. "You're old enough and smart enough to see your dad's not getting better."

This time Andy didn't bolt off. The dog resumed its calculations of *leash, human, yard.*

"Instead of getting better, though, he could maybe live differently."

"What do you mean?"

Stretching her eyes, she stayed their tears. "Well, he could live with other people like him."

"Who else is like him?"

"Or with a nurse." His eyes were on hers now, also wet, and she went for it. "But not with me. I don't want to live with your dad any more. Don't cry, honey. Lots of kids are better off when their parents are divorced. Come here. An — drew, come here."

She focused solely on his hand trying to squirm out of the leash's looped handle, so she, too, forgot about the dog. Free of the leash thrown from Andy's grasp, perhaps stimulated by the run, the puppy bolted.

Glaring back at his mother with his teary, rotten-apple face, Andy slammed the fence gate so hard behind him that the latch did not catch. Yelling after him, Pat watched the gate jerk shut and fling back open. Walking quickly, grateful for the consumption of worry after the corrosion of guilt, she reshuffled the remaining cards in her hand. *There or not, I can't make him any healthier.* Or *I'm better for you if I'm happy.* Or maybe even *We only have one life.* These crisp, reassuring cards filled her mind's hand, and she did not immediately notice the puppy's turn for the open gate.

"Andy. Andy, the dog."

Andy had long since run around the building and out of sight. Quickening into a ridiculously fast walk, Pat could see the blatant geometric impossibility of her reaching the gate before the dog did. "Here, girl. Here, girl," she called, half running.

The bright blue leash dangled behind the galloping dog, and as it passed through the open gate, Pat hoped its handle would catch on something. There'd be a yelp, but they'd get her. No such luck. Passing and shutting the gate herself, Pat rounded the corner of the building to see Andy running into a field on the opposite side of the road, and the puppy, leash snaking out behind, following.

She saw so much. The driver's lips moved as he talked, head bent just slightly to his passenger. The speeding tires locked suddenly on the dark pavement. Her boy turned back at the sound of the brakes. Caught, finally, the blue leash snared under one tire, grew taut, and whipped the dog under another.

"Don't look," she thought to yell, already running, already undoing her coat. "Don't look," at the unbelievably fluffy chest split and pumping fast blood, at the small, sharp teeth broken into red and yellow pools. Pat made it to the body before the driver could even open his door.

Unwilling to ask her to move, looking now at the top of her head, he temporarily forgot about his window crank and yelled over talk radio into the solid window. "I'm sorry. I didn't see — Where'd he come from?" Only the passenger saw the boy approach then freeze at the sight of this tall woman gathering up the dog in her own coat. Her bloody hands were long and slender even as they strained around the weight gathered in her darkening coat.

A few years later, arguing with his mother on the phone again, Andrew recalled those hefting arms and her cheque-book euthanasia. "You helped the dog," he snapped at her over the phone.

"Who did I help?" she asked him back, asking but not quite saying, *I was helping you.*

28

Another bright pill lolls on the highway's black tongue. As soon as he notices the roadside daub of canary yellow, his pace quickens slightly. His thighs, hounds trembling on a scent, suspect that the bright yellow in the distance is another cyclist. He cranks out another few kilometres, thighs straining at the leash, without knowing whether the jolt of yellow is indeed another rider or, if so, whether the rider's coming or going. Will he meet or chase the other rider? Meat or cheese?

Finally, he sees a gap between the yellow dot and a distant white house close. Speed and colour all but certify that the shape is another rider, not a runner, in this brightest of sports. More even than those for running, cycling jerseys, jackets and helmets leap out in the highest voltage yellows, high-frequency magentas and radioactive blues. Cycling socks usually collar the ankle in bands of colour, if not some flag or image, reggae or tartan, cartoon or psychedelic, while, the jogger pounds on in mute white. In part, these jolts of colour are designed to awaken the sleepy eyes of drivers, to be anything other than asphalt grey, minivan blue or evergreen.

Cyclists have an honour roll of the fallen, riders killed by drivers, firm legs crumpled by tired eyes. Thousands of kilometres ahead of him on the Trans-Can, near Sault Ste. Marie, Ontario, Dugald Christie, a BC lawyer, was struck down on his third cross-Canada ride to campaign for better legal aid. Australians lose their Olympians to drivers; Amy Gillett and Darren Smith were wiped out on training runs. Mark told Andrew that urban bicycle couriers annually ride a silent midnight vigil for their fallen.

Henry Ford is credited with inventing the assembly line. He didn't. He adapted the assembly line from the disassembly line of the slaughterhouse. Carcasses, then cars, strung on a line.

But more than just safety brightens cycling clothing. Every squirt of primary colour is also an homage to cycling's industrial origins.

The near nudity of runners is surpassed only by swimmers. For cyclists, colour squirts into their clothing to thank test tube and lab, to flag this enduring fusion of a natural skeleton to an engineered one. The only earth tone on a cyclist is mud.

Lab, indeed. Snorting above his curved handlebars and breathable gloves, he switches his cycling computer over to its stopwatch. If he had a sextant or some kind of calibrated looking glass, he could clock the seconds the other rider takes to travel between two points and then calculate his speed. Or hers.

Shrewd fatigue finally tables a debate, solemnly lists the casualties of his pointlessly chasing Yellow. What does this three-kilometres-an-hour leap in pace and pulse yield? What does it cost? Why are you faster for someone else? And your pace — if it ain't broke, don't fix it.

Fatigue's a saboteur poisoning the ear, an isolationist. Yellow and I could chat route and chafe, swap tales of flats and broken chains. *Have you ever been without patches and used a fiver to keep yourself going? Money in lieu of a patch? Why not a piece of your map? Money is stronger.* Or we could build a communal meal. *My chili and your...* please don't have chili. Maybe he (she) has vegetables. A starburst red pepper. A buttery avocado. Does he (she) know that "pannier" originally meant "bread basket"? Companion. Company. We'll break the bread we carry. (Keep your Nutella buried.)

These bright marbles roll in a green bowl. Peak to uneven peak, this valley stretches for nearly ten kilometres. On flat land, free of the panniers, one pedal stroke, one plunging shank, would roll Andrew's frame roughly two metres. Here on the New Brunswick highway's curling ribbon, fully laden, spilling down one hill, falling back the next, he'll sink left then right more than five thousand times to end this valley.

Who doesn't want to be faster? Riding trails in Kingston or Halifax, he had been certain that some guys rode just to hunt out a race, ears cocked for a distant rustle in the leaves or the zip of fat tires along dirt. Every three or four weeks some single rider or, even more ominous, a silent pair, would find him unawares, sliding noiselessly into the bottom of a narrow switchback climb or shooting a pocket of coaster. These grandsons of men who were paid to sweat now paid to do it.

Their unannounced races started with nothing more than a shaking of the trees. Asses inched back on seats. The balls of the feet were rediscovered. Knees swung out to cut finer corners, and yet no race was officially announced. If someone pulled onto the main artery beneath the power lines, when he turned into your already burning climb, you could no more declare, "To the willow tree" than you could ask for a handicap. And yet everyone knew exactly what each turn or run meant. Fingerless gauntlets were everywhere thrown. When he had described these unannounced but unmistakable forest races to Betty, she asked, "Are you riding bikes or rulers? Me, Big Dick. Ride money bike fast."

Yes, Betty, yes, yes, yes. And yet here he is gunning for the yellow jersey in the distance, all considerations save for the pass wiped away. The thrill of pushing past and the fear of being swallowed are hardwired, undiscussed but unforgettable.

The yellow rider hits the bottom of the climb out of this valley. The road is a tailor's tape measuring rise and fall. Still on the flat, Andrew has a specious gain on Yellow, crunching the space between them but not the time. The bottom of the hill will bounce him back, flip time Yellow's way. Ascent is mapped with the burn in heart and lungs. A climb actually taxes slightly different muscles in the legs. Ground is won or lost on the butcher's wire of a hill, two strung hearts scraped on the inclined blade. Five-time Tour de France winner Miguel Indurain, Spain's Big Mig, lived his climbing years with a standing heart rate of twenty-eight beats per minute. Back at UNS, nearly forsaking his bike for a library carrel, Andrew had felt his heart rate climbing back up to the average sixty-eight.

Now he's close enough to the other rider to see a glistening calf (androgynously shaved, impressively chiseled). In the pass of an actual race, *attacking* as it is accurately called, the attacker would surely fuel off the smell of his opponent, must push for that mossy aluminum whiff just when it's most needed. Entering the climb, Andrew realizes that this could also flip, that this very air would also be traded. The passing fuel you take from me will soon give me yours.

29

"Prison saved us from batch," Andrew told Betty one night over dinner. "When you're young, you can live with a phrase, especially a phrase of your parents, for years without catching all its angles. *Batch lots*, Dad used to say of the two of us. It was years before I got *bachelor*. After Mom left, when I stayed with Dad, he'd say we were *batching it*. He'd already been teaching in prison for a few years."

"Bachelors by day, bachelors by night," Betty concluded. "What was it, wieners 'n' beans on Monday nights? Fish sticks on Tuesdays?"

"Pretty much. But more than just our diet changed. Something about prison, all that control, all those rules — he got more managerial, sure, but that could have been just the disease. It was a long climb down, but not a steady one. Ability would plateau for years and then drop. He still drove until I was seventeen."

"He drove until he could stop."

"No, really, he was okay. Just errands in town. Got himself to work and back. But prison, it made him more scheming."

"Don't tell me he tried to join a heist crew."

"More like a painting crew. One night, eating dinner right here, he just looked up and said, 'Yellow.' He suddenly wanted the dining room painted yellow. We didn't always admit what he couldn't do any more. Repainting? That meant admitting you now had to pay someone to repaint the walls your old hands, your hands and your wife's hands, had painted a few years ago. Let it grey another year. Get a bigger TV and let the scuffs hang."

"Maybe he just read some advice in a magazine. My mom probably *wrote* articles about divorced dads and redecorating."

"It was more like training than decorating. He hired a painter to paint and to teach me to paint. Older guy, more expensive, but he had the moves and was willing to share them. *Set the brush, then move it. Look and your hand will follow. You find wet roller seams with your ear, not your eye.* I'd grown up doing this, listening to instructions, guiding my hands with Dad's instructions. If he was no longer able to advise me, he hired somebody who could. He always said, 'You can buy anything, if you pay enough.'"

"That sounds like a dad, all right," said Betty.

"When everything was limited — the shirts he could wear, the chairs he could use — his brain changed. *Evolved* is probably the word. The arms lost reach so the imagination gained."

Stan thinned everywhere save for a little paunch, his "goody bag." His shoulder blades sliced through his sallow back. His collarbone was a bow. Most relevantly, his sense of touch diminished with every millimetric curl of his fingers, every hidden fraying of nerve endings.

His tracheotomy tube, that arc of silver respiration, was replaced twice a week. Working slowly, usually after a shower, air-drying in his saggy boxer shorts, Stan would boil a small aluminum pot of water on the stove to sterilize the alternate tube, its two inserts for night and day and the glass jar that would house them. The bent fingers of his tented right hand could fit into the wide grips of a pair of rubber-handled tongs while the idle left was indeed quick work for the red devil of the glowing stove burner.

Younger, Andy simply assumed there was no *other* cause than Disease No.1 for the blunt, nail-less fingers of his father's left hand. Surely the fingers were also curled by the foul gravity that was changing the orbit of his ribs. In the kitchen at four years old, when he saw Stan's left hand support his right and a saucepan handle in it, when the dangling left fingers brushed the angry red spiral of a maximized stove burner, when the burned fingers came up weeping, Andy thought adults, not his dad, felt less pain.

"Dad, your fingers."

"Oh, damn."

Two, maybe three years would pass before some casual question of Andy's about the blunted, penile fingers of Stan's left hand prompted Stan to clarify their history of partial amputation. "No, no. I lost them to infection," he said. "If the fingertip gets really infected, the nail becomes like a roof. Off they went." Stan drew the clean, bent fingertips of his right hand over the butt ends of the left.

Betty didn't wait, couldn't wait, more than a week between hearing about Stan's hand and asking to feel Andrew's imitation of it. Love lets you out of one cage and puts you in another. Andrew rubbed the knuckles of his fist across her hips. Not his fingertips, not a tongue, not even his smooth palm. Knuckles and then knuckle pinches. His whole fist sank between her thighs to give her a slightly gentler version of what wrestlers call a crotch tilt. Her message had been unmistakable. Show me. Show me. No one had ever cared so much about what he cared about. But then, after a meeting with his father's lawyer and a dinner with his mother, he could no longer hold on to the two things he cared about most.

Coaxing him to sleep one night, she'd given him her yoga advice. "Your body is the past, your mind is the future. Your breath unites them in the present." That winter he stopped breathing easily.

30

Fewer than two hundred metres of hill separate Andrew and the nameless rider in front of him. Although this distance will quickly double, then double again, seconds after the yellow-jerseyed rider crests the hill, Andrew feels the math is in. Unless Yellow is playing the touring cyclist's version of cat and mouse, unless his (her) pace in this valley was an alluring feint to draw him in, Andrew will claim the next valley. What a charming prelude to a shared dinner. Say there, Crushed One, do you have plans this evening? Oy, Vanquished, got any cheese?

Once, twice, he glimpses the silver in Yellow's mirror but nothing more. No concerned eyes. No revealing whiskers.

Up until this final inclined stretch of the race, he has told himself he only wanted the challenge and then, honestly, the company. An evening of chat. Stories of the road. But the climb doesn't believe that. You want to win. Win what?

In Kingston, when he had learned to ride trails with Mark, there had been plenty of post-ride chats, but Mark was the exception to many rules. Meeting other riders on Kingston's Fort Henry trails or the Long Lake run in Halifax, Andrew found that the chiselled calves and thighs were usually accompanied by a wiring shut of the jaw. Most riders don't speak; they just spit and change gears, maybe leaning over to pointedly examine the transmission on your bike. Groupo? Skins? If anything, they ask, "How many k?" In ways, Betty was right: they ride rulers not bikes.

Late sunlight pours down on both climbers like boiling oil. To meet in the next hour might mean sharing camp with a stranger. He'll miss his chance to walk around half-naked airing his swampy nethers.

Nothing unites them more than Yellow's refusal to brake or waver. Andrew will almost certainly take the next valley, but for now they're fighting tooth and metal claw. However much his thighs burn with fatigue and lactic acid, envy makes them burn hotter as he watches Yellow scale and crest the peak of the hill. Yellow raises his back to stretch it out, while Andrew remains cramped in a climbing crouch. Yellow rolls his head left then right before pouring himself into the drop. All the while Andrew is hip-deep in pain. What pure, murderous envy.

When Andrew crests the same hill, his envy turns into fuel. Yellow currently has the descent, but Andrew has the legs. He draws some water, stretches his neck and prepares to scream downhill into a pass. Yet he doesn't crank the pedals. He stops pedalling but doesn't brake. The distant yellow dot moves. Inertia seeps from Andrew's tires. His dwindling stop is comically slow. Finally, his right toe clips out and comes down. He dismounts and stretches to guarantee Yellow a lead. Christ for a beer.

Gulping tepid water in fading sunlight, he finally sees valley, not road, province, not climb, and he lets Yellow go, gladly. This will be his turn from the brothel gates, his bride at the altar, the predictable career he abandoned. Pursuing and passing the other rider would have reduced days of this trip to a simple chase: attack then defend. Introspection and wisdom would have been tossed aside as dead weight. And, having let Yellow go, he can return to wondering if it was a man or a woman. Paused here on his hilltop, watching Yellow fade into the sunset, he can concentrate on his erection without fixating on man *or* woman. He can think person or body. He definitely thinks *legs*.

31

Andy and Stan also had their races. Races with each other and against each other. Races against time. Once, they raced together slowly on a crowded bus from Kingston to Toronto. They would race again when they got off in Toronto, travelling from bus station to doctor's office. All of those races in bone.

Andy was thirteen years old, and soon — four to six months — he'd be taller than his dad.

"You just wait, Stanner; I'll give you progress reports on your bald spot."

"Evil, evil boy."

"Or *spots*, I should say."

"You remember what a *will* is, don't you?"

Whenever Andy saw Pat — Christmas, the once or twice they got away in March — his height was always the first thing she mentioned. "It's what I do," he occasionally said or, "It's my job." He never told her that Stan was shrinking.

Despite fading muscle and warping bone, Stan had still been driving in Kingston. His job at Allenville Correctional. Grocery stores selected not for value or quality but for their immunity from left-hand turns, their proximity to slow side roads. Always the dry cleaners. For years Andy thought that's just how men's pants got cleaned, making no connection to Stan's races to the washroom. Stan could drive around for small errands in Kingston. But a drive into Toronto? Impossible.

Once a year they devoted a whole day to thirty minutes with Dr. Khan, one of the specialists. Even today Andy couldn't say whether Khan was Neuro or Rehab, OT or PT. Back then he didn't know what those acronyms stood for, didn't even know the name of Stan's disease or if it had one. If his were a condition Andy had ever seen in a doctor's office, on television, in a movie, maybe Stan would have used a name around the house. In life before a web search, *syringomyelia* was a private noun, a unique coin. If it were something exclusively internal, a hidden worker's strike in the pancreas, a length of intestine blown like rails in war, a name might help carry Andy in. But here, arms bent ruinously, one leg curling out, the other frozen, what was in a name? By the time he met Betty, he had said the word aloud less than five times.

By the second hour, Andy felt entirely coated in bus, slick, infectious bus. He could not avoid overhearing multiple conversations about what someone reckoned was a good idea for starting up a business, and what *They* said about this, and what *They* were now saying about that. If he heard a single adjective, it was *different*, and invariably it was used approvingly for some junk you could buy. Although the ride there always felt longer than the trip home, he knew that nothing would be as biblically interminable as the wait in Dr. Khan's excessively bright waiting room. The hands on the beige clock wouldn't move any faster than the orange squares and green cones of the office's huge, ugly painting. Each year, a few ambitious weeds grew among the tar and pebbles on the rooftops beneath the one (sealed) window.

Mid-route, the highway blurring along beside them, Stan dropped his magazine to the gummy bus floor, and Andy knew they had a rush on their hands. "Let's go," Stan said, meaning *piss crisis*.

First Andy had to get him up. He stepped over Stan's sharp knees and into the aisle. Surging with the pitch and roll of the bus, Andy steadied his legs and reached down for Stan's hands, finally looking into his face. A drawstring of alarm had tightened around each eye.

It would be another few years — not until Andrew regularly rode trail with the swelling balloon of his bladder folded palpably into the sack of his insides, bobbing there above the saddle's wedge — before he understood his father's binary bladder. Not until he himself pissed off a tilted bike frame did he realize that Stan and his pissing were inseparable from his body's other warps and retreats. Here at thirteen, Andy did know that Stan's sense of touch was diminishing radically. The burns from a stove element. The way he'd consensually let his shoulder fall into a door frame to break a fall. Shadowing this body day in and day out, Andy was beginning to understand that for Stan, standing upright was a largely visual operation. He had to glance around just to stay in place. And what difference did understanding a degenerative condition make to living with it? Thursday's epiphany did nothing to Friday's chores, to the recurrent challenge of pulling up pants. What was theory compared to the necessity of a sandwich? The internal body, inside was a foreign, unpronounceable worry, each organ a continent away. So many shop windows were smashed nightly that neither of them fully attended to the disease's backroom legislation that was quietly seizing all of Stan's assets. Really, Stan was only feeling extremes, inside or out. A half-full bladder wasn't even noticed. Three-quarters was a nag he couldn't quite place.

Stan's arms seemed to fade a millimetre or two each time Andy hauled him up. Halfway between sitting and standing upright, Stan's hands and arms began to pull away from his chest. In their living room or here in the bus aisle, Andy had to arc his spine, bend his knees, step back if he could to take up the slack, Stan's hands coming at his shoulders like the paws of a huge but aging dog. Stan's too-vertical arms looked as if he hoped to fly out of his seat.

Upright and semi-evolved again, Stan exhaled victoriously before proceeding to battle-test his legs and knees, leaning from one foot to the other. The brown scrubland adjacent to the 401 rushed past on either side. The bus droned.

Andy had pulled Stan up in the only direction he could, toward the driver. The washroom, of course, was in the rear. The long march back could not begin until they managed a complete about-face. Two children began to stare. A pale woman with a scarf over her head averted her eyes. A man in a plaid bush jacket clenched his jaw.

Unnecessarily, Stan looked into Andy's eyes and nodded. Okay, round two. Twisting and tugging Stan while propping him upright, plucking one leg, guiding the other, Andy waved his ass in all their neighbours' faces. Excuse me. Sorry. Just be a minute. Successfully reversed, all hands locked, Andy checked once behind his feet while Stan said, "Damn."

Andy followed Stan's gaze to see the washroom's red *Occupied* sign light up. A preschool girl stood on her seat in yellow rubber boots and looked from the sealed door to Stan and Andy then back again. She wore a green dinosaur T-shirt. Eventually, her mother pulled her down.

"Just keep stretching." Andy had his own knees slightly bent for the roll. While Stan's gaze never left the *Occupied* sign, Andy's alternated between it and the driver's wide mirror. Visorlike sunglasses. Walrus cheeks. Ginger moustache.

The intercom coughed awake. "I'm sorry, sir; there can be no riding in the aisles."

Stan would have ignored him fifteen minutes ago. His feet were shifting too frequently. His eyes saw little. "C'mon. C'mon."

"Sir, absolutely *no* riding in the aisles."

Andy stopped looking forward. Land, brown and grey, rolled past.

Finally the washroom door opened. Stan jerked Andy's arms like a horse's reins, not noticing that Andy was already stepping back. Part owl, part minesweeper, Andy craned his neck from side to side as he pre-checked each step and gauged the stability of Stan's feet with each passing glance. My left, your right. Fred and Ginger in the small aisle.

Stan's every movement was propelled by a high buzzing note at the back of his throat. The dinosaur girl's hair was unbelievably, pastorally blonde.

Flattening himself between Stan and the unfortunate passenger tucked into the seat beside the washroom, Andy held back the spring-loaded door with first a hand and then the raised toes of one foot as he guided Stan in ahead of him. Stepping as far as he could, Andy steadied his uneasy father with both hands and didn't watch as he permitted the door to shut against his own outstretched leg. Wrapping Stan's fingers around a knurled safety rail, Andy pressed himself into a corner before reaching back for the tiny bolt of the token lock.

"C'mon. C'mon."

Reaching under Stan's arms, Andy tried to ferry him across the few remaining inches to the stainless-steel hole of a toilet. A sudden turn threatened Stan's besieged balance and shifted his whimpering into overdrive. "In the sink. In the sink." The rectangular mirror showed him nodding his head between crotch and metal bowl.

"That's where people wash their hands."

"The zipper. Hurry. Pull it out. Pull it out."

Andy had to turn his head and press one cheek into Stan's left shoulder blade in order to reach. Glancing around, Andy saw them half-reflected in the steel walls, toilet and seat. Only Stan could have seen the actual mirror, precise reproductions of buttons, belt, zipper and meat, and his eyes were closed, beatific. Andy looked from the many versions of their humped, greasy reflection to the blue floor's coin-sized circles of raised rubber. Traction was improved. Spills contained. Collected near the neglected toilet were multiple hairs and aging, viscous stains. What to listen to other than the urine sliding over the smooth steel of the sink? Chat on the other side of the door. The steady growl of the bus engine.

The sharp bones and thin muscles of Stan's back relaxed steadily against Andy's cramped cheek.

"Sorry, Andrew. I won't forget this."

"Makes two of us. Finished?"

"Yeah, all done."

Andy packed his father away.

"Better hit the water."

"I'm not stupid."

The tap opened to nothing. Again and again Andy unscrewed the single metal tap. Nothing. Should the walls have cast accurate reflections, Andy's disapproving eyes would have met Stan's for just one second before the bus took a severe bump. Instead, two pink orbs traded vague stares before the big hit, when Andy shot his hands out reflexively. One hand grabbed Stan's chest and the other the nearest good grip. His right still held Stan after the tremor faded from the bus. He slowly withdrew his dripping left from the pissy edge of the sink.

"Oh, Andrew —"

"Shut the fuck up."

Twice, Andy scraped his nose over Stan's back while holding him up and searching for paper towel, Handi Wipes, anything. Voices from the other side of the door floated back. He wiped hands, counter, sink and hands again with thin scraps of quickly dissolving toilet paper, then flushed the whole mess in a blue swirl.

32

As a Visual Culture major, Betty shouldn't have underestimated the power of Andrew's cycling shorts. That fall, she didn't consciously tally all of the pheromonal math that found her an only child of divorce underexposed to a noseful of testosterone. In the programmatic self-design of an education, in which one was both volunteer and conscript, she was currently devoted to the eye, and so didn't anticipate a surprise attack by smell. At first she had tried to deny that the fragrant cloak he wore home after a ride, with its baseline of musky sweat, its rub of cedar, that brief squirt of oil, was an attraction for nose not eye. Her reluctance to admit that arousal could bubble up so strongly outside of her daily trade of eye and mind, that shifting see-saw of image and word, of colour felt then indexed, found her trying to rewrite her own perceptions and memories, to push away an alluring smell in hopes of pulling in an image. Sitting in classrooms, ostensibly listening to lectures, she was also performing daily autopsies on yesterday's lust.

If present, smell is the fastest conduit to memory, the most teleportational of senses. But an absent smell, a past smell, is not recalled as easily as something visible, and for a while Betty was able to sit in class or meet a friend for coffee and see in memory the mud or blood on Andrew's calf, could precisely recall the crisp, finite shapes of torso, tush and thighs packed into their jersey and shorts.

The shorts. The word *lingerie* didn't quite apply to his cycling shorts, what with its curves and soft edges, its complicit consonants concealing and revealing its trio of arousing vowel sounds. *Lingerie* — each consonant is an offering. The upright *l*, the plunging *g* dragging the action down low. Naughty little *n* and *r* bent and rolled over. For Betty to even say the word, spilling it down her tongue then briefly munching the *g,* offered more cunnilingus than most so-called men on campus.

Andrew's tight cycling shorts were the male equivalent of lingerie.

The thin black Lycra, simultaneously pliant and snug, collared the cascading muscles of his thighs. At their top, they made his hips into a neat black tray eager to serve. And of course, there was the plucked black tush. More than just her eyes drove her to unwrap that Lycra present. The smell of his post-ride, pre-shower body, like tin rubbed with grass, brought her fingers and more to the thin border of jersey and shorts. Her hands and eyes loved the Murphy bed of the tight cycling shorts and their jack-in-the-box spring. The shorts revealed plenty but also covered a massive area, eclipsing roughly twenty per cent of his body in blackness. She would peel that warm layer to climb into caves of smell hidden from the sun above. Here was the pure animal waft of him, the hibernating bear, the spraying tomcat. This musk she had become addicted to further marked *in* from *out*.

Sated and elated at home, she tried to tell one half-envious, half-disapproving friend or another that no man offers a woman the visual, tactile and ritualistic pleasures of lingerie like a cyclist does.

"He buys the gear. He loves wearing it. He even washes it," Betty told Jenn over coffee.

"Just as long as he knows where the runway ends in this little fashion show," Jenn warned. "Homo*erotic*'s one thing; homo*neurotic*'s another."

"Oh no. Andrew's not gay. No way."

Neither of them said anything for a moment.

"Really," Betty added.

33

You never forget how to ride a bike because memory sits deepest in muscle.

Marathon runners speak of The Wall, that border of endurance and pain beyond which the sensations are unknown, shocking, incommunicable. Your body is inescapable yet also not quite yours. Andrew's wall is made from red Maritime mud. Past it, he is amazed to feel the addiction deepen and widen. Here is the alcoholic's terrible relief at a full bottle, the junkie's last stop pulled. Healthy or unhealthy, of an exercise or an exorcism, these distinctions are too heavy for a climb, too cumbersome for a screaming descent.

A star of pain burns brightly in the back of his neck, stretches into his skull and dips between his shoulder blades. Knees, bottom lip and cheeks have all been branded by the daily sun, have burnt past red to freckles. By the time he hits Quebec he should see the sun written more forcibly on his left side than his right, see his passage on the East-West Trans-Can mapped onto his skin. Salt scurries from his eyes into his tawny whiskers.

Each discomfort is a toll gladly paid. Time has finally become binary: on the bike or off the bike, spinning or still. More than just understanding Tom Simpson — the British cyclist who died climbing the Tour de France's Mont Ventoux — Andrew repeatedly hears his dying, amphetaminal words: "Put me back on the bike. Put me back on the bike."

Dissolution with a chain. The rolling rapture. The spinning annulment. Here is absorption, totality, metal breath. Today, the desert fathers would be a riding club.

When a cluster of New Brunswick houses finally emerges in the near distance and a few billboards appear in the fields adjacent to the highway, Andrew instantly sees himself riding into the post office of this village he is approaching. Now that each kilometre is hauled through sweat and he has become a nylon nomad, a post office, even a small one, is empowering infrastructure. He'll mail home some gear to dam some of this sweat, to lower the flame of each climb. Any desire is a weight, and he's willing to cull. He'll further minimize his minimal gear to reduce the pull of gravity. No matter how carefully he had packed back in Halifax, he has pushed beyond those theoretical expectations of the trip and bikes here in pure practice. It's time to lighten his load.

Turning off the highway, thinking of his gear and what he can do without, he becomes a Minister of War, captain of a sinking ship, an alpha wolf in lean times. Who goes and who stays? What has pride of place in the panniers? The useful must be separated from the potentially useful, the daily from the possible. Street signs and a stop light nominate the moss-coloured vest he hasn't worn in days (back left pannier; but it's my pillow) and the warmer SmartWool socks (back rear). By the time he stops to ask for directions, he has rolled into divisive speculations. Warmer already, not too long before I turn south; do I still need the Wick Dry gloves? I could use mud instead of soap. I have read the novel before.

This mental culling skips past the sacred postcards in more ways than one. He's biking to a post office. Although Betty's trip is "entirely fluid" and "open to chance," they had at least mentioned embassies and *postes restante* to give themselves the illusion that he could mail her too. With a squat brick post office rolling into view, flag unfurling languidly in a slack breeze, he finally becomes more than just a postcard reader.

> *My Good Bet,*
> *Sweat is clear.*
> *You wrote of Greek men moving worry beads between their fingers. So's my chain. Worry uphill and down. Worry past, worry future. Worry us.*
> *Just noticed 'worry' is almost 'sorry.'*
> *— A*

He writes care of an embassy in Madrid she may not visit or may have already visited or may no longer want to visit.

Next he writes out his own Kingston address. Already, a pen in his hand is a strange tool, writing an effete game. This gear will fly ahead of him to Kingston, then sit in a post office, more of his stuff packed and stored. By now the house should be empty of tenants, home, now, to just memories. Daily and hourly he wants progress, distance, speed and kilometres, yet he'll arrive to an empty house. He may be going home, but he may also just be going.

The large padded envelope into which he stuffs vest and socks is its own little pannier. Wait, the cold-weather gloves too.

34

After a relationship, which do you remember more, the sex or the arguing? Sure, the sex is sex, unforgettable in general, but the details do fade. Actions are memorable. But tastes? Textures? Whereas the arguments were words and remain words: if you remember them, you think them.

Andrew and Betty didn't fight until January, and then they did, endlessly, about one thing and everything.

The Argument of Timing

"This MA in Halifax," Betty asked, "you're going to study travel literature instead of travelling? That's like going to a lecture on the symbolism of gardens but refusing to water houseplants. Try life."

"*Before* travelling, not *instead of*."

"Backpacking isn't an exam."

"Anything worth doing is an exam."

"Okay, sure, but you can read all summer. You can read while we travel."

"Read, yes. Write, maybe. I churn out essays for this travel lit guy, he could set me up with someone in the biz. Then I could sell pieces. Think of what a difference that would make."

"Yeah, two years."

"Year and a half, tops. What's fourteen months?" he asked. More than twice as long as we've been together, she didn't say.

35

Teaching inside a prison, Stan was mostly voice. In his first few years with Correctional Services, his disease still not announcing how far it would descend down its staircase of paralysis, he had circulated between Kingston's dozen prisons, sometimes even changing institutions for morning and afternoon classes. Seniority and the expected occupational fatigue of the Correctional Services teachers were the acknowledged factors that finally reduced his teaching to only the Allenville Transitional Facility. Stan's rogue bones and mutinous muscles were the unacknowledged.

Procedurally, Allenville Transitional combined the gender isolation of a private school with the latent ferocity of a military academy. Inmates there were counting down sentences of less than a year, either the end of a long stretch served mostly elsewhere or the full duration of a token sentence. Six months for a tax cheat. One year less a day for the marijuana kid's first bust. Among the teachers, at least those sober enough for conversation, this arrangement was known as "lions and lambs." Here was a final check on the lions before they re-entered civilian life, this stroll among so many fluffy, little lambs. As for the lambs, this was designed as a nasty scare. Clean up your life or next time it could be the infamous Collins Bay, better known as Gladiator School. Stan herded lions and lambs both with a red pen and a voice.

Not long after Andrew took up mountain biking, Stan was keen to leave work for his physiotherapy appointment so he could vicariously relay Andrew's stories of the torso-thigh wrestling match of riding to Susan, his physiotherapist.

"He should try yoga," Susan once replied, hoisting Stan's arms into the air. "It shows you who's lazy. 'Raise a leg,' you say, and most people never give it a chance. You can coax, demonstrate, give them visualizations and still most people treat raising a leg like an intermediate step, not an end in itself." She tried to let Stan's arm drop to show him how little he was raising it himself, how body must first be mind, but he was already palpably proud of his reply.

"You should try teaching," Stan said.

After twenty-four years of teaching at most levels — elementary during his own education, secondary by choice, peers at workshops, adults in or outside of prison — Stan knew a good class had ten to twenty per cent of its population willing to really do the work, to leap and then keep going, to change. Most want to coast, with or without your permission, with excuses or hostility. I'm here, but don't expect me to change.

Throw acne and hand-held electronics at the Allenville inmates, release barely dressed girls among them, and they'd be ordinary students: lazy, some version of cowardly and resentful of their own who wanted out.

Trained for work inside a prison by various men in acrylic sweaters, Stan was repeatedly warned that he would certainly be — each of them would certainly be — approached to mule. *Help a guy out.* Or *I'm protecting someone.* Or *Everyone needs favours.* Or *This letter's for my girlfriend, but they'll send it to my wife just to fuck me.*

"That's how it'll start," Stan was warned repeatedly. "They pretend they need you, that you're doing them a favour. Carry anything, I mean *anything*, in or out, and you're breaking our rules for them. Friday's favour becomes Monday's job threat. They pretend you're helping them and then they start to squeeze. The only game you can play is a zero-weakness game. Never, ever give them an inch."

The mule requests came as described. Stan's dragging left foot kicked up pleas like dust. Letters, small packages, sealed cassette cases. But the threat didn't come disguised as a favour.

36

Their sex was only partially verbal. *My dirty* this and *give me your* that. Whereas their arguments were almost exclusively verbal. Now, in memory, language pushes at him. Old taunts. Guilty admissions. Language pushes at him, pushes him on, pushes him down, while sex pulls at his balance. Here on every day of the ride at least one of their winter arguments between travel and study finds him, strafing him in the middle of a valley, adding weight to his climb or scorching his tent at night.

The Argument of Desire
"Of course I want to travel. With you. But I want to be ready to make the most of it," he said.
"If you wanted to travel with me, you would."

Their debate — travel versus grad school, change with a knapsack or change with a book — has mapped itself onto his daily debate of whether to remain on the bike-hostile Trans-Canada Highway (the hit-and-run way) or to strike out for the half-finished Trans Canada Trail, that carless utopia, that flatter club that would gladly have him as a member. Back in Nova Scotia, the Trans Canada Trail was off-puttingly intermittent, bursts of trail here and there that would require inefficient side trips and connecting jaunts. But here in New Brunswick, the trail lengthens, calling to him with its sweet, carless music. Here, and into Quebec, most of this patchwork trail has been converted from old rail lines. These old railways should be a dream, yesterday's explosions and rock-breaking leaving him a blessedly flat four per cent grade. On the highway, he's currently taking hills at seven, nine, or even an eleven per cent grade. When he'd first begun cycling and heard others speak of percentage grades for hills, he ignorantly assumed that a hundred per cent grade would be a vertical wall of asphalt. Oh no. Mark had eventually explained to him that a forty-five-degree hill, already impassable by car or bike, was a hundred per cent grade. Road grade is calculated by dividing the rise (height increase) by the run (horizontal distance). If he migrated to the Trans Canada Trail, his rises would be flattened into his run.

He's tempted by the trail's reliable grade, not just its ease, and also by its steadiness. His lungs could find their own rhythm. He'd feel his pounding heart as all friend and no enemy. On a trail, he could let his mind go even more, fling it to the day's kilometres. He could be like the somnambulant minivan driver or the robotic commuter. All of that release would spare him the raven corpses of blown truck tires and the foul wind of engines, *and* he'd be faster, do better as tortoise than hare. But for now he's come to want the hills. This way he takes the land into his body. And for every up, there is a down. Where would we be, as individuals or as a species, without our masochism?

To get back home, to get back to his home, he needs an up for every down.

The Argument of Honesty
"If this is so important, why not do it in a way that counts?" he asked Betty, somewhat genuinely and somewhat snidely. "Why travel for a hobby when soon we might be able to travel professionally? I want to do more than just run away."

37

After the divorce, Stan rarely saw full-length mirrors. The cheval mirror that had been his wedding gift to Pat left with her at his quiet insistence and went unreplaced by both negligence and design. After forty, he only caught his full-length reflection in a random encounter at a friend's house or semi-annually in the crash-victim's dance hall mirror of an occupational therapy clinic. The feeling of deflating horror got worse each time. When Stan watched an eighteen-year-old Andrew begrudgingly, then intriguingly, slide into the suit jackets that he had bought for himself in his mid-twenties, he was secretly proud to see a little slack hang on his son's shoulders, to see that Andrew still had some space to fill. Teaching Andrew to wear a suit properly, Stan had asked him to point out the widest part of a man's body.

"The shoulders," Andrew said immediately, not pointing anywhere.

"Where? And I said *point* to the widest part, not grunt about it."

Andrew glared and slapped the tops of his shoulders with one hand, one shoulder then the other, a huffy self-knighting. For a moment there was no disease, just a teenaged son and a father in his late forties sharing their universal looks. *I already know everything, so don't dare try to teach me*, said Andrew's set jaw, compressed lips and upthrust chin. *You know you're an asshole*, Stan's eyes calmly replied.

"You're relying on what you think you know, instead of actually looking. The widest part of a man's body, a normal man's body, is just below the ball of the shoulder, muscle not bone."

They had traded those half-looks in the half-length mirror above Stan's bedroom dresser, and then a month later Stan had found himself once again in a hospital's occupational therapy clinic, staring into a wall of mirrors. Just shy of fifty, Stan already had the frustrated sexuality of a prostate cancer sufferer ten or fifteen years his senior. Stan stared into the wall of mirrors, alternating between horror at his body and the burning knowledge that at several dance schools around town, flexible young women in tight clothing were staring into mirrors exactly like the one in front of him. Unlike these fantasy ballerinas, Stan's legs *did* quit, and far too often.

Worse than the bowed shoulders (his once-broad shoulders curled into an elderly woman's osteoporotic clutch) and the crimped limbs was his defecting torso. The deep ruin of Stan's body was nowhere more evident than in his unevenly hanging ribs, their slosh from the left side of his body to the right. The ribs are the saloon doors of the body. Something had flown out of Stan's saloon in a rage and twisted the doors on its way out.

With teaching for Correctional Services, the mutinous ribs and half-functional arms were generally more asset than hindrance. Grease for every joke, extra gravitas for every lesson, the swing up from a visibly hard deal. Stan had worked for Corrections for eight years before being transferred to minimum security, settling first along the gradations of medium security, which washed up everything. Men in their forties, neither old nor young, trying to resign themselves to a long, boring path from prison to clerking in some bad TV store, walking to a small apartment and heating tinned soup while young bloods hoped that enrolling in classes, just enrolling, never actually doing any work, might reduce the demerits they racked up breaking jaws and fermenting ketchup. In there, inside, Stan cut a rug.

To film Stan doing his English Language Sentence Dance it would be best to use different angles of him in front of the same chalkboard, one dialogue track stretching over multiple shots with the muscle-bound pupils changing year in, year out.

"Everybody up on your feet," Stan said to one hulking class after another. "If I can do this, so can you: you're the body crew. All right, put all your weight onto one foot. This is a verb. Say hello to the verb." For years, Stan hadn't been able to raise the opposite foot off the ground and made do with a flexed knee and shifting shoulders. "*Verb. Verb.* Funny word, isn't it?"

Funnier still — side-splitting, whisky-pouring, vote-denying funny — was the fact that most of these less than monolingual bruisers who only used language to make excuses or leverage couldn't recognize a verb for a day pass and a hooker, and yet they themselves were all verb. Whole lives of verbs. Verbs done to them, then by them. Verbs unavoidable, habitual, or delightful. Verbs by the mustachioed guy in the dirty red toque. Verbs by the guy who insisted on wearing a sleeveless shirt in November to flaunt the tattooed pillars of his arms.

"Verbs are action words. Your words," he continued. "What's the action? What's the operation? All right, other foot. This is the subject. It causes or receives the action. It can be victim or perp. The doer, not the done." Inside, they were all in a way station between doing and done. "Now, rock from one foot to the other." Stan simply shifted shoulders and hips while in front of him several thousand pounds of muscle shifted from one leg to another. "Without a verb," one foot, "and a subject," the other, "you can't stand up. Got it? Verb. Subject. Verb. Subject. Action. Actor. Action. Actor." There it was, the loudest pedagogical applause he could hope for in here: silence. Ten, twenty seconds without a joke, a snub, or a taunt, just piles of muscle dropping on one foot then another. "All right, take a seat. Now, let's get a basketball player up here and I'll show you the semicolon."

In hindsight, he would see Nick Vickerson's sleeveless shirt in November as the mark of premeditation and the tip of a threatening iceberg. As class ended and the other students filed out, Nick and his bulging arms stayed back. He stopped at Stan's Spartan desk and removed an envelope from inside his abbreviated shirt. Staring down at the seated Stan, he tossed the letter into his open briefcase.

"You'll deliver that for me." Nick jutted his chin at Stan. "Wouldn't want any *incomplete sentences* around here." For punctuation, Nick flared the uppermost layer of muscle clamped on top of his swollen shoulders and arms.

"Have a seat." Stan nodded at the single chair bolted to the floor beside his desk. "Sit. For the details."

Nick swung a leg over the chair and sat on it as if crushing a cat. Stan, meanwhile, was not idle. He had turned his own bent torso over to the desk's metal drawers. With his right hand he opened the drawer wide enough to dangle in his left pinkie. With his finger wedged in the metal drawer, he finally looked back into Nick's face, eye to angry eye.

"The next time you threaten someone," Stan used the force of his right arm and chest to shut and press the drawer against his skinny finger, "pick someone who feels pain." Nick didn't move. "If you're going to start punching, be sure to land one on my head. We're insured at about thirty grand a pop, plus the LTD, and, frankly, I could use a nurse around the house."

Nick seethed and twitched before spitting out, "Fucking cripple shit," and hoisting himself out of chair and classroom.

Withdrawing his pinkie, Stan pressed it into the desktop to see if it was broken. His left knee withdrew from the panic button mounted on the inside of the desk's leg bay.

By the next day, Nick was out of the class. By the end of the week, so was Stan, suddenly "rotated" to the minimum security Allenville Transitional. It took him nine months and three applications under the Access to Information Act to find his friend Paul Tucker's signature on the bottom of his involuntary transfer order.

38

The next motorcycle isn't so friendly. The roar growing behind Andrew has enough insectile whine and a nearly instantaneous acceleration that he needn't check his mirror to confirm the approach of a motorcycle. Here comes the Cyclops' wink. Christ, he's flying.

The motorcycle approaches with such ballistic speed that as soon as Andrew recognizes the second helmet of a passenger in his mirror, the bike is suddenly behind him. At such a speed the motorbike should fly past him and leave the valley in seconds, and yet Andrew clearly hears the decelerating groans of low gears engaged at high revolution, of brakes and engine both working to slow down. Having swooped in on a scream, the motorbike drops its speed by eighty per cent to suddenly hang two bike lengths off Andrew's rear. The motorbike begins trailing him, hanging back just five metres.

Here at day's end, Andrew's long shadow almost touches the two-stroke stalker. The roar behind is inhumanly steady, an inescapable shawl snug on Andrew's shoulders. His tiny mirror duly records the rider's unchanging visor. Even their helmets are bigger.

Two kilometres, three, four. So, what, you've got a skinny fetish? Yes, you and your polluted heart are faster. Go ahead, give me your startling shout, insult my ass and get on with it. Obviously I can't sell you on self-propulsion, on the aerobic trance.

Six eternal kilometres with this burning shadow. Most alarming is the obvious boredom of this speed. From fifth to second gear just to trail the skinny primitive. Cocaine to herbal tea. Finally, Andrew turns and stares, leaving just four outstretched fingers on one handlebar, still pedalling, to look: *What?* Nothing. Engine, visor, leather. He yells it now, "What?! . . . Quoi?!" Still they hang back.

He's thirsty from the increased pace. He wants to swat the dusty nub of his water hose into his mouth but is afraid to show any weakness. No, it's foolish to go without water, to weaken himself for their sake. He drinks. He even spits a little, onto their side of his bike, not into the ditch.

What can he throw or swing? Tucked into his fist, the compact cylindrical pump may strengthen his punch a little, but then again it's designed to be featherlight and could crumple or splinter at the first crack. The engine snorts, and the motored fatty lurches up another two feet to hang just inches past Andrew's rear tire. Recalled here is the boyhood nudge of front tire to rear, the cyclist's trip. Breathing, cranking and sweating, Andrew finally gets one image. His helmet. He'll throw his helmet, pull his goalie. One quick hand under his chin, then a flick back to send the hard dome under their front tire. Feed them to the road.

When the motorbike pulls up alongside him, passing his rear tire but then holding again before running completely flush with his front, he thinks of the metre advance as a wolf's snarling leap. Brushing off the flash of panic that would have had him roll into the ditch, damn the consequences, he sees, not beside him but in the mirror, the passenger's right arm extending a tiny bundle of tinfoil. (Woman or slim man?) The driver levels off this offering with Andrew's own arm. This is how they could finish him: wait for his hand foolishly outstretched, grab it, then kick the bike (or his ribs) out from under him. Still, a biker's tinfoil ball. The speed. The offer between moving parallel lines. His exposed fingertips brush the passenger's hand as she presses the tinfoil into his gloved palm.

Focused on the bridge of their arms, on proximate threat, he has been slow to notice the passenger's other arm stretched around the driver's far hip, its quickening stroke on the winded red pole of his exposed erection. A small white moth splatters onto his leather chaps before they roar off.

When the valley is his again, when his pace is down and his mouth rinsed, his hands crowd together on his profile bar to open the foil while he pedals on. If this is the weed he's hoping for, the proper leaf of this country's flag, this unpeeling of the foil could spill crumbs or drop a valuable nugget. Or maybe they've wrapped up a dead bird for you. Your bird, crushed beneath your tire. The one mercy kill you did make. On a journey, memory tries to become action.

Ten more metres of poor steering and a sideswiped pace as he unfurls aluminum leaf after leaf. To nothing. This is just metal foil, an effective lure of shine alone.

39

By the time Andrew was seventeen, the medical trips to Toronto were done by car, not bus. Strap Stan in, negotiate CBC Radio versus CDs, advance and retreat with the volume dial, slip into the fast weave of traffic.

"Oh, for Christ's sake, give him some horn," Stan barked.

They were in the left lane, the *passing* lane, of North America's busiest highway, yet held back by a car in front of them content to travel at exactly the same speed as the one beside it.

"That's right, buddy, the skinny pedal," Stan was saying. "You can do it. Go any slower and *I'd* be able to give you the finger. Oh, sorry, glasses please."

Andrew waited until he returned to the centre lane to reach over and nudge Stan's sunglasses back up his nose. Half an hour later, Stan announced another plan. "You're smooth between lanes. You keep your eyes open and moving, and I'm willing to bet you don't keep those fingers near the horn just to impress me. Drivers ed taught you well. When we get back home, phone around to find a decent package for renting a standard."

"We Porsche shopping while in T.O.?"

"They taught you to drive," Stan clarified. "I'll teach you to drive fast."

On rented cars they progressed from frustration in empty parking lots to endless trips though town — "Stop and go traffic'll give you the chops like nothing else. One more round" — to larger and larger highways. "Throw it fat on the curve. Fat on the curve," Stan ordered, but joyously, urging Andrew to engine-brake by dropping into fourth. "Who's dancing with a big one now?!" Stan yelled. Andrew hadn't seen him grin like this in years. "All right, we're out. Don't burn your power."

Here, beside Andrew's legs on the drum kit of clutch and gas, Stan was almost all voice. Once again Stan was a disempowered body and a

managerial, almost imperious voice. You'll find a... You'll want to...
Bend down to look... Hundreds of times Andrew had wanted him
to shut up. A few times he said so. Then, there in the fast night, he
wished he could close his eyes to get just voice, swing hand over hand
on that baritone rope. And this time the voice was different, crackling
with fun even when it was full of care, maybe even peppered with a
little daring.

"Think of chess," Stan half-counselled and half-commanded.
"Don't just look at what's moving, but also what could move. And
from where. Rank *and* file. What's beside you? Either side? What's in
front *and* behind? Take the Accord and do a full right sweep."

The surprises were as numerous as the lane changes. That Stan
knew all this, had once done it. Ghost muscles, the atrophied sacks
at the tops of his arms, hid days of fast youth. Imagine those bent,
cabled hands dissolving into pliant fingers, an easy palm, into the
flick and snap of third to fourth gear, the right hook into fifth.

"No. No. Stay here. There's space, regardless of how fast they're
going. You can fit. Gain on the Prelude. More. More. C'mon, you're
not even in his lane. Good. Steady. He's a fixed distance in front of
you. Feel that. Know it. Don't lose or gain any speed, just slide left.
The Neon's not going to hit you. Slide. Slide."

And the waste. The rented car. The scorching fuel. Insurance. A
possible fine. "You handle the speed. I'll handle the speeding," Stan
said more than once.

Andrew had got the balance down from paid lessons, got the
clutch-and-gas Tai Chi, and took every prompting to use it. Stan
didn't need to close his eyes to remember the yin and yang of the
pedals. Every kick and release rippled through the seat backs, each
chuck and pull echoed through the floor. The kid was all right, all
pink meat and reflexes, earning his confidence in five-kilometres-an-
hour increments.

"Always know what's happening to the space you're leaving," said
Stan.

"Yeah. Got it."

"Why?"

"So you know what's happening and what could happen."

"Be more specific. Your life depends on it."

"To know where the cars are."

"You're repeating yourself. Always know if you can move back. A leap's fundamentally different when you can't leap back."

"That's what I meant."

"Is it? Anything over one-twenty, you're dead in seconds. I'm a train wreck. You, we need to keep whole."

That night, wired and splinted into bed, Stan could still feel the speed, the old narrow tunnel rush of it. Staring absently at the ceiling, he remained in the pouring lanes, was still in the fast tile game of moving cars. *You handle the speed. I'll handle the speeding.*

Mercifully, Stan's intended police charade had gone untested. For the bond with the boy, for this one rush he could arrange, Stan had thought himself ready to pretend to a police officer that the visible mutiny of his body had suddenly become worse, that the hostages of his bent shoulders or tented hands or half-paralyzed limbs were now in even greater danger. If a cop car had pulled them over, Stan told himself he would have gone horse-eyed and gestured with one of his paws at his silver tracheotomy tube. He'd swap badges across the boy's chest, mouthing *can't breathe,* work spittle all the way to the ER. He'd been slipping though the medical cracks for years, repeating syringomyelia so narcoleptic interns and pudgy GPs could make it to the nearest reference guide. Spine mechanics, trachea mechanics. *Wow, same thing happened years ago. Some kind of blockage. I'm fine now.*

This was what his parenting had become: reckless, pointless speeding protected by lies and schemes, weakness a badge. Sorry, Andrew, sorry — playing my hand.

40

The wetness in the highway air has changed once more. Again his cheeks wear a moist blush, but something in the wet air is different. His curious chin prowls about ceaselessly, a dog dissatisfied with every corner. Finally his flared nostrils understand. He can feel water but no longer smells it. The salt is ending.

Ferris-wheeling over the next New Brunswick hill, he sees a flash of river snaking through the trees. Mentally he leaps ahead into the shaving clean of cold moving water. This keen leap should be regarded as the fruit of a fourteen-minute climb, should be tied to his three-digit pulse, and yet he is already a series of wet crescents. His chinstrap floats among the reeds of his whiskers. His crotch is a swamp. If saturation won't change, though, temperature certainly will.

Down the hill, up an oiled gravel side road past a faded Dead End sign, he lugs the hot machine until the river curls and gurgles in front of him. He digs beneath his jaw for the helmet's warm buckle, removes and cups the bright yellow beetle in one hand. Exposed, his sweat-drenched hair begins to cool in the breeze.

As soon as he dismounts he begins scraping his pale, wrinkled feet from the tight, hot shoes. The wet jersey comes over his head like a sail in scorched wind. Glancing briefly around the gravelled shoreline of weeds and squat shrubs, he finally tosses the balled jersey ahead of him into the river.

The water's cold bite is just a nibble compared to the icy mud's ceaseless, severing gnaw. Strips of mud seal around each toe, buzzing constantly with a frigid electricity. Beneath his heels, the mud sucks playfully at first, then jealously, entrappingly, as he tries to stumble forward into the water's filleting cold. Wading in past good sense, he is disappointed to see streaks of dirt still visible on his shins beneath the thin brown gauze of diffusing river mud. How can the cold hurt his skin so much without cleaning it? A thin, frigid line inside his skull may be a logical argument for a higher water temperature at the river's surface but may also be the thin edge of a hypothermic wedge as this long body of sun-cooked sweat, this strip of plunging mercury springs forward into brain-dissolving cold. He turns onto his back to hold his skull together with a series of lung-emptying whoops. Inside his recently molten shorts, his testicles mutiny and burrow into his pelvis. Sliding the shorts off, he either kills two dirty birds with one foul stone by using the balled Lycra as a washcloth or he simply smears bacteria all over himself. Each armpit gets chiselled with soap. As the cold deepens, chest, thighs and feet are lathered and rinsed with increasing haste. Contrary to both experience and expectation, his crotch remains warmest and invites a scratchy, prolonged soaping.

Returning to the gravelly shore he watches purple spill over his skin, cheap Chianti barfed from every vein, before he's even out of the water. Fingers jerking on a pannier zipper, he rips his way through to the car-care chamois which *250 Touring Tips* assured him would make the perfect camp towel. He shoves the faux-sheepskin chamois, a silly beige rectangle no larger than a placemat, around his body in absurd shapes — a scrotum-to-stomach codpiece, a nipple-to-nipple flag — to arrest the growing chill. Still, cold spills in. Fleece, rain pants and toque stall but don't reverse the purple tide. He needs a burn. Back left pannier for the sealed bag of dryer lint, lid-pocket for the waterproof matches. He has four sources of paper.

When he had read touring sites refer to dryer lint as "puffy gasoline," he was skeptically stupid enough to take matches along on his next trip to his apartment laundry room. To his very abrupt surprise, the pink cloud of lint in his hand had exploded its already puffed nature, maximizing the three-dimensional sprawl of its shaggy molecules in a nearly instantaneous leap from end ignited to end burning. Although he had hoped to drop it to the ground and extinguish it with his shoe, the lint was even lighter when it was ablaze, and it floated, a tiny Hindenburg above dirty, cracked linoleum.

Now at the riverside, Andrew retrieves his already diminished sack of lint with shivering fingers. He is by now a graduated sapper and knowingly laments the charge's meagre supply. Cold continues to race out of the river and fling itself at him. Arctic cleavers take one kneecap, then the other, as he piles twigs, sticks and snapped lengths of dead branches. The match's tiny flame wobbles then stands before briefly igniting the lint's inadequate store. Again the cyclist's razor parcs mass from priority. He wants fire. Toilet paper, novel, Betty's postcards, or map? Choose now.

No single garment is less welcoming to life without toilet paper than cycling shorts. Given the snugness of the cycling shorts, their value and a crotch itch that he fears is becoming constant, he reaches instead for the map and slices off its unnecessary provinces. Newfoundland, off in its columnar time zone, is the first to go, then Thunder Bay and a panel of Ontario from the other edge. The useless southern row, New Brunswick's porch door on the States, also meets the press gang. In less than a week and with the help of his knife, Quebec will finally separate.

Warming, finally, he begins to refold the heartland remnant of the map then recognizes that he has already biked off its neat squares. The red highway line stretched between distant Maritime towns has no relation to two and a half days of sweat. The map's lime-green hash marks are too quaint for these acres of trees. Older than the nascent Trans Canada Trail, the map doesn't show him the one thing he can't find himself. This gap between paper map and daily muscle is a small epiphany, the mere actualization of theory learned with a burning thigh. More important is his acceptance of a deeper, simpler navigation. He doesn't need a map at all. Just take the highway west. Chase the setting sun.

Before this trip, before every single thing he carried had to have a present or impending use, he would have burned the rest of the map now to mark this wild new leg.

41

In December, Betty stuck an enigmatic Post-it Note a metre and a half up a door frame in the front hall and changed his Kingston house again. *PRISM NAVEL.* The note made him even more impatient for her to come home. *Home.* The word bent up now, not down, the *M* a trampoline, not squelching mud. The dirgeful *O* had become buoyant, flung.

Crossing to the thin blue shingle of a note, he easily dodged two pillars of guilt, one new, the other eternal. The gone-Stan was as certain as the here-Betty. He flexed the bottom of the note with a fingertip, bent its inked letters.

"Hey," a returning Betty called out through the closed front door. Stepping into the entranceway she said, "Don't move it an inch," while dropping her bags.

"Not moving. Just bending."

"Hands off."

"Hands off what?"

"You'll just have to wait and see."

"Wait how long?"

"Until you see."

Nearly ten days passed with the *PRISM NAVEL* note unexplained. Eventually, tape was necessary to keep it in place. Finally, on an afternoon home, Andrew sat reading a Canadian novel boring enough to be required university reading (the *divine* what? what's so *divine* about whining?) as a beam of December sunlight strained through one of the bevelled edges of the front door's leaded window. The thin winter sun refracted through the bevelled glass to land in a knot of colour on the door frame three metres distant, precisely on Betty's *PRISM NAVEL.*

The house had never seen so many cards and notes. A robin's egg blue envelope propped between triangles of brie in the fridge, or a small envelope the colour of oatmeal tucked into his Shakespeare.

Translucent scarlet on his bike handlebars. Where did a woman who routinely read past midnight find the time to buy cards of all sizes, textures and styles? Could he just write a Post-it back? No, apparently he couldn't. Not with a frosted tobacco envelope riding his pillow.

> *Andrew,*
> *I don't know if you've been thinking of the L-word.*
> *People usually want to use the word before they need to.*
> *Frankly, I'm proud to never have wasted it on a prom guy*
> *or someone nursing his first sideburns. Here, though, I do*
> *wonder.*
> *I might be in love with you. Mom always said love*
> *should mean need to live with. Not want, need.*
> *I am ridiculously happy living with you.*
> *I might be. I could be. I want to be*
> *Your Bet*

As winter froze and bleached autumn, Andrew had trouble matching his opening move of September. He had made his initial, extravagant invitation to Betty. The orange room, half a house. She cooed for an hour, but then what? He didn't have another trump card until the opening of the *Strapped* art exhibit.

At an art gallery, she was definitely *Betty*. In second-year she had wavered. Maybe *Elizabeth* was better for the sweet white wine and track lighting of galleries. At nine and ten she had hated the stuffiness of the full, birth-certificate *Elizabeth* but soon grew to delight in its adaptability and its long list of usable parts. When boys her age were discovering the technological and marketing wonder of a toy/cartoon character that was both one aggregate machine and several constituent machines, one giant robot or airship and several smaller, more specialized vehicles, she was scouting ground with Liz, Liza and Lizzie, was flying around in the slightly differentiated small planes of Beth and Betty. Most comfortable with Bet, she occasionally admitted that she never stopped loving how affectionately that word came out of her mother's mouth. Post-divorce, there'd been mother-daughter spooning and sleep wherever and whenever they found it. *Bet* was a friend. Funnelling down from Ottawa to Kingston to study contemporary art, she did audition *Liz*, thinking it more appropriate for the organ meat suspended in fishbowls, the shredded phone books stuffed into kilometres of coiled transparent hose. In the maelstrom of young dating, who could forget a name that rhymed with jizz? But, no. *Betty* was Ping-Pong and flipped hair and a palpable step for the tongue. Betty was ready.

Exhibition openings were mandatory for the serious Visual Culture majors, but only the casually and confidently intelligent students relaxed enough to recognize that openings were for the artist, not the art. The conscripted audience, Betty and her classmates partially set down the conceptual toolboxes they built up during the day. Their usual attention to material, scale, cohesion and context was, and was not, suspended as they reached for little black dresses and lip gloss. By her last year, Betty knew she wanted a freelance curator for conversation, not a staffer, and who would be getting stoned in the receiving bay and who had wandering hands.

Late one Friday afternoon she phoned home from the gallery where she volunteered to cancel the pre-opening dinner they had planned. "I've been suckered into set up," she consoled Andrew.

"What, they need more genuine human urine? Used tampons not fresh enough?"

"Not quite. We fan and refan the pamphlets. We expand and contract the distance between cheese and fruit trays."

"Do you need anything?"

"Nah...Oh, wear something nice."

"Mesh? Latex?"

"See you at eight."

He was already smiling as he hung up the phone and reached for the Scotch. He'd drink to Stan then wear one of the suits he had inherited along with the house. Walking upstairs to the hall closet, he had made his decision before he'd reached the top stair. The two-button charcoal. High lapel notch. Slash pockets. Unpleated pants.

When he strolled into the gallery, indigo tie resplendent, he stopped her in her tracks.

"Wow," she said, "come back here."

42

Nutella, chocolaty, gooey Nutella, has become his sex. Bicycle, bi-sexual, then unisexual. At least with Nutella he's monogamous.

How can a — no, not a food — how can this spreadable candy so ensnare him when a month ago the cloying smell of it turned his stomach? From his education, from that slow maturation into his mid-twenties, he's no stranger to first reading of emotions or actions and then finding them more easily or frequently within himself. But to date, he thought this immersion belonged solely to good novels, great films and indicting porn, not cycling blogs. More than one tour blog consists of nothing more than daily distance juxtaposed with a volume of Nutella: *127km: 150ml approx (on crackers, spoon).* Nauseating, industrial Nutella has become sweet, fuelling Nutella. Chocolate's cocainic climb broadened by earthy hazelnuts (with their illusion of sustenance and nutrition). The European hazelnut fuels this European sport and spares him from the even more vomitous North American peanut-butter cup. Maybe that's the allure: (slightly) better chocolate, less North American wax. Without the francophone diet, this addiction would have been harder to manage. In Quebec, Nutella, cheese, beer and wine can be found in corner stores.

There's a red, measly rash growing in his crotch. That couldn't be from too much Nutella, could it?

Stopping here on the roadside to dig out his dwindling jar (front right pannier), he's able to deal his fix without even stepping off the frame. Licking the brown goo from his knife blade, he glimpses Vienna in the chocolate haze, has one toe in Paris.

He now knows the taste of Nutella better than the taste of Betty. Nine months ago, he felt like he lived between her thighs. Undeniably, her crotch was the focus of his life in the house. Oh sure, her feet were attractive, her shoulders, her neck. No harp ever played sweeter music than her hips. His life divided into before and after his relationship with the soft warmth of her breasts. They were young in the age of truly ubiquitous porn. No part of either body went unexplored. And yet nothing enraptured him like that private mouth at the base of her body. Her scent of soft cheese. Her taste of buttered blood. The texture of her clit, that key left above the door, is now becoming vague to him. He is starting to forget her body.

Riding pain day after day, rolling over land he flew over nine months ago, pushing his now and pulling his past, he is surprised but not ashamed at the tears that suddenly begin falling out of his eyes. Inexplicably, he pictures that other, yellow rider he let go. This, this is what he wanted, his own quiet road. He doesn't stop pedalling to cry. The sobs are steady, not jagged; no muscle gets wasted pumping out the tears. They just leak from him silently then get yanked by the wind across his sun- and wind-burnt face before they're buried in his thickening auburn beard. He can feel their wetness on his cheeks, a wetness that continues for kilometre after kilometre. Lower down, beneath the grip of his hands and past his bobbing knees, he can also feel the faint weight of Betty's postcards. Hard shame and bright knowledge spill out with the tears. There's an extra little flutter in his lungs but no waver in the legs, no sag in the pace. The bald digits of his speedometer blur beneath his tears. This is what he's been biking for.

43

Kids, dogs, teams (corporate or athletic) and those living under the yoke of disease all appreciate routine. So one Friday evening during Andrew's final year of high school when Stan called him up to his room, he was surprised to see a rarely used closet door hanging open. Andrew was even more surprised by an unopened bottle of Scotch sitting on Stan's dresser. He glanced from the bottle to his father standing crookedly in the centre of the house's dull master bedroom.

Stan declared, "You're going to learn to drink whisky and wear a suit. Don't laugh at my suits until you've got one on, and no ice. Those are the rules. Water we'll live with, but please, no ice."

The bottle was multiply surprising. Liquor store, beer store, Andrew had long been Stan's bag man even when he was still driving. Here was a full bottle out of the blue.

"Stanley, are you having an affair?"

"Dial-a-bottle."

"You ordering anything else on the phone?"

"Kiss but never tell. All right, listen. Proposition time. Friday nights aren't exactly pleasant for either of us when you stay in, and when you are out, you're not coming home with the grace of a ballerina. That sprint for the toothpaste isn't fooling anyone. Give me one night of the weekend and you can stop haunting parking lots, waiting for some stranger to float your bottle on the other night. Stick around and learn a few things.

"Time to meet a proper suit. Me, I'm for the monkey-wear these days." Last week Stan had paid fifteen dollars to have a full-length zipper added to the front of a twenty-dollar golf shirt. Using a door frame, he could lever a buttoned shirt on or off his shoulders, but his fingers couldn't manage the buttons. Pullovers used to work, but now his head was becoming an unpoliced outpost unreachable by his weakening arms. "Time to tie a tie on you for a change, and with something a little more elegant than the schoolboy's knot. Now, grab two glasses and pour a little cold water into a measuring cup for yourself."

Andrew fit a tumbler into Stan's wide paw, setting it there and holding it until he could feel Stan ferry the weight. When they toasted — to a good fit — Stan simply nodded his head, too slow to raise his glass. The whisky tasted like steel wool dipped in gasoline.

Stan's parents had both died unexpectedly at the end of his teaching education. The impecunious austerity of his university days was abruptly replaced with both principal and income. The inheritance would go to a nest, the income to its occupant(s). Daily trains sped east and west from Kingston. The same travel time and fare would land Stan in the Toronto or Montreal of the late 1960s. For suits, he had headed east.

Now his nearly grown son stood down the hall, not really looking at his once-prized, custom-made suits.

"All brown? What are you talking about? Actually separate the hangers and look at them. No, we can't start with that. Because it's double-breasted. You might never go back. Try again, please. Yes, the charcoal. Well, then, go get one of yours, preferably not a band T-shirt. That's right, then the trousers. Okay, turn toward me. Smashing. Broad in the shoulders, but you'll grow into it. A suit's never the garment to hide in. Let its shoulders settle on yours. Feel the unseen seam at your back and realize that it follows your spine. Let the jacket hem advertise your hips.

"You'll see notched lapels far more often than the curved or shawl collar. How deep will the notch be, and how high or low will it ride? Also consider the width of the lapel. Just be thankful I wasn't casting my net in 1974. Art, life, a suit — look for pattern and variation. C'mon, find me two related angles. Well, yes, inside and outside lapel edges, sure. Dig deeper. Yes, notch and pocket. Slash pockets, jaunty notch. This is order. Deserves a drink, absolutely. The taste is an invasion, so don't bother trying to hide. Get washed in it. Chew it."

Next weekend, another suit, another drink. This time, Andrew held his glass accessibly low. "C'mon, if you can get it to your mouth you can get it to my glass." He surreptitiously tilted one hip to lower his glass still farther so Stan could join him in a toast.

"To proclaiming the man," Stan said, briefly but audibly touching his glass to Andrew's.

44

Then, with Betty, the same house, once a dungeon of care, became a bright nook, a pad, a glowing balance of prospect and refuge. Clothed prospect and naked refuge. They were pleasantly surprised to find themselves preferring house paint on a Friday night to yet another student pub with bad music and diseases of gossip. Each was quietly relieved to be within grabbing distance of the other, with their music on the stereo and better pizza in the oven. Here, finally, was a dinner companion delighted by his marinated tofu, equally committed to roasting nuts and insatiable with salad. Household objects he had stopped seeing a decade ago suddenly leapt into view again. One day a floor lamp wore a new shade. Cups and saucers that hadn't seen the light of day in fifteen years were dropped off at the Sally Ann en route to the hardware store. Weekend archaeologists, they pried down through worn carpet, past a brittle subfloor, to three-inch Douglas fir floorboards.

"It's not home to me if there isn't sawdust across a floor and paint cans stacked in a corner," she said. "When other people were addicted to cocaine or divorce in the eighties, my mom was addicted to flipping houses. Eight in twelve years. I didn't have a bedroom; I had luggage. For her, why date when you can hire and fire contractors?"

"Remind me to buy a tool belt."

"Mmm, and film for my camera," she said, whacking his ass.

After pizza and wine, she reached across the table to rub paint off his wrist. "And what are you going to do with this place?"

"*Do*? For now I'm just going to exploit your taste for as long as I can."

"I'm serious. Beyond this year. Are you thinking of —"

"Hey, wait," he said, leaping up and slipping to a nearby bookcase. "I've been meaning to lend you this." He handed her his parents' copy of *St. Urbain's Horseman.* "One of my all-time faves."

"Great. This from a course?"

"Are you kidding? Study English in Canada and you get two choices: Blighty's poesy or novels of the oppressed, by the oppressed, for whoever's oppressed enough to have to read them. Besides, this is funny."

She was thumbing through the novel's opening pages, no doubt reading Stan's spidery inscription. "This was —"

"A courtship bauble, then a spoil of war."

"I thought *I* saw too much," she said, comparing parental divorces again.

Two nights later he wrapped his arms around her tired shoulders as she studied. "I just cleaned the tub. I've got candles."

He returned upstairs knowing he was starting more than the bath. The first time she had seen him in his cycling gear — taut black flanks shining, snug jersey blazing — she had asked when she would get to shave his legs. Now, immersed limbs laced wetly together, small candles burning, he finally raised a calf.

"Want to make Saturday's ride a little faster?"

"Saturday's? More like tonight's," she said, reaching for her razor. She gelled his calf.

45

As he is about to ride into Quebec, his third province, he passes borders of vision and perspective, in addition to those of government and law. After a week of riding, his eyes no longer lead his body. Or his mind. Although normal humans share several key characteristics with birds rather than quadrupedal mammals, the cyclist loses one of those and hangs between sky and ground. Like birds, humans are more active during the day than at night. Our young both depend on extended care. And our eyesight is our dominant sense. Watching Andrew dress for a ride, Betty once pointed out a fourth comparison between birds and humans. Well, at least cyclists.

"The males have bright plumage," she'd said, toying with the zipper on his magenta jersey.

But the bicycle is a mammal's skeleton. His eyes and nose are now closer to the ground. Finally, his eyes cease to be the advance scouts of body and mind. Instead, they are now just pushed on ahead of him like dirt in front of a stable broom. Visually, he's losing detail. Leaves shimmer en masse. The highway's painted yellow line is an endlessly spinning disc. So when a fully loaded red Mustang approaches head-on and too slow for its crew of young men, Andrew genuinely cannot remember whether he saw its tail lights whip past him a few minutes ago or not. Four thick heads turn his way as the car passes. None of them conceals his idiot grin. They drop over the hill behind him, and his mirror becomes a photograph he wishes would not develop.

He should roll through the ditch and stand by the treeline, should grab a handful of rocks.

He doesn't.

His knife hangs in the right-hand pocket of his jersey.

The Mustang's nose and grill come back smirking. The front tires advance like shark fins. The front passenger, all hockey jaw and beer T-shirt, works steadily at a cigarette as the metres between grill and bike close. Andrew will always remember this determination to get the cigarette down to size but understands it too late. As the car passes again, the two in the back are already laughing, heads moronically craned, and Andrew reluctantly follows their gaze to the front passenger leaning back out the window, then flicking a cocked finger.

The burning cigarette hits Andrew's chest, an unfathomably hot bullet that bounces rather than penetrates and hits him again on his left knee before dropping out of sight but not smell. Ill-timed and misplaced, his left hand swats at the pain, causing the bike to wobble sloppily and nearly take him down. The two burns continue to deepen long after the laughing thugs squeal away.

The anger shooting down each calf banishes his inflamed heart and swollen lungs from both reason and wisdom. Taking an avenging leap in pace, he tries to match the conqueror's steel directly when he should have just slipped between the trees. He could have simply braked and let them fly ahead. He could have avoided them, and definitely cannot catch them, but he tries to bike away from these irrefutable facts, tries to hitch his pace to his two drilling burns. Chasing them will exhaust him, take him into metabolic red zones he should not enter. If Mark were here, he'd tell Andrew that once he bets everything on his pace he is in his enemy's control. But, of course, Mark isn't here.

As he snorts and rides through the valley, he grows to appreciate that at least there are two burns. He can transpose the dual pain of chest and knee to the regular pain of one leg and then the other hurting in a climb. Or front tire and back tire. Upper body and lower. Two aching lungs. The fools, he's used to pain.

46

Betty found it appropriate that the artwork that most enraptured Andrew was a piece of sculpture. Of course someone devoted to "the animal machine" of the bicycle would fall for three-dimensional, thingy sculpture. In January, when she learned that Ottawa's National Gallery was launching a retrospective of the "viciously realistic" sculptor Ron Mueck's work, she had thought *term paper* and *road trip* simultaneously. Only as she raced home to invite Andrew did she think of Mueck's signature sculpture, *Dead Dad*, with its "hyper-real" frailty and its well-known shrinkage of Mueck's father's body down to just one metre in length. But Andrew was all enthusiasm. He wanted them to avoid their mothers and get a hotel. He proposed eating Indian and renting skates.

Later that night she tried again to slow their plans as she remembered the crumpled fusion of Mueck's realism, with its individually applied hairs, its layered tones of indictingly fleshy paint, and the shrunken, metre-long *Dead Dad* laid out on a floor. Drive, hotel and skating date all hung in the balance as she tried to warn Andrew. But he wouldn't be dissuaded, shared an interest both personal and vicarious.

"He did high, high-end mannequins in London," she warned, "he did film work. Super, super accurate, and there's always this manipulation of scale. *Dead Dad* is tiny and, well, it's *his* dad. Not *a* dad."

"A lot of people have dead dads," he said. "This is one of the things you realize. Thanks for checking, though."

"You sure?"

"What is sure?" he asked honestly.

Andrew was keen and helpful to get to Ottawa. He compellingly proposed cutting his Friday afternoon class so they could be at the gallery on a weekday for extra elbow room. His art chat in the car was better than what she got from most of her classmates. She went through Mueck's sculptural oeuvre, informing him about the use of scale then quizzing him.

"*Dead Dad, Old Woman in Bed*; they're tiny, smaller than life. What about a young girl, big or small?" she asked.

"Seven young, or twelve young?"

"Elevenish. Growing, so extra skinny. Long legs but no real tits to speak of, more like boobettes."

"Oh big, for sure. Do the opposite. Or size to potential, something like that. Definitely big."

"Yep, all seven feet of her."

"No doubt. Seven feet of the creeps."

"Okay," Betty pressed on, "what's she wearing?"

"Oh, you're merciless." He thought for a kilometre or two. They raced past frozen farms and clacking trees. "I don't know, a sleeveless sundress?"

"Worse. A bathing suit."

"This guy hits below the belt."

Each of them could spoon up this chat for hours. Lust might start with the body or how it's presented, but it blooms fully in the private language of love. Foretalk, give me this foretalk.

"Wait, she's not wearing a bikini, is she?" he asked. "I don't think I could take a bikini."

"No, no. A one-piece. You don't want to see a larger-than-life girl's belly button?"

"I'd rather see a woman's life-sized one," he said, smiling and reaching for Betty's shirt.

"Wait, one more. A pregnant woman. Big or small?"

"Big. No question. We're talking *force*."

All of this talk about the sculptor's work, all of this preparation, and yet forewarning Andrew did not adequately prepare him for the sight of Mueck's *Dead Dad* lying face up on a little morgue-like slab. When they changed rooms in the gallery and finally saw Mueck's dead father, Andrew's had been dead for five months, though he continued to let Betty believe it had been seventeen.

The head and the heart know in different ways. His head knew all about Mueck's hyperrealism. Theoretically, he knew that the *Dead Dad* of art would be removed from life in various ways: dead, laid out on a pedestal close to the floor and reduced in scale to just three feet in length. Yet for the second time in his life, his heart saw the blatant uselessness of a corpse, that unfiring engine with its few residual stains of vitality. Simultaneously, he stood in a gallery above someone else's dead father and yet he was also, once again, standing over Stan's body in the entranceway of their house. At least with Mr. Mueck there wasn't any blood, not outside the body anyway.

The sculpture said *death* with its pale, immobile limbs, its un-openable eyes and its nudity, yet it still had echoes of life. Colour, that deep grammar of art, juxtaposed pale stillness with the vigour of dark hairs on the calves and shanks and the scouring pad of pubic hair. Black, indomitable black, held out beneath a revolution of grey in the eyebrows and the hair on his head. The miniaturized nipples lay like discarded pennies.

However unique Stan's body had been with its bends and twists, it never stopped saying that it was a version of a man's body. A fallen man. A man so rudely stamped. But a man nonetheless. Standing above either man, Andrew saw the familiar, ruddy trinity of scrotum, testicles and penis.

Unlike Stan's, Mr. Mueck's corpse was surrounded by a crowd. More so than the sculpture of a pregnant woman, or a mom with a child, or a baby's head, Mueck's career-making *Dead Dad* constantly had a crowd around it. Shrewdly placed close to the floor, the prone corpse said *morgue* and *grave* in equal measure.

Surrounded, Betty and Andrew had so much to see and to hear. Andrew saw two dead dads, and also saw Betty's fear for his fear, as well as her helplessness and maybe just a little of the double vision of love. She could see the sculpture but also Andrew's difficulty with it. And yet that view was false. Just as a fresh wave of guilt caught him, they each overheard details that threatened to capsize Andrew entirely. Mueck had become an internationally famous artist with this sculpture of his father, who had been a toy-maker. He went on from this piece to others in the same hyperrealistic mode with individual human hairs. Betty and Andrew knew all of that and barely batted an eye when a bystander said, "It's his dad."

Only when another viewer added, "Not just that, he put his own hair on his dad's body," did Andrew finally say, "I need a break."

Betty let Andrew wander off in search of a courtyard. If she'd been ten years older she might not have felt guilty while she continued to wander around the sculptures alone. She wouldn't have felt so tethered to him in his grief. Care, yes. Coddling, no. But she was young and in love. Curtailing her last circuit of the mind-blowing, ego-dissolving sculptures, she sought out Andrew. She found him on a stone bench near an interior pond, took his head into her arms, her chest, wore a few of the tears he half-tried to hide.

"Do you need to leave, or can you make do waiting here with a book and a cup of tea?"

He did wait a while off in the gallery sidelines, but quickly enough he sought her out again, even told her he needed to see the flattened little dead father one last time.

When they finally left the gallery, they tried to resume their twenty-four-hour itinerary. There was hotel sex with its white anonymity and soulless décor. There was a long vegetarian feed at an Indian restaurant, each of them surprised that other people could leave the Mueck show and go off to eat flesh. Dinner and drinks were sweetened by the filial hooky of each of them being in Ottawa but not seeing, or even calling, their mothers. And yet throughout it all he felt the pull of a guilt he thought he had buried. Each of her consoling touches was chilled by the lie he had told her five months ago on that sunny Kingston ferry. There in Ottawa, she'd squeeze his hand thinking that he was nursing the scar of Stan's loss, not its still-open wound.

Only when they descended down onto the frozen Rideau Canal to rent skates and slide out into the cold darkness did he feel any relief from the strain of guilt. His legs still worked. His lungs stretched reliably in the clean air. He was grateful for the seemingly endless ice of the winter canal, grateful to skate forever forward, not in dumb circles, skate past her patience for cold fingers and clamping aches. Moving across the hard, even ice he tried to push ahead of the pull of guilt. When she became too cold to enjoy herself, he parked her in a warm-up hut and assured her he wouldn't be too much longer. No matter how much farther he skated, however, distance, pain and movement withheld their usual annulment. Each cutting blade and all of the cold, twinkling night said the same thing over and over again. *Tell her the truth and she'll leave you. Don't and you're not really together.*

47

After the flicked cigarette, Andrew's chest burns doubly. The actual burn, small but intense, a third nipple of pain, floats atop the conductive heat of his regularly pumping chest. A scorched hole in his jersey allows the wind to poke steadily at the circular burn. Both chest and knee add their own heat to that of his increased, enraged pace. Cresting one of his last New Brunswick hills, he sees that his heightened pace may not be useless after all. Thirteen kilometres into his pursuit of the Mustang, he finds a truck stop in the next valley. He will fill his water bag and get better fuel for his chase.

He swats the dusty water hose into his mouth and draws several deep mouthfuls while his intestinal chorus sings *four eggs, two sides of beans, stack of brown toast, cream cheese, and a vanilla shake.* Temporarily immune to fat, he mentally fills and refills his stomach and panniers. Four yogurts. An ice cream sandwich. Old nuts. A litre of chocolate milk. Tired bananas. A couple of power drinks for the parking lot. Woody oranges. He can practically feel the gummy ooze of a factory butter tart on his teeth when he bumps into the parking lot and sees the red Mustang tucked in among the waiting cars.

His shoulders and neck actually flinch as he squeezes to a complete stop and only relax after he checks and rechecks both the empty car windows and the nearest windows of the restaurant. Fear, then anger. He wishes he could admit otherwise, but fear flashes through him faster than anger. Their numbers. The size of the car. Their love of cruelty and his vulnerability in the open air. But then this wash of fear trickles down into his arms as anger. Step inside the restaurant and do what, though? Trade stares, then get jumped in the bathroom? Meet that mockery, all those tough nudges? Attempt a citizen's arrest of four guys? His pinch of burns tightens. He stops moving toward the restaurant's entrance, toward food and water, and buries himself instead in the depth of the parking lot. Blessedly, a minivan sits on either side of the Mustang. Thank you, soccer parents.

Every day for the past week he has kept his knife in his right-hand jersey pocket. He can feel its stiff outline, knows it is warm with his heat.

He stops himself from leaning the bike against their car, not out of any consideration for its paint job, but because it would attract too much attention, declare fender-scratching war to anyone else crossing the parking lot or glancing out. To keep the bike upright and ready, his parking options include leaning it against a Dumpster or a picnic table. The Dumpster would hide the bike, and to the Mustang crew any glimpse of the bike is a glimpse of him. But the Dumpster is also deeper into the parking lot than the car, whereas the picnic table is even closer to the road. He prefers a fast getaway and props the bike against the picnic table, careful to point it toward the road. Setting his hands into the low of his spine, he arches back into a stretch that allows him to surreptitiously slide the knife up and out of the deep jersey pocket. With the knife closed and hidden in one hand, he pretends to dig out coins with the other, then drops them and chases them toward the Mustang's tires.

This knife, purchased in Kingston by Betty then half-stolen by Andrew, is less than a year old and has never cut anything more substantial than cheese, apples, or packaging. As he pretends to stoop for fallen coins he isn't even sure the blade will be able to penetrate the thick hide of the car tire. Nonetheless, a two-handed shove driven by the weight of his chest slides the bright silver blade in to the hilt. Twisting the blade is like opening a tap of fetid air. Despite its stink, he showers his face in the tire's spray of hidden air. Briefly, he even tries opening one leg of his shorts to direct the cool air at the rash he feels there even now.

Expert in flats and patches, he twists his squat little Excalibur in the opposite direction as he withdraws the blade and then reinserts it to lengthen the gash. The steady buckling of the corner of the car increases his nervousness. When he duckwalks back to stab the rear tire, he knows how firmly the rubber will hold his blade, that a kicking foot could reach him long before he could withdraw it.

Stowing the knife in a jersey pocket releases another fear. He hasn't bought any food or filled his water bag. He's a brightly clothed vandal travelling slowly in broad daylight away from a lopsided car, and he's running low on fuel.

48

When Betty and Andrew finally started arguing, all fights save the one that started in a restaurant with his mom were about "clinging" versus "running away." He was accused of clinging to the house, to his past with Stan and even to their own recent past in the house, nostalgia already. She was accused of running away on a borrowed fantasy or, worse, a marketed fantasy. Rail passes, hostels and anything to do with the indicting term *backpacker* were all baubles of consumerism. Freedom prepackaged. Dharma in your size and colour.

Sometimes the fights lasted for an evening, sometimes they were just quick jokes. Travelling now on separate continents, they each feel the half-life of those old arguments burning away. They resurface on his bike, clinging arguments rising on one knee while another sinks and runs away. For months, they had both thought she was running away, but look at him now, slashed tires just one problem behind him.

He should have paid more attention to the contradictions. What is a lover if not her contradictions? They each contained multitudes. Academically, they had been equally motivated, chasing skill, knowledge and personal expansion in equal measure. And yet she didn't like his plan to do an MA. She didn't like it or her plans didn't like it. Every week she had some little gem to share with him mined from readings or class, and yet nothing could dissuade her from pausing that growth to strap on a knapsack. "Anyone can go to Europe," he once resorted to saying.

A taunt one day, and then two days later one of them would have some new wonder to share. She once told him about a contemporary artist, one of the gallery pranksters normally devoted to manipulating the surface of some ready-made thing, anodizing a shopping cart, dipping an inflatable bunny in gold or blood or both. For one piece, he simply dropped a few basketballs into a rectangular tank of water. The sealed, transparent tank showed four or five beefy basketballs floating in a row. Because air and water refract light differently, the submerged fraction of each tan basketball appeared to be offset from the top fifth left floating in the air. That little perspectival gap, that wonk, that was the piece. Kids at the beach submerge sticks in the water to see this difference between air and water, this undoing of what we think we know.

When Andrew and Betty drove home from their *Dead Dad* pilgrimage, he did not bring his stick into the light of truth, but left it to bend between light and water, left it floating among half-truths. And yet he did want her to hear the truths.

"Dad was the first one to tell me that dads die, parents die, that's the usual deal," he said, speaking honestly but staring into the middle distance of the drive, not her face. "But missing him, it's like I've lost the star witness to the trial of my life."

"We get new witnesses," she said, raising a cheekbone and shaking her face a little in self-nomination. "We earn new witnesses."

They had travelled, talked and seen enough that he had driven into an emotional quadrant that wouldn't let him keep quiet. Thirty minutes later, he started to tell her how long Stan had really been dead. At least, that's what he thought he was starting to tell her.

"And many have it worse. Imagine losing your dad at seven, at nine. And hey, what's a dad compared to drinking water? But all the same, hope is an exercise of the future. One of my philosophy profs defines despair as the inability to imagine change. You can't even *think* of a future different from your present. This is chronic starvation or totalitarianism. Dad and I could think of a future, all right. We couldn't help but think of a future, and it was worse."

Know this, Betty, know this.

He drove on, running away beside her.

49

Until now the knife has been a tool. Riding here on the New Brunswick – Quebec border, the border into his third province and his second language, he cannot stop feeling the outline of the knife against his back. All of the gear is ranked according to its proximity to his body. The shoes with their unseen metal cleats (the cyclist's equivalent of car keys), his brain-sealing helmet and the ass-protecting shorts — the holy trinity of cycling — all ride on the body, crowning the top, banding the middle and grounding the bottom. The jersey, part clothing, part luggage, holds in its pockets enough food for a half day's ride. Curved bananas, apples weightless with their lack of taste, PowerBars softening from the dual heat of the sun and his endogenously warm back, all ride in the tall jersey pockets atop the low of his back. Along with the knife. With the slashed Mustang ten, then eleven, then twelve, kilometres behind him, he feels the prioritized spiral of his gear all over again, feels not just the knife at his back but also the emergency blanket and tool kit beneath his saddle. A tool kit loaded with tire patches.

Back at the slash site, he wasn't able to see whether the gas station had a fully operational garage. If so, would they have the right tires in stock? What, thirty minutes for installation? Surely he cut deeper and longer than a patch could patch, didn't he?

He may or may not be pursued, and the carload of thugs may or may not be his only pursuers. The same knife he wants in his jersey for the Mustang could be problematic if he's overtaken by a police car. Legally, are they able to search his clothes but not his bags? In the pain of his increased pace, a pace higher than he thought he could maintain, he's still able to chuckle at the absurd thought of *searching* cycling clothes. Only the thong is more revealing than cycling shorts. Lycra and spandex follow every curve and are designed to offer no baggy resistance to the wind. Mark used to joke that there are no closet Jews on a bike trail.

Eventually, humour nibbles away at fear, but the unpredictable ripples of laughter also release waves of doubt. The drilling burns on chest and knee don't let him forget that this is happening. He is light-headed with more than just hunger. Hours of a red-lining pace, all on the electrolyte poverty of a day without one of the bioengineered sports drinks gas stations sell to overweight drivers.

Fear, hunger and fatigue, those thin, dirty siblings, run up and down the alley of his body. Thirty-seven kilometres an hour robs him completely. Thirty-seven. Grandparents don't even drive that slowly.

In the radius of importance that travels out from jersey to saddle-bag to pannier, his water bag is closer than the simple luggage of the panniers. It is closer, and draining quickly. There can be no ride, fast or slow, without water.

50

To his shame, he and Betty came home from the *Dead Dad* road trip even closer. Imprisoned as he was in delusion, caged by fear and shame, he even began to think that he had already told her when and how Stan really died. This heightened closeness, with its confidence and ease, surely this was a new them, a more together them. This themmer them was undone by a series of phone calls.

Because he'd grown up so close to Stan, he met the utterly relaxed pleasure of two people reading quietly in the same room through family first, not romance. Although he already knew the readerly pleasure of inhabiting the same room as someone else but being in a different world, each inhaling a private smoke out of their common air, he didn't know until life with Betty that, to him, this would be one of his very images of love. He didn't know he'd been searching for someone else with smooth feet and a warm crotch to read with at the other end of the couch until he found her. One blanket, two bodies, five or six books scattered around them, they were together yet distinctly parallel. For various reasons, some barely conscious, he was content to let the phone keep on ringing.

"Your phone's ringing," she said.

"It's no longer *my* phone."

"You just don't want to get up."

"I don't want either of us to get up."

This call was no problem left to the machine, a classmate phoning about some token group work. The very next night, however, the desolation of January prompted three people too many to check up on him by phone. He came home to a trident of piercing messages.

First his mother: "Hello, Andrew. I wonder how you're doing there. Please give me a call."

Second, even his old friend Nathan was a liability: "Hey, Day, thought I should keep in touch. Hang in there."

Lastly it was Larry, friend of the family, lawyer and, potentially, chief whistle-blower: "Hi, Andrew, hope you're well. Could you please give me a call? Home or office is fine." What if Andrew hadn't made it home first? Macbeth's finger reached for the delete key.

By the next day he had to widen his liar's miserable gulf, had to further bury that sunken, lying ferry of September. Biking home from class, he had a whole body glow. Love draped down from his shoulders and jumped up from his knees. When he looked up to the familiar brick house, he saw through to the new blue and orange paint inside, could hear the house's former soundtrack — all hangdog cello and netherworld bassoon — replaced by sunny violins and sugary guitar. Everybody let their hair down.

As he stepped inside he saw Betty already on the couch, sipping tea, glasses pushed up her nose.

"Larry phoned, said he's your lawyer. Wants you to stop by. Who are you suing?"

"My Classics prof. Did he say what it was about?"

"Would you want him as your lawyer if he had?"

Andrew stepped around the entranceway phone to head upstairs. After flushing an empty toilet and running an unused tap, he slipped into his office to call Larry back. Returning to the couch, he had a book in one hand and his poker face snug.

"Anything wrong?"

"No. Just form X by date Y."

"God, it's taken a year and a half to settle your dad's estate?"

"Mmm? Yeah."

51

In the late 1960s, the undergraduate Stan zipped through no exams more quickly than he did those of a baffled campus physician, then one specialist, then another as he complained of an inability to breathe in his sleep. Almost overnight he seemed unable to sleep in a bed. Suddenly, his lumber-mill snoring deepened into abrupt jolts in his throat. "It's like I hiccup myself awake," he told one doctor, then another. Finally, he was admitted to a neuro-psych ward for tests and observation. For loved ones who come to know the sweep of hospital doors and the sharp smell of their bright corridors, admittance is very much an admission, a confession of seriousness.

Lying in a hospital bed, not even twenty-five, Stan then had no trouble getting in or out of bed or dressing himself, save for his lack of anywhere to go. Unknowingly protected from pain by the same neurological failure that was expanding its paralytic reach through his body, Stan was relieved one evening to hear his friend Larry's voice down the hall, long after visiting hours had ended. He inflated a little with each approaching footfall.

"Mr. Day," a nurse announced from her starch and whites, "your lawyer is here to see you."

Suit. Hardback briefcase. Confidence. Even Stan agreed that Larry the law student looked like a genuine lawyer. "Thank you," Larry said to the nurse, turning to her with the complete expectation that she would draw the curtain closed before leaving.

"Well, Lar, thanks for stopping by."

"Stopping by? Thank me for the beer." Setting his briefcase onto the bed beside Stan's already skinny legs, Larry snapped it open to reveal six shining cans of cold beer.

Few positions are as conducive to honesty as sitting up in a hospital bed. Cranked up, sipping beer, Stan told Larry of how surprised he had been by the neurologist's questions about his balance as a child. "In six minutes he reshuffled my entire childhood. I could ride a bike, but couldn't walk the rails. The bad dancing was more than WASP repression. Something's really wrong."

Growing up, Andrew heard these stories more than once, but Larry had actually been there. After Stan's death, Larry was a little more than professional with Andrew. Each of them held different fractions of Stan, and like all partial owners, they admired, needed and condescended to each other.

When Andrew was with Stan, his body had a second language. By the summer before Andrew started university, remaining at home to care for his dad, Stan's body stayed with Andrew nearly everywhere he went, even alone. Leaving a cinema and stepping onto an escalator, Andrew could turn his body into Stan's. Lock the left leg, collapse the right hand then drop it onto the moving rubber handrail. Riding an escalator, Andrew could see Stan's body in his own hands and legs riding the folding stairs, knowing all the while that this body could not make the final roll off. Food packaging was opened for Stan, with Stan, or evaluating whether Stan could handle it even if he weren't there. Only in sex or on a riding trail was Andrew's body exclusively his own. Yet, just when Andrew thought Stan was so thoroughly in his own body and mind, he'd get a glimpse of Stan's past before the bankruptcy of disease, an anecdote from Paul, a reminder from Larry.

Once, when Andrew had chauffeured them home from another round of domestic errands, Stan spoke before Andrew could reach across his dad's chest to undo his seat belt. They were parked in the driveway and staring up at the house. On this dully busy afternoon, when Andrew was eighteen, Stan spoke revealingly of the divorce that had occurred ten years earlier.

"Larry told me I was getting off lucky, that the deal she took would have meant resisting her own lawyer. We were in his office. He had a pen set on his desk. He paid different people to clean his house and office. We sat there, talking about a love he had seen bloom and fade, and all the while we could remember each other when we were twenty-two."

Andrew got Stan's seat belt undone and reached for his door handle.

Stan wasn't quite finished. "Hey, how many divorced men does it take to screw in a light bulb?"

"I don't know."

"Neither does anyone else. The man never gets the house."

Andrew unloaded his dad and then their groceries into the house.

52

Last February, a card of Betty's taught him about admission prices. Now, making camp while fleeing the hobbled Mustang, he certainly agrees that all admission is paid admission. If you want to go somewhere, you have to pay to get there. Balancing paranoia and protection, he slogs uphill on a side road to hide his campfire.

Wisps of smoke climb off his small fire. He can feel both the smoke in front of him and also the rush of fetid air from the slashed tires of four hours and seventy-eight hilly kilometres ago. That rushing air is one of two sense-memories he cannot shake. The dwindling of his water bag is the other.

The map he finished burning two days ago was his traveller's visa for the country of lean. The pages of fire starter he now tears out of his novel are his application for full citizenship. Even when he first started to burn the map, that post-swim chill had been a hypothermic Iago urging him to burn all available paper. *You've read the novel before! At least burn the pages you've read on the trip.* Now, bad wind and unknown furies at his back, he agrees.

Because he has been reading a cheap paperback whose paper is essentially an unbleached, unquilted version of the toilet paper he carries in another pannier, he's able to rip out his first stack of pages without disturbing the gluestick spine. The suddenly gap-toothed novel looks like the sadistic smile of a purging despot, the smug grin of Stalin or Pol Pot slaughtering the intelligentsia. But burning a book is so easy, so effective. Fire starter couldn't be packaged more conveniently. Sheet after burnable sheet lie tucked together between the burnable covers of this box of tissues, this sedimentary, flammable brick. This combination of compact efficiency and weight management will unquestionably make book-burning Andrew's contribution to touring websites. Fear of being labelled a fascist has apparently kept anyone else from thinking of (or sharing) this most sensible of ideas, as if torching print one night would have you clipping in jackboots the next morning. "Burn your read," *250 Touring Tips* should say, burn whatever you can. Lighten always. (But don't burn your crotch. Tonight he undertakes his first non-sexual powdering of his tackle, spreading the medicated powder solely to relieve his growing rash.)

And yet, even though this paperback edition is not the actual courtship memento then spoil-of-war of his parents' marriage, simply a squat mass-market reprint with endless blocks of manically tight leading that cost less than a glass of good Scotch, this graduate, this teacher's son with an MA near completion, can't help but feel that these are a monster's fingers digging down to the novel's glutinous spine. The novel's unspooling voice, this nightly transport, is also just paper.

Another message emerges from the flames. The book remains a densely efficient piece of tech. Andrew's only visit to his undergraduate campus radio station had included a stroll by an archaeological strata of obsolete audio technology — LPs stacked between larger 78s and a top pile of various tapes: quarter-inch reel-to-reel, the ubiquitous cassettes of the 1980s and some recent, indeterminate DAT. Books last. One century of recorded music has mutated through at least ten different media. Cervantes's *Don Quixote* is still riding across the same pages while Mozart's *Don Giovanni* has been pushed into wax, shellac and vinyl, then pulled from metallic tape and polycarbonate plastic.

One chase or another possibly behind him, he's suddenly unable to read the book he's burning. Old pieties had prompted him to rip out the first pages but to leave the paperback's cover intact. As the fire beneath him grows, and a small amount of creek water begins its very slow boil, he pulls off the book's front cover and burns it too. He already knows what he's carrying. At least in the panniers. He scratches his crotch again. What is he carrying down there?

Inside the dome of the tent, when he once again piles the cleansing snow of the medicated powder onto his crotch, he finds a third heat in the grip, admits that his fingers are scratching as much as they're stroking, finds himself rubbing *beside* his unit. What is this, a Celibately Transmitted Disease?

53

Although there certainly aren't any actual mountains in Kingston, the nominal distinction of *mountain bike* and *mountain biking* helped Andrew roll away from the biking of his young past. The bicycle is the machine of childhood, balancing dependence (what child buys his own bike?) with independence (even a child can bike more kilometres than she would ordinarily walk). Children progress through a mammalian crawl to the uncertain walk of a toddler and then, finally, to the transposed feet of a bike's rubber tires. Just when many mutate fully into lifelong drivers, sacrificing their lives to one more cushy chair, they could be reaching for a mountain bike, a bike designed specifically to go where cars do not. Like many new mountain bikers, Andrew biked away from habit. A new bike made him an immigrant in his native city. More than just new trails were opened up.

In February of his year with Betty, when Larry's incriminating phone calls to the house prompted Andrew to finally make an appointment, he biked downtown to Larry's office, despite the snow and cold. Nearly two decades of cycling and he'd never ridden in winter. A mountain bike changed the city he thought he already knew. He held his helmet in the crook of his arm when he was finally ushered into Larry's office.

Larry half-rose from his chair. "Andrew, good to see you. Still bringing home the *A*'s?"

"Trying to. So, what are we up to today?"

"Just wanted to talk. See how things are going, off the record and off the meter. Frankly, I'm curious about your plans for next year."

"I haven't really thought past next month."

"What about development work? Maybe ESL in Asia?"

"Maybe in the future, yeah."

"Andrew, I wonder if you've read your father's will very carefully."

"After 'all to my son' I kind of glossed the rest. Why?"

"You'll want to look a little more closely. You get everything, but not forever. He didn't want you to hold on to the house. Don't dwell, Andrew. Take this as an opportunity to move on."

"Sure, absolutely. I realize I've got certain options once I'm ready."

Larry tapped his desk. "Your dad took steps to help you get ready. Take a look at Item Twelve. You have to sell the house within a year of graduating."

"What?"

"He wanted you to move on. This is kind of the opposite of an old move of the Catholic Church. *Mortmain*, it was called. Hand of the dead. This is a nudge, Andrew. Take it for what it is."

"But I don't want to sell the house."

"Andrew, they're not called *wills* by accident. This is what Stan wanted, to see you move on. Graduate and go."

54

Above a campfire, on the second night of his possible pursuit, science and magic swirl together in the wispy smoke. He burns more of the novel, burns more than just what he needs to start a fire. He's proudly committed to this efficiency, lightening his load, starting a fire and sterilizing water all in one stroke. Rationally, he has equated warmth and hydration with the diminishment of the novel and its reduction of mass. Yet he also stands above this warm efficient fire wondering if he adds the right number of pages or the right chapters and squeezes hope hard enough, will the map he burned days ago somehow re-appear unharmed, as if tonight he could bake what he destroyed three days ago. Fantasy is a sure sign of fatigue.

Now he wants the obscure back roads he has thus far avoided, those storeless, restaurantless strings of potholes haphazardly flung between Maritime ghost towns that half-support the resentful grand-children of miners or those reared on stories of the good old days when the mill was running and the fishing nets were full. Yesterday's roads may be best for him to avoid the Mustang, and yet to run out there would be to run without witnesses. On the old or new Trans-Can, telephones and maybe even heroes might protect him a little from a roadside beating. On a crumbling country road, a road he can't find reliably without a map, only mercy would save him, and he cut mercy away with a knife.

Before his counterattack with his camping knife, he had essen-tially stopped reading. Lobotomized with fatigue each night, he'd really become too lazy to read, as well as suddenly, profoundly dis-interested. Until the novel became fire starter, its urbane emotions had become too effete for him, too alien, fine china on the *Titanic*. Now, fear sharpening his mind, he reads again, reacclimatizing to the novel's adult emotions of envy, ambition and guilt in less than two pages. Its well-dressed lust is welcome. Despite his possible chase, he now steals a few minutes reading in the morning. When he finds a restaurant for lunch, he once again takes the book in with him, freeing up the night's fire starter with one hand while clearing his mind a little with the other.

In the panniers, the novel is given the most dramatic of seat upgrades, summoned from the economy class of pannier bottom to the executive class of pannier top. The novel finally wears the robes of highest aristocracy in this land, a plastic bag.

Burning print nightly, reducing his load, what of her postcards?

> *Andrew,*
> *Arcachon — unbelievable corner of France. Ocean and lakes. Heart of the Bordeaux region. Bike trails galore. Best is the 3 km long sand dune. I'm at the top — 3, 4, 5? — storeys up. Rolling ocean in front, sweeping pine forest behind. (The sand/pine looks like G. Bay). The dune advances every year, quietly claiming a few more pines.*
> *This is what I wanted, beauty that doesn't give a damn.*
> *— B.*

55

Running scared but also a little elated, more self-reliant than he has ever been, Andrew finally has to wonder if Betty was the first or the second woman he let go. When his parents had divorced, they each told him repeatedly that he could choose whether to continue living in Kingston with his dad — same house, same school — or he could move to Ottawa with his mom. Just as frequently as they told him that the choice was his to make, they also told him that he'd still have two parents, no matter what, still be loved by each of them, that things wouldn't be so different. "If everything was really going to be the same, I wouldn't have to decide where to live!" he yelled back at them on one of the rare occasions when he had them both within earshot.

Given the way he'd been told about the divorce, he didn't take the schoolyard advice and sobbingly ask for a dog as a consolation prize. Nonetheless, some of the schoolyard wisdom did prove accurate. *You'll definitely get a video game upgrade. Ask for a new Superbox.* Check. *The first Christmas, you won't be able to count the toys.* True. *Your Mom's new guy will give you money. Not stepmoms; they're too cheap. They'll feed you and try to hug you, but any new guy's an easy touch for money.*

When he chose to stay with his dad, Andy could not have said then how much of the decision was to stay with friends, how much to stand by his dad and how much to avoid Gordon Gamlin, the man he'd seen drive his mother home more than once. For all the honesty he did meet during the divorce, he now wishes that someone had assured him adults generally don't know why they do what they do any more than kids do. Pat came closest, telling her son, "Sometimes you want what you want, regardless of why," but instead of listening he used a glittering piece of fresh injustice to pry himself away from her. He definitely couldn't bear to hear her talk about *want*.

Go with Gamlin was definitely Patricia Day's slogan, the catchphrase that moved her front and centre in Gordon Gamlin's esteem and election campaign. In hindsight, *Go with Gamlin* was also her resumé, calling card, battle cry and prophecy. Gordon, a man with an MA in the 1970s and an undefined job with the school board, was a distant colleague of Pat, a woman with a BA, a palpably higher IQ, a lower salary and less career mobility. When Gordon won the nomination for a federal political party with vaguely centrist policies and unprecedentedly deep pockets, Pat followed him, dropping to part-time teaching at Foulton Elementary to manage his spring election campaign, for starters.

Pat's going with Gamlin found Andy and Stan in the kitchen working their way through a limited repertoire of fish sticks, bacon sandwiches and omelettes draped in processed cheese slices. For two. Andy earned praise by learning to make coffee. Pat shoved things in the nearest drawer or cupboard on Tuesday nights before the new cleaning lady arrived on Wednesday mornings. She didn't ever quite show her grade four class the draining math in which two "part-time" jobs were more consuming than one full-time job.

For an election campaign before computers, Pat often drove typed press releases to the mail slots of the papers (at ten p.m., eleven p.m., twelve a.m. or later). She quickly learned that the Whig building was only dark and silent at the front. Around back, men in caps and greasy coveralls smoked in nearly flammable air and steadily went deaf among the clattering presses. The noisy oily press room became an oasis for Pat. Last night, before the pamphlet catastrophe, she had wanted to lay on the horn until someone opened up and she could charm her way in for a drink from one of the many bottles she knew were secreted in desks and cabinets. When she did leave, she sped home close to prayer, the bed ahead of her just a shelf to set an overused tool.

Then morning. Alarm. Coffee. Muffin and banana for the drive. The high brown boots. Lesson plan? Lesson plan? (*The teacher who fails to plan plans to fail.*)

Still in his pyjamas, Andy radiated a gauzy kind of heat. She looked into his face in the mirror while she slid in an earring.

"Are you still taking me biking after school?"

"I said I would."

She continued to discuss her life at the school with Stan. She never stopped wanting to talk to him. Stan, not Gordon, was the perfect audience to hear about how Nancy, the school's youngest secretary, lorded the intercom over Pat. "Mrs. Day," Nancy was now saying regularly over the crackling intercom, "you have a phone call." Mrs. Day, the intercom wanted to know, are you going to leave these children unsupervised, again, as you tend to your moonlighting? Striding down to the office — yikes, one boot is going — Pat saw a teacher's face in every doorway, correctly inferring that Nancy had paged the entire school rather than just her classroom.

With or without the principal hanging beyond his door, Pat fired at Nancy from the doorway, "Nancy, I don't hear it when other teachers get phone calls. Surely I'm not that special."

"I can't keep track of your running around, now can I?" Nancy launched the swift carriage return of her electric typewriter, eyes tightened by that high school diploma she'd missed by half a year, by the bus she took to work, by her unpaid summers.

"Three-twelve, Nancy. I run around room three-twelve." At that, Pat picked up the blinking phone to the breathless, irate, pleading Gordon whose voice she'd been waiting to hear.

Two hours later she had a coffee stain on one thigh of her skirt (and possibly a mild burn beneath), a kink in her neck from endlessly cradling a phone and Gamlin's son Ben drawing in blue ink on parliamentary reports. A glitch at the printer's, some inconsiderate bastard's mangled arm or burst hernia, some traffic jam non-delivery, meant another delay on the pamphlet or running without proofs. She'd argued for the delay and would be returning tonight to recheck the pamphlet and prepare questions for tomorrow morning's visit to the aluminum plant. Returning, she'd been adamant, after a meeting with her son (and a change out of these boots).

At home, she couldn't do anything — explain her lateness, order Chinese, break the news that she'd be going back in just two hours (Don't wait up) — until she had clawed her way out of those boots, had a drink and flopped, however briefly, onto the couch. Andy's unanticipated absence made a ten-minute flop on the rocks entirely doable until she reached for her boots. The zipper tab on the already torturous left boot broke in her fingers, broke painfully and then jammed. Free leg shorter than the trapped one, she hobbled down the basement stairs. She should at least have mixed a drink first, but she was down now and the hunt for needle-nose pliers was becoming an even bigger priority than gin. Stan didn't use the fucking things, so why should he have been more likely to know where they were?

"Mom!" Andy bellowed from the doorway. "I'm ready. I was at Kenny's and saw you drive by so I ran home. So I'm ready."

"Okay. Say, do you know where the needle-nose pliers are?"

"Oh no. My bike's fine. Let's go."

"Yep."

Sinking her other leg back into the one obedient boot — twenty-seven when she bought these; what was she doing? — she honestly contemplated a swig of gin from the bottle. Instead, she slipped out into the garage and was ruined by the sight of Andy holding the next door open for her.

"This time I can make it," he said.

In the sunny driveway, Pat didn't quite say, "Bike away from your own fear" but relied instead on old standbys like, "I've seen you almost make it" and the vaguely hepcat, "Just keep going." Now, twenty years later, Andy would be cinched into a bulbous helmet and bike-savvy parents would yell out practical encouragements like, "Look where you want the bike to go." And they'd practise on grass or a forgiving recreation trail made from recycled tires and fine gravel. Here, all they'd had was the side of a quiet residential street, Andy's thin moth skull and Pat's distant but distinct memories of herself riding.

You never do forget. Somehow, surely, she could get the memory of riding out of these boot-trapped legs and into his little body. Standing alongside, she could hold the bike at both ends, but this demanded a brisker sidestep she would have had trouble executing in sneakers, let alone boots. Worse, she couldn't see much of Andy's body and so had no idea why he barely lasted a single bike length whenever she let go.

"Mom's going to have to go behind."

"No."

"I need to see what you're doing."

"Then the handlebars won't go."

"You control the handlebars, kiddo, not me."

Andy abandoned verbal protest for some bottom lip work, and Pat gripped the seat under his little coconut rump. Sadly, her skirt and the back tire didn't get along, leaving her in a hunched run no faster or more convenient than the sidestep.

"Andy, you're putting your own foot down. You've got to pedal."

It wouldn't be until he met Mark sixteen years later that Andrew would fully abandon this boy's timid instinct with the foot. "If you can choose to put a foot down, it's going down too soon," Mark would later tell him. The quick-drawing body will always get a foot down if it can.

"Pedal, Andy," Pat coached with diminishing patience.

"I am."

"Andy, I can see that you aren't. You've got to keep going. That's how it's fun."

They tried and failed. Again and again. She understood that he was lying because he was afraid, but that didn't make his snappiness any easier to handle, his imperious, bike seat-throne snappiness. The hobble of her boots was worsening by the minute. The weight of bike and boy was firmly registered up her arms and into her phone-cradling neck. She didn't need this sweat behind her knees. So, yes, she was impatient and did push a little extra. He needed to feel the bike move. Andy, meet inertia.

Sadly, Andy met a ditch, a full ditch. Pat couldn't even think to yell, "Steer," and just watched the silent slapstick comedy. A bike was moving toward a watery ditch. Boy. Ditch. Boy. Ditch. C'mon, kid, they're handlebars, not handcuffs. Thankfully, his total refusal to steer meant that he entered the ditch on the angle at which he had approached it, so the abrupt stop of front tire meeting submerged ditch bottom sent his body northwest instead of north. Yes, he landed in green, scummy water, but at least he didn't hit the handlebars first.

The sight of the algae-speckled water rising in one small wave up his arms to his chin sent the words, "Oh, Andy, I'm sorry" out of her mouth. She disagreed with *sorry* as it passed her lips, but in an abstract way. A fleck of cartoon-bright algae clung to Andy's quivering chin. His small eyes were stretched fully. She was stepping forward to ask if he was hurt, where? She was bending down.

"My mom pushed me in the ditch," he hollered, looking away from her to the road he began to run down. "My mom pushed me in the ditch." She was left to retrieve the slimy bike. She limped home to a fading, "My mom pushed me in the ditch."

Back at the house, Stan had none of Andy's speed. Using one arm to lift the other onto the railing, raising one leg, then the other to climb each stair after the returned Andy, this took just enough time for Pat to come back, drop the wet bike in the yard and head for the stairs herself. When she stepped out from behind Stan at the top of the stairs, she realized that she had seen Andy do this dozens of times, squirm past his dad.

With both parents in the hall, Andy whipped open his door to scream, "Mom pushed me in the ditch." Pat took a sharp right and headed for the bathroom, neither closing the door nor looking back down the hall, just scrubbing her hands.

"Andy," Stan coached from the middle of the hall, "the only way to stay up is to pedal. Pedal, then steer. Take it from me, kid, in life you either push or get pulled."

The bastard.

56

Betty's postcards are now his only map. Fleeing the phantom Mustang, he barely sees the signs counting his way down to New Brunswick's Botanical Garden / Jardin Botanique, doesn't yet appreciate that this garden near the Quebec–New Brunswick border is one of the places where the Trans-Canada Highway and Trans Canada Trail flirt enough to briefly kiss. He remains in the dumb hamster wheel of the chase even after he sees the public garden emerge in the distance.

An entrance building is thrust out from a high green fence over which tall lamps peek their heads like giraffes. When he is close enough to see that the fence is not solid as he had thought, but rather a standard diamond-wire fence with strips of tough green plastic braided through, when he sees that this fence is designed to quarantine beauty for paid admission, he thinks of one of the Germany cards riding just inches from his burning left knee.

> *Munich.*
> *Am I for or against Dachau being on a municipal bus stop? (Dostoevsky: Man grows used to everything, the scoundrel.)*
> *I knew about Nandor Glid's memorial sculpture here, lecture knew, book knew, but am really smashed by it. The simplicity: a mass of starved limbs = a barbed wire fence. Knees = barbs = elbows. You stand here and think* fence *over and over and over. In here, the absolute worst. Out there, buses, shops, radio every night.*
> *Learning,*
> *— B.*

This garden fence moans in a warm breeze. In flight not fight, he needs to go to ground, why not well-tended ground? He, too, will hide behind the admission-price-only fence. Provided he can get the bike in. He rides past parked cars and small beds of cheap flowers that border the parking lot and front the entrance building.

In a grad school seminar, someone once tried to paraphrase Aristotle's notion of aesthetic logic with a half-remembered, possibly apocryphal, Monty Python line, something like: there's no problem if three men walk on stage dressed as carrots, but the one guy dressed as a piece of celery will have to explain himself. Celery-Andrew wants to take his vehicle inside a garden with a parking lot. Because he can, this may be a problem.

Near the entrance, the alienness of small, polite signs and cement and turnstiles is brushed aside by a physical dig for cash and a silent audition of various arguments for the ticket taker. *I believe this is called smelling the roses. Or I don't pollute. You let in the planet killers, but not me? Oh this? Seeing-eye bike.*

The turnstiles in front of him leave no hope of slipping the bike past. Drained as he is from fleeing the Mustang, could he even lift the bike over? Approaching the admission guy (guy — damn) he's still debating aloof expectancy versus some calibre of plea when he hears, "'ang on, let me get da gate for you."

Stepping out of his booth to ease the bike's passage, the young clerk with his whispered moustache asks, "You come up the Temeese?"

"No, but I'm looking for it."

"Right over dere."

At the other end of the parking lot, a metre-wide trail reaches into the trees. Small square signs point to Le Petit Témis, a long section of Canada's incomplete Trans Canada Trail and a bit of cycling heaven. "Merci," Andrew says, stepping inside the garden.

Incongruous with flower beds both ordered and sprawling, with patterned groves of saplings and cascades of shrubbery, are the ambitiously tall lampposts with their ballpark halogens and suspended speakers. Sealing the adjacent highway from sight, the botanical gardens try to replace its muffled roar with Vivaldi audible at every step. Andrew is delighted. Every violin stroke is like a wipe from a clean cloth. Bed after flower bed is even more compelling than the fragrant cafeteria. Laying the bike on the ground, he is combed by serrated leaves and showers in greenery. The complete spectrum of green, from the most sprightly bright greens to the most brooding and umbrous, are punctuated by dissolutions of burgundy and brief frosts of blue. Flowers hang their various lanterns. Ladies dangle bright slippers. Around and around he goes.

Returning to the pavilion, he eats three tasteless bagels greased with slabs of dull cream cheese, drinks two bottles of grapefruit juice and reads photo panels devoted to the region's rail history.

Le Petit Témiscouata railway ran for one hundred and twenty-five kilometres, from Quebec's Rivière-du-Loup into the most westerly point of New Brunswick. Designed to connect New Brunswick's serpentine Saint John River to the massive St. Lawrence, up towering hills and through almost constant curves, Le Témis remained profitable after other private rail lines lost freight to trucks as nineteenth-century rail was replaced by twentieth-century trucking. Entire forests of lumber were hauled through this curved chute blasted through rock and cut through forest. In its day, Canada's national railway was the largest civil engineering project in the world. The world's second-largest country built a railway from the Pacific Ocean to the Atlantic, then squandered it in favour of perpetually running diesel trucks, those warehouses on public roads. Some of the freight currently passing behind Andrew on the Trans-Canada Highway arrived in Halifax by ship to be trucked to warehouses in Montreal before being returned by truck to retailers in Halifax. The Trans-Can isn't a road; it's a river of oil.

Cut and cleared, then eventually abandoned, Le Petit Témis was finally reclaimed as part of the growing rail-to-trail initiative, that funereal dirge sounding across a continent content to rip up unused rail so every citizen can have the freedom to buy groceries with an eight-cylinder Supermarket Utility Vehicle. Linked once again, Le Témis has become a segment of the growing Trans Canada Trail.

Here, inside a public garden sealed from public view, at an intersection of highway and trail, Andrew digs out his half-novel to wait for night to fall completely. In this, the first in a series of hidden waits, he isn't able to bike away from memories good or bad. Betty's postcards continue to ride prominently on his bike, and sometimes her arguments ride even closer.

The Argument of Honesty, II

"Okay, sure, you want to travel with me to some degree," said Betty. "But obviously, indisputably, you want something else more. I don't blame you for wanting tea and books in a cold apartment; I blame you for not admitting it."

57

The ride has him eating constantly, with unprecedented nutritional demands but also an inconceivable nutritional licence. He could eat ice cream by the pound without gaining any. Eating alone, squirting twice-warmed but uncooked food into his mouth on the bike or packing himself in a restaurant, he often pictures Betty in one European restaurant or another. He doesn't yet know the monotonous, tepid reality of bread-and-cheese travelling in Europe, so to him she is eating risotto one day and miso-baked tofu the next.

Because the start of the trail runs vulnerably close to the highway, he waits for the cover of darkness, passing hours in the garden cafeteria reading, eating and strolling up to one informative display after another devoted to the now extinct railway. Rivière-du-Loup and Edmundston were, as rail enthusiasts call them, *the ends of steel*. Long after Andrew has read each display panel at least twice, he thinks as he eats of the nutritional museum exhibit he could create for his own culinary evolution, the cuisine he inherited giving way to one he chose.

The Kingston house that hangs in front of Andrew, waiting 850 kilometres beyond his handlebars, has finally relinquished its gendered kitchen appliances. Even when divorce turned the house into a men's club, neither Stan nor Andrew would ever have allied himself to antique phrases like *her kitchen* or *her oven*, and yet in ways, their kitchen fossilized at Pat's departure. No *Lady Convection* warmed their hearth, no *Kitchen Maid* housed their meals, but gender still lurked in their cupboards and haunted their drawers.

For the first few years after the divorce, emerging, finally, from numerous mediocre restaurants, Stan and Andrew cooked together, opening bags and cans, double-checking the instructions on the sides of small boxes. Aside from the day's barbecued or fried meat, they subsisted on the astronaut food of the early 1980s, with vegetables frozen into bricks or stacked into their canned pillars. A few years after Pat's departure — Stan shrinking, Andrew growing — Andrew unearthed grey memories and dug out the already aging electric frying pan Pat had gladly abandoned. Freckled with pepper, pork chops were fried until they achieved the colour of lead. Sausages hissed and spat.

On her weekends with Andy, or in the phone calls he made to her, Pat quickly deflected any questions about cooking. She talked over him if necessary — *roux*-this, *parboil*-that — or bribed him off with more TV time or asked him to first grate the cheese she knew he'd silently snack on, anything but make him into Stan's butler, maid *and* chef.

At home, Andrew had no complaints. Back bacon sandwiches for dinner. Boil-in-the-bag corned beef. Frozen pizza. Mac 'n' cheese 'n' wieners again. Tucked there at the back of the house, the kitchen was their forgotten, Atlantic province. Stan relented to a microwave only after a VCR and a video game console had long ago made their way into the house. When Andrew was stretched on the rack of full adolescence, when their freezer was piled deep with frozen entrées he didn't then realize were made by a company that started its meat empire removing dead animals from farms, Andrew was unfazed when Heather, his first girlfriend, said, "You don't cook; you heat. Has this kitchen ever produced a salad?" Mouth and inner body slept a few more years.

He never did get to ask Betty's mother if architects and real-estate agents anticipate the architecture of argument. The kitchen and dining-room arguments about meat between Stan and a late-adolescent, quasi-vegetarian Andrew spread throughout the house. Triumphantly raising an arm off his bed during some home physio, Stan had the audacity to boast, "See? Protein," as if their now con-tested meals of meat and two tasteless veggies were getting his weak arm up in the air, not exercise or Andrew's daily coaching.

"That's just it, though," Andrew retorted, resisting Stan's raised arm. "North Americans consume twice as much protein as we can handle, let alone need. You think any other mammal needs a maga-zine to take a shit?" A week later, standing over a phone book in the front hall, they debated a pizza order.

"Ordering one vegetarian pizza won't infect you for life, Dad."

"What other pleasures do I have?" Stan said, shuffling off. He wasn't thirty seconds before calling out, "Just order two."

That spring, if he hadn't had to lift Stan off the toilet ten minutes before starting dinner four feet away, if he'd known more food than the meat, potato and one vedge of two decades ago, if he hadn't been greying meat in an electric frying pan, hadn't biked his way into a friendship with the vegetarian athlete Mark, he might not have gone fully vegetarian, might not have later fallen in love with Betty. But Stan's defecting ribs were still palpable in his hands after two washes in the kitchen sink when he dropped two pork chops into the pan. The sizzling, bloody meat aged steadily along its dagger of bone. A phlegmy nugget of fat bubbled in a notch at the bone's base. With a large fork he plucked up one chop half-cooked.

Years later, Betty and Andrew strolling home from an Indian restaurant, she once again took up their periodic inquiry into why they had fallen together so thoroughly and so quickly. "All right, look, I'm not asking for the number, but your lovers — how many, and how many were vedge? For me, any time a guy reached for a burger I knew this was just temporary sex, and not the best-tasting fuck in the world at that. The two of us haven't spent a month in church between us, and yet we know all about the challenges of interfaith marriage. A guy wants non-human ass in his mouth, and I cue the curtain."

"Can't leave the tofu tribe."

"This thing with your dad, you so easily could have been an asshole. I don't just mean scowling at him when he wanted a hand up the curb, though that was no doubt Option Number One. Outwardly, you could have been decent, maybe even good to him, but still let yourself be an asshole the rest of your life — *excused, entitled, exempt*. A taker. You chose to avoid that."

"No, a saint I wasn't."

"That story about the bus, that's nothing. We all lose our patience. A week with you and anyone could see what you haven't become. A lot of guys think foreplay is pushing your skull to their dick. A guy has to do a lot of work not to wind up an asshole. You helped. You cared. I can tell."

"I did what had to be done, that's all."

"You did more, and you should admit that. What, it's a coincidence his body was falling apart and you went vedge?"

Reaching home, they made a bowl of their pelvises, spilt milk worth crying over.

58

The cafeteria of the botanical gardens is about to close so he loads up before leaving. Sick of the tasteless bagels, he settles for multiple bananas, peanut butter and mildly bilious orange juice. Only when the clerk bends beneath the counter for another handful of peanut-butter packets does Andrew notice a pink highlighter jutting out of a Styrofoam cup beside the cash register. "Actually, could I get a few more?" By the time the clerk rises again with a double handful, the pink highlighter has leapt into one of Andrew's deep jersey pockets. "What about a spoon?"

Ostensibly racing or fleeing the Mustang crew, Andrew doesn't last more than an hour on the darkening cycling trail before he stops at a picnic table (oh, the civility) to dig out postcards, novel and highlighter.

Austria:

> A,
>
> *If you're lugging any brain at all along with your pack, travel will make you a Marxist, though Groucho's your man, not Karl. Vienna is a conveyor belt. Starfucks on one side, DickFondles on the other. I want to see architecture. Instead I see fatties looking up from their guidebooks.*
>
> *I hear rumours of an annual summer convention/ competition for pickpockets. They choose a city, descend en masse, and pluck away. No wonder. Another day here and I'd pick my own pockets.*
>
> *Heading to Turkey to skip class,*
> *You Betcha*

What, he only now wonders, is he doing on this ridiculous bike?

Prague,

   Even I love Czech beer, you idiot.
   That's a chandelier made of human bones. Very huge.
Very thrilling. From an ossuary outside the city. S'posedly
there's at least one of every bone in the human body. Short
ones connected to the long ones.
   What's that bike of yours made of?
   — Plan B

Here and now, riding what should be a cyclist's dream, an unhilly, carless trail of more than one hundred kilometres punctuated by hand pumps of potable water, he wants Betty more than he wants rolling speed and the aggregate pleasure of the kilometres rolling on by. Opening his half-novel and turning it sideways, he writes perpendicularly across the type with the pink highlighter.

   YOU ARE
   MY PUSH &
   MY PULL

Conserving paper for fires yet bursting on with telegrammatic brevity, he flips onto the next pair of hinged pages and continues. In the moonlight he can just make out how the translucent fuchsia ink of the highlighter picks up random black letters from the novel, like stray iron filings plucked from the sand.

   His cyclist's half-gloves could be the hand protection of a tombstone engraver. In this privately lapidary mode he is finally wise or honest or both.

   MISS YOU
   LIKE CRAZY.
   LIVE W/ ME.

Or I'll live with you. The bike is now a stockade. Clipping back in is punching at the cancerous factory, crewing up on the low-riding fishing boat. Something like 115 kilometres left to Rivière-du-Loup. Until now, his credit card has been useless mass, a precautionary rectangle. He could book a flight at the nearest 'net café and ship the bike to K-town. Train to Montreal. Flight to Madrid. Clothes some-how, somewhere.

Home may well be where the heart is, and biking to Kingston in the dark of night, halfway there, he realizes that his heart's no longer in Kingston. In one of their winter arguments she'd asked him why, only then, was he ignoring Stan's wishes and pressing on with what he wanted despite Stan's plan that he sell the house.

"Aren't you defying the father a little late?" she partly asked and partly taunted.

"Every time I shave, I rinse his whiskers from the sink. If I bend my wrist, like on the bike, I see his hand in the back of mine. I've had to leave his body behind. I'm not ready to leave our house."

Nine months ago he was utterly certain of those feelings, yet now, cheeks and neck covered in a beard drenched with sweat, he finds his father with him wherever he goes. He gets back on the bike.

59

Only as wide as the muscular legs that have carved it, a single-track bike trail can start on nearly any run of land. Beside an arena. Behind a medical centre. The unassuming, unannounced brown trail at the rear of a neglected municipal park could be one thread of a gigantic network spreading across the city into the bordering scrub and distant forest. Heterogeneous terrain and topography are pulled together by the hard-packed trail. Chalky limestone and low, tight trees give way to tall grasses then clusters of pine, seams of maple. Soon enough these thickets yield again to littered urban scrub. Car tires dumped in the night. A washing machine rusting on its back. The narrow trails wear no signs, endure no bylaws and easily go unnoticed.

In Kingston, Andrew had been guided to the trailhead of what would become his favourite ride by a vague rumour from a half-acquaintance met at a grocery store. Been riding? Yeah, up behind the base, the north side. To hunt for a rumoured trail was an exercise in patience. Chasing the promise of a new route, his legs would chomp at the bit to ride quickly, when in fact he had to ride painfully slowly, eyes peeled for any break in the shrubs or for muddy incisions in the grass. Trails were often purposefully hidden, entrances cut between two slim trees or behind a boulder. Hidden from hunters, landowners, even other riders. Some people ride for the adrenal and aerobic rushes or the self-propulsion or the changing land. Others, Andrew grew to suspect, ride for the isolation, the removal from daily life. Aside from the Prairies and southern Ontario, most Canadian cities still have patches of forest around them. Judging from the hidden trails he has seen and the riders who prefer to ride on rather than stop and chat, Andrew concluded that some riders were trying to bike away from useless small talk and a life of just working and shopping. Other riders, he also discovered, were already half your friend. If this is how you like to spend your time, you're okay by me.

Picking his way along one stretch of Kingston's Fort Henry trails, looking for a rumoured extension, he once heard the telltale zip of another rider snaking through the trees. Andrew looked up to see a rider about his age in a sleeveless blue jersey racing along the trail atop a yellow bike. Forests crawled and reached with their greens and browns, while riders shot through them in the brightest of test-tube colours.

Here, at an intersection of new trail, Andrew paused as the other rider approached. He did some sustained drinking and spitting as the other became audible, visible, then finally close enough to chat. "Nice curves, eh?"

"Yeah. Total roller coaster." The other rider stopped, clipped out and straddled the frame, the cyclists' equivalent of idling his pickup or drawing up a barroom chair. He was a few inches shorter than Andrew, but beefier. Chiselled, tanned arms sprang out of his sleeveless jersey. A vaccination scar rode low on a shoulder rounded with muscle.

"What's your usual route?"

"I'm up and down off that double-track ridge most of the time. String of pockets on the right. Two left near the end."

"That's it?"

"Hey, lead on if you've got more."

They were off.

"Andrew, by the way," he said to that bright blue back.

"Mark."

They traded maps with clicks and snorts, ground a little borrowed land.

60

Everybody begins with just one jersey. After the bike, after helmet and pump and tools, usually after the cushioning gloves (function before fashion), certainly after the padded shorts comes the breathable, synthetic jersey with its sweat-wicking tech, its tall pockets for the low back, its zippered Nehru collar. This is another migration. You ride away from your densely packed closet, your bulging drawers, into slick singularity. For life, you have one or two dozen shirts; as a new rider you have just one. Absorbent cotton is inadequate for the new land, the new machine and its new body.

When, sick of wearing yesterday's reek, you graduate to a second jersey, you search store racks and catalogue pages riotous with colour. Fear of cars driven by people who only notice other cars, or fellow riders cutting around with night lamps, or deer hunters who shoot first and look later pours only the brightest colours into cycling jerseys. The uniformly black cycling shorts are offset with canary yellow shirts straining for flight. Magenta spills from test tube to shirt back. Yves Klein has gone cycling. Here, at last, women's sport clothes are spared the infuriatingly condescending pastels.

The centuries-long international race between inventors of all kinds — blacksmiths, wheelwrights, even coopers — to perfect the "feedless horse" was a race to wed the human skeleton to a constructed one, to replace the expensive horse and the fixed route of the train with a self-propelled machine devoted to individual whim. Now, today's sweat-clever jerseys emblazon the logos and icons of contemporary bike manufacturers onto the chests of riders willing to pay a company to do their marketing for them. Chemical brightness and syntheticness continue along the shop racks of jerseys to emblazon cartoon characters across adult chests. Even in his cycling apprenticeship, Andrew disapproved of this garish arrested development. More than just immature, these cartoon mascots are also mutinous, a bright agreement with those drivers who think of the bicycle as the tool of children, those Westerners who let their bike chains dry and rust, their tires deflate and crack with the acquisition of a driver's licence. Opposed to this frat boy consumerism, and clearly speaking from the side of the road, are the message jerseys. World Peace springs from a kelly green jersey atop yellow chevrons. Choice, choice, choice stacks into a downward pointing red delta on the women's rack. In cycling, gay pride's rainbow banner is a jersey.

Only at UNS would he learn that more colour in a garment generally equals more pollution. Find a shirt, any shirt, that hasn't been dyed in Asia. T-shirt, dress shirt and cycling jersey all make their dip where the labour's cheap and the environmental laws are non-existent, unenforced or dissolved with cheap bribes. The Tirupur region of India exports nearly half of that country's T-shirts, and more than ten per cent of the toxic dyes are dumped directly into local rivers. Every year the colour of river water changes depending on the latest Western fashions. Yet no ride is possible without drinking water. Eventually, the pull of thirst will beat the push of the legs.

Early last spring, when Betty rushed upstairs with a package from the day's mail to change into a new *Girls Love Dirt* jersey, a jersey she had presumably ordered from one of Andrew's catalogues, her grin was as uncontainable as it was enigmatic. This olive green jersey combined slogan and image, so the phrase and a faux hand-drawn female stick figure (complete with bulbous helmet, stringy hair, double-scoop boobs and a determined grimace) rode Betty's breasts together, snugly. This terrain and her irrepressible grin made the jersey's baptism of fire a short one. She walked down the stairs, they traded smiles, then walked back up together. For ventilation, jersey zippers generally go to the solar plexus or even the navel. They took hers down slowly. Inaccurately, he had thought that her new jersey marked an increased interest in cycling, that Tuesday's private fashion show of the snug *Girls Love Dirt* jersey would be followed by a week-end ride together. Thursday morning, however, she came downstairs riding dirt to class.

"You're serious?" he asked, pointing one of the fingers he had wrappedaround a juice glass at the jersey. If she hadn't been loading a knapsack she would have noticed that his finger was quite specific-ally aimed at the jersey's low-riding zipper.

"I can't let the BFA students hog all the synthetic clothes," she finally replied, crossing the room to squeeze his outstretched finger and steal his juice.

"*Clothes?* Off-trail that's not a shirt; it's a tit-delivery system. Have you seen you?" He cupped evidence.

"Easy . . ."

"No, it's not easy. Not easy to keep my eyes off you, hands off you — off them, this." He pinched the dirty shirt.

"Eyes are not hands, are they?" She disengaged then crossed to another cupboard. "Relax," she finally said, "I know where I ride."

61

As an architect, Elaine had showed Andrew how older homes such as his don't always hide their renovations. A square of paler hardwood floor announces some later desire, a duct replaced, a chimney removed. Incised mouldings say *new wall*. A thoughtlessly severed joist confesses that the basement predates its staircase. The same is true of roads and trails, but who sees this from a rushing car? Surely much of the fun in the speed of driving is its immunity to distraction, its totality, its blinding absorption. This captivation is monotonal, though, unidimensional. Tour on a bike and you will occasionally miss that speed, will marvel at its kilometre-devouring efficacy and recognize the allure of its Prozac vapidity.

Riding on the old Petit Témis railway after reading illustrated displays about it just two hours ago, Andrew constantly sees the old rail in Le Petit Témis's new trail. When his skinny bike slides through the first pass blasted out of solid rock, he can feel the evolution of transportation on either side of him. With its paradigm-shifting movement to two in-line wheels, not two or more pairs of wheels, the bicycle is so uniquely a machine of the two-legged human body. Yet the curve and grade of land beneath him hold memories of rail. He pauses between sheer rock walls of two to five metres, walls blasted and cut with nineteenth-century dynamite and muscle.

Between these chutes of solid rock, the surrounding land develops unevenly around the former railway. For stretches of three to five kilometres at a time, cross streets intersect the trail regularly, adding one or two shops and making cafés out of old train stations. Farther ahead, new homes abut the long-abandoned railway. Free from much light pollution and rolling quietly, he can smell lake water just before it appears alongside him. Lac Témiscouata sparkles and gurgles in the moonlight. If he had biked south instead of west after hobbling the Mustang he would eventually have hit upstate New York's Finger Lakes. Here in Quebec, riding alongside the moonlit Lac Témiscouata, he sees both its inky water and the maps of it he'd been staring at in the garden hours ago. Like New York's Finger Lakes, Lac Témiscouata is long and skinny, but unlike its New York cousins, this finger is long, skinny and sharply bent. On a map, Lac Témiscouata looks like one of Stan's unamputated fingers, crimped into its lock of bone.

When Andrew reaches the middle knuckle of the lake, water, trail and a secondary highway are all yoked alongside one another. A quaint lakeside inn is ready for the traffic. Braking for a historical plaque, digging out his flashlight, Andrew acknowledges that he has read more local history in the past three hours than he has in the past decade. This one's written in French only, so his legs get a longer break as he dredges his translation out of the plaque's heavily embossed brass letters. On this, ye olde merry spot, a rich man kept his mistress. Enjoy your stay.

There's probably a dock around back of this tiny inn. He's tempted to dive in for a brief swim to soothe his rashy crotch. This finger lake could give him a good scratch. No, still too public.

Finally the trail is swallowed in total darkness, its gravel line almost lost to sprawling, unlit black. This immunity from surrounding traffic questions the days he spent dodging trucks on the side of the highway. He relaxes into the evenness of the trail's steady grade and the privacy of his ride, finding them perfect for this first and unplanned night ride. He should have switched from highway to trail long ago, as soon as he could have. This is a different league, not a minor one. Soon it's also absurd.

Just one metre before he will roll onto what he swears is an endless lawn, he spots bilingual signs announcing that he is about to bike across a golf course. No locked gate bars his ride through the links. Motion sensor lights do not fire on and off as he slips onto lawns even more manicured and carcinogenic than those he normally passes. Utterly skeptical of this green intersection, he passes into even greater absurdity at a fairway traffic light. Negotiations, land deals and bylaws combine to spread today's golf course around yesterday's rail line. A small traffic light attempts to spare runners or cyclists from drives sliced or hooked. Protected as he is by the cloak of deep night, he nonetheless obeys, then more than obeys, the traffic light.

He doesn't just stop; he dismounts. He gets off the bike and stretches his tired body out on the smooth lawn.

Poisoned though it is, the soft, endless lawn is irresistible. Stooping to stroke its choked greenery, he can't help but drop his bare knees into its cool, damp, agri-chem softness. Stretching his hands out here on the world's largest yoga mat he isn't two minutes before he empties his jersey pockets so he can loll and uncurl. Neither clammy skin, nor knotted muscle, nor burning crotch (*What is going on down there?*) can feel the herbicides that skin frogs en masse and drip tumours into the drinking water. A golf course, that realtor's jousting field, is also a sore back's dream, a masseur's table. Here in the dark, the lawn is felt more than seen and the feeling is good. Oh, to tack out his shoulders. The back of his skull becomes a pestle to the lawn's green mortar. Spread-eagled on the indecently soft lawn, he wonders at the stars and the unknown black around him. Simultaneously, though, he is crushed by an exhaustion built of more than just the ride. He was right a few days ago in thinking we wouldn't be the culture we are, maybe even the species we are, without our masochism. But that masochism is part of an equation, and pleasure, possibly even wisdom, hangs on the other side. His bike frame has become an un-balanced equation.

62

Why did Stan feel the cold more than the heat? If he could burn a finger without even noticing, what, in fact, *was* cold? Andrew would continue this autopsy for years after Stan's death, slowly understanding that crumpled body that during Stan's life constantly had him doing damage control. Cold on his night ride, Andrew finally understands his father's fickle body. Numbed, Stan was even less coordinated, felt even less. He wasn't grimacing and snarky out of pain, but fear.

For the human body, cold is almost always an encroachment, a slow invasion up extremities toward the warm core. With severe loss of blood, with surgery, heat is lost from the core. Most operations find the body kept warm with heating pads and lithe electric blankets. When the doped-up body is finally wheeled into a ward room, the thermals are obvious to the caregivers and bystanders. Blankets, clothing, even a toque — fabric can only hold heat, not generate it.

Stan had never looked so angular, so sharp, as he did following the surgical attempt to relocate a paralyzed vocal cord. One, two, three extra blankets (requested, pleaded for and finally demanded) and still every joint was an arrowhead, each limb a rod. Delirious with blood loss and annihilating anaesthetics, Stan drifted in and out of consciousness and sensibility. Whether ordering "Lock down! Lock down!" or coughing up the intriguing "Never speak to me," he always returned to "Cold, cold."

More than words spoke. Stan's eyelids became a slow percussion for the trembling limbs, tambourine shakes before the timpani barrage. Shivers went impressively global. Twitches plucked at the little dishrags of his quadriceps. The arced shoulders were tireless semaphores. An urgent but unreceived Morse was tapped out by his toes. Knowing that the well of the nurse's station had run dry for him, that after three searches no thermostat was to be found in the hospital room, that rubbing Stan's thin, unresponsive limbs wasn't doing enough, Andrew began sliding his body into the narrow bed beside his father. Hauling his last, chaste foot off the floor, angling hips and torso and draping a connubial arm across Stan's chest, he wondered if — in for a penny — he'd be better to remove his jeans, whether the thick denim dispersed or taxed this thermal delivery.

"Oh no, no," Stan was just able to mutter, his eyes briefly their most open.

"Shh. Please, seriously. Shut up about this."

The weak body that Andrew had puppeted or supported so often jerked now with shocking force down his own abdomen. The legs he usually guided or compensated for, or even doubled, now twitched along his own. The smells of antiseptic alcohol coming off Stan's face were avoided with a burrowing of Andrew's forehead, a move that conveniently spared him the sight of a salmon run of blood vessels up Stan's neck and scalp. Finally, Andrew draped the inevitable, chicky thigh across his father's.

"Oh no, Jesus. Jesus, Andrew."

"Quiet." He tried to lead their breath, pace out the old, skittish horse, all the while clamping a bar of heat across the thighs. "But you get an *inch* of wood, and I'll smother you in a second."

Father, then finally son, sank into uneven sleep.

63

The first run on a new trail unfurls spontaneously. Each new metre arrives suddenly, leaves just as quickly and feels almost unconnected to the remainder. Accelerating one minute then braking the next, too fast on a sharp corner, then too slow for a climbing curve, a rider on a new trail juggles various balls.

On Andrew's first ride with Mark, each of them unknown to the other, each just a first name, a bike and a visible speed, Mark was faster, tighter on the curves. Even more impressive than his pace was the grip he had on his own force. When Andrew pushed more energy into the pedals, he lost precision in the hands, bumped out of the trail's sweet groove. Bobbing his compact chest, tucking an elbow or a bronze, shaved calf before leap or landing, Mark kept the shadow of his force trim to frame and bone. Andrew was always behind. Mark's breathing was steady; Andrew's ragged. He hated Mark for waiting ("Water break? Pee break?") and hated him for rolling on.

Deep roots cut across the narrow trail just as it doglegged into a nasty climb. Learning to traverse the exposed structural roots of trees without losing too much speed is a requisite trail skill, especially at the start of a climb. Andrew had previously paid the admission price of bruised shins learning to fluidly cross a washboard of hard roots, some of them five inches tall. Here, though, one escarpmental root towered at the base of a climb, and Andrew slipped across its merciless ridge. When he clipped out one foot to stabilize himself, the noise felt as loud as a pistol shot. Then he was forced to take the hill cold. The click and set of cleat, then gear, was thunderous. Ever climbing, Mark's spins and snorts poured into the leaves ahead until he paused rebukingly. Mark's lean into a hilltop tree, his loaded pause, reduced this forest soundtrack from stereo to Andrew's own mono. Because he had slowed Mark to a halt, Andrew heard more clearly when Mark started riding again. He didn't know this ribbon of curving mud beyond the metre immediately in front of him, but Mark did. Making the next climb, Andrew stopped trying to ride with his eyes and concentrated more on what he could hear. Mark's clicking derailleur would prompt and caution his ride. The click and flick of a downshift meant the climb ahead was steeper than it looked. A click and toss meant the climb was about to end and they were in for a drop. Soon their ride was fluid, tandem. Andrew shoved his body forward into not only a space, but also a shape Mark was just vacating. He learned to ride, to really ride, to ride out of his body and into a new one, by chasing this bright, living ghost in front of him.

At the close of each ride with Mark, Andrew was battered but amazed. Alone, he would have been less. Slower. More cautious. Andrew thanked Mark for his introductions to new lengths of trail or, early on, the occasional tip, but he had tried to keep his deeper gratitude private. Then at the close of one ride, vis-à-vis no comment of Andrew's save the pumping of his chest, Mark announced, "Each of the four or eight people in a rowing shell pulls harder than he would alone in a solo shell."

Until that moment, the two of them together hadn't said as many words on the entire ride.

64

Deprivation holiday. Lying (absurdly, he admits) on a golf course lawn, closer to sunrise than midnight, fleeing a car chase that may or may not be happening, these two words pour down on him from the starry sky above. Deprivation holiday. So far he's been able to tell himself that the trip, this earned distance, isn't anything so bourgeois as a holiday. He biked away from an apartment he'll never enter again. By day, he powers himself up indomitable Maritime hills, and by night he lives without electricity, running water, or solid walls. And yet he's still a white, middle-class North American with a credit card in his saddlebag and an affluent mother one phone call away. However arduous the biking, the deprivations he's putting himself through are all chosen.

If Betty had been travelling in the East, not Europe, sending postcards of monks and seeking enlightenment as well as cheap hotel rooms, he might have thought of the Buddhist notion of chosen suffering earlier. Without the one shining statement he does remember — in fact, he can't forget it — he'd readily agree that his knowledge of Buddhism is superficial, nothing more than an afternoon's reading from a borrowed textbook and then a few web searches over the years. Without this one phrase he can't forget, he'd say he knows nothing. But the noble truth "All suffering is created by desire" finds him once again, this time on an empty golf course chasing the wispy gleam of religion. Enlightenment doesn't care whether he knows one Buddhist thought or a hundred. Right now, cold, sore, exhausted and wishing he didn't have to get back on the bike, he sees the unbreakable chain between suffering and desire. Suddenly this is more solid than a phrase, stronger than an idea. Push desire and you pull suffering. Sitting up on the grass, he utters the truth aloud, amazed by its combination of brevity and profundity. Pound for pound, *All suffering is created by desire* must be the wisest statement in human history.

Finally, caught by one phrase, he crawls across the fairway to dig out Betty's postcards and search out another.

> *Dubrovnik. There are bullet holes in the famously gorgeous marble walls. This whole coast is, as the cliché goes, ruggedly beautiful. Cooked beige. The rocks look straight from the oven.*
> *In her Chardonnay, Mom likes to say there are four walls in the house of love. Taste. Humour. Morality. And of course, lust.*
> *Tell me, did we get three or four?*
> *Scaling the walls,*
> *—B.*

Temporarily enlightened, he's glad he had offered Betty Stan's house before he got caught in the lie(s) that drove her out of it. If it's love, ego-dissolving love, you'll bet whatever farm you have.

Betty's postcards are beside his feet, and their Kingston arguments are never far from the top of his mind. When he had tried to reconcile himself to Stan's will nudging him out of the house, his first revolutionary plan had not necessarily been the stalling tactic of a graduate degree, but nominally selling the house to Betty.

January saw their nasty fights, then February, with its lean toward sunlight, saw mergers of defence and offence.

The Argument of Inheritance
"So you stay in school for two more years," Betty genuinely asked, "is the house going to be any easier to sell then?"
"Depends on who I sell it to," he said, poking her.
"Oh no, wait —"
"Not marriage. Just two people who love each other and share a house."
"No. No. No. Your dad didn't lose this house to divorce. How would you feel if you did?"
"What's a relationship without trust?" he replied, still lying.

65

Compared to the tired bureaucrat of English, French is a richer language in the mouth, with its elastic vowels and chewy consonants. And topographically, Quebec is a mouth. The open throat of the St. Lawrence lolls among a varied set of craggy teeth. Mountains, escarpments and hills rise and fall throughout the province. Drumlins, those old, single molars, stand alone in plateaus and fields. In the east, the province is one sharp incisor after another. Hills and valleys. Hills and valleys.

Riding toward Rivière-du-Loup just before dawn, he sees yesterday's religiosity still burning in today's valley in the form of a red glowing cross. A metal cross several metres high rides a promontory overlooking the city. Its lipstick red glow gives the cross a campy, neon Gothic look, yet the province with the highest per capita rate of agnosticism still has the architecture and infrastructure of homogenous faith. A towering metal cross punctuates this landscape of steeples every three hundred kilometres. Metal remembers.

The red cross's unmistakably electric glow charges his sagging pace. The distant beacon of right angles, roads and power grids now advertises new trinities. Food, beer and a doctor. Cheese, fruit and pints.

With the city growing in sight, he again appreciates the railway's blasted grade. This old gash of industry will funnel him to the St. Lawrence, the national birth canal. The St. Lawrence also returns salt to the air and slips its fine hooks into his nostrils.

Three or four kilometres from the riverside city's puddle of white light and its Christian prick of red, he is a pinball driven up its narrow, loading trough. Arriving, he shoots out on the top of the city's raked tiers. Knowing nothing save the few metres of road in front of him, he jinks his way down a hillside of the city, randomly passing through one stoplight then veering off another, silent bumpers for this rolling pinball.

Between the city's top shelf and the moving field of the river below are two other tiers. Adjacent to the river is a surprisingly wide flood plain. Pollution-cook an ice cap or two and this downtown becomes a coral reef. Above the fertile first floor is a second tier nearly as flat and wide. Andrew rolls from the hilltop houses with enormous windows into a polite second tier of smaller homes, lawns cut and trim, two cars to every drive. A teacher here, a manager there. On the bottom tier, the cars are older and rustier.

The St. Lawrence River made Canada. The great blue umbilical cord to the Old World challenges its banks and isn't at all intimidated by the mountain range flanking the north side. It isn't still, but the river is so wide that it can't be seen as running alongside the bordering land. Wide and deep and as long as any schoolkid can doodle, the St. Lawrence is perpendicular, never parallel.

This long night's ride of the soul has put shakes into his hands, squeezed his vision down to just two dimensions and made the bike frame into a rolling iron maiden. Spoiled by the lost railway, he is utterly bewildered by local traffic and may not have survived a midday arrival. The sweet pull down hill after hill hides a burr of incompetent fear. Additionally, Andrew is lost to the siren song of water.

As the sunrise finally pours down into the valley, he wobbles toward a park marked *chutes*. A smaller, more rivery river runs downhill to the St. Lawrence, and Andrew soon discovers a deep gorge cut into auburn rock. The roar of rushing water echoes up the rusty rock walls to hum in his ear as he rolls over a scenic bridge with the St. Lawrence to his left and a small hydro dam high on his rocky right. Only in Quebec would producing electricity be cause for a park.

He's tempted to sleep on the nearest patch of soft grass but also wants to press deeper into the park for privacy. Having crested a small pedestrian bridge, he lets gravity lead him into a dark trail on the other side. He wouldn't even look at the trail if it weren't downhill. As is, he's willing to abandon the trim lawns and rectangular flower beds behind for the shady forest ahead. Free speed and the roar of water merge to sing *here, here*, a song he resists not for any competing desire but from a laziness so thorough he doesn't even want to pull the brakes. A footpath offers a peek of the rushing river on his left while levelling terrain slows him to a wobbly stop. Old, gnarly apple trees surround him as he brakes and dismounts. He is in an old orchard, and he flops contentedly in the fragrant air, an itchy dog keen to make his shade.

66

"Come on," Betty argued as Pat's proposition beeped to a close on their answering machine. "I'm going to show you mine."

They had returned home to a surprise message from Andrew's mother announcing she had been suddenly called to Kingston and would they like to meet for dinner.

"No. No. No. No," he said.

"You can't be serious."

"You live with me, not my mother."

"Free food. Better wine. Stories about you when you were a wee laddie," she said. "Come on."

"That's just it, her stories will all be about how I was never a wee laddie. She'd prefer if I showed up tonight on Rollerblades and blew bubbles in my milk."

With less than two hours between their receiving this message and the proposed hour of invasion, with the fun of showers and gin, of pinkened bodies tucked into layer after layer of familiar clothing, he simply forgot to worry about his mother and his lover possibly discussing when his father died. His only thoughts were of lowering the thong he had watched rise, and of whether Betty would confirm the rumour that the presence of a (common-law) mother-in-law makes a young woman even hornier. If they'd known of Pat's visit days, not minutes, in advance, he might have made one quick case or another to Pat to ensure that Betty wouldn't be told so casually of the lie upon which their relationship was based. Given how infrequently he and Pat talked, let alone talked about Stan's death, he probably could have left her a brief voice mail or email, a simple *Please don't mention exactly when Dad died* and he'd have been fine. Even at the restaurant, working on the fly as Betty went to the washroom, if he'd leaned closer to his mother and made a quick request for secrecy, he would have earned a disapproving look from her but still found sleep that night in the usual way. He might even have waited until Betty was approaching the table and tried a shotgun pass; "It's easier for me if she thinks he died *two* Augusts ago."

Yet the pleasures of living with Betty were both constant and evolving, and he couldn't always remember that their household was founded on a lie. The surprise of his mother's visit and, unbelievably, its laughs, further blinded him. To his shock, that evening's three-way conversation with his mother was the first loss. Dinner between just him and Pat had been more or less perfunctory since he'd graduated from Happy Meals. His choice of restaurant, her credit card. See you in two weeks. Suddenly, Betty in the mix, the laughs flowed more freely than the wine.

"I'm serious," the well-dressed Pat assured the well-dressed Betty, "a snowsuit, a balaclava and a diving mask. In July! All so he could free a bee from the car."

Endure this embarrassment and he'd soon be back in Betty's arms, back in the body trade. She had become his night, his lust and sleep, his home. Until Pat reached into her purse for a khaki envelope.

"Look at this," Pat held up a mid-sized Revenue Canada envelope. "We've been divorced for sixteen years. He dies, and six months later I get his tax forms. Honestly, what do we pay for?"

"Six months?" Betty asked.

Andrew froze.

"Counting's still the same since I was in school, isn't it? August. Now. There isn't a *new* new math, is there?" asked Pat.

He actually preferred the hatred in Betty's face to the confusion and the diplomacy which preceded it. She had every right to put on the visor of nastiness that fell from her quickly peaked eyebrows onto her burning eyes. He deserved her sharpened jaw, her compressed lips and much more. Or much less.

Betty calmly announced, "Pat, thank you for the meal and company. I'm leaving now. I'm sure Andrew can invent some explanation."

"Betty, wait, listen —"

"No. Not one word. Do *not* follow me." Rage boiled in her face.

Watching her push herself across the restaurant, he could just recognize the envy beneath his own guilt and shame. Yes, Betty, I'd run away too if I were you. Absolutely goddamned right.

"Andrew, what is going on?" Pat asked.

"We started seeing each other in September. I told her Dad died *last* August, not this one. We'd just met." When Pat said nothing verbally but spoke volumes with a piercing look, he added, "I didn't want her pity."

"So you say."

67

In Rivière-du-Loup, he wakes in a series of hot bags. The tent burns with an afternoon sun seemingly hot enough to ignite the grey nylon walls. The sleeping bag, half-opened and half-drenched with sweat, lies crumpled beneath him. More forceful than the sun are his gouging hands and their tireless, unconscious scrape at his measly crotch. In the bright light he can clearly make out sideburns of red spots at the apex of each thigh and sprinkled across his scrotum. The Gold Bond hasn't been medicine enough.

His crotch shrinks from the cycling shorts like a pound dog from a raised hand. From the bottom of a pannier he unearths his single pair of hiking shorts. He slides into the civilian clothes then checks the cycling computer's clock. Early afternoon. A pint and a meal? Undoubtedly. A potentially interminable wait for medical attention? Maybe he could just buy some calamine lotion and ride off. Perhaps the blind wash of kilometres will keep his scratching fingers out of his crotch. But he has seen that red-eyed stare below, knows the Martians have taken Central America and covet the north.

He'd have bathed even without the intended medical examination of his grand canyon, bathed for city life and the crisp delight of a cold scrub. Port after stormy seas.

Walking from the overgrown orchard where he camped, toward the rushing river, he sees again why rivers have always made such obvious borders. Despite the machine-cut wood chips that blanket the larger trails behind him and the monospecial humanness of the old orchard, the park behind him is positively sylvan compared with the parking lot that towers above him on the opposite side of the river. Curves and chlorophyll behind, concrete ahead. And up. The riverbank he picks his way down descends from a metre of dirt and brush into a metre of jagged rock, whereas the other side rises in a towering, coppery cliff. A parking lot tops the cliff, allowing *grandmère* and *grandpère* to enjoy their ice cream from the comfort of their idling

Crown Vic while Andrew picks his way half-naked into the rushing, frigid water. Sitting against a slab of rock while the water cobbles his feet in cold, he watches a carload of teens drop a bag of fast-food litter out their car window before squealing off and wonders how much anyone bothers to see him below.

What, really, is so wrong with a little nudity? Sitting on one of the larger of the riverside boulders, he slips out of his hiking shorts. The gaping shorts rise and fall so quickly and promiscuously compared to the cycling shorts he has rolled on and off every day. Smashed rocks along the shoreline prolong his chilly, wading dangle to comic lengths as he sends one scouting foot after another between the sharp shards. Even in the shallows the current is strong, so his glances at the towering parking lot are largely abandoned for a tight view of the next step and the next. Pain and navigational challenges leave him, perhaps thankfully, to hear the floating, indistinct murmur of voices without seeing any pointing fingers or faces split by leers or fury. Though what, really, would they see? Where is the crime in a distant delta of fur, a genital daub? Finally, he reaches a pool, adds his bent knees to the sharp points of the rocks. Cold slices a strip off his back and temporarily smothers his speckled itch. Rolling over onto his stomach, he reaches down for a hold against the current, hangs a nightshirt of icy water from collarbone to hip, hears the first cheer from above.

Returned to his change-room rock, slopping wet feet into the wide legs of the hiking shorts, he can feel the rash's burning itch through a skin of frigid water, and the hospital question shifts from *if* to *when*. Back at the campsite, hunger, dread at the anticipated emergency-room wait and a reluctance to sweat another drop from his stippled crotch finally ignite a dormant underbrush of laziness. Rather than break down his tent and re-sling every pannier, he simply drags the entire kit into denser brush. While he can lock his bike downtown, he can't lock the gear to it, and he could be hours at a hospital. Sometimes you just have to trust.

Thankfully the only shirts he has are two cycling jerseys. Without a jersey's tall pockets he would no doubt have succumbed to the speed of rash logic and taken nothing but cash off to town. As is, he adds the amputated novel to the centre pocket (hospital wait) and his wallet to the left. The knife already sits in the third pocket. He grabs the post-cards at the last moment because he has a thirst for more than water. In his beer, he'll think of the postcards, will want the familiarity of her flowing handwriting with its peaks and curls, its loops and cross-overs. Rationally, he thinks of patriotism as manufactured consent or brand loyalty or mass delusion, yet the sight of the word *CANADA* written out repeatedly in Betty's hand swells his heart a little, even if they are addressed to a Halifax apartment he has already vacated. In her hand, from foreign shores he hasn't seen, *CANADA* becomes a pet name. Normally it's hard to love the worst per capita water and energy use in the world, or a nation of civil servants. Stan once told Andrew that there are more education administrators in Ontario than there are in all of Western Europe. In a newspaper, *CANADA* refers to the idiots keen to torch and pollute the Canadian environment to fuel the American economy and the unimaginative meekness of a country that exports twenty per cent of the world's lumber but no furniture. Nonetheless, across the twenty-seven postcards, the common denominator *CANADA* evokes how much Betty and Andrew knew of each other before they even met, the similar props and scenes and activities and overheard comments of each other's childhoods. At their first kiss they could almost see back to the insides of the family cars of their childhood, could guess what kind of sandwiches their grandmothers had made. Biking off in search of a restaurant with a patio and strong, unfiltered Québécois beer on tap, jersey pockets stuffed with half a Canadian novel and Betty's postcards, he has never felt more Canadian. He doesn't yet know that the Québécois beer he seeks is now owned by a Japanese brewery.

Why did he ever ignore the touring recommendation to sling a pair of weatherproof flip-flops on the back of the rack? His uniform shoes mercilessly pinch these furlough feet.

A rash isn't going to get him anywhere at emerg, especially a crotch rash. Oh, put it where you shouldn't, did you? Just make yourself a part of the furniture and we'll have someone who's currently think-ing of applying to med school glance at you dismissively within the decade. Might as well eat first.

Never in the history of this body has he sat down to table and menu with such ferocious ability. Each bite of salad is a cambered bite of green air. Then the buttered, earthy breast milk of soupe aux champignons. He's quickly off the menu, thinking that crème brûlée has melted gooey stuff, so "une baguette avec le fromage brûlée" should get him some melted cheese. "Mais avec les oignons et champignons dans la moitié." Another Maudite, *oui*. This high-alcohol beer, essentially a pint of wine, doesn't help him keep his hands above the table and not scratching at his rash. Back and forth his knees swing, fanning his crotch. "Oh, et un potat — pomme de terre, s'il vous plaît." Pie and a cappuccino for desert. Three Maudites? His high-rev metabolism takes the beer like water.

The fact that Canada has two official languages but most Canadians only speak one and a half affords both tolerance and strangeness. Where else can you feel like an immigrant in your own country? English and French Canada, these two solitudes, endure the same offshore queen on their stamps and money. A Canadian summer drive with a flat tire twists simple data into phenomenological poetry. *The others, not the back ones, they will have need of the same impression please.* Stop to walk your dog while driving through Quebec and you become a crazy uncle. *The best fashion in which to make the acquaintance of a dog is with the bum of your hand. Like this.*

"Oui, une autre bière." Back into the half-novel. Both hands above the table. Above. The. Table.

68

Divorce, career and character had kept Betty's journalist father, Jim, away from most of the dentist appointments and dance recitals. To her partial surprise, this removal, this track record for stocking RESPs but not kitchen cupboards, made her email him, not her mother, when she was leaving the lying Andrew. After running from Andrew and his mother at the restaurant, she'd spent the night at a friend's.

Lies were like tar, sticky and toxic. If she had tried to fight Andrew's lies, she would have just become ensnared herself. No, she ran. From the restaurant. From Andrew. Even, finally, from the relationship she'd been running from when she had first run into Andrew. Emotionally, she knew the exhilaration of wind at her back. When she emailed her dad, that bird of a feather, she didn't need to explain a thing.

Will you take me to lunch? Tomorrow? Tues. at the latest?

Her mom would have speed-dialled before she'd read the entire email. Yes, Elaine would have offered unconditional support and immediate vengeance and broiling indictments, would have accurately mapped the distance between *boy* and *man*, but the shape of it would have been all wrong. Short questions. Personal tirades. A hypothetical yet demanding tactical debate. With her dad she'd be free to speak in paragraphs or monosyllables as it came, or didn't.

Tomorrow, yes. Do I pick you up or meet you? (The Piggy, ya?)

Stepping into the restaurant, Betty saw her dad as an island once again. Afloat there on the raft of his table, he was, as always, so variously removed from the dad she had once clung to. Age, time and Elaine's running caricature all kept Jim and Betty in a very loose solar system. They hung in some balance, but not a tight one. He was just shy of forty when they stopped living together, and was now partially clothed in nostalgia and mystery. In her memory, his shoulders were broad, muscled and tanned from their early life at the waterfront house, Black Rock. Today, the man at the restaurant table had smaller, more sloping shoulders.

He rose to greet her. Thankfully he didn't try to offset baldness and turning fifty with safari clothes. Jeans and a blazer. Small, low eye-glasses. Divorce had kept him thin.

"Well, whatever's wrong, you're still walking," he said, hugging her shoulders roughly.

From Sunday night email to borrowed morning shower and into her walk downtown, she had had no idea how much she would tell her father or what, if anything, she would ask him. She knew this want by picture, not thought, and this was it. A clean, well-lit restaurant with plenty of space around a table half in the sun. Maybe she just needed a really good lunch.

He had already studied the menu. She knew she was being treated tenderly when he didn't ask, "You're *still* a vegetarian?" and stated, rather than wondered, "We'll get wine. Have you ever had a white Bordeaux?"

Chat, chat, until one coffee, another, all right — let's share a piece of cake. As the table cleared, she shifted from conversation to a small-ish monologue, describing Andrew despite herself. By the time he replied they were almost huddling.

"The greater the love, the more you feel death for the deceased. Those first days are all shock or terror or loss for a life you haven't yet really realized is gone. You dwell on the how. You tabulate future losses as if they'll hurt more — friends unseen, holidays unenjoyed, even food they won't get to eat. All of this you still count for the dead. Eventually, though, you realize none of this matters. You matter. This is the hard part. You're the one who needs attention. You're the one losing. Go through a big death and you'll learn to anticipate this second, larger death, the you death. Loss from you, for you, not the dead. That knowing wait is horrid, one of the things you'd rather not learn.

"It's great to have a survivor in your lifeboat but maybe not in your bed. For all his loyalty to his dad, your man knows he's the one left standing. He knows that or he's gotta learn it. Decide whether you're willing to teach him."

The bright sun slid past.

69

Fittingly, Andrew is still tipsy when a doctor in Rivière-du-Loup tells him the red crotch rash that has been burning for days is a topical yeast infection.

"A yeast infection?" Andrew's quietly incredulous tone carries the shame of an STD diagnosis plus the fear that he has biked himself into hermaphroditism.

"*Oui.* It is not only a gurl ting."

Pervert of the microscopic world, yeast love the wet, dark and warm. While their cousins are content to produce bread or the sweet clouds in the unfiltered beer in Andrew's stomach, another strain of yeast has been baked into a scarlet rash below.

"Your shorts," the doctor continues, "all these days. The sweat."

Touring has given Andrew a monastically low standing heart rate and rock-crushing thighs but also a cramped high back, a rash-sprayed crotch.

"What do I do?" Andrew hikes up his underwear-less hiking shorts.

"Wash your shorts regularly and dry them in the strong sun. You will need this cream."

Rolling away from the clinic, a tube of ointment riding in his jersey like a single bullet, Andrew the Monistat man releases the bike to the fading pulse of Maudite still inside him and surfs the city's long, tiered hill. Without the cumbrous panniers and the weight of the tent and sleeping bag, the bike feels whimsically loose. He is suddenly more nimble, and faster, though the city has temptations to slow him down. He sets out for the park and his neglected gear, but it is so easy to surrender to gravity, to take only the turns which ease allows him. He reaches another sunlit bar patio without having to climb a single hill. Entering the bar, he heads straight to the bathroom for a second, radically premature dose of the slick cream and only then to a crowded, sunny balcony. The river's enormous flood plain and the angle of its valley and a joyously hopped beer all combine to show him that the spring sun is beginning to win its arm-wrestle for the sky, is growing into summer. His delight in the first strong and lasting sun does not, however, survive his discomfort below. Within minutes he relocates to a table in the shade.

A yeast infection. So this is a private medical affliction, a failure of the body which is at least hidden. Kingston had been small enough that he and Stan were hardware store celebrities, known at their grocery store, spotted around town. The ruined man and the flesh of his flesh.

Back on the bike, tipsy — okay drunkish — he cuts and drops toward the park with sweet-potato french fries in his gut. Rolling over the bridge of the gorge, he has warmth in his belly and cold, moist air brushing his limbs and face.

Once again he turns into the trail's descent, bumps toward his nylon base. He will sleep easily in the tired, old orchard, will nap his beer then wake for dinner, perhaps a fire. Burn these fallen limbs. Smudge the sky with appley smoke.

70

Fleeing Andrew, his precious house and their rotten relationship, Betty began to wonder if only the young, possibly only the young and those educated in the arts, could think that love is the permission to say absolutely anything. Blocking his emails, deleting his phone messages without listening to them, Betty began to see that no relationship could survive total honesty. *I know you're afraid to love me.* Or *You're different when you have an audience.* Or how about *I still think of X when I come.* Andrew and Betty learned the hard way that love does not invite you to say anything you feel. But that same school of hard knocks also showed them that love enables you to say more than you thought you had to say. Your ability to talk, not just your desire to, is increased by love.

All this time they'd been disagreeing about next year, he'd offered her every excuse for keeping his house, every counterfeit emotion possible save the truth: *I still miss him. I can't let go yet.* Instead she got:

The Argument of Possession
Betty told him, "You've got a home you don't want to leave, that's fine. I don't, though, I don't."
"You did once. You could again."
"Not without leaving first."

Asshole. Asshole. Asshole. His lies had mutated her, forced her into nasty corners she should never have been in. Nastiness like:

The Argument of Change
"You nursed your dad to death and you still think the humanities are taught in school?"

71

In the city, biking into his park campsite, he sees that young jerks are not restricted to country living or eight-cylinder cars. As he approaches his tent, he spots two male teenagers sacking his campsite. One half-crouches over an emptied pannier, flicking through his clothes and small bags of food. A pot lid lies decapitatedly at the end of this sprawl. Past it, a second youth stands with his back to Andrew, pissing on the tent wall in sharp smirks of urine.

The crouched sacker is the first to spot Andrew. His quick rise into a stand wordlessly alerts the pisser. A hood of anger tries to rise from Andrew's shoulders, but the fear between nipples and hips is arresting. As the squatter stands and the pisser ceases, Andrew must look between them, one foot resting his weight, fingers still half-gripping the brakes. He can feel a palpable triangle of earth beneath the ball of his resting foot and the shoe's sharp cleat. The pisser tucks, zips and turns. Andrew doesn't have time to think properly. Instead he feels the edges of his thighs. He watches the two of them while they are watching only one of him. More recognizable than thought are the twins of fear and rage. Then everything is wiped away when these two glance back past his shoulder at a rustle in the leaves.

In his mirror, Andrew sees a third punk stepping out from behind some shrubs with a bastard's grin and a pannier held open at arm's length. The boy is proudly exclaiming some French version of *steamer* when he spots Andrew and his briefly idle friends. Time becomes entirely space. The two at the tent leap to close the fifteen metres which separate them from Andrew's front tire. In the vulnerable arc, Andrew turns to cut back left. He must temporarily turn his back to their charge and lose them from his line of sight and then the too-slowly sweeping disc mirror. In front now, the shitter crouches slightly but doesn't yet drop the pannier. His spine-sinking, knee-flexing crouch could be designed to meet or avoid Andrew's charge.

The chase behind grows. In front, the fouled pannier finally gets chucked aside.

Now their numbers are felt, not counted. These three are a net of young muscle tightening around him. Legs, legs, legs.

Because one eye keeps checking the (filling) mirror and the (too-distant) trailhead, he can't really tell how thoroughly or not the shitter in front has raised his arms. Only when Andrew brakes suddenly in the second before meeting the shitter do the young arms rise fully, and they are not shield enough for the quick lance coming. Braking both tires then briefly turning the handlebars away from the youth, Andrew opens a column of space his freed right leg can fill. Unforgettable will be the small, preparatory heel twist of his right foot, the minuscule dab of lateral force necessary to free his kick.

Although he has never once forgotten the cleat waiting at the bottom of this whipping leg, Andrew is somewhat surprised to see its ferocious bite into the kid's splaying cheek. More than force — no doubt pain, perhaps horror — drops the shitter to the ground and frees Andrew's path.

72

Of course, twenty cents didn't really end Pat's first marriage.

Shoe leather should be a labour index on any job. Her classroom and the Gamlin campaign had Pat running around for twelve to fourteen hours a day. When she walked into the campaign office at six-thirty that night, marooned in the mutinous, knee-high boots, a disastrous cycling lesson with Andy behind her, the heel was knocking. The refrain *My mom pushed me in the ditch* still hadn't left her inner ear. By nine p.m., the heel clapped. When the last of the others filed out at ten-thirty, she wasn't going to let the now flapping heel rob her old term-paper stamina. Gordon wouldn't see that.

He stood by a window reading a letter. Cars, the cars of their co-workers, could be heard starting and leaving from the parking lot beyond him. Extra light spilled briefly across the broad province of his shoulders. In the nearly empty office, the ka-clump of her heel and her compensatory shuffle became ridiculously loud.

"Why don't you just take them off?" he asked, turning.

A committed problem-solver, Gordon Gamlin will — "Obviously I've thought of that. The zipper's broken."

"Will you think I'm campaigning if I offer to take a look at it?"

"I'll know you are and have a camera ready."

He emptied his hands while walking toward her.

She was ruined when he gave the desktop a demonstrative little double tap with all four of his fingers. "Hop up." Her boots nearly reached her knees. Her skirt didn't.

"The tab's not entirely broken," he said while remaining bent over, sounding every inch the able diagnostician. "Hang on." He stood back to fish change from his pocket. "Don't ask how I used a pair of dimes in school. May I?"

He raised an eyebrow, she a leg.

In his hands, it was and was not her calf that filled the boot. His strong, collaring grip around her calf both added and released pressure.

Immediately she felt the difference of his hand, of his body on hers, but there was also the distinct sensation that his hand gave more space to her body, expanding the very muscles it pressed. Gordon's encircling grip finally confirmed what they had each known since the moment they met: together, they had a *them* body. One plus one equalled a sweaty three. Exhaling through her nostrils she could send part of her breath down into the grip of his hand. Her breath glowed inside his hand like the bones in an X-ray. His pinching dimes pulled the boot collar tight before opening the longest zipper of her life. At thirty-three, this zipper was the back of every dress she had worn for the past ten years of her marriage. The pants of her past, present and future were tugged open in his hands. The boot leather unclenched, but they did not. Because of the boot, she couldn't feel his wedding ring at all.

From sit-bone to heel, yes, she turned her knees out to curl her legs without actually spreading them. Her jaw rose to bare a little neck. Freed, the boot poured down her calf into his hands. Still cupping her heel in one hand, he looked at her just long enough before setting the other hand above and inside her knee to claim the leg entire. What agreeable gravity.

Her only moment of anything less than joyous acquiescence, the moment when she pressed and angled not to complete a shape but to change it, came during his early chest-leaning push to get her on her back for the full prone offer. No, no, you're going to look me in the face. Let me get that belt and fly, do more than just undress you, but you keep your face close to mine. This doesn't happen without you knowing who I am.

73

Physically, the two other tent sackers could probably catch him as he bikes off from the body he just dropped with a kick. However quickly he bikes, plunging his legs so frantically that he rises in the frame and all but leaps off it, he is still biking uphill on a soft trail. For the first few metres, the runners should have more acceleration. But, wordlessly, they stop their pursuit at their fallen comrade. Physically, they could have him. Global war, contact sports, gang violence — intimidation is always the meta-weapon.

He climbs chipped wood and adrenalin up the park trail. Swelling lungs, bursting heart, a still-empty mirror. Trail and panic flatten as he makes the bridge.

Speed is downhill, and he chases it. Shooting out of the park, he follows the steep hill down toward the river. He slaloms between moving cars, cuts into oncoming traffic when necessary and blows through an intersection. After just three blocks he has biked past the area of the city he knows.

If they call the police — *if* — they'd have to run for a phone first, then wait for a cop on the scene, a scene that includes piss on his tent walls and shit in one of his panniers. That won't change his guilt at kicking the kid, but any doubt it can muster might slow or even curtail a pursuit by the police. Then again, what paper-pushing cop wouldn't like a manhunt with the pedal down? He pours himself downhill toward the St. Lawrence and then turns left. The roads are flat alongside the river. He'll see the police coming for miles, but they could also see him.

His lungs, heart and legs hurt too much to feel guilty. He pushes them so they're too busy to feel fear either.

74

Pat and Gordon kept having sex. The consolidating and demonstrative second time. The flatteringly committed third. Experimental with the fourth. They were together more than once, so the sex was more than curiosity, novelty, campaign fatigue, revenge, or indulgence.

Pat evolved into a creature of guilt. She had selected the family shot to be used in Gordon's pamphlet because of the way one entire half of his body (arm, shoulder, undoubtedly a fraction of hip) seemed to reach out for the body of his wife, Sandra. Let other candidates clutch at their children. Pat had wanted to emphasize that Gordon's first successful election was by a woman.

In her private, unvoiced defence she knew that guilt was now her element. Her father, a natural history buff with a worn library card, had given her a better explanation of evolution than any classroom teacher ever had. The big evolutionary moment didn't occur when creatures simply crawled out of the sea to walk on land. Eating on land wasn't even the end of the line. The big moment, a moment recorded best on Canadian soil yet unknown to most Canadians, occurred when marine creatures began to reproduce on land. Pat had already been breathing guilt for years before she met Gordon, guilt for her fears about Stan, her impatience, for how unconnected she felt. Even guilt about her fear. Careerism had been the slope she'd been climbing to raise her head above the sea of guilt. Now, the sex was just a conclusion. Evolution is a matter of survival, not choice.

More than anything else, motherhood had taught her to distinguish surviving from thriving. The eighteen years of middle management that finds you pushed and pulled between your child and everything else: friends, school, your husband, the whole big world. Kids could be weeds or prize flowers, could grow by accident or design. Somehow they'd grab enough light and suck enough water to grow, but would they thrive? Family life, that expected, genuine stake here in the guilt, was also crucial in her amphibious evolution into a creature who could breathe guilt. Family is the crucible of guilt. Just as it teaches you the weight of guilt, schools you in its challenging, enduring mass, so it also teaches independence. Always this background lesson of the family — fuck guilt.

The neighbourhood guilt she could deal with easily enough. She'd move out. The whispers and raised eyebrows among fellow teachers in a staff room or at workshops wouldn't be much of a problem if she quit. But there was Andy. Live with a lover, and you live with a full-time witness and part-time judge and jury. Even more intense are your children; they'll judge you their entire lives.

I can't do it, Stan. Selfish. Weak. Scared. Shallow. Whatever you want to call me, yes, guilty as charged. Not in sickness, no.

75

As soon as his breakaway pace sags a little, he has to think. Spinning his legs madly, hitting and maintaining a pace he has never held before helps him avoid calculations of risk or probabilities of exposure. Leaving behind the last borders of Rivière du Loup, the cheap strip joints and public storage garages, he relies on routine rather than planning. Keep going west.

He can only run so hard for so long, yet he had this same sobering thought yesterday morning with the slashed tire and now, after the kick, he's trying to bike even faster.

Inevitably, thought returns. To get away, what is he willing to do without? What would he have to do without in prison? Go to ground. You win this by hiding, not running. Hiding now is part of the long run. You must endure boredom before you endure pain. Cunning, not strength. Get off the fucking road.

He's finding survival to be a matter of will, not skill. Pushing one aching leg then the other, he hears the question *Do you want to survive?* grow into *How different are you willing to become?* Now more than ever, ego is the heaviest thing he carries.

He slips into an empty cemetery and rolls toward the curtain of trees at its rear. The mercifully sylvan Maritimes. No city east of Quebec City lacks a visible treeline running its borders. The capital city of New Brunswick is positively besieged by trees, with forests abutting its shopping malls. Edmundston and Rivière-du-Loup are francophone coins briefly weighting endless blankets of green. Rolling toward the cemetery's treeline, he is hit by a bizarre combination of laziness and boredom. No, I don't want to drag this thing over a fence and into the woods. Four or five more hours to full dark. No food. No water. Christ, this burning crotch.

Mostly he doesn't want to be alone and still. For the epigraph of his application essay to UNS, he had chosen Pascal's dictum that much of human suffering stems from man's inability to sit contentedly alone in a quiet room. Hiding in a forest, this large, hot and temporary room of the woods finds him tracing the circumferences of the cigarette burns on his chest and knee. No tent. No sleeping bag. No water or food. Once again, his chase may be only hypothetical, but the blood underneath his shoe is certain. Be alone, wear tight, bright clothing and the whole world wants to fuck you up. To police, would his use of the shoe's metal cleat constitute assault with a weapon, not just assault?

When he had begun planning this trip, he had emailed Betty repeatedly with varying versions of two recurring answers to the obvious question of why. Why undertake such an arduous trip? *Because it's the right way for me to return home, to that home. And because life isn't life without tests. I don't know what exactly I'll learn about myself, but I know I'll learn something.*

Now, thirsty, angry and afraid, he finally grasps a lesson that has been building for years. Possibly on the run again, only possibly, he either has a new enemy or maybe even the need to have a new enemy.

76

The disease of one body in Andrew's childhood home eventually changed every body in it and even the house itself. His childhood home turned sour. Betty's parents each claim hers started out sour.

Before their restaurant conversation with Pat dissolved the *and* of Betty and Andrew, these two children of divorce had talked about this powerful little conjunction and its evolution through the generations.

"Jim *and* Elaine. Stan *and* Pat," Betty announced. "What's responsible for that sound? Don't they *sound* different?"

"Man first? Age of the names maybe? Mackenzie and Gabriel doesn't sound so... so —"

"Gluey. One divorce each, and yet I'm sure your brain does it as well as mine, plays this little *and* recording, just staples the names together."

"Trudy and Dave," he sang.

"In the eighties, two performance artists actually tied themselves together for a year. Like maybe six feet of rope."

"You mean at a gallery?" he asked.

"No, all day, every day. The life was the art. Tehching Hsieh and Linda Montano. I want a shower, you have to stand outside the tub."

"Were they lovers? A little rodeo? Take turns whipping the bad boy or girl?"

"Don't know. They sure weren't lovers after. One year together and twenty years publicly bickering about it."

"Oh, I did see that. It was called *My Parents' Marriage*."

"For my parents, it was Jim, Elaine and a rock," Betty said, telling him what she knew of the contested family legend.

As an architecture student in the early 1970s, Elaine studied within a roughly 4:1 ratio of men to women. For the first couple of years, she'd enjoyed the attention or at least the convenience of never having to look far for her next date. But by her last year she tired of meeting the same guy over and over again. Trevor or Neil or Roger, each one certain that he was a future starchitect, steadily filling a sketchbook with jutting this and towering that. Jim, a journalism student, was utterly different. Part new journalist, part town crier, part documentarian, he knew what to ask and when.

"And remember," Betty told Andrew, "this is decades before email. My dad wooed her with a pen."

One day, walking across campus toward the house she rented with Barb and Megan, Elaine once again rolled that powerful little word *home* around inside her mouth. She disapproved of the realtor's smarmy swap of *home* for *house*, but she wasn't always as enthusiastic as her classmates to constantly say *space*. A parking lot's a space. A cramped, mouldy laundry room is a space. A closet's a space. She was going to need more than just space.

"Meg, Babs," Elaine called out to her roommates as she stepped into their small house.

Megan, another future teacher, was upstairs working on a Shakespeare essay. "Unless you're a ready-formed paragraph, I don't want to see you," she called out.

"Seriously. Get down here."

Barb shuffled out of another room. "Where's the fire?"

"Black Rock," Elaine replied, grinning as she raised a stiff envelope.

"Unless that's a new Leonard Cohen album, I'm back up the stairs," Megan said.

"No, it's Jim."

"Oh, love, big deal," shot Barb.

"I've lost two, three sentences for this," Megan said, retreating.

"His family has some land on a lake, a place they call Black Rock. He's invited me there for Easter." Elaine fluttered the envelope. "Written invitation."

Barb and Megan reversed their exits. Barb was first to snatch away the envelope. "My dearest Elaine. You have taken me to so many wonderful places, I would now like to do the same. (What, *you* finally get to come?) Please spend Easter with me at the black rock of Lake Iwannalayu — all right, all right — Apple Lake."

"Tick, tick," said Megan. "Think it's question time?"

"It better be," Elaine replied.

77

Waiting in the Quebec cemetery, he peels the bike with his knife, undoing in fifteen minutes the safe, preparatory work that took him three-quarters of an hour two weeks ago. The reflective See-Me tape, which he had wrapped in two vertical strips up and down the front forks, cuts away like pant legs to reveal supple calves beneath. From the rear forks the tape, once started with the knife, comes down more easily in his pinching thumbs, comes down, he can't deny, like stockings off an extended leg. He does not forget this image as he raises his yellow helmet to pare one long circumferential peel from its brow. From the backs of the pedals he scrapes at daubs of tape as tenacious as fungus on a horse's hoof.

Collecting the sloughed-off tape, he is caught in the classic waste management debate. His new desire to *not* be seen at night results in a small pile of useless waste. It's easy enough to collect, but does he store it and carry it around with him? If he's caught with it by police, is it evidence of evasive guilt, conspiracy to commit...hiding? Flight is guilt, especially night flight. Looking around at the expansive forest floor around him, he sees why so many Canadians are wasteful. What minuscule fraction of this soil would be needed to bury this little ball of tape? If it can go in a landfill there, why can't it go in the land here? He uses his right shoe to dig a hole. By the time he's done digging, the bottom of his shoe is entirely covered in dirt, including its sharp cleat. He buries the ball of reflective tape with both hands, hoping that the dirt he mounds with his hands will help him scour off some of the tape's residual gum. Instead, his now filthy hands simply grow darker stripes of resinous dirt. Stamping down the mound of earth with his shoe, he watches a sharp imprint of the cleat roll into the damp spring soil.

Rechecking his diminished gear is the only chore left before empty hours of waiting:

- knife
- wallet ($60 plus emerg $40, Visa, licence, health and organ donor cards)
- saddlebag tool kit (tire patches, one emergency foil blanket, waterproof matches, two tiny bungee cords — previously useless)
- one tube Monistat-Derm (almost full)
- one half-novel
- one pair hiking shorts, breezy
- one short-sleeved jersey (dirty)
- one pair cycling shoes
- helmet
- sunglasses

The sight of the helmet is unnerving. Yes, it's necessary. Yes, he's glad to have it, now more than ever — spare the brain from whatever gets thrown. But it alarms him to have to think of the helmet as a tool, as an asset. One piece of armour isn't much.

Despite his boredom and his need for distraction, the half-novel remains untouched for one quarter-hour after another. He knows too many of the novel's phrases and scenes already, recalls its various trials and tests of loyalty. One remembered phrase, *his moral editor*, tempts him to burn the novel outright. Travel lightly. Again and again, he looks away from the ripped coverless novel that helped his parents fall in love. His parents, and then, despite or maybe even because of their romantic failure, he himself fell in love with advice from a novel he now won't look at. On the uneven ground, he tries to sleep but fails.

78

On their ferry date in bright September when Andrew lied to Betty about how long Stan had been dead, when he hid this truth beneath what he thought was the better, more relevant truth of wanting her to move in, he didn't yet know how uniquely wounding this would be to her. Only their slow talks of November and December began to show Andrew the additional costs of his September deception. Weeks before Betty left him, she told him about her mother and father falling for, then fighting over, a lakeside plot of her father's land.

Nearly a week after Elaine's Easter departure from campus, her housemates, Barb and Megan, perked up at the rare sight of headlights in the driveway of their rented student house. Barb plugged in the kettle and asked Megan if she'd been able to keep herself away from the last bottle of Mateus.

"Well?" they both asked as Elaine floated in from her first weekend away to Jim's family land.

"The lake is deep and dark, but clear."

"Get the chocolate."

"These huge pink rocks, they just seem . . . kind."

"Where's the corkscrew?"

"And the pine trees, so brave. Impossible pine trees growing up the sides of cliffs."

"C'mon, Elaine, quit with the star talk or we get ugly."

Sitting on a couch between the two closest friends she'd ever had, Elaine smiled from ear to ear. "He didn't make one proposal; he made two. The second was would I design a house for us there on the lake."

Even Megan cheered.

But after courtship became engagement, and as a wedding and house designs eclipsed graduation, Jim was torn between the land he had inherited and the life he wanted to build on it. Betty would describe the lakeside house her mother designed as "an argument with a roof." Jim tried to tell Elaine that architecturally she had carte blanche, but she didn't find the carte very blanche when he asked her to sign a pre-nuptial agreement guaranteeing him ownership of the land.

Riled, Jim finally replied, "My great-grandfather cleared that land with an axe, a chain and a horse. Of course I think of us together, but the land —"

"Needs a pre-nup. You say The Land like it's a person. Right, The Land went off to this lawyer's office for a pre-nup. What does The Land think of this baby going into French immersion?"

"Elaine, I love you. We live together and this is a non-issue. We can build whatever we want. We can do anything."

"Except change. Except evolve."

"That land has carried two names, the Queen's and my family's. I can't — no, no, you're right — I *won't* give it away."

"Oh, poor man's worried about losing the family name and something precious."

"Elaine, I'm asking you to design our home."

"*Your* home." Elaine stormed off.

"The poor fools," the narrating Betty had concluded, nodding *yes please* to the wine bottle angled in Andrew's hands. "The lake where he spent his childhood summers. An architect designing her own home. Could the stakes have been higher?"

"A *pregnant* architect. They ground it out until you were what, six?"

"Almost seven. We'd already moved into the city by then. For a year we tried treating Black Rock like a summer place. When he moved out for good, at least Dad knew where he was going. And the arguments were great for my vocabulary. *Modular. Labyrinthine. Unitized. Imprisoning.*"

"Such a head/heart debate."

"Dad doesn't think so. How is it unemotional to protect your emotions?"

"Yeah, but I can see her point — poison trees, poison fruit."

"Maybe, or maybe my mom just made a mistake. It was her first house. Notice she *redesigns* houses now."

"So, your dad's bringing it all down?"

"Yep. After two decades of renovations and adaptations and excuses for his moods or his career bounding, he's celebrating his fiftieth birthday with a bulldozer."

"I got a light bulb joke to rework," Andrew admitted.

79

In nameless woods outside Rivière-du-Loup, he waits for the cover of darkness. Waiting alone, scared yet bored, he thinks incessantly of the kick that has sent him here to hide, the kick he can still feel in his leg. A whip from hip to toe. Higher even. The tucking coccyx, the up-swept ribs, a pliant lung. And deeper than that, a kick forged by every metre of this ride and each of those that brought him to it. The body he remade through cycling, then again by cycling with Mark.

He stands up, steps around in the piny heat, steps nowhere. Brought here by a body now made idle. Idle and itchy.

Stand here. Stand there. Squat again. Dodge the sun. He does not read.

His growing hunger displaces some of his guilt but augments his fear. If nothing else, hunger is reliably self-absorbed. And thirst *is* fear, that rusty ache in the mouth, that empty bite. His eyes tighten but do not stare. If he could see them, he'd notice his pupils reduced to pinpricks, even when his head's hidden in leafy shade. Pine boughs, maple branches or dirt in his empty stare. Pine boughs. Maple branches. Dirt. And the inescapable sun. Although the heat won't yet last through the night, here now is the staggered roast of direct and residual heat, the burner and its heated room.

Without his own wind, without a distracting ache in thigh or lung, he feels imprisoned by the sun's hot, red stare. Cheek and forehead burn. To turn away is merely to trade off the triceps or offer up the neck. Regardless of where the sun hits him, blasting shoulder, chest or neck, sweat gathers on his itching thighs and even trickles into his rashy crotch. Unfairly, sweat finds his yeast infection even though he's hiding, not riding.

He stands again, grateful for the distraction of a chore. With time on his hands he's able to undertake a thorough quest for shade. None-theless, no matter how much he expands the radius of his search, no matter how distant the bike becomes, each tree he auditions still leaves some patch of him vulnerable to a prodding finger of burning sunshine. A red pinch on the ear, a hot stain on a pink thigh. Again he rises, squats, or strolls, amazed at the pure research of an investigation free from a ticking clock. He's a military scientist, a scheming convict, nothing to do but think. Finally, he switches tack. If he can't find shade vertically or perpendicularly, he'll find it horizontally.

Hunting out the largest, shaggiest white pine, he begins to raise its hemline with the saw blade of his knife. Only now does he really think of the book he's not reading or the toilet paper he abandoned as starting out like these tree branches in his hands. At UNS, he met a young librarian who referred to books and paper journals as "treeware." Hardware, firmware, software, treeware.

Computers show you how other people think: the programmers who anticipate how you work, the designers who try to chart what you'll do. All of the commerce and connectivity remind you that you are one of many. Hacking off long pine boughs feels utterly removed from reading or the daily world of computer use and other people. He cuts away, piling the boughs beneath the shortening skirt of his chosen tree. Tree parts fill his hands, yet he won't read the treeware of the family novel or, worse, Betty's postcards. Witness and jury, the postcards sit tucked into the remainder of the novel off with the parked bike. Betty, would you still write me now, with blood on my cleats? To his every protest of self-defence against these random attacks of male violence, he can hear Betty or his more enlightened self reminding him that he alone chose to travel on the vulnerable side of the road.

As a young teenager, when he began arguing with his mother on the phone, picking fights on the most irrelevant grounds, glorying in the sting of an accusation, she'd often reply with the word *victim*, smearing it with such disdain and revulsion that now, years later, he will not say that he was a victim of cigarette violence from the Mustang crew. He's equally unwilling to say that he victimized the kid he kicked. They'd been pissing on his tent and shitting in his panniers. That was symbolic violence more than it was petty theft. But then Betty's voice catches him again. Symbolic violence doesn't require reconstructive surgery, though, does it? In each of their liberal arts educations they'd discovered how limited binary thinking could be. Victim *or* victimizer. Mother *or* whore. Heterosexual *or* homosexual. What about life in between? What of the intriguing shades of grey between black and white? And yet here he is, inconvenienced and disadvantaged but unharmed, awaiting night to avoid being a victim.

The severed pine boughs make a half-comfortable bed, offering a dense layer of softness. His cycling jersey, however, is too thin for him to lie comfortably on the innumerable pine needles. His first thought about his bed of pine needles compares it to a funeral pyre. Now, nearly two years after Stan's death, he can still hear that shockingly procedural question: *Did he ever talk to you about funeral arrangements or discuss what he wanted done with his body?*

Amazingly, the familiarity of lying supine yet unable to sleep finally prompts a deep stirring in his still body. This sexual desire, his first since confronting the campsite sackers, lights up as suddenly and as brightly as a lamp after a power failure. His hiking shorts are quicker to enter than the now abandoned cycling shorts. With his eyes closed and his shorts open, he chases the one erotic image he has been given, so grateful for this reliable distraction that he doesn't care that the fantasy and memories that currently drive his hand are of Mark, not Betty.

80

At UNS, Andrew learned more about the bicycle than he had ever thought there was to know. Early Chinese manufacturers made bikes with bamboo frames. A bicycle tire can support four hundred times its own weight. Today, the adult tricycle is the under-recognized workhorse of the megalopolises of the developing world. The nouveau riche entrepreneurs in New Delhi who want tricycles banned so they can get across the city more quickly in their BMWs forget that the vast majority of parts and goods they need to do business are shipped around the city on tricycles. In Manhattan, traffic and stoplights make the average car speed just ten kilometres an hour. The bike should be everywhere.

Physics, sociology, geography and economics all ride along on the bike frame. Carry Freedom, a non-profit project to encourage the use of bike trailers in the developing world, argues that the panniers Andrew abandoned back in Rivière-du-Loup are actually less energy efficient than a low-mounted bike trailer. With every single stroke he made to Rivière-du-Loup, the force of one leg caused the bike to lean a little to one side. The weight of each pannier had grabbed that lean, deepened it, and forced him to pull the weight back to centre. His arms had to correct that lean thousands of times each day. No wonder his neck and high back ache.

Now, utterly idle as he waits for dark, becoming delirious with thirst and fatigue, the image of bamboo bicycle trailers rolls down the old rail trail he took to get here and kicks up a childhood memory of a televised grammar lesson. The memory and the delirium invite him to ponder a single word with all the concentration that bored isolation can offer. Nearly twenty years after he watched a so-called educational cartoon commercial, he can still sing "Conjunction Junction, what's your function?" He can't remember all of the images, but he's sure single words or phrases were presented as the boxcars on a train. Conjunctions — *and, but, or* — were the dramatically opened and closed couplings between these wordy boxcars. With his bike still beside him and the railway miles behind him, the word and its antonym, *coupling* and *uncoupling*, poke at him incessantly. Betty and Andrew had coupled as they shared their stories of parental uncoupling. By the time those parental uncouplings had been described in full, Betty — or Andrew — pulled the release lever on their own coupling.

Describing his parents' divorce to Betty, Andrew delivered details he was surprised to remember, details that immediately swamped him with questions, Betty's questions as well as his own adult questions added to old questions remembered from childhood.

Stan had a slow body and a quick mind. When he fell in love with Pat, part of what he loved was her bluntness, her honesty. But the young man who fell in love hadn't been given as much to fear in life as the prematurely aged husband still in love with a woman who had worked late every night on Gordon Gamlin's political campaign. In the few conversations he got alone with his wife during the campaign, that siege of pamphlets and phone calls, he never brought himself to ask whether she was having an affair. The closest he came was mentioning her endless hours away from home. Pat's reply was accurate but unconsoling. "Children grow and change, so should families."

When the election was over, with Pat and Gordon victorious in public office, Stan knew what was coming in his private life. She left for a weekend away in Ottawa with no more warning than a brief note on the counter. On Monday, a private courier arrived to hand-deliver a slim envelope to Stan during the brief interval between Andrew's leaving for school by bike and Stan's leaving by car. These elaborate preparations dissolved his last shreds of doubt and hope. A laboriously delivered — but skinny — envelope, not even its contents, told him that divorce was no longer a question of if, just of how much it would cost. That male, early eighties dread of divorce's financial ruin was his first misconception.

Stan waited until he reached the Allenville Correctional parking lot to open the letter. One hooked finger dragged at the envelope's thin seam. Unfolding the single sheet of paper he could, damn it, still see the old letters of memory, still see *Stan my man* heading notes and letters from their early days of clutching and joking.

Stan,

You're smarter than I am, better than I am, but you have to be, don't you? (There, that teary grin, hold on to that.)

You have taught me more, of life and of myself, than anyone else alive. For this alone I shall always adore you. I can see the bridges I'm burning here, and wish friendship with you were not one of them. Of course that's impossible; I do realize that. This letter is also an offer of undying friendship, affection and a kind of loyalty, should you ever want them. (Please reach past that snorting derision. Read this again in a month, six months, a year.)

Our friends and family are starting to put a halo on me which you know I don't deserve and I know I don't want. You told me from the start that you wanted a wife, not a nurse. I'm prevented from being one and I'm gambling that it's better if I'm not the other. Better, yes, for everyone. I've never risked more, and I've never admired you more than in thinking, at some incommunicable level, you agree I should go.

Until you and I had Andrew, I could never have understood that bravery can be shared. Please believe that I think part of the compulsion I feel is bravery, and it's a three-sided bravery: yours, mine and Andrew's. No one else's, ever.

Respectfully but shamefully yours,
Pat

Hoping to blunt the wounds he knew this letter would deliver, Stan read it in the prison parking lot just before a shift, the time when he normally had to seal off all emotion. But he had waited in the parking lot too long. Another vehicle approached and idled. Stan looked up to a stone-faced prison guard idling in a rugged pickup truck. A mounted shotgun bristled the cab's still air. To those who patrolled the borders of a prison, you were either going in or out; there was no in-between.

81

Back in their September and October, Andrew could barely pull himself away from Betty to go riding. He cancelled on Mark twice in a row and began to lose the hard edge of speed he'd sharpened all summer. Consenting to a ride late in October, riding behind Mark once more, Andrew saw his shaved calves again as if for the first time. One ascent shed trees, shrubs and grass as the trail climbed a giant slab of naked pink granite. This bank of Canadian Shield held just a few patches of soil and supported only the most tenacious of pines, the most gregarious tufts of cedars and then finally dead patches of grass as the incline increased. Direct sunlight and the rock's store of ambient heat made the steep climb triply hot. Slower, they were finally caught by the sweat they'd been fleeing. Drooped foreheads poured. Arms and calves shone.

Rational thought, let alone liberal thought, was too heavy for the hot climb. On flat land Andrew would never have agreed to a statement like, *Women shave their legs; men don't.* Live and let shave. But here on the climb, two sleek category mistakes bulged and gleamed in front of him. Tiny sub-strands of Mark's muscled calves glistened like facets of a jewel, individuated one minute in the late afternoon sun, then gathering into a cohesive whole the next. Even overweight men can have fit-looking calves. Hang thirty extra pounds between a man's nipples and his knees, give him that heart-attack pouch, and his calves can still look muscular. For the lithely fit, take away hair and how different is the male calf from the female? Tanned and glowing in front of him was not only calf, but also the naked, hairless cleft behind the knee, that sweet spot of — Climb, Andrew, just climb.

At the top, when the waiting Mark pointed to Andrew's legs and said, "It's all that hair slowing you down," Andrew tried not to betray his alarm. (He's more fit than you, not telepathic.) When he later thought he had closed a gap between them on the trail, Mark shot on ahead and slipped a corner. Cursing inwardly, bleeding sweat, Andrew cornered to find Mark pissing off a cliff. Mark had turned his side to the trail, not his back. The black rim of his lowered shorts spilled down square hips and strung twice-naked balls.

"What, you didn't know a razor could go this high?" Mark asked.

Back on the trail, Mark took a brutal pace.

Later that week, in the warm glow of the Kingston house, Andrew had started to tell Betty about this glimpse of Mark as she shaved his legs. His slick legs aroused her as much as him, so he'd told her that Mark took the razor even higher.

"He showed you his balls?" she asked.

"No, no." Andrew's lie surprised him. "No, he just mentioned it." What was he hiding? Looking wasn't doing. And Betty liked his gender-bending. Besides, wasn't a same-sex experience monogamy's Get Out of Jail Free card?

"Hey, name part, will shave," she offered. "Now can we get some sleep around here or are you going to start talking barrettes and scarves?"

82

Awaken is not really the verb for how Andrew rises from his forest hiding spot in Quebec to start his night ride. After hours of simply sweating and itching, of a boredom so total he had begun counting how often bugs crawled over him (count abandoned at fifty-two), of hunger and a hundred worries, he had, at most, slipped into a more fluid fear, a general anxiety with a low pulse. Bored or occasionally even dozing, he never lost track of the likelihood that he is being hunted. For prey, even sleep is a cower.

Opening his eyes fully in the darkness of night, he's a camp worker moving from bed to labour, a soldier on the rhythmed push. His lack of food spares him any camp chores, save for a piss. Here is the bike. The cleats make their familiar bite into the pedals.

On this long night's ride, the frame seems designed to isolate his gurgling stomach, a luggage rack to sling this empty bag. Then darkness and his spinning legs draw the hunger out of his stomach. A black cape of fear settles about his shoulders. Each knee slops through hunger.

More than just his stomach notices the absence of the panniers. He's been back on the road for less than two hours. With the Trans Canada Trail still incomplete, and its erratic quiltwork of linked local trails, he has decided to return to asphalt for his night run. Although he wants a road, the Trans-Canada Highway is too popular and too illuminated for his slip through the night. Instead he hopes to hitch the bike to national history. The Trans-Can runs parallel to the river at times, but the highway is much younger than the river. There must be older highways closer to the river. After all, the majority of the country's population still lives within reach of the St. Lawrence or the Great Lakes served by it.

In road time, he has been pannier-free for less than two hours. The bike is a carriage horse suddenly free from harness and team. Pulling cumbrously out of Halifax, what, eight days ago (just eight?), he'd been sloppy on the turns, amazed at each laden pannier's mutinous gulp. Now he misses the long arcs of steering with the panniers. Sure, they made him slower and less nimble. They taxed his upper body as he resisted them thousands of times a day, but they also reassured him with their mass. Every turn they weighted showed his body that he was carrying a home, not just going home. Without the panniers, the handlebars have become a midnight switchblade flicking left or right with the slightest unevenness. Even a distant set of headlights sends tremors through the metal frame.

The mere sight of the growing headlights has him checking the severity of the ditch and inching closer to the roadside gravel. He has already chosen his line into the ditch when he fully recognizes that he has stripped his bike of reflectors and now flies below the radar of visibility. The growing stain of a second pair of lights behind him doesn't deter his return to the centre of the road. No reflectors wink between his handlebars or glow in the rear. No stroke pushes a glowing little bar on the front of each pedal. He cuts wide S-curves in the growing light, spins silently and privately in his dark envelope until his heels begin to glow.

Idiot. The lights in his lane pick out the reflective heel patch he forgot to remove from each shoe, igniting them with a leaping, indicting conductivity he feels as a palpable shock. He races to the roadside and prays these nicked heels look like a scurrying coon. Enough light spills in from the approaching headlights to reveal the looseness of the roadside gravel and its steep slope into a rock-strewn ditch. His erratic unweighted front tire snags in the gravel he hasn't properly anticipated by balancing his chest. Because the cleats dutifully keep his shoes locked into the pedals, most of the bike, not just its rider, begins to fly over the front handlebars. When the rear tire rises past the point where his shoulder should be, he lets go of the handlebars to meet the approaching, inclined ground. His padded gloves, like so much else, are back in Rivière-du-Loup, in vengeful or prosecuting hands. Only one foot disengages in time, so bike and body wind up in a deformed mule-kick of sharp angles. The caught downward calf is punctured on impact by at least one rock. The bracing hands don't absorb enough force to spare his forearms and elbows from gash and smash. In this jumble of inclined pain, his first realization beyond ache is that each knee has been spared. Then there's the blood.

His right calf isn't quite a hose of blood, but the puncture wound beside his shin does pump steadily. Lengthening trails of blood on each arm go unobserved a few minutes longer while he tries to swallow all the jagged pain and concentrate on the steady leak of blood coming from his shin. The passing spill of light stays his reflex to hop up in an attempt to walk off the pain.

After the headlights fade, he feels the severity of the bleeding more than he sees it. Hopefully, the rivulets of blood on his forearms will seal with just time and dust. The bleeding in the oddly weightless-feeling leg won't quit so easily.

Removing his jersey he is hit by a wave of the post-orgasmic, cannabine reek he and Betty used to find daily under his arms. Bleeding in the cold night air, he raises an arm briefly to check his scent. Yes, unmistakably, there is the skunky, weedy smell he normally exudes immediately after orgasm. That smell is one reminder of Betty from the jersey. Removing her postcards from a jersey pocket is a second. As a bandage, the breathable, sweat-wicking jersey is inadequate, a failure over civilian cotton. He knots the shirt to the outside of the leg, but can see blood already sliding down his leg before he even grabs the bike. Now pain finds him, slices into him as he reaches for the flung half-novel. He rips out a small stack of pages to make an absorbent pad for the leg and reties the jersey around the paper bandage. Now he packs the knife in his saddlebag. He doesn't like even looking at the postcards, let alone touching them. They could be left in the ditch. Burnt before he rides again. With one of the two tiny bungee cords, he lashes them to the pannier rack, images up.

However thin and porous the jersey had felt in the night air, he now feels absolutely naked without it as he pushes his bare chest into the cold night.

83

When Pat left, Stan could still sit in the brown easy chair and manage a proper glass of Scotch. The chair, at least, had sturdy arms.

However much it had claimed humility and contrition, Pat's farewell letter was still the record of the victor, the glorious public monument with a jaw upturned and a fist raised in the air.

If Andy had kept the kitchen drawers properly organized, there'd be a box of wooden matches in the junk drawer. Stan could pin the box under his left hand and, eventually, get one stiff match lit. Or he could ignite the letter on a stove burner. He knew they worked. But her letter took Andy hostage.

The earthquake of divorce shook his land so thoroughly that he spent months convinced that her contrite letter was designed to be discovered by Andy. Have children and you no longer know how much you will say or hear about yourself. Every family is a little KGB of eavesdroppers and information-selling. Pat's farewell was a letter, not a speech. These words were designed to last. And to reach Andy, their mutual target. Each of them knew that Andy was still far from choosing where he would live. Pat had sent the letter to a house she had abandoned. Maybe she hoped it would be discovered.

He could burn it in the kitchen sink then rinse away the ashes.

And what of the letter she didn't write, the motives she didn't confess? Above all else, I want a lover, a second body, sweet annihilation.

Go ahead, Pat, woo him with words. Two can play at that game.

84

In the eventful August before Betty moved in, Andrew wound up swimming naked with Mark. Every gesture either increased or decreased a view of hanging cock. Asking Mark about the gorilla tattooed on his shoulder, that would involve less cock, not more. Get him talking.

"Our high-school wrestling team," Mark explained. "But it's more about freethinking, not team spirit or anything like that. Gorillas are vegetarians but strong enough to rip your arms off."

They'd gone riding despite a heavy heat and had mutually agreed to swing down to a section of brook with a few pools and half-submerged rocks.

"Duncan, our coach, started with one question: Do you want to win or eat burgers? Wrestling's all about weight."

"Yeah, in order for men to be anorexic we need the excuse of throwing each other to the ground."

Warm water curled around their pale, submerged hips and across their buzzing thighs before pouring over their knees into a greening pool. Warm, firm rock stretched beneath them.

"That's the struggle, strength versus weight. You wrestle weight. Whole sport's full of guys living on nothing but Popsicles and water days before a match. Duncan laid out the math: you need maximum protein and minimum fat per mass unit. That's never going to come from some animal that's storing food on its body."

Each treed side of their tiny valley, the rocks coppered with sun and the water they wore in place of shorts allowed Andrew to half-glimpse a circuit running through him. Reflex, politeness, modesty or some other current sent his eyes away from Mark's glistening chest, from the water curling over hip and fur.

"Duncan wasn't an animal lover, just efficient. In fact, he advocated lentils cooked in blood."

"In technical parlance I believe he's known as *a vampire*."

"Most guys resisted. A hamburger tells you who's lazy, who's selfish. For me it was like a light went on. I wasn't great when I started, but after a year on the beans I got what I wanted. The gorilla asks me what I really want."

Andrew then Mark rolled off the solid rock to sink into a pool of moving water. Heads and toes broke the gurgling stream as they floated one way then another. Floating on his back and reaching out with his feet for a snared log, Andrew submerged all but his nose and mouth to float fully. Smaller currents surrounded him as he pulled his torso to his heels and pushed it back again, bending his legs into angle brackets then straightening out over and over again, sack and balls swishing up then down in their own small tide. Mark could worry about turning away.

The damp cycling clothes they'd left in the hot sun had nearly dried. As Mark dug his arms into his blue sleeveless jersey, Andrew nodded once more at the gorilla.

"What do you want now that you're done wrestling?"

"We're always wrestling something."

85

Riding in the dark, he can smell the rain coming for miles. Despite a bodysuit of cold and sleeves and pant legs of sweat, despite racing stripes of blood, he feels wetness growing in the night, feels a slight smothering of the wind down his naked back. This dampness brushing cheek and knee is a piano's tinkling prelude. First he expects a single poking finger of rain on his neck or a few potshots at his back to precede a machine-gun wave. No. The clouds crack open severely enough to dissolve earth from sky. Instantly he wears a skullcap, jacket and gaiters of frigid water. Cold expands across his back, growing from strips to bands to plates before reaching around for rib and nipple. The rain falls hard enough to bounce off the pavement, creating a second rain for his spinning shoes. Cold water squirms between his toes. Water gloves each finger, flies up his baggy shorts, straddles each hip. However temporarily, however speciously, the curtains of cold rain douse his burning crotch and draw attention away from his growling stomach. Cold replaces the inside of his body then expands its cavern of hunger with a frigid chisel.

Thunder cracks through the valleys frequently enough that its waves and echoes combine to overwrite each valley and cut a new landscape of boom and roar. Lightning tears the sky left and right to seam a new, vertical world. Still pedalling within this wet avalanche, he worries that he might be a horizontal lightning rod, a ripe fin of conductivity. Metal wedges up his middle. He holds a metal bar in the rain and repeatedly throws one circuit switch after another with feet clamped into metal pedals that ride metal crank arms. Supposedly the rubber tires on a car protect it from lightning. A car contains much more metal, but it also lays much more rubber across the ground. Do his bike tires meet the necessary minimum in the rubber-to-metal ratio? Is *grounding* really a function of having rubber on the ground or a deceptively tempting verb? Once again he sees how this entire trip rides on two thin sleeves of air.

Heavy, endless drops of rain flick his cheeks. This veil of driven rain and his defensive squinting hide the road. He pushes blindly into a road more felt than seen, relying on his legs to keep the hard road beneath him. A single lane of the highway is 120 times wider than his tires. For longer than ever before, he rides with his eyes closed, finding balance without seeing it. More than anything else, this blind balance would have been impossible for Stan. Daily, they had concentrated on keeping Stan's arms moving, keeping him feeding himself and dressing himself as much as possible. His sense of touch, that inner terrain, eroded steadily but invisibly. With his feet internally numbed, Stan stood upright more by sight than by touch.

Each time Andrew opens his eyes he checks for headlights raking this wet valley. There are none. The cars have pulled off. You can't see the road. I don't need to.

86

Pat endured nearly a year between her desktop defection and her supervision of Gordon's mounting the two dimes that he had used to undo her boot into the front door frame of their new Ottawa house. Drill a shallow hole into each side of the door frame, then use the strongest glue you can find to hold up those two dimes. I will walk through this gamble every day.

Leaving her job as a teacher to become what was essentially Gordon's Ottawa secretary scared her senseless. She had plenty to resent about teaching — the neglected parenting she was expected to redress thanklessly, the annual repetition of adjective lessons, pioneer lessons, the life among small minds. As a teacher she had felt under-stimulated and underappreciated. Once, when her mother had shown Andy a composite photo of Pat's graduating high-school class, Pat had taken the department store frame in her hands and counted off the women. Teacher. Nurse. Secretary. Teacher. Nurse. Secretary. How she had hated that crudely piercing trident. At least teaching meant university, although each of her parents (mother, how could you?) implicitly and explicitly clarified that finishing her degree was not the primary objective.

Beneath the fatigue of the first few years of teaching there was genuine challenge and interest. The near-total independence, the steady performance. She had discovered depths of strength, discipline and humanity she had never so thoroughly plumbed. After a few caffeinated years, though, she wondered if she'd been confusing career satisfaction with trench survival. Unquestionably, teaching was the most complex, varied and sustained challenge she had ever met. Having met it, though, she had to ask how much it could change, evolve; how much could she? Teachers are field soldiers, not parade soldiers: fit but tired, malnourished but battle-tough. Where was the retraining? The fresh assignment? Sparring with ten-year-olds brought her into shape, but what then? A lifetime of small teeth and secreting hormones? There were no promotions to strive for, no awards to covet. A teacher she began; a teacher she'd remain. Thanks, but no (never enough) thanks.

Gordon, I'm smarter than the shoppers and breeders in the staff room. I'm smarter than your wife. Damn it, we both know I'm smarter than you.

Leaving husband, child, home and job, Pat literally drove away from her life to go work with Gordon, and she treated the three hundred kilometres between Ottawa and Kingston like an ocean. At first she wished they could have been farther away from Kingston. Be the MP for a Prairie wind patch or a Maritime ghost town. Drive from the fowl suppers to our foul bed.

She spent less than a month lying to Stan (until after the election: who was she any more?), while Gordon took six months to leave Sandra and Ben. If education is indeed change, what's more educational than divorce? Love should be courageous, not safe. Gordon, your son will survive your leaving if you let him. Mine must.

On those early, interminable weekends Gordon spent "home with his family" (that land mine of a phrase), she hated that she could be with him in under three hours, be with that skin she couldn't stop feeling, that body he was sharing with another woman. There were a few impulsive nights with him in her car in a Kingston parking lot, all this before cellphones or email. Sandra's icy voice on their home phone. Gordon's back-seat oscillation between passion and distance. He'd be in someone else's bed while she wound back to Ottawa with the smell of him, of them, still thick in the car.

He would joke about Sandra's equine stupidity, her blunders at dinner, her garish taste. And then he'd pack bags for Kingston, load shirts she had ferried to the cleaners.

"What do I do here, Gordon? Leave another job? Another man? I've given you time enough. What you call difficulty, I call one in every port. Her or me. If you don't choose, I will."

On her weekends alone she could not dwell on the fact that in Kingston, Gordon was sleeping with another woman while across the same city, Stan now slept alone. She was alone in bed two nights a week, while Stan was alone seven, alone with that mutinous body. She couldn't tell him, couldn't tell anyone, that instead of running off with another man, she had simply run off. Stan, my real selfishness here is leaving now so I can remember you at your best, so I can remember you, not your disease. If it's any consolation, I don't want children with Gordon.

While she was drinking gin and guilt in Ottawa, Stan wanted to jam his mitten fists into his mouth and scream while biting his knuckles. But his had been a long study of the possible and the impossible. He wore a straitjacket of impossibility, an armour of impossibility.

During her time as The Other Woman, the Ottawa touch, Pat tried to live off more than guilt, longing and fear. Night-class pottery. A little toe-wetting French. In her month of Tai Chi classes she had learned that the bones of her body had already set by the age of twenty-four. Twenty-four. Waving Hands Like Clouds, she looked back to herself at the altar at just twenty-three. All those troubled bones.

Twenty-three. She could easily have been swept out to sea by the cultural pressures to marry, pressures that would eventually see couples in their mid-thirties undoing all of the matrimonial work of their twenties. During her engagement, sensibly neither too short nor too long, her mother concentrated on Stan's Montreal suits and the report of his keen intelligence rather than on the crimped hand, the slight bow to his shoulders. Her house was small, her dresses too frequently mended. Her carpenter father simply asked, "Any debts?"

Only Lois, friend and, because of her question, maid of honour, dared to ask, "This disease, how bad does it get?"

"It's like a staircase going down. How far, we don't know. This could be as bad as it gets."

"But children. Is it —"

"No. A one-shot thing."

"So you're sure?"

"What is sure? I know he expands me, he makes life different, better. And I know I want smart kids."

Although she was able to use the word *bravery* with Lois, she couldn't quite share her image of Stan as a knight. Precisely because his armour was dented and bent, she saw past cliché to see genuine bravery riding for her through the banal mists of engagement. She knew without being told that she could marry a boy or a man, a fun boy or a slightly ruined man, this was another of life's deals. As courtship neared engagement, he gave her a copy of Mordecai Richler's sensational new *St. Urbain's Horseman*. The cover image was indeed a mounted knight (again, he silently fingered her thoughts, put noun or image to her instinct, shook coals when she smelled smoke). Inside, he had taped a one-word cover note over his brief inscription, requesting *After*. Only read the full inscription after you have read the book. Yes, dear.

What enormous private wheels turn in love. Those last few months she had known her feelings were deepening, had used the word *love* to herself and then to him, but had been unable to specify or itemize this growing respect until she spent hours behind Richler's corny image of a knight, until, three-quarters of the way through the novel, she read the line "I can be your wife or nurse, not both" and realized plenty. She thought of that line all through the next day's teaching then raced home to uncover Stan's inscription.

> *I agree, wife or nurse. I may need both, but I'll only want one.*
> *Test everything, especially my courage.*

Reading this novel he adored, talking with him a thousand times, she grew to see that the sparkling intelligence driving every one Stan's articulate sentences, that mogul skier's descending bounce off felicitous adjectives and judicious verbs, was itself driven by will and bravery as much as talent. Target first your own assumptions, your own vanities. Once, after she thanked him for finishing a thought she wasn't quite getting out, for switching tracks in a political disagreement they'd been having, he winked and said, "Hold nothing." How often she would later wish that he could conclude his adult life, not just begin it, with that motto. Hold nothing. *Tene nil.*

87

First to surrender to the cold night rain are his hands. Although the hands are not as distant from the core of his body as are his feet, the hands are completely exposed to the dual wind of the storm and his ride. Unlike on a mountain bike, where sometimes even your toes are needed to help you corner, on a touring bike the feet are basically stumps wedged into shoes. However cold, the feet are at least by now used to their reduction into mere blocks. But the proud hands prefer the individuated labour of thumb or forefinger changing gears or their synchronized curl around the handlebars. The cold, wet night undoes the evolution of his hands and chops off his opposable thumbs. For hours he has not gripped the handlebars, but simply rested clenched fists upon them. Gears no longer shift by finger or thumb. Pressing corners are found on fists squared by cold. His naked knuckles alternate between shades of white and purple. Even his wrists have gone numb.

Victorious in its coup, the rain has relaxed into steady totalitarianism. Sheets of cold rain oppress the dark kilometres. His frigid crotch no longer burns with itch, but he can feel it marinating anew in the constant wet of his soggy, ill-fitting hiking shorts. Any warmth his body finds will cause this freshly watered rash to grow. Water soaks him from tip to toe, and yet he hasn't swallowed half a litre in hours. Whatever heat he has comes from the endless pedalling, but what is he burning? The knees, knees, knees slosh a thinning blood through aching muscles and sprawling hunger. He regularly opens his mouth to the rain. Held up to the sky, his mouth is an aching funnel. Lowered back down, jaw dropped, it is a tiny net swept through cloud after cloud of rain. He trolls so long that his jaw aches, and still he rarely collects enough to swallow. After thirteen foodless hours, even his hunger has grown weak.

Thirst, hunger and fatigue, those mewling triplets of inescapable need, force him off the road in search of water. Cracking open his fists to slow and turn onto a side road, he is tackled by a numb dizziness and finds a cold, naked shoulder hammered into the pavement. Neither hand nor foot breaks his fall. One entire side of his body — a spurred ankle, a stalled knee, a blind hip — falls heavily to the wet asphalt. He tries to crawl under the shelf of pain, mines the bright minerals of it glowing on knee and elbow. Perhaps he will stay here, spoon his machine into sleep.

Headlights pour into this bowl. He crawls out from the frame and limps into deeper shadow.

All water falls, and in this endless run of valleys besieged by rain, his is an unnecessary thirst. Water, water everywhere. Despite the steady trickle in either ditch of this hilly side road, he steps over one brimming ditch to momentarily forage in the woods, briefly deluding himself that minimally higher ground could yield cleaner water, or that this forest of slick branches is actually penetrable. He manages four zombie steps up a treed incline before stumbling. A conscious turn of the heel converts his near fall into his descent back to the flowing ditchwater. What sweet trickling music. At first, he doesn't plan on dipping his face into the ditch, but his brief search for a small dam in the flood soon has him kneeling in front of a tiny mud bowl. The first handful does little more than splash his beard and disturb the bowl. Small stones poke out from the mud beneath his knees as he lets the bowl clear. Finally, he simply lowers his mouth into the water. Rain splatters his back and slides down his sopping shorts while he camels away at the passing stream. A faint taste of salted mushrooms passes his wet lips as the sucked millilitres swell to litres. Christ, he'd love some cheese, a fat bomb of melted cheddar soaking into some greased vegetable. A zucchini heart attack. An eggplant aneurysm. Sitting back, he turns and looks down at the still bike and beyond to the dull stripe of the highway. He could piss here, now, shrouded in rain. He gets up.

After another hour on the road, gravity waits for his eyelids to flutter with sleep before snatching the front fork with a quick hand. He wakes just in time to see he is about to fall. Free of the panniers, he's able to counter with a hip toss, and rights the bike before his knee goes down.

His heart pumps waves. The cold is the panic, the panic the cold. Now that he's awake, his teeth begin chattering beneath his chin strap. His stomach, that abandoned old man, steadily moans.

88

Pat and Gordon leapt for each other at the last moment when North Americans admitted that work was arousing, that time spent together workday after workday exchanged more than memos. When cars were the size of islands and neckties were as wide as tree trunks, a man — even a politician — could still leave one woman for another and be just an individual monster, not the willing extender of monstrous and historic systems of oppression that victimized and blinded the feeble, impressionable Pat with power and cock. They found pleasure in his underwear, not hegemony. Here was the last possible moment in North America when they could be a simple philanderer and home wrecker, cut by friends but not newspapers, from dinner party lists but not the national party.

> *Happiness is not a crime. Please, Andrew. Eventually, if you let yourself, you'll understand.*

For more than a year after she left, Pat kept a journal. Divorce was a new country with new ways. She didn't question that suddenly she was writing in bed, not reading, hushing Gordon when he was there and better enduring his absence when he wasn't. Yes, she needed some talk with Gordon, and she got a passable version of it. But the old chats with Stan, even with Andy, these chats did not and would not stop. So she kept them going, privately but not futilely. Paradoxically, in leaving Stan she wanted to talk to him even more, to talk about what hadn't worked, who she was becoming, even what she missed. But that would've been unfair, reopening old wounds she had hoped to cauterize with the bluntness of her departure. If she could no longer talk with Stan, she'd talk at him.

A few years later, her journal put aside but not thrown away, she'd advise any friend who was divorcing to do the same. "Write it down first. That way you get it out and then you can decide whether to share it." A decade after that, she'd recommend a similar kind of journal to those early widows who began to appear in her circle. By then, she had resumed her own journal, writing to an even more absent Stan and an errant Andrew.

89

Only between four and five a.m., deep into a stupor of frigid fatigue, does he realize that the postcards and the partial novel he had parked behind him on the empty pannier rack have been in the pouring rain for hours. His first reaction to this recollection is not to worry about the fate of the book or cards, but to wonder if they could somehow warm his naked chest. If he had thread, could he sew together a paper shirt? Of course he has no thread. He doesn't even have dental floss any more, not to mention a toothbrush. A wet paper shirt wouldn't be very warm, but it might blunt the wind a little.

He doesn't turn around to look back at the stack of soggy post-cards. Instead he simply reaches back with one finger to blindly touch a wet corner.

> *Notice how the word travel is very close to the French travail, to work? Lug the pack to Hostel 1. Wait until it opens. Find out it's booked. Slink on to No. 2. Find out 2 is full then watch later arrivals get rooms. Be insulted to your face. Starve. Bathe rarely. Race for trains. Wait for trains. Always carry too much of the wrong currency. Master the Italian phrases Bathroom? How much? Hello? Please, Thank you and Excuse me just as you move into Germany.*
> — *Working Girl*

90

Riding with Mark he was always behind. The younger brother. A shadow stretched out. At the start of a summer ride with Mark, Andrew was grateful for the company, grinned at the protracted stereo of shaking zippers and clicking gears. By the time his swollen lungs had melted from his spine, though, the very air was merciless, indicting. Fifteen rides together, twenty, and he could feel a harder body emerge within him, could feel his heart annex more hot space. The last three rides, he had shot through the stump field perfectly. Now he too accelerated toward a dirt jump built up alongside a tree, loaded his shocks on the fly to clear a log on the other side before splashing through a stream and rambling up its bank.

Mark waited until Andrew finished the fast climb before announcing, "Never going to get your girlfriend to ride that section" and then sprinted on ahead.

Long past Fort Henry, a string of metal power line towers cut the forest as far as the eye could see. The wide strip of cleared land beneath the towers was divided into short and tall grass, with uncut green cover beneath their tires and two-metre-high brown stalks swaying in the breeze to one side. This rider's expressway served multiple pockets of single track, each carved by the unseen riders of yesterday.

Trails are communal veins pumping through the muscle of a landscape. No trail is ever built in a day, so when Andrew saw a passing, skinny stretch of broken grass he thought it could be a possible trail start, the recent exploratory work of just one or two riders. Andrew called, "Head on left," then turned into the half-track of broken grass. He slowed down to start a recon in the man-high grass. What was Mark doing riding so quickly behind him? A nudging front tire was inferred, if not actually felt.

While the numerous blades of bent and dog-eared long grass in front of Andrew clearly recorded some passage, the ground itself had barely been touched. Andrew was not following a burgeoning trail but an abandoned one-off. "I don't think this is anything," he said. Tall grass swayed above them.

No brakes squeezed behind him. No indecision slowed their rolling pace. Why bent grass but not cut mud? Mud will hold tire tracks until the next big rain. "Seriously. Nothing. Wait, wait, stop."

The line of grass broken at mid-height ended abruptly in a flattened circle. Andrew and Mark stopped and dismounted, bewildered at a one-metre circle of flattened grass.

"Deer bed," Andrew finally concluded, extrapolating a deer's body from a large teardrop of toppled grass. The eerily stamped patch had them standing still in awe. Mark was the first to release his bike from his hand to let it drop into the tall grass beside him. Two-metre tall grasses swayed above their heads or drooped alongside them, sweeping and clattering in a thick August breeze. With no traffic audible in the distance, with a deer's absent body stamped here in front of them, Andrew recited, "But charm and face were in vain / Because the mountain grass / Cannot but keep the form / where the mountain hare has lain."

"What the hell does that mean?"

"It's Yeats," Andrew replied.

"That's what you do, memorize other people's words?"

Andrew would always wonder if Mark's stepping toward him at this moment, if the challenge in his jaw and step would've made "Fuck you" a better response than the "What words don't belong to someone else?" he chose, and what difference, if any, that would have made.

"That's the trouble with words," Mark said, standing directly in front of Andrew's chest. "They're unclear." He punctuated this last word by gently setting the knuckles of one fist against Andrew's damp, hard stomach then dragging them *un*-left and *clear*-right across his buzzing hips.

When Andrew set, but did not punch, his own fist against the hot wall of Mark's stomach, he felt none of the relief he had hoped for. Mark immediately set his second fist against Andrew's other hip. Each fist felt and looked ready to turn screws into Andrew's hips. To set his own remaining fist to Mark's free hip would exhaust this brief arms race. Then what? Each of them stared from tinted plastic glasses, flexed their jaws against the chinstraps of their helmets.

Rather than square off all of their arms, uncertain but not uninterested, Andrew used his free hand to smack his padded glove against the side of Mark's hip. And ass. Because his hand sought Mark's hip, he habitually expected it to meet some give and curve, the harps of his heterosexual past. Instead, Mark's hip practically slapped him back. His sedimentary layers of muscle grinned at their Newtonian return of force, their palpable rewriting of *ass*. First to leave the swaying grass was the slap's echo, then the sting in Andrew's hand, then his control.

Mark smiled as he reared back to knock the brow of his helmet into Andrew's.

91

If he finds what he's looking for within this string of rural houses, he might get in as many as twenty more kilometres before he pukes.

Elaine could tell him that the houses strung loosely along this rural Quebec highway rarely go on the real-estate market. When they are sold, legally and nominally sold, they are sold to children or nieces or nephews. When you see your great-aunt several times a month, you live in the country of house transfers, not house-selling. You live in deep country, family country. And you may not lock your car.

Food does get left in cars. Food of a kind.

If you were starving in the woods, friends, acquaintances and strangers love to ask a vegetarian, wouldn't you eat meat? If I were starving in the woods, Andrew invariably replies, I'd eat you. Rarely does he add, We're not starving in the woods, though. We're in kitchens, supermarkets and restaurants; we're in lineups, and never far from the bank.

The growing depths of hunger and fatigue have him so delirious he feels as if he steps away from the bike into an afterlife. One minute he is leaning against a tree, clipped into the bike's strong metal frame. Two steps away from the bike he is a ghost, shimmering with each squirt from his empty stomach.

And squirt his stomach does. The gurgling pancreas and dripping duodenum squelch on his approach to the first parked car. The parched liver thumps its tub in disappointment when the car is locked. By the third house he does find an unlocked car, a Chevette, but no food save for one hard little brick of gum in a waxy wrapper. A barking dog redirects him from the fifth house. There is food of a sort at the seventh.

Asking a car to be fridge or pantry, he might find a protein bar and maybe even a bottle of water in some urban car, but such a car would be locked. Instead, here are two rural pepperoni sticks for the taking. For the brief walk back to his bike, they are arrows in the quiver of his hand. By the time he reaches the bike, before he even mounts or rides, the first arrow flies at his stomach.

Just as you never forget how to ride a bike, you also never forget the sensation of chewing meat, no matter how long you might be a vegetarian. This Herculean mouth-work is unforgettable. Betty and Andrew liked to joke that vegetarians are made, not born. Meatless living is their chosen country, not their native one. In this second country there are inevitable translations and comparisons, even unwelcome ones. Kalamata olives are the seared beef of vedge kitchens. If frozen first, firm tofu crumbles into shepherd's pie and chili to forge the protein and texture of ground beef if not its (dyed) colour. Phyllo pastry basted with soy sauce can be baked into the skin of a kinder, less toxic chicken. But no food other than multi-processed red meat has this tenacious elasticity, and not only in texture but also in its density of taste.

From years of distance if not disdain, Andrew knows that meat is the food of the long haul, a haul few of us actually take. To him, to date, the energy one's body spends breaking down meat's ropy strands doesn't seem profitable for daily life. Given our mouth full of flat teeth that grind well but tear poorly, red meat seems like the food of emergency savings, yet North Americans use it for daily chequing. Eating meat is the hard-rock mining of digestion.

Shiela, a friend of Stan's, taught ESL for decades and so met a changing cultural mirror of both Canada and the world in that meeting point of those who needed to emigrate to Canada and those whom Canada needed to attract. The initial contact with Italian and Chinese communities of Shiela's predecessor gave way to a shifting map of Southeast Asia and a brief spike of Eastern Europeans for her. As so many writing assignments involve photographs, Shiela saw glossy print after glossy print of one post-Soviet student after another smiling incredulously in front of an entire wall of meat at the grocery store. Juris proudly held a steak across the majority of his chest. Smiling, Vlad cradled a basketball-sized ham.

When disgust does finally squirt into Andrew's mouth (after joy and relief and a deep-burning pleasure), it's not for the death, the absent piggy squeal, or because of the cannibalism glimpsed in this unforgettable chewiness, this mouth-leather; it's for the tenacious oil spill. Here in his mouth is the exact taste of his bile below, and it lingers far past the lengthy grind of molars or the forced cram of the epiglottis. His repugnance is not that of the abattoir, but of the ingredients list. His years hoping that clean food coming into mouth then body will clean and clarify his life are here not disproved. His molars and tongue are slopped with chemical waste.

Back on the bike, he injects the second stick as well, but not so easily. A series of wet belches temporarily level stomach and mouth and physically remind him again and again that he is eating bile. The final cylindrical morsel is practically a bulimic finger going down his throat. He quickly loads the tablet of stolen gum into his mouth, although this, too, is an entirely predictable failure. This cloying squirt of sugar in his mouth is a purely synthetic taste, some saccharine tang, and its cheery pink burst is no antidote for the bilious spiced pork. The new taste of the gum simply layers onto that of the meat. The fake sweetness of the gum's syntho-berry taste hangs over the rank, vomitous smell of the pepperoni stick like some counterfeit floral spray spritzed over the jagged smellscape of a horrific shit in some cramped bathroom. His naked chest heaves.

92

Pat should have known that Stan would get her back through the mail. Her letter to Stan had been, she'd hoped, mercifully brief. His reply, mailed to Gordon's new Ottawa office, wasn't even a letter. It was a list, and a short one at that.

Divorce, with its unwelcome comparisons and radioactive knowledge, suddenly made Pat into a forensic typing expert. Sorting through the office mail in Ottawa a week after she had written Stan, she found a slim envelope with a typed address but no name. Every other envelope to cross her new desk was addressed with the crispness of an electric typewriter. In her hands she saw the old wispy hammer strokes of the portable typewriter Stan had used throughout university. Now he'd used the typewriter to conceal his doubly shaking hand. But of course she could still see everything, the dust riding the case of the old typewriter, paper in the third drawer, the cranked arms of machine and machinist. She could even hear the brief, one-fingered pecking climb up the stairs to Andy's room.

As for the envelope's lack of a name — not even just *Pat* — she immediately had two theories, each of which she knew he wanted her to have. Whatever distance they still had to travel to a legal divorce, she certainly wasn't *Pat Day* any longer. He could have used *Patricia Thompson*, her maiden name, but they both knew she had outgrown that name as well. She was no one's son. What ridiculous phrases. *Maiden name. Keep her name.* What century was this? Of course these too familiar, too simple thoughts simply meant she was stalling, her brain slipping into its indignant neutral, not opening the envelope that, in ways, she had mailed to herself.

One page. An unintroduced list, not even a title. Not "Four Conditions." Certainly not the inarticulate "Four Things." Not even "Consider." Without the numbers, it would have been the worst poem she had ever read.

1. He decides.
2. The house.
2. Never speak to me.
4. St. Urbain's.

As her eyes clouded with tears, she understood the second reason why Stan had addressed the envelope without a name. He didn't care if Gordon saw her letter. Consider everything Gordon got to see.

93

Contrary to expectation, Andrew was not hurt when Mark's helmet butted into his beside the deer bed. This fundamental lack in what was still a delivery of force, this jerk from abs to crown, destabilized more than just his feet but injected no significant pain. Mark stepped forward as Andrew stumbled back into the tall grass. Thoughts stopped coming in lines and now pulsed irregularly. The grounding of Andrew's heel and his leg's redirection of Mark's next shove was like the fluid loading and unloading of his bike's rear shocks. The load and transfer of force rose from inarticulate sensation but didn't quite become thought by the time that force had passed Andrew's hips and swum into his arms to grab the advancing Mark and pull him over a braced thigh. Seeing the brief arc of Mark's head and chest toward the grass, Andrew definitely had the thought — spun a small roulette wheel of *ifs* — that he must now retreat from or advance onto Mark's briefly prone body. But Mark wasted no time calculating *ifs* and *whats*. When his arms met the ground, he loaded his body weight into them while hooking Andrew behind the knees with one leg. Mark sprang back and pulled Andrew down simultaneously. Turning his head slightly, Andrew took the fall on the brow of his helmet and was again briefly amused at the absence of expected pain. Then a knee found the back of one of his, then a mouth the other.

He could never forget the helmets. When Mark's lick and nibble leapt from the back of Andrew's knee to the low of his back, he expected and wanted the curve of a forehead, not a helmet, to hang above the munching lips and flicking tongue. In the logic of appetite that sex stretches over the flesh, the mouth leapt from the unexpected to the inevitable, yet that same expectation couldn't quite compute the hard, bulbous crescent of a helmet wheeling in the low of his back. Lines hard and soft were drawn and redrawn in the tall grass.

94

In the middle of the night, riding on a dark highway, the rolling belches of spicy pepperoni aren't as worrisome as the sloshing at the other end of his stomach. Recurrent rehearsals of vomit help him to ignore the wet mutiny hatching even deeper in his intestines. Fear, cold, exhaustion, shame, pepperoni and the ditchwater he drank have been percolating in his empty stomach for hours. Given this intestinal cramping, the angles of the bike frame, with their levelling of ass and head, feel like the most vilely attentive scatological demons of Hieronymus Bosch hunched there with their numerous teeth and dutiful scoops. When the diarrheal sneak-attack finally makes its intestinal putsch, voluntary defecation is only its first casualty.

In a bid to save his shorts, Andrew locks his brakes and drops to the road as quickly as possible. His years of contentedly urinating from astride a bike make this sudden, quick lowering of it feel much like the lowering of a toilet seat. This comparison occurs just before the sight, sound and stench of his bottom-spray causes or permits the pepperoni's rise back out his mouth. Few human bodies will travel life's years without at least once suffering this simultaneously bi-directional revolt of the intestines, this viral flossing, but many can hope for the helpful porcelain furniture of toilet and sink, not a cold, hard road. Out-wrestled by the deepest muscles of the body, he is quickly dropped to hands and naked knees. Cold sweat smears his dirty brow. Last to join this prison break of internal liquids are the hot tears that pump out with slightly different abdominal heaves.

Betty, you're right. I can't keep it together.

Dropped to all fours on an asphalt so cold it feels hot, heaving and weeping, a tiny bit of his brain still knows this is temporary. He is palsied by a total lack of warmth, by fatigue, hunger and bacteria, but still he eludes the obvious permanency of Stan's disease, that chromosomal tick, that glitch in DNA or chemical bond, in ring or strand ruinously bent, in enzyme over- or under-secreted. Two wet and busy tear tracks run down his cheeks as he climbs back onto the frame to roll one foot, then the other. A single thought keeps him going, has, in ways, always kept him going. Better him than you.

95

After Andrew watched Betty flee their restaurant dinner with his mother, he walked home alone to the fallout of his lie, knowing fully how wrong he had been, how singularly hurtful he had been to Betty. They were bright enough and had read enough to conceive of a life beyond the cheap psychology that related all adult shortcomings to childhood pain, yet no illuminating novel or dollop of cultural theory or memorable lecture offered an actual alternative. Everything that had brought them together, and not just together but together as *them* — the failed marriages, vegetarianism as a quiet revolt, remaking themselves with the right stack of books — also taught them how to wound each other uniquely.

The first night alone he left the door unlocked, didn't drink and wrote her self-reproaching emails late into his nearly sleepless night. The next morning, when she blocked his emails, he cut class to wait by the phone, knowing she wouldn't respect that but doing it all the same. He didn't let her prolonged silence shift him into defensive indignation about his being left to worry in complete ignorance of where she was or how she was doing. Finally, on the third day, he began packing her a bag: clothes, textbooks, saline solution and a three-word note that wasn't wise to send. He'd catch her on her way into Film. Tonight he'd lock the doors again.

He winced most with her first dresser drawer. He should have started with sweaters, not underwear. Job commenced, shame and idiocy acknowledged, he tried to ignore the swell of desire and keep on diplomatic schedule. The taunting thong, less offering so much more, had no place in a peacemaking bag. Reaching for cotton panties and non-black bras, his plan met its first doubt. How long? Two nights would seem too hopeful, even controlling, an underwear leash. At four pairs of panties he might as well throw in a list of available apartments. Three pairs in (still folded — how? — into her neat little squares) he worried about seeming too prudish, too protective down under, and in seconds he was standing in front of her closet holding up cleavage shirts and ass pants. Also inappropriate were his favourite clothes of hers. The blue corduroy bell bottoms would be smeared with unwelcome affection. The French cuffs he so admired would become handcuffs. The simple task of filling a bag with her clothes suddenly found him auditioning outfits, holding shirts at arm's length then up to his chest. Skirts and sweaters were laid out on the bed, mixed and matched, combined and discarded. Holding a shirt up to his own chest, then checking it in the mirror, he found his first smile in three days.

She had moved the full-length mirror in with her, but they had never mounted it properly. For the past five months it had just leaned against the wall of what they had called the dressing room. Now, as it appeared that she was moving out, he found himself cross-dressing vicariously. Chuckling at this, chuckling in part because he knew it would make her chuckle, at least the old her, he crossed the room to the notepaper he had left on her dresser top. He'd bought the flaxen notepaper specially, though his message was short enough to fit on a matchbook. *It gets worse.*

96

At dawn, soaking wet and spastic with cold, Andrew attempts to cut himself another bed of pine boughs. His jersey remains knotted about his wounded leg, so his back takes countless scratches as he bends beneath the tree that will be his inadequate shelter. Although the bleeding in his leg has stopped, he waits until his bed is made and he can stretch his leg out before he gingerly removes the jersey-and-booklet bandage. Blood has drained through the paper dressing to create scabs of type. Fortunately the blood appears to be dry.

The rain has also ceased, but by now the ground and leaves around him are saturated. His putting on of a soaking wet, bloody shirt is as desperate as his opening of the emergency blanket's cheap packaging. Without the shirt, the pine boughs would scratch and pick at him ceaselessly. Even with the shirt, his back feels perpetually stung by the hundreds of pine needles. The foil blanket is so thin he can't risk wrapping it beneath his back and having it punctured.

A need for warmth, regardless of cause, is exactly the reason he bought and carried this assembly-line emergency blanket. These little foil wonders are so popular they are available at dollar stores. And yet surely they stay unopened in their crowded first-aid kits or get forgotten in glove compartments crammed with tire warranties, pamphlets and maps. Unfolding the emergency blanket, he's relieved and hopeful, but also dubious and worried. *Blanket. Blanket.* According to whom? Cut the legs off a chair, the philosophy cliché asks, and at what point does it cease being a chair? What is the essence of a thing, of a blanket? Heat retention, sure. Yes, this crinkling metallic film, which can fold into the space of a handkerchief (and weighs even less), holds a heat he hasn't felt in days. Despite his being thoroughly soaked, the reflective foil traps whatever heat he has. His teeth stop chattering within minutes. Where, though, is the comforting thickness? The private insulation against the world? And the sprawl? When it covers his shoulders, the millimetre-thin foil barely reaches his knees.

Cold feet and a fear of punctures in the back are not his only concerns. There's also the admission. *Emergency* blanket. How do you keep breathing calmly after you have broken the in-case-of-emergency glass?

He is warmer but far from warm enough. He cannot remain both cold *and* hungry, so he digs the knife out of his pocket and cuts a rectangle of the blanket off one corner. Removing the bungee cord from his leg dressing, he secures the scrap of blanket about his head to form a small, crinkling kaffiyeh. Tired enough to sleep on a picket fence yet too hungry for an easy sleep, warming finally, he remembers an email of Betty's. This past year, while he studied and she travelled, he'd emailed her when he discovered that before Lawrence of Arabia rode camels across the desert he had ridden a bicycle across France as an undergraduate.

You'll hear people say he died in a motorcycle accident, Andrew wrote, *but no one tells you the cause of his accident was avoiding two boys on bicycles.*

He'd been thinking motorcycle versus bicycle and experience versus innocence. She'd titled her reply *Lawrence of Suburbia*, teasing him once more, but the body of the message wasn't so jovial. *I can understand wanting to avoid two boys on bicycles.*

Now, hunting sleep as dawn breaks, perspiration clouding up his metallic kaffiyeh, Andrew remembers the opening of Lawrence's *Seven Pillars of Wisdom* with shameful recognition. *Some of the evil of my tale may have been inherent in our circumstances.* Yes, Andrew admits as he drifts off, *some.*

97

In Andrew's restless sleep beneath a half-denuded tree and a foil blanket, he is invaded by the strangest memories and images. Not just Betty, or Mark, or Pat and Stan, but old jokes, TV memories (those copies of copies), T.E. Lawrence and, the second-last time he wakes, of Stan's professional rise and fall with Correctional Services Canada.

Paul and Stan had been friends since teachers' college. Fed up with a bloated, self-serving Ministry of Education, yet devoted to the Kingston sailing, Paul left the traditional classroom and colleagues complaining above chipped coffee mugs for Correctional Services work in this, the country's prison capital. Surprised at the speed of his own promotion (and ignoring the rate of burnout), Paul quickly moved from applying for work to interviewing potential employees. One night, he came by Stan and Andy's house for some after-hours recruiting. Andy poured them beer and snuck a sip from each glass before delivering them.

"All right," Stan said, palpably intrigued by Paul's offer, "when do you finger the horseflesh?"

"Now. This is it. Just me and a pen. And we actually have an office staff. Call this number and they'll type your résumé."

"You do realize my billy club will need Sure Grips."

"We leave the billy clubs to the officers. Somebody has to hire wrestling fans."

When Paul — no longer a Kingstonian but another Ottawa bureaucrat — returned to the same kitchen a dozen years later, Andrew sat on the floor of an upstairs hallway to listen. Of course he couldn't see through walls and floors, but he felt Paul down there in a kitchen so unchanged from the night of the job offer to this, its opposite. Paul's even, timbrous voice floated past tired wallpaper and glasses gone cloudy in an aging dishwasher. The kitchens of Paul's other friends had, no doubt, gone through this decade with more redecorating than pullout shelves, long-tab sink taps and photoelectric light switches.

"Stan, we can get you early retirement without a second glance. We can get you a farewell bottle on the government tab."

"Are you selling anything I might actually want?"

Paul paused. Managerial oil squirted into the room. "They'll deal to a point. A voluntary acceptance will get you the full package without any long-term disability. We're talking substantial money here."

"I see. Is Roger also getting a package for his rubber elbow? The guys have a betting pool on when Henry will snap. Nimble I'm not, but at least I teach. Amendment number two: I teach well."

"Nobody's denying that."

"Come again? You've got a team of drunks and losers sliding their way to divorce number three or four. Behind the plate, I'm as good as I've ever been."

"When you're there."

"Slow, yes. Poor attendance, never. I'd have to be able to feel, to feel bad."

"Stan, every trip to the bathroom, and every minute it lasts, is a liability. The feeling is, the strong feeling is, that you dilute officer time. Even at the halfways, they want maximum readiness."

"Keep that doublespeak away from me."

"Call it whatever you want. Their union's lodging a complaint."

"Why, because suddenly I've dropped below the fitness level necessary to fend off a career bruiser who pumps iron five hours a day? What kind of locks do you have on your house, Paul? You got infrared? Your windows all wired? I didn't think so. We get by on chance, pal. I didn't get this job for my drop kick. Why the hell should I get fired for losing something I've never had?"

"You're not getting fired; you're getting freedom. Take the package, the strong package, and volunteer with adult literacy or an immigration centre."

"Fuck off and get out."

Paul did. Upstairs, Andrew knew the imperious face that had just been turned from Paul's, knew the feel of his quiet exile.

Andrew didn't wait very long, or apologize for overhearing, or say that adult literacy sounded heavenly compared to daily masturbation jokes and ketchup wine. He walked in and put his hand on his father's falcate shoulder to say, "We can fight it."

"And what do we win?"

98

He wakes up keen to steal. Beneath the foil kaffiyeh his hair is damp with sweat. He thinks of removing the blanket to lick it. One way or another, he'll eat tonight.

Betty, I'm the person you've hated or been afraid of every waking moment since your plane touched down. You wear that stained money belt because of the length of my fingers, the reach of my appetite.

First he needs clothes. One shirt, possibly new shoes, and he'd be incognito. How long is his radius of infamy? Maybe it stops in Rivière-du-Loup. If 132 kilometres won't spare him, what will? (You know what will: 400 k, 500.) Again, police or thugs? If every gas station in the province is looking for *un cycliste caucasien avec les cheveux auburn, chemise pictographique de rouge et bleu*, then he eats garbage, steals table scraps from beneath cold coffee grounds, forages for a restaurant's cornucopia packed in dirty napkins. If the campsite punks are after him themselves, do they even have a car? Are they stopping at *every* store? And the cops, what, have they put a bird in the sky? Telephoned everyone who sells power drinks and chocolate bars?

Choose poorly, get weak and your life is very, very different, undeniably lesser. Be lazy or careless and you get stomped or a criminal record. With a criminal record, you won't be able to leave the country. A hundred times with Betty he reluctantly chose not to leave Canada. Now that a departure is threatened, he'd go in a second.

To walk into a store for food, he needs different clothing. To get clothing, he must find laundry to steal, but only after night has fallen fully. He needs laundry left out on a country clothesline. Have gone to bed without bringing in the laundry. Have fucked. Be drunk. Have had a child shriek in fever. Anything to leave your threads strung out.

Brash stealing, a sudden theft with opportunity knocking on his door would be so much easier. Instead he must hunt and wait, all the while maddened by his empty stomach. He's too hungry to have slept from dawn until dusk and must now endure a few more hours of evening sunlight before he can begin to search out clothes and food to steal. He busies himself walking through his woods looking for water to drink. The groundwater he slurps from a brook sluices countless bacteria into his gut, but it's that or more nothing. Ultimately, he spends nearly three hours simply lying on the ground beside the stream, drinking whenever he can. His hunger is both similar to and opposite from meditation. In ways, everything but his stomach fades from his consciousness, and yet he is too tightly focused on this one growling, grumbling, squirting little bag.

Eventually, he can see himself lying there on the twiggy stream bank as if he were looking down from the treetops. This is the image he would file in court as proof of his guilty mind, what Larry taught him to call his *mens rea*. The simple fact of him patiently waiting for nightfall, enduring hours of utter boredom, even sharpening his already sharp hunger to do so: this is premeditation.

When dusk finally falls, he returns to the bike, the evil twin. Together they ride. Pausing his straight flight west, he begins a spiral forage for neglected laundry. If this laundry hunt goes on too long it may threaten his already precarious night route west. Since Rivière-du-Loup, luck or possibly francophone history have had him on a route he's sure is parallel to the St. Lawrence and the Trans-Can. He'd like to think he remembers some fifteen-year-old history lesson in which the farm lots in New France were cut back in narrow strips from the St. Lawrence. One road then another and another punctuated the ends of the lots and ran parallel to the river. Should these roads exist, should he be remembering history and not Québécois folklore or, worse, fiction, they will be perfect for his planned series of night flights but also make his current laundry search a long one. The first hour of tonight's ride is spent cruising along one country road, then back along another. All this pedalling and no distance gained.

My kingdom for a sweatshirt. Or a toque. *Toque*: a Canadian word, a Canadian necessity. Bike into a store and one is yours. Again, warmth or secrecy?

When he does eventually find a laden clothesline he must wait again until the house looks quiet with sleep. So much time waiting beside trees with a growling stomach. How do criminals stand the boredom? Finally, circling back past midnight, the boredom vanishes. Creeping around the side of the small house, he picks his way around plastic toys littering the lawn as if he were stepping through a mine-field. Rounding the corner into the back, he tries to keep his eyes open, glancing at everything save for the clothes he wants. Already, associative logic makes him salivate at peripheral glimpses of civil-ian clothing. Look left for a light coming on inside or a figure at the window. Check right for a lunging dog. By the time he reaches the clothesline, he's nearly ready to settle on the first thing he can grab. Ah yes, a powder blue nightie would be perfect. Trying to squeeze out courage as he moves down the line, he eventually recognizes his luck. This is family washday, two loads left here for the country night. Litters of socks. Boy's jockeys. Doll-sized panties. Broad jeans. Past halfway he finally sees this lemon-scented portrait of divorce. The clothes of a boy, a younger girl and their mother; another couple of kids growing up without men.

Mom offers him a pair of track pants and junior an oversized sweatshirt. In for a penny, ruined by a southern itch, he grabs — okay, two — pairs of mom's neglected, utile underwear. Half a kilometre away he stops to pull on the loot. The sweatshirt has room for his chest, but he has to cut off the sleeves. Its warmth feels like an em-brace. And who cares how ugly and ill-fitting it seems? This is North America. No fashion is impossible.

For his itchy nethers, he slides one foot then the other into the panties. Don't look down. Although they settle worse than a German swimsuit, although contents may soon spill container, he's prepared to use almost anything to ease his chafe. Perhaps they'll allow his cream to sit for longer. Off the bike the mom panties would divide more than they contain, as if a ribbon were trying to cradle two kiwis, but in the cramped geometry of the saddle this narrow cotton is just wall enough. Opening the cuffs of the sweatpants with his knife, he steps into the world's least fashionable culottes then caps them with the wet hiking shorts. The spare panties go in a pocket and are his only luxury. A bandage, a handkerchief, tomorrow's freshness.

Right. In-cog-nito.

99

By the time Betty fled Andrew and his mother at the restaurant, they knew each other's class schedules intimately. Whether she wanted to leave him or not, she knew where and when he'd grab a coffee between Transgendered Transnational Fiction and lANguAge poE-Try. He knew when she worked out and that she wore skirts to The Art of Time, pants to Technology and Ritual and tighter pants to Performance Art, the class with the tall, thin TA with a half-beard who was always going on about Fra-hance and Brooklyn.

If she had stayed in Kingston and not gone home to Elaine's, she'd certainly be going to class again after two days, so he waited for her outside of her Film class with the bag of books and clothes he'd packed for her. Arriving early, standing still and waiting while other students came and went, he himself felt like a six-foot strip of photographic film. The sway of Betty's hair, the cut of her collar and every movement of hip or eye burnt indelibly into him. Condemnation, reproach, spite and perhaps disdain polished the facets of her cheekbones and sharpened the blade of her jaw. She slowed but continued as she saw him. He concentrated on her eyebrows, watched them grow from distant chevrons into individuated lines then precise fossils. Unable to wait for her first words he held up both palms. The pack slid down to the crook of his elbow. He waved his arm to indicate the laden bag.

"Underwear, clothes, books. No strings attached," he said.

"Fine. Thanks."

"Decide if you want to meet me later." He handed her the bag, brushing her hand just once before walking off. She wouldn't countenance distraction before class, so his brief note would go unread for at least an hour. The note — *It gets worse.* — sat like a time bomb in her bag, but she, not he, controlled its clock.

He went grocery shopping while she was still in class, then cleaned the house maniacally. Finally, he sat down to some neglected reading and green tea, not beer. She phoned at a noncommittal 8:30 p.m.

"You were definitely in better shape before I read your note. Why should I track you down with more questions?"

"I can't tell you, Betty. Not, I won't. I can't. I can show you one more thing — really, just one — that might make a little sense of why I would lie so much when I love you so much."

The pause ached.

"Come meet me," she said. "JJ's."

"Give me an inch and I take a mile, I know, but I need to show you. Here."

"This is totally unfair."

"I agree. You don't even have to step in. I'm not trying to trick you. Please come to the door." He could hear her breathe. "Can I meet you and we'll walk back here?"

"Okay," she finally said.

His breathing resumed.

100

Awkward question, given the tiring circumstances, but he does wonder as he rides who will be the face of justice for his campsite kick. Did the punks ditch his stuff then claim a cyclist had randomly attacked them? No, that wouldn't show la Sûreté that they want a touring cyclist, someone headed out of town. And look at those kids. They had *asshole* written all over them. Young little takers. Then again, they also look like future cops. And what about the fact that he's *maudit anglais*? In rural Quebec, is that more likely to let slip the dogs of justice?

Running would be so much easier if he knew that he absolutely *had* to run. Running *just in case* taxes his patience and widens a grey area of doubt about what's possible and prudent. If there were police choppers in the sky and cops at roadblocks he'd bike across fields or portage down streams. As is, he knows two things: (1) he'll do what it takes to see Betty again, and (2) he's finally able to drink chocolate milk. First daylight then traffic thicken around him. By the time he spots a gas station, it's early morning: late for a fugitive but early enough for some people heading to work.

Peeling paint on a wooden garage and the one hand-drawn digit on the price board for gasoline hopefully say *out of the loop.* Then again, a phone call's a phone call. He's six feet of dirt in absurd clothing. Little work would be required to see him riding off on a bicycle. At least, he'll have been fed.

He approaches in the midst of a little morning rush of single men who idle their trucks and yell jokes across the parking lot to one another. Andrew parks the bike by the garage's air hose, a move both natural and concealing, then walks across the parking lot to join the small lineup of men who prefer to drive for a takeout coffee that costs ten times what it would cost to make at home provided they could stand the company.

Door to cooler to brown milk carton, his vision's a narrow line.

Chugging sweet brown milk here, in front of the cooler, is the opposite of inconspicuous, but it's sweet and thick and just keeps coming. After a litre, something like vision returns. Cheese curds are available by the bag. He begins filling his arms with small yogurts. Speckled bananas await him. Wine, chilled wine, is his for the buying. By the time he makes it to the counter, he can actually hear again, connects tinkling bell to opening door, anticipates sirens or screeching tires, and so reaches now for a fat-bomb butter tart. Collecting bananas and an orange, he's even able to think again, realizes that a baritone voice means a man is speaking near him. No, at him.

"Don't even look at those," a fit man behind Andrew says in English. Andrew looks back to see a clean-shaven man nodding at the apples and oranges in his hands.

"Tasteless." He's early forties, well groomed, likes to show some money in his clothes and watch.

This guy really should know that Andrew's smile is not friendliness, just the best he can do to avoid laughter. Kick a kid in the face then chat about snacks. Kick. Chat.

"When I toured, I dreamt of fruit," this stranger continues, "would have given a few toes for berries. I've actually got some melon in the truck if you're interested. Name's Glen."

Andrew doesn't reply, simply pays for his carbs, aminos and trace fattys then follows Glen outside.

"You doing many centuries?" Glen asks, wondering how often Andrew bikes a hundred miles a day. "It's just over there. The Pathfinder."

One foot, then the other.

"Honeydew melon. Some mango too. Cut up and ready." Glen leads him to his truck and opens the passenger door. "Let me move the seat back. Here, take as much as you want. Go ahead. God, my mouth used to just bark for the stuff. Haven't been out in years, though. Marriage, mortgage, management. Notice 3M's a glue company? Pass me a few grapes. Boy, you look bagged. What about a morning off? We'll throw the bike in the back. C'mon, stretch out."

"Sure."

"I'll get your bike. You just eat."

He does.

101

One August night six weeks before Andrew and Betty's ferry date, Mark phoned to invite Andrew out for a night ride.

"I still don't have lights," Andrew replied.

"Not required. We go urban."

Andrew glanced past an eavesdropping Stan at the kitchen clock and asked Mark, "Where do I meet you?"

Stan and Andrew had stood exactly like this around the hallway phone hundreds of times over the years. By the time he was three years old, Andy could reach the phone faster than his dad. After the divorce, they'd wordlessly developed a little theatrical routine of overheard dialogue and unseen mime. What adult callers thought was extraordinary politeness on Andy's part was actually family code. When Stan's friends would call they'd think that Andy was coping with the divorce well and really maturing as he'd reply "Hello, Paul," or "Good evening, Shiela," when in fact he was asking Stan whether he wanted to take a call. With his prepubescent voice, he could get away with slightly corny lines like, "You're right, Mr. Dunbar, my dad might be interested in life insurance." Andy's purposefully overheard lines would give Stan time to haul himself within sight of the hallway phone to shake his head yes or no. If the phone was for him, Andy reflexively turned away from Stan and the living room. Neither of them acknowledged that this made it easier to take the rare calls from his mom. Before cordless phones of the late 1980s and cellphones of the late 1990s, divorce and infidelity were marked by phone cords stretched around door frames, those borders within borders.

This decade-old ritual of Stan looking on with a raised eyebrow as Andrew talked on the phone continued when Mark called to propose a night ride. Hanging up, Andrew partially asked Stan and mostly told him, "You're all right for an hour and a half" while bounding upstairs to change.

"Nice black tights," Stan said as Andrew trotted back down. "Seriously, shouldn't you wear something brighter?"

"I'll be fine." Andrew pulled on a long-sleeved jersey.

"I just heard you say you don't have lights. Andrew, this doesn't sound safe."

"I'm going with Mark. He's an excellent rider. It'll be like the buddy system." Andrew began filling up his water bag. "Do you want to do the tube now or wait?"

"What I want is for you to come home in one piece."

"Both of us want that. Relax. The paper's on the table." Andrew avoided Stan's alternately stern and beseeching look by stepping into the living room and fixing the TV remote to the strip of Velcro on Stan's chair. "Remote's up. I'll be back before midnight. Okay?"

"Do I have a choice?"

"I'll be safe, Dad. I always am." Andrew shut the door behind him.

102

Andrew can't stop squirming around in the Pathfinder's wide seat. Even in the few minutes before he remembers *seat controls*, he shifts left, right, fore and aft, amazed at this county of ass space. Out the window, every metre of blurring land brands him a traitor. One hundred and twenty kilometres an hour. An hour in a car, a long day on the bike.

"Here," Glen offers, all but abandoning the steering wheel to lean across Andrew with his right hand to grope at the far side of his seat. "Lumbar support." The leather seat actually inflates at the base of Andrew's spine, pushing his hard stomach a little closer to Glen's lingering arm.

"Is one of us actually going to drive?" Andrew asks.

"Thought you could use some comfort."

"*Alive* is very comfy."

Glen returns at least one hand to the wheel. "Oh, honeydew melon," he says a few minutes later, motioning to another container in the back. "With lemon juice. Somehow the lemon makes the melon taste more like itself."

Two, three bites into the bright green melon Andrew replies, "There must be a name for that, a thing that makes another thing more itself."

"Yeah, alcohol."

That Glen happens to have not one but two bottles of chilled white wine behind the seat is notable enough. Then there's the conspicuously new mini-cooler in which they're chilling. However keen he is for the wine, however delighted at the cool touch of the bottle's slender neck, Andrew finally admits what's happening here. The fruit Glen feeds him has been taken out of a dozen plastic shopping bags which have been relocated around his bike. Whatever domestic situation has this moneyed family guy piloting his Stupid User Vehicle in the early morning has him doing so with a load of family groceries.

The groceries have probably been in the car overnight, but the chilled wine and the cooler in which they sit have been purchased this morning in this *belle province* of gas station wine. Within a second of grabbing the bottle, Andrew knows it's a screw-top, not corked, but he digs the knife out of his pocket anyway.

"Oh, screw-top. How convenient," he says, briskly tapping his unopened knife on the neck of the bottle. He waits until he's had a deep swallow before asking, "So, you saw me when?" He pauses just a second, smiles just a little, before leaning over, dropping a hand onto Glen's substantial thigh and raising the bottle to his mouth. "I've got it. I've got it. You just drink."

"Mmm. Maybe half an hour ago. I thought someone with a thousand-dollar bike between his legs and five dollars' worth of clothes on his back might have a story to tell." Glen motions for Andrew to raise the bottle to his lips again.

"Storytime's over." Andrew drinks again, guzzling wine that tastes like green apples spritzed with honey. "What if you didn't find me on the way back — take the cooler home for family picnics?"

"I don't think my family's what interests you."

Glen smiles, and so, sure, does Andrew. Kilometres whiz past every minute they drive, chat and drink.

103

Andrew had been evasive and dismissive of Stan's questions about his night ride with Mark but was then a little annoyed when Mark rode up as taciturn as usual. On the phone Mark had been inviting, almost imploring. Collecting Andrew at the house, all he had to say was, "Let me know when you've warmed up." On residential then downtown streets, Mark took corners and assumed Andrew would follow. They didn't say a word until their approach spilled them toward a towering parking garage. Andrew kept even the question "This it?" from leaving his mouth, listening instead for Mark's confirming downshift. As they slipped around the dropped yellow entrance barricades, Mark finally broke the vow of mileage to offer gearing advice ("Middle-middle") before they commenced a race up each level of the parking garage.

"You can start on the inside," was all Mark said.

And then they were off, racing up the parking garage's constant incline, struggling from one corner to the next. Beside them, the still, dumb cars shone under caged fluorescent lights.

Despite the bleaching light and the layered reek of dirty concrete, exhaust and leaked engine oil, there were pleasures in this parkade's spiral of right angles. Unlike any climb in the surrounding woods, the stained concrete incline was invariably even. By the second storey, will, lung and leg were as much freed as burnt by the steady slope. Pain was the third racer that night. There was also the electric novelty of riding at night, the long leash of light. The banks of caged fluorescents lined the ceiling as regularly as the strips of yellow paint carved up the concrete. Andrew had investigated but still not purchased cycling lamp systems capable of lighting his way through dense forest for hours. The parkade race was as novel as night baseball or skiing at nine p.m.

Here, finally, was width enough for a proper race. Week after week on the single track, Andrew had raced Mark's pace, but from behind.

Now each lane was at least as wide as a road, and he rode faster with Mark beside him, not in front of him.

The wide concrete lanes also afforded them the track racer's lateral cat and mouse game. Block left defensively or pour it all ahead in a fleeing sprint? To not be cutting a line was to be cut by one. A moving obstacle came from above in the shape of an exiting sedan. Mark didn't hide his excited grin as their change of play approached, whereas the driver's face swung visibly between paralyzing confusion (movement without a car?) to projected rage (Because of you I might actually have to steer). The riders split to either side of the car like wind around a sail and were sucked together at its red close. In their parting, Mark must have released his pump because suddenly Andrew's ribs took a token whack from the pump's light rod as it played his triangle of ribs, arms and top tube. Andrew retaliated by drawing as large a mouthful of water as his burning lungs would permit, then spitting it in a thin jet onto Mark's blue side. He laughed and choked and gulped while gunning for the next turn.

Parked cars calibrated the burning race, those bright turtle shells, those smirking gas boxes. The occasional tinted window flashed briefly with their greasy, deltoid reflections, chests bent into the climb.

Finally the choked, muzzy air began to loosen, and the envelope of their echoed tires spilled open. Had this climbing spiral ended in a cliff, Andrew would have gone over it as well. Oh, the steady push. Everything for the end. Here, finally, was the complete meeting point of strength and weakness. By surrendering everything to the pain, he could claim the pain for fuel. He painted each toenail with pain. Pain was speed; it was worship. Mark wasn't ahead of him.

The cooler, fresher air of the parkade's rooftop pulled them into an open-air decline. City lights pushed up against an overhang of stars. On the road below, a strip of red tail lights passed into the half-dark city. They didn't stop until they reached the exterior wall of the parkade, a metre-high battlement for this castle of cars.

Four cleats clicked out. Helmets were dangled from abandoned bar ends. Water was gulped and spat. Finally, Andrew leaned his back over the low wall to stretch his head out over the noise and light of the traffic below. "We gotta get more guys." A crown of sweat slipped back from his hairline. He rolled his skull back and forth, taking air so easily now. That tight little sound was a small zipper, but he didn't look up. Then he heard the rasp of a match being lit. Ah, sure, the fug of weed. When Andrew began to lean forward for the joint he felt Mark's hand in the middle of his chest.

"No, hang back," said Mark. "Take it like that." Mark kept the hot joint in his fingers and raised it to Andrew's lips, suspended where they were out over the traffic.

104

In the Pathfinder, the wine bottle Andrew feeds Glen passes back and forth in front of the car stereo.

"No CDs?" Andrew asks.

"A few here and there. Mostly I just troll the radio."

"Mind if I give her a spin?" Andrew doesn't wait for an answer.

In rough terms, a radio's seek and scan are all the GPS one needs in Canada. A sludge of US commercials marks a southern dip along the border. *Do you suffer from vague paranoia and/or inexplicable hostility and/or emotional distance? If so, Centrax may be for you.* Not just French but the abundance of talk, the actual human discussion of issues and events, heralds your entrance into Quebec. The Anglo bridge posts east and west of Quebec differ radically by density. If the radio's seek stumbles every few seconds, you're in Ontario. Here in rural Quebec, the receiver numbers climb and roll by the dozens, up and down the entire band, with just a few snags. The inevitable country music sanding down its planks of you, me and regret over and over again. Always surprising is the metal. In rural areas with population bases that make hospitals difficult, who's bankrolling the thrash? Second most objectionable is the so-called contemporary rock, that emotional marketing of women pimped up and down the entire industry or male voices so thick with counterfeit feeling that you can hear their whiskers and see their squints. There is, of course, the reliable CBC, the radio birthright. Equally popular (but unsubsidized) is also classic rock. The state has laid one radio rail across the country, and the baby boomers have laid the other. From sea to shining sea, somebody's angel is still the centrefold.

"How long have you been driving with just this shit?" Andrew asks.

"Mostly shit." Glen raises a jaw to give Andrew an unmistakably appraising look. "I don't just listen to music; I listen to chance. You're probably just old enough to remember a VCR coming into the house, yes? That's your generation. Not mine. Not the one after. You saw the shift into movies on demand, whereas younger kids don't know any different. They can't imagine that you used to have to catch movies. Sure, no one wants to go back to hanging off the mercy of TV, but movie rental spoiled us. A certain cartoon company fought like hell against the VCR before going on to make a fortune from it. Before that it was chance. Preferable? No. Totally annoying? Not at all. Back with thirteen channels or fewer, no DVDs in the mail, no specialty channels, a pair of rabbit ears bringing it all in, you got blessed. Late night at a cottage, too hot to sleep, voila — Bond at eleven."

Andrew sits on both Glen's passenger seat and on a frayed orange couch as a boy at Paul Tucker's cottage, his short legs dangling between Paul's and his father's, a tiny screen glowing in one dark corner. Beside him here in the SUV, Dr. No is becoming Mr. Yes.

105

In the winter, when Andrew met Betty to walk her back to the house to explain his deception of September, he didn't bring flowers or hot cocoa in a travel mug or her favourite little toque. He didn't joke or grab at nostalgia, trying to rescue the them of now with the them of then. His hand didn't accidentally brush hers. Instead, he thanked her for coming and told her directly he'd missed her. Only after they walked for two silent blocks did he say anything mildly ingratiating.

"I've always liked walking beside you."

Given what he was about to say at the house, even that felt schemingly casual, but he had to let her know. Her jawbone wasn't entirely sharpened with hostility.

At the house he simply said, "Front doorway only, I promise" and stooped to prop open the aluminum door with its imperfect little metal toggle. He opened the main door, stepped in to the base of the stairway and turned back to face her.

"Dog hygiene was my dad's other big joke. You've heard this? Why do dogs lick their balls? Right. Because they can. I lied to you about when he died because I could. Not to hurt you; no, please, I promise. It was fear, not cruelty, fear and shame. I lied because, quite simply, no one was going to correct me. I wanted you, and he was gone. I knew these two things in the same way: what was gone, what I wanted. I'm still getting used to how permanent death is. In ways, though, you also see it right away. Over and over, you process the one big fact you see with your first glimpse of the body: never again.

"I'd gone riding at night, with Mark. Dad was okay every other time I went riding, but this was at night. He was needier at night. His trache tube. His hand splint. The electrodes. I was guilty and elated every minute I was out. The guilt fuelled the elation and vice versa. I'd resist taking a piss because I'd have to think of him needing to go, the seven to ten minutes he'd spend just getting to the washroom. Was he okay? Still I kept riding. And he fell.

"I knew as soon as I was back, as soon as I saw him. I jerked at the door, but I had my bike in my hands. His head was...his head was right there. I had to drop the bike, then move it before I could open the door. Do you understand? Doing these little things? Turning a door handle? Setting something down? All that time his head was draining. Not pumping, not squirting. Draining, balancing out.

"He would have called my name. Like at night, if there was ever a power failure and he was standing, he'd call my name like a kid. *Andy. Andy.* I know he would have yelled my name as he fell, but I was out riding. For fun."

Neither of them acknowledged the climbing pitch of his voice or the tears on his cheeks — or hers — until she stepped through the doorway and he wasn't speaking any more and she had him heaving in her arms. After a few minutes his shoulders did a little half-squirm as he pulled back his raw face to say, "I didn't want you like this."

"Shhh," she said, "come here. Come here." Eventually she reached behind her to shut out the cold winter air. She walked him to the couch in the next room. Crying, stroking ("Just let me get my arm out"), they lay braided together. A wet kiss, two. Her breasts, his shoulders and thighs, were brushed then clutched, stroked by a finger then grabbed in a hand. Wordless mouths made deep kisses and they chased a quick living-room fuck in the glow of the street lights. He apologized endlessly. He left her the blanket while he phoned for pizza. She held it out like wings as he hurried back.

"This is it, right?" she asked eventually. "You're not also a three-time absentee father or a life support system for various STDs, are you?"

"I was also high, a little, with Mark. I was high when he fell. Other than that, no, no more skeletons in the hallway...I've got to sell the house, though. That's what Larry has been phoning about. It's in his will, graduate and go."

"Oh."

106

Crucially, and perhaps strategically, Glen leaves Andrew in the truck while he books their motel room. Andrew's trust and comfort rise as he's left alone with Glen's cellphone, the remaining booze and a full name and address on his vehicle registration.

When they enter the musty motel room, Andrew proposes, "I'm gonna take the world's longest shower. Seeing as you have my vehicle inside of yours, how about I take your car keys into the washroom with me?"

"Why not take me in there with you?"

"Nobody can want it this dirty," Andrew replies. He sweeps up one wine bottle and holds out a hand for the keys.

"Take this too," Glen says, offering a translucent shopping bag with a visible can of shaving cream.

"Boy Scout Glen."

In seconds Andrew isn't so much in a shower as in another dimension, a dimension not only of sight and sound but of wine, and of heat, cleansing, unknotting heat. Sleeves of dirt fall from his arms. The tan lines that cuff his thighs and arms are so precise he looks to be wearing an antique, one-piece male bathing costume of paleness, his body mapped into provinces of public and private life. His feet are so privately pale.

He drowns his filthy hiking shorts at the bottom of the tub. When he finally gives them a scrub he tries not to stare at his own stains, at the abject spectrum of his recent intestinal struggles. Already, yesterday's hunger, dehydration and diarrhea are vague to him. As the shorts come clean, he feels both embarrassed and dethroned at the thought of hanging them here to dry, as if he should be the laundry-less hooker, the mistress without utility bills. If they were his cycling shorts, he could at least hang up the male-male equivalent of a thong. As is, he looks like a waylaid tourist.

Glen would no doubt prefer that Andrew put the razor he bought to a more central environ, but Andrew's fading yeast infection still forbids it. Instead he simply begins unearthing his face, shaving away at ten days' worth of whiskers, peeling himself down to urban smoothness. He showers again to do his calves.

Stepping out of the small bathroom with a thin towel tied around his waist, Andrew is glad that all men are not created equal. Glen has been waiting in the bed wearing nothing more than a white sheet pulled halfway up his body. When he turns to stow some documents he'd been reading into a soft leather briefcase, Andrew is relieved at the modest size glimpsed between the sheets. He once heard a gay comedian list the three sizes of penis: Small, Medium and Keep That Thing Away From Me. His memory for jokes like this has been pulled through his brief adult life by uncertainty, curiosity and secrecy. Why *do* men buy so-called fitness magazines with bare-chested, ab-racked men on the front? The staff at some sports bars wear referee's uniforms to serve a mostly male clientele. What are they really refereeing? Right now he is clean, warm, tipsy and fed. *Bisexual* is just a word, whereas his dick is cylindrically hard. As he crosses the room he sees his slim back in a mirror. He can feel the strength in his thighs despite the wine in his thin blood.

Andrew stands beside the bed and reaches under the sheets for Glen's tackle. Ah, sex with men: he doesn't first have to use four-syllable words to talk about well-respected novels, indie film, indie rock or fantasy travel — and undressing is the only foreplay required. When Glen reaches to undo his towel, Andrew says, "No, up first" and spreads his legs in the towel. This perpendicular start launches a sex of purposeful reaches and grabs that seems so much easier than anything commencing in a horizontal embrace. And why bother with the kissing? Fully, gleefully naked, Andrew raises and plants heels or knees, offering one minute, taking the next.

The manageable sight and heft of Glen in hand or mouth complete the drop intuitively commenced when they had walked across the gas station parking lot. He likes meeting this plummeting decision, is relieved to lash himself to its falling weight. You will give me highway miles. I will take you inside. Of course I know how to do this.

Accelerated by wine, relief, surrender and a transgressive arousal he'll later wonder if the fully gay ever lose, he drifts from the strokes, gulps and licks into a quasi-telepathic link with Betty. Inclining his weight back past the fulcrum of his knees and lowering a jaw to the mattress to enable and entice Glen, he moves also into some future when he can describe it all to Betty. He'll tell her how easy it was to turn his body into a version of hers, to angle his own hips as he had angled hers, to receive the exploratory thumb he used to give. He will only ever find words for this moment in her presence, could relate to her alone the undilutability of this fit.

I thought of you the entire time, the adulterers half-lie, trying to forget about the orgasm they can't forget about. Near the finish, this telepathic link with Betty is scrambled briefly by difference. When Andrew straddles and posts he meets longer, stronger arms. Where you have clutched at those two faceted pools at the base of my spine, this one can reach up and down my entire buttocks, marks ripples on the surface of my back's disturbed water. A pelt of chest hair is in Andrew's fingers and Betty's. What power to deliver this inside, to crest and deepen his every whinny. Already this experience is a memory, something to share with someone not here, someone who should be here. With its unstoppable pushes and multiple pulls, memory is an orgy.

107

Betty stayed over again on the night of Andrew's hallway confession. After a few restorative days of constant hugging and classes cut for hours in bed, for movies, for reading novels, for yes sex, again sex, thank you sex, how dare you sex, we've just had a shower sex — for confidence and disclosure, Betty pulled off for a day. Class again. The library. Errands.

That night he found a moss green envelope waiting for him on the dining-room table. Taped inside a card of calligraphic Japanese flowers was an image of a small cockroach rolling a Timbit. No, wait, smaller than a Timbit, and with tiny bits of green leaf sticking out everywhere. Maybe she wanted him to be as strong as an ant, capable of carrying numerous times his own weight. Switching from the image to her looping inscription he read:

> The male dung beetle spends countless hours tirelessly building a ball of dung before parading it past potential mates (think of the new trucks cruising Princess St.). Females require the insulated, nutritious dung for a nest. They, too, need to see that a man has his shit together before mating.
>
> You were afraid I'd condemn you for letting your father die. That's just not possible. (In fact, it's a little crazy, but one step at a time here.) There's simply nothing for me to judge there. Do remember, though, that I contest your note. With us, the way your father died is not worse than lying to me. Please look beyond your grief to see that.
>
> Healing is the admission price we pay for love. I'm your celebration. I'm your preventative exercise. I'm not your treatment.
>
> Let's heal.
> — Your Bet

108

He wakes in a bed to layers of panic and a new pain. Where am — What's he — The bike.

The rest of the bed is empty, the room still. His bike leans against a wall of the motel room, extra fruit hanging in a grocery bag off one handlebar. He is stupefied at the vulnerability of this coma. It's 4:14 in the afternoon, and he'd been dead enough not to hear an exit or the entrance of his bike. Exhaling with relief, he rolls onto his back. And pain. How am I going to put this on the saddle?

Another hot shower and a snack don't even take him to six p.m. Before every small chore he peeks out the curtains, perpetually debating the tactical necessity of waiting for the cover of darkness. He didn't gain more than seventy kilometres in Glen's truck, a distance he'll make himself by morning. He had thought a milking fuck delivered on cabled calves and glistening flanks would score him hundreds of kilometres.

Reading naked in bed, he staves off the growing hunger as long as he can, defending himself with underripened bananas, decent oranges and a final whiff of grapeshot. The sun looks tireless as he mines his own lammy cliché and watches television news in a rented, ugly room. A split face wouldn't be national news, so he flicks channels looking for the newscast with the cheapest decor and the most flashy anchorwoman. Listening, he understands maybe a third of the French, but the pictures and icons help. A labour strike. Something about doctors. Pollution and water. Nothing about a cyclist on the run.

Face it, you got away. Relax. Be human again.

Miscalculate or drop your guard and you'll never leave the country, will work shit jobs forever, would drag a partner down.

Eventually, he burns the day's novel pages, that useless mass, in the bathtub and upends the food bag hoping for something other than fruit. A new jar of Nutella rolls onto the bed, *Cheers* written across its label with his pink highlighter. He eats the Nutella with a finger.

109

Initially, Andrew and Betty's shared status as only children and only children of divorce gave them similar landscapes of emotion and experience, rolling hills of uncertainty, plateaus of loneliness that rose into bluffs of independence and watercourses of boldness. Eventually, though, they found difference as well. Her parents' divorce had been a ceasefire in a hostile war of hurled insults and slammed doors, while his had been one person walking briskly out the door. Fundamentally, everyone in her house had said too much, too loudly and too often. Whereas his parents hadn't said enough. Not, at least, until the divorce started.

Andy would always remember that Stan had sat for his custody speech, sat at the kitchen table and invited him to do the same. He was straighter there with all of those right angles, all that firm support. Pat had been gone for a week.

"In ways, I shouldn't tell you any of this. You won't end the day without agreeing with me on that. Right now, this moment, your life, it's splitting apart. A huge chasm is opening between who you thought you were and who you need to be. I know that. Worry about the circumstances of change, not change itself.

"So, here it is: I'm in the shit. We all know that. Your mother, we're splitting up. And yeah, you're the rope in this tug-of-war. You didn't get to choose whether you wanted to choose. I agree; that sucks.

"Please know, forever, that I will always love you, whatever you choose to do. Yes, I'll be sad if I only see you on weekends. But that's not the only sadness here, is it? Promise number two: however much I need you, however much you help me, you're not expected, by me or by anyone, to stick around. You're my son, not my nurse. I'll still love you if you go, and I'll get by. But here's the thing it might be easier for you not to hear. A boy might go because I'm in the shit, cut and run for higher ground. A young man might stay for the very same reason. Andrew, no one is accidentally strong. I've got a fight I don't want, and I've got to fight it all the way without getting bitter. And, son, that's life."

110

When he had biked around Kingston, Andrew had been happiest to create circular routes that didn't see him doubling back much. Returning to Kingston from Halifax by bike was conceived of as a route with *no* doubling back, at least not geographically. Ever forward. When Betty returned to Andrew's house that winter, his lie and fear now acknowledged, she too preferred not to double back. After the initial bliss of reunion, after the grinning pleasure of meals and sleeps together, she had to admit, to herself and to him, that she hadn't, in fact, *returned*. They'd started again and were a slightly different them. Phase Two. They remembered their past, but, however recent it was, they wouldn't get back to it. Could not, should not, would not and, she began to wonder, maybe even didn't want to. They'd changed their emotional arrangements; why not their living arrangements?

Walking home from campus one day in February, she was trapped on the sidewalk behind two so-called fellow students, walking prisoners to their idiocy.

"There's no way you were as wasted as Tony."

"Dude, absolutely."

"No fucking way."

"Six shooters, three —"

Betty hated them even more when she stepped out from behind their leather jackets and baseball caps to cross the street and their loud, thick voices carried effortlessly to the other side, amplified, no doubt, by necklaces of coral or hemp. Raising her collarbones, lowering her shoulder blades, she tried to fly away from these fellow Canadians. At "Chelios is back in tonight," she thought again of how she had never been in Paris's Georges Pompidou Centre. The dumb, efficient pace of these dudes tirelessly matched hers, exiling her to Morocco's Tagghdite Plateau at "fucking killer tits, man" and too temporarily sending her off to an austere Warsaw.

At first she was elated to open the door to Andrew and an uncorked red. Two glasses sat patiently on a clean counter. Garlic roasted in the oven. "Making hummus," he called.

She'd just set her bag down and his (Scotchy?) tongue was in her mouth.

"I got my Monsters essay back."

"Well?" she obliged, aware of how close the front door remained to her back, of how she was standing in a corner with her coat still on.

"A-pahluss."

"Hey, wow. Great. Great." One kiss. To his neck. "You pour while I run up to the washroom."

One floor up, she now had the bathroom door, not the front door, behind her back as a surrogate spine. She just needed a breath or two alone. The comfortingly firm door was not, however, thick enough to keep out the eventual sound of clinking glasses and footfalls on the steps. She ran the taps, flushed an empty toilet, watched clear water spiral away.

"There's more." His voice drew near the door.

"I'm sure there is. Give me a second here." One minute, two, what difference did they make?

Maybe her mom had a point. Maybe there is a right and wrong room for everything. Betty never lost thought, word or sight of *hallway* as she stepped out to a glass of wine and Andrew arranging a floppy white term paper in his hands.

"You ready? Andrew, this is quite simply one of the strongest undergraduate essays I have had the pleasure to read. The numerous strengths herein (an unwavering attention, a focused imagination, a sustained eloquence) will obviously live beyond the scope of this paper, and so, too, could its principal assertions. Your central idea of self-monstering — of monstering both chosen and demanded — could and should form the basis of an MA thesis. You will be extremely competitive for scholarships. Consider working at UNS with Nigel Ryan."

"Wow. Andrew, that's —"

"Yes. Yes. Yes."

He was clutching the paper so tightly he appeared to have one hand and a white flipper.

"I mean, you barely think something — you hope, but you don't want to hope because that might ruin it — but sometimes you do get what you want. Hey, can I buy you dinner? Jezboto or Split Yellow?"

"So, you want to do this?"

"Not necessarily. I don't know. In ways, yeah. I'm just excited about the recognition."

When these waves of wine, hope and endurance finally broke on their walk home, they each found how cutting one could now be, how discrete knives had been custom forged for single hands and hearts. The first of many battles in their war of Europe versus grad school began.

"Go off in search of praise," she said. "Go chase your check marks."

"You're right. Running away is much more admirable."

111

His play with Glen wasn't the smartest indoor sport for someone interminably on a bike. The small, hard saddle now feels like a meat-hook.

How did Betty wake up and go to class after this? How did she walk around?

But he's fed, bathed, hydrated and rested, more than willing to take the saddle sores. The clean edge of speed. Beneath the cramped, stolen track pants, he's got freshly shaved legs sharp in the night. His crotch's red tide seems to have turned.

Back on the road his body continues to remember the softness of last night's mattress, and he's grateful to no longer be slinging around an empty stomach. Free of hunger, he can see again. The valleys have flattened. Retracing European settlement, fighting the westerly wind, he can see the Maritime valleys behind him as a natural defence, row after row of sharpened stakes driven into the ground. Here, finally, is flatter farmland, the agricultural sweet spot of Quebec. The highest of these now manageable hills affords him a horizon of electric light. Lingering, unnatural light stains the far distance. Cities have returned.

Even this rural highway has signs announcing that he is en route to Quebec City, directing him to *le capital national*, the province's capital and proud home of a provincial legislature named Assemblée nationale du Quebec. The National Assembly in Quebec and Queen's Park in Ontario — Europe's grip cast off in one place then clung to down the road. Here in the lonely dark of a provincial highway, no longer within the parade of licence plates he left back on the Trans-Can, he recognizes that Quebec's licence plate slogan, *Je me souviens,* is the only Canadian poetry going. Here is a society distinct from the sales pitches of wild rose country and ocean playgrounds.

Je me souviens. The *viens* looks like conjugated iterations of *venir,* to come. Here in the dark of night, *I remember* is also *I come back.*

Quebec City. Some version of six hours by car to Kingston. With distance at least he remains bi- not uni-lingual, remembering or calculating distances by car, then translating them for the bike. Six hours by car will put him back in Kingston in a few days. Leg it home.

Or leg it back to his house. All those months fighting with Betty, telling himself and her that in part he was doing his MA to maintain ownership of the Kingston house — had he really wanted the family brick and mortar, or just Betty? Had he, as she once claimed, wanted her on his terms (in the house), not hers (bumming around Europe)? Their honesty was cutting one moment then inviting the next. When he had told her about his first significant girlfriend, that late high school pairing off, she'd interrupted his description of an anniversary dinner to ask about Stan.

"Whoa, whoa, whoa. Your dad checked himself into a clinic so you could get laid?"

"No, that's just when the —"

"Appointment was, when you were seventeen and having your first anniversary with your first serious girlfriend. Pimp Daddee. Pimp Daddee."

"How did I not see this?"

"Sex. Parents. We build walls," she commented quickly.

Three weeks later, tired of arguing over plane tickets and Plato, she found new game to hunt. Questioning some phone calls and emails he'd been trading with a female classmate with long hair and a longer list of past boyfriends, she was suddenly yelling, "He's dead. He doesn't need any more vicarious ass."

"What the hell is that supposed to mean?"

"What it does," Betty snapped. "Maybe career options aren't the only options you're looking to expand next year with this MA."

"Couldn't that be said of your Grand Tour, as well?"

"Could and should."

"Super."

In the court of love, anything you say can and will be used against you.

House aside, timing aside, ambitions temporarily ignored, in ways their fight was head versus heart, history and personality be damned. His grad student plan was orchestrated and accredited, with clear expectations and semi-predictable outcomes. Here is a reading list. These are the deadlines. Find what you can. Make what you must. But then one of them would realize that this was also true of her proposed Grand Tour. For four years she'd been looking at art in textbooks or on slides or websites. In London, major galleries had free admission. What does that culture *feel* like? You've either stood in front of a Rothko or you haven't.

When they traded confessions, not insults, they agreed each of them was chasing a fantasy of the heart and calculations of the head. At a calmer moment, he tried to sell her on his joining The Centaur Project at a university in Halifax.

"It's not just an MA. It's an interdisciplinary bike project. A physicist. A social geographer. A human kineticist."

"So what are you and the gym teacher actually going to do?"

"I take courses in Travel Lit, another Monsters in Lit and The Body in Theory so I can write about the bicycle as social projection. Not just history but social context. Why leisure here but daily life in China?"

"What about The Body in Practice?"

"Theory first. Horses were expensive. Walking was slow. Rail was the big break, but it didn't last. Why did we misstep in the evolution of train, bicycle, car? Why did we forsake affordable travel that makes us fit for debt, pollution and getting fat?"

"Bikes don't have a back seat."

The arguments weren't frequent so much as constant — making dinner, walking for groceries, late into the night, with or without wine. Making lunch, it would be a rational argument, a chess game of voice and mind over common, gridded ground.

"I'm not pushing you out of the nest, your dad is. It's his *will* for fuck's sake," she tried to say.

Cleaning that same kitchen four days later, they'd fight to wound, tugging their rope between tuition and plane tickets. In the night's grey air, each was sniper and surgeon both, piercing the organs they'd soon patch together again. Arguments of timing, desire, honesty, possession, change, everything that mattered and several subjects that didn't. Other nights, in bed, there was utter sweetness, brief confessions while spooning, hope and doubt acknowledged equally.

112

He couldn't have said so at the time, but he stayed with Stan in part for the double vision. Like any member of a marginal community, the sick and suffering are entirely fluent with how the central culture works. As a boy, Andy knew the social pecking orders, or loyalty fighting against curiosity or the very public record of who got breasts when — but he also had this other huge life at home. Sadness and fear turned every wall in the house into a mirror. His shadow had a separate life, was a character of secret worry. There were also hidden treasures. Endurance. Adaptability. Even the reach and courage of Stan's humour. "It sure took the sting out of going bald," he once said.

Truth was, Andrew didn't much miss Hug Me Mom. He had checked out of that just in time then looked for it where every other man does. A few years later, in early adolescence, when Shadow Boy dropped his shifts to a surly minimum, one parent was enough to find in constant contempt.

Slogging away here in the dark night on the cold machine, wearing that loneliest of costumes — cold sweat — he recognizes which voice he had missed in the house. He had missed Battle Scar Mom. He has just enough memories of a wry rye voice he didn't get enough of. Divorce put both mother and child on probation, meant they only ever saw a conscripted good behaviour, a scenario they each hated.

If he were closer to thirty years old, not twenty, he'd be comfortably at ease with sex and *all* bodies, would see bisexuality as a scale from one to ten. At the bottom of the scale would be the toxic closet, bent, denied lives of hatred and violence. Up at eight or nine, women would do only in a pinch, preferably the small-breasted and slim-hipped. Ten, extreme ten, would be cock-o-rama. It is Mark's point he's remembering, still an accurate one, when he acknowledges that no matter how faggy two men might be, they still have two male sex drives, that double-barrelled shotgun of testosterone. His explorations with Mark and Glen spike his scale up to a brief five, but he thinks of himself on the ride as remaining a casual four, curious but largely theoretical four.

All this and he's still hard for Betty every day, despite not having seen her in nine months. There are still many experiences he can't even conceive of doing with another man. A little sex, yes. Sleeping? No. He stares up into the dark sky and thinks of not one, but two women, Betty and his mom, sleeping somewhere under this same dark blanket beneath which he rides. His thoughts sometimes linger on male shoulders, abs or cock, the way a fit male ass tucks into itself, but they'd never concentrate on a man in the peace of sleep. Meanwhile, he's cranked off the last thirty kilometres imagining Betty somewhere far behind him in the east and his mom ahead of him in the west. He doesn't overestimate what Pat can do for him on his half-fugitive night flight, although of course, he has always known that, in fact, she's money just one collect call away. And he's not so sweat-drunk to expect a healing reconciliation the minute he finds a phone booth. He simply admits that he can trust her. What a charade it has been to pretend she was untrustworthy for doing what she wanted. Trust a bounder, just don't rely on her. One hundred kilometres from now he might doubt he could tell her anything, might think it prudent not to mention his Lady Macbeth right foot, but for now, she's the one person to whom he can say anything. (One of two?) He can ask his mom whether he loves Betty or whether he just loves love.

Precisely because love is daily and Andrew and his mother do not actively love each other, do not labour for each other, he can ask his mother how he can tell if he really, really loves Betty or whether he just thinks so because he has made her more unattainable. They're not tremendously close, but they're honest.

He rides nearly three more hours before he finds a gas station, and by then the bruise of dawn has already begun spreading above the eastern horizon. Stashing his bike behind the garage, slurping endlessly from a wall tap, he finally crosses to the phone booth, trying to avoid his multiple reflections in its panelled glass. A tiny grey sweatshirt. Eyes bulging in their sharp sockets. *You have a collect call from —* It's Andrew.

By the time the call pulls Pat from sleep to a dressing gown to a trip downstairs, Andrew admits he is bone-weary, wishes he too could curl up with a blanket for this chat. Slow to wake, she's eventually all business.

"Do you know, exactly, where you are? I can hit Quebec City in less than five hours."

Will she wake hubby to tell him or leave a half-informative note? She'd know that *potentially fugitive* isn't even worth mentioning.

"No, no," he replies.

"You didn't call me for directions."

"Well, directions of a kind. Before all this started happening, I'd been thinking so much of Betty. Maybe *thinking* is the wrong word. Hour after hour, she's just there in my head. You know when you're not talking but there are still words — mine go to her. Missing her, admiring her, I've thought of you too. I wish things were better between you and me. But no sooner did I think that and I got myself into this mess. How do I tell her about that kid?"

"Andrew, I'll talk with you. I'll send you money. I'll come get you. But if you're talking about love, let me tell you right now, you need to have a conscience, not marry one."

113

S/he didn't dump him/her. Betty and Andrew stayed together, one roof, one bed, as his transcript, letters of reference and application essay moved him closer to Nova Scotia and her passport application and vaccinations moved her closer to Budapest and Marrakesh. All this time they'd never been more busy. Senior papers week after week. Politely demanded attendance at lifeless, mumbled public lectures and gallery openings of pathetically diffuse work.

From each of them, *I love you* lost part of its daily currency, temporarily ceased to be the couch's punctuation, the dark bed's echo, only to be soon replaced by *I do love you*, or, *I love you, you idiot.*

With their desires now painfully clarified, the sex became prismatic. Self-interest was parsed into commanding violet, generous blue and greedy red. Neither overtly acknowledged the gratitude and respect each felt for the other's purposeful self-design, for the clarification that their lives were definitely parallel tracks, not a single one. Betty took them closest.

"Mom had an interesting line. Selfishness is the mother tongue. We all know selfishness, can always do it. If this MA is what you think you need to do for you, then do it."

They fucked now with the skill and efficiency of temporarily reunited ex-lovers, yet talked openly about the sadness awaiting them come end of summer, come plane journeys large and small. When she started her trip purchases with a giant knapsack, he playfully hid it around the house again and again. Beneath the kitchen sink, in the freezer. Permissible too was doubt.

"This may be one of the biggest mistakes of my life," he said once in their nightly clutch.

"One of?!" She reached back to cup and shake half his ass.

The next night, lingering over the supper table, she gave him

The Argument of Protection

"Dad worked at the tail end of the old school, the wet school of journalism," Betty said. "It was a man's game for a long time. When I was going through some bitchy high-school shit, he once said — and remember, this is Mr. Weekend Wisdom here, but it has stuck with me — Sweetheart, I have friends, and I have people I drink with. One of the people he drank with was ex-military. This guy once told my dad that at Royal Military College, feeding you what they want, when they want, clothing you, all these tests, they find who they want very early and then enable them, advance them, throw resources at them. The Executive. The Tribe. The Cult. These doors that open for you, though, maybe they're also prison walls. Why are these profs opening doors for you? Yes, because you deserve it. Yes, darling, you're clever as fuck. But isn't there also vanity here, a fan factory alongside the scholar factory? Do they want you in their tribe for you, or for them?"

A few weeks later, when he tried casually using the word *supervisor* around the house, she cut even closer to the bone.

"Supervisor? *Super*visor?" Betty had asked as winter began its slow exit. "What's so *super*? He's able to leap tall footnotes in a single bound? That X-ray vision for plagiarism is something you covet?"

"Mentally, I'm in shape. I don't want to lose that."

"The Tate isn't a lobotomy clinic. Travelling, especially travelling with me, isn't going to make you dumb."

"But it might make me lazy. Or rusty. I'm still growing."

"Old men are not the only people who can help you grow."

"What do you mean, old m —"

"I mean white, male, fifty-something Prof A is sending you off to work with white, male, fifty-something Prof B."

"That is so irrelevant. I'm being offered money for thinking here, because of my work, this... this —"

She did reach for his hand. He should have noticed that.

"I'm not trying to fight here, but can we say *father figure*?"

He didn't see or feel himself shake off her hand, didn't seem to choose the words that flew from his mouth. "You just don't want to travel alone."

114

Stan country. The remainder of the ride is evenly punctuated. Two days from Quebec City to Montreal, then another two from Montreal to Kingston. Montreal. Andrew had been there with his parents, with Stan, with friends, with other girlfriends, by himself and then with Betty. Approaching it now, he mostly thinks of Stan, thinks of him going there repeatedly in *his* mid-twenties to have his suits made. Like most of the rest of Andrew's stuff (and some of Betty's), those suits are tucked into the Kingston bedroom he had converted to storage. He'd like to wear one now. Throw the bike off a cliff, shower for an hour, then slide himself into the brown with rust pinstripes. Eat in a restaurant with Betty. Gargle wine.

Of course, he could be well fed and properly clothed right now. Here on the approach to Quebec City he begins easing himself off the vampire riding shifts. He still rides into the evening and sleeps later in the morning, but last night he was finally sleeping again at three a.m., not pedalling.

If he turned off the highway and fought his way through Quebec City traffic, he could buy a new pair of bike shorts and some more gear and be back on the highway in three hours. Comfort aside — and in the hiking shorts things certainly don't get properly swept aside — the baggy hiking shorts will probably cost him three hours in aero-dynamic losses over the next four days. The open legs of the shorts are beginning to chafe his thighs, sliding up and down several thousand times a day. Yet these same sloppy openings send a steady stream of air up to his fading but still noticeable rash.

Why buy more gear when he's finally in sight of home? Sure, he'll wind up buying new cycling shorts anyway, but to head downtown to hunt out an outfitter would be both tedious and tempting. One sight of a bivy sack might crumble his resolve to make-do with a foil blanket, pine boughs and a sweatshirt-sleeve-and-bungee-cord toque. As is, the lack of camping gear has actually put him on the bike more hours per day and upped his catch. Biking into the higher population density of central Quebec, he's now able to buy food every day. He's been refilling plastic bottles of water. He'll get by.

Turns out only the shoes are integral. Late in the trip, his ass as hard as a walnut, the padded shorts are an endurable loss. Everything is proving replaceable. At least everything physical. Deciding not to turn into Quebec City, cranking out the miles, he reaches up once again to finger the now scarring cigarette burn on his chest. More than a year ago, Betty told him that healing is the admission price we pay for love. That's all the map he's ever needed.

115

Mass versus utility. For at least nine months, first theoretically then hyper-practically, he has thought of the cyclist's debate between mass and utility. In ways, the bike frame is a scale, weighing a thing's usefulness against its weight. On a bike, cost-benefit analysis is measured with sweat. He's sure that one of the reasons most hard-core riders prefer weed to booze is the difference in the weight and volume they claim. That, and the muscle relaxation, and the lesser threat to balance and dehydration, and the immunity to hangovers and calories.

For nearly his entire life, and certainly into his MA, the bicycle has been one of the human inventions he admires most. Mobility. Self-reliance. Fitness. Speed without pollution. Incredible efficiency. More than ninety per cent of the energy a cyclist puts into the machine comes back out. But humanity's greatest invention is much, much lighter. Living with Betty he'd been amazed at the tininess of the birth control pill. Less than a gram in weight, smaller than the eraser on the end of a pencil, that little dot changed their lives, allowed their lives to be what they wanted them to be, not what they had to become.

In the Kingston house, as spring turned to summer and their separate flights away were less than a season away, Betty wasn't sure if she was being a jerk absolutely or just relatively when she came home from the pharmacy with a very full prescription bag. She left the swollen white bag on top of her dresser, not in one of its drawers.

He asked as soon as he saw it. "You're staying on the pill?"

"What? Oh, yeah… Aren't you maybe coming over at Christmas?"

"Yeah, hopefully. Good time to give your body a break, though."

"Isn't any time? We could start wearing condoms now if you'd like."

"Obviously those aren't all for me — for us." He nodded at the bulging white bag.

"Long, significant list here," she said, raising a hand. "One, my body, *mine.* Two, it's harder on *any* body to go on and off. Three, I have all but begged you to come with me, and every one of those pills could be for us. And, quite relevantly: we have chosen different paths for next year."

"Five, six, seven: ecstasy, raves and hooded cock. I'm just wondering what protection you're taking on your little path. Does *Lonely Planet* offer multilingual translations for getting tested? What's *chlamydia* in Serbo-Croat? Portuguese? Perhaps we should make up some flash cards."

When he stormed away and pounded down the stairs, she couldn't have seen that he was heading for his bike but she guessed as much. "What is it about bikes anyway?" she yelled.

116

The Buddhist notion of chosen suffering has been one of his most frequent thoughts, dredged up hundreds of times a day by the left leg. Newtonian physics has come up almost as often with the right. The energy required to keep something moving is only a fraction of the energy required to move that thing in the first place. Rockets, billiard balls, economies — the big energy is paid up front. Relationships aren't so simple.

Cycling for sport requires one to bike away from the pedal-and-coast leisure of childhood or adult errands. Genuine cycling is constant spin. Two wheels, two pedals, two lungs. Pedal your breath.

On his approach to Montreal, the jukebox of the bike finds one reedy refrain. Long ago he biked past rationality and the conscious mind and knows by now that he has no choice about what songs he will recall or sing, sometimes even loudly. Before a flicked cigarette and a sacked campsite pulled this trip of peace into a trip of war, before that kid's face launched a thousand predatory kilometres, he had embarrassed himself with a near-total recall of most of the AC/DC oeuvre. For days, the ride had him ringing "Hells Bells." In the next valley he'd abruptly stick on the title and chorus of some song of Betty's, *something, something, exTRAordinary machine*. He had no interest in riding with an MP3 player. Touring, you shuffle your past, not your iPod. And today, that past his past is stuck on Neil Young's "Helpless." There is a point in fatigue and loneliness beyond which there are no clichés. Deep into a marathon, in the double-digit kilometres, if one thinks at all, one thinks with wonder. And gratitude.

Andrew has read maybe a dozen poems that describe someone walking through a neighbourhood with front lawns awash in the blue glow of televisions. House after house, each one a link in a glowing blue chain. Most of Canada has a similar view. Eighty per cent of the Canadian population lives in the twenty per cent of land immediately north of the US border. Granted, that's also the warmest part of

Canada and has the longest growing season, but still. English Canada has its nose pressed to the American window, watching what they watch on TV. A Canadian sees or hears cultural references to Canada one time for every hundred references to New York, LA, Chicago or San Francisco. So, cleansed by sweat, his legs moving more than they are still in twenty-four hours, Neil Young's "town in north Ontario" has a hold on him. "All his changes" weren't made in Kingston, not with blood on his sole now and a bed literally under the stars, but enough changes happened there to call it home. And for him to finally want to leave it.

Pat told him he needs to have a conscience, not marry one. Betty has also given him more direction than he thought another person could. And he wants to tell all of this to Stan. More than anything else, he misses Stan's voice. He was inescapably body yet indisputably mind, and they came together in his voice. He wishes they could talk once more, precisely to talk about him being dead. Andrew wants an afterline, not an afterlife.

Tell me what you couldn't, wouldn't. Enumerate your fears. Describe your sins and what took you to them. What should I look out for in life? Here, take a little Scotch.

He wants to hear Stan talk, and then he needs to tell him about Betty. The appetite she has, the need for life undiluted. You can feel the hang of her collarbone from one glance at her jaw. She just floats.

Andrew had followed Mark on trails but Stan in life. He was the first man. The lead man, guiding me with a voice.

Avoiding the numerous highway exits for Montreal, maintaining his spin, he sees past the city's sprawl, sees ahead three hundred kilometres to the Kingston house. Avoiding the city, keen for home, he's impatient to drive a particular kind of flag into his lawn upon his arrival, to claim his own island. He can already see his new flag swaying stiffly in the breeze.

117

Under a Montreal overpass, bike temporarily beside him not beneath him, he sits with the damned in shrunken light. He had watched the rain gather, felt the air dampen and thicken, watched it squeeze the city's light. When the undersides of leaves began flashing regularly, he switched from flight to a fuel-up.

In the concrete sprawl outside a major city he no longer looks like an excommunicated touring cyclist. Finally he's just another guy in dirty, ill-fitting clothes, someone poor or crazy, not able or permitted to drive, another skeletal, grumbling reeker who sets chilled beer onto the counter of a corner store. Transformed from fugitive to trash, sweating in the one Canadian province free of paternalistic liquor laws, he has beer, bread, fresh cheese, yogurt and more cheese at every corner store.

Hunkering down in the fug under an overpass, sitting on the sloped, grimy concrete, he uncorks a strong beer and launches the cork across both lanes of traffic. The first sweet gulp goes down with the cork's burst still ringing the muzzy air. The pictorial label of the large brown bottle depicts a canoe flying through a burning sky. He guzzles the high-alcohol beer, trying to hop into that canoe.

Before a supper lecture from Betty, he had thought a wine bottle of strong, unfiltered beer all the explanation necessary for its name (*Maudite*, the damned) and its image of a flying canoe. Drink this and you too can sky paddle.

"No, no, no," French-immersion Betty had explained, "this is a crucial French-Canadian myth. All the big themes: isolation in a merciless wilderness; humans fighting an inhuman climate for home or profit; hairy men alone in the woods. These guys — all guys — are chopping down wood in the middle of Nowhere, Quebec. This is pre-electricity, pre-Confederation. No light other than the fires of their camps as far as the eye can see, nor woman either. Saw wood in the winter; tend your farm in the summer."

"Tend your wife in the summer."

"And make the annual new mouth to feed. Hence the isolated wood cutting."

"Ugh, get wood, cut wood." He shuddered.

"They cut their trees and make their cash. Christmas approaches, but they won't be getting out. Too much snow. Too much money to be made. Tyrannical boss. Greed and need keep them working in the woods while their wives and kids huddle somewhere under the same sky trying to make the apples last. Whammo, here comes the devil to take bets on a cold night. Hey, fellas, who wants to toss down the axe and head in for a night of soft flesh?"

"Or who wants some titty with their shag for a change?"

"Right. Everybody's game, and that's the clincher. Voila, one wave of the devil's hand and here's a flying canoe. Sometimes the canoe's on fire."

"Soundtrack by Hendrix."

"To keep their souls, they all have to come back, together, before sunrise — one big canoe. They all want sex as individuals, but have to work as a team to get it. The very reason the sky canoe is tempting is that they *don't* want to be with each other. But give in to the need to leave and who's going to return? So they all go down. Individual versus communal want."

Now on his wet concrete perch Andrew eats a lonely meal out of grubby hands. Drinking his beer, he watches car after car pass empty save for the driver, sees the individual match and the collective SUV fire.

In his debates with Betty, when they each temporarily became a bloodhound for hypocrisy, she didn't have to say much to disparage his (inherited) car compared to the Eurorail pass she had bought for herself. Yet he was the cycling advocate.

The Argument of Slavery

"Nearly one-third of North American car trips are for five kilometres or less. Nearly one-third of North Americans are obese. Any connections here?" Andrew ranted. "Slaves used to be skinny, used to be housed; now chemistry has let them go fat and free-range. Get in the car to get cigarettes or chips or pop. Gasoline and nicotine. Gasoline and trans fats. Where's my Prozac? Chemical warfare. Class warfare. You can even get jerseys: *Riding is revolutionary.*"

"You have a car," Betty pointed out.

"Which I don't use to get to work or to do most errands and rarely drive alone."

"Aren't you going to use it to move out east? Won't you be a driver out there?"

"No, I won't. I'll leave it in the garage," he said, surprising each of them. "I'm trying to be part of the solution here."

"By doing the grunt work for your *super*visor? By being a slave?"

Now, under a Montreal overpass, he tips his orange canoe and drinks, already keen to make various appointments in Kingston. He'll give concessions then confessions.

118

In a breakup, you might get officially pushed or pulled away from your partner's family and friends, but friendship and affection don't honour custody agreements. Not only does the ride finally have Andrew thinking affectionately of his mother, he's also been thinking repeatedly of Betty's parents. As he returns to his own house, he thinks of the week when part of the furniture of her childhood home moved into his.

Aside from having to clean ("So, that's dusting?"), Andrew had been keen to finally meet Elaine just before Easter. Elaine was Betty's mom, not his, so he had chores but no worries. Betty, however, dashed around all week, acquiring a suddenly crucial lemon zester, two kinds of German chocolate, Polish vodka and South African white wine. Foolishly, they cooked a joint along with their late afternoon snack, so by six p.m. Andrew suggested she just bring the mirror down to the kitchen rather than going up to check on herself every eleven minutes. They were recuperating in each other's arms when Elaine's knock finally found the door.

Andrew genuinely regretted that his eyes weren't the only thing noticing Betty's mother. Throughout the evening he'd forgive himself a little, reminding the court that her ecru shirt could not possibly have been intended to cover the visible straps of her black bra. Here in the entranceway, shaking a ringed hand, trading cheek kisses as brief as whispers, he could feel all too well how long she was in the leg and spotted a familiar volume in the chest. Damn it.

"So you're the young Bluebeard she doesn't stop talking about." Elaine handed over a tall bottle of chilled wine.

"It's hardly a castle."

"Or a prison, Mom."

"Well, Andrew, let's with the tour. Betty, are you getting us drinks? Hey, bevelled baseboards. Somebody once cared. Were you ever here for these French doors? Don't worry, inside they just take up space.

Oh, thanks, Bet. Cheers. Mm, chilled Gertz, you peach. Was that once a pantry back there? Oh, that inherited lamp, just tear off the old shade and recover the frame with rice paper. Then rice paper blinds here and there. At Toronto's Hoa Viet, they must rip them right out of the prison workers' hands they're so cheap."

"Mother."

"What, Andrew's a big boy. You ever have to sell, Andrew, you'd pay dearly for this little gab. The work, though. However you acquire a house, you sell it on your knees. Scrub. Scrub. Scrub. Oh, a Turkish rug would be perfect here. Just go to Turkey. Shall we go up? New railing. Home Despot really can't be beat on the retrofits. Nice orange there. Skylights would be perfect here. Have you thought of a reno loan? Remember, parents buy houses, not kids. Enlarge this bathroom into that bedroom, pave the thing in the tile and let junior have a smaller room. All right, Betty, but as we walk back down, I want Andrew to picture a deck off the kitchen. Trust me; I've seen it a hundred times. Renovation is the best way to mourn."

"Mom, that is not appropriate."

"Well, Betty, it just happens to be true." Turning to Andrew with a complex smile, she added, "I say death makes us live."

As they sat for dinner — "Stuffed eggplant. I'm probably impressed." — Elaine slipped off to the washroom and Betty dropped her forehead down onto her empty plate.

"I'm so sorry," Betty murmured. "I think it's men. I'm so used to her with other women. I had no idea. Be flattered if you can."

"She's a scream, an absolute scream."

Betty rolled her forehead to one side of the plate to look up at him. "I get fucked after this, right?"

Always.

Wine and conversation flowed. No glass sat empty for long.

"Andrew, do you mind my asking if your father got funnier as he got sicker?"

"Well, it was such a steady — I was really, really young — no, yeah, absolutely. He did. I never realized, but sure."

Flush with wine, Andrew started in on the leg bag story, was just about to get to Stan's astronaut jokes when the ringing phone gave way to a man loudly barking into their answering machine.

"Where's Betty Craig? I got these walls —"

Betty rushed to the phone.

"Hello. Hello. This is Betty. What? No, that's no longer true... No, the nineteenth was once *a* date. Then *the* date became the twenty-sixth... I left a message. Of course messages count. No, that's impossible. Impossible in a variety of ways... I agree. I will have to take them. On the twenty-sixth, no — impossible. Do you think the Better Business Bureau would agree, It's now or the dump? Sounds like we're threatening each other... Your warehouse is not my concern... Not at that price. Do it for two and I'll leave the porch light on... Cash in hand is what it is. Fine — 149 Collingwood."

Betty returned to the dining room, looking at each of them in turn. "Andrew, I'm going to hold you to that *mi casa* speech. Mom, Dad's walls will be here within the hour."

Elaine, Jim and Betty's house of hope, their house of resentment and their house of unwelcome cards had been intended, Elaine always claimed, as a "modular" set of cubes. This "unitization" included built-in, floor-to-ceiling bookcases for the walls of Jim's study, walls he quickly found demanded he sacrifice a view or fresh air for excessive storage space. Redoing the house at fifty, he now wanted windows and agreed to let Betty sell off the wall units.

"I couldn't have heard you correctly," Elaine told Betty.

"The storage walls. You know he's demolishing. I've been selling off the pieces for very good money. These walls are sending me to Europe. Would you rather they go to the dump?"

Andrew checked for frost on Elaine's collar. "Maybe I'll step out and think about that deck," he proposed.

"Stay there, Andrew. I'd never want to be accused of driving a man out of his own home."

"Mom, don't."

"Wouldn't want you to feel caged within your own walls, Andrew."

"It's just wood, Mom, saleable wood."

"Selling crack would also get you to Europe."

"You started a career with his fear of commitment. Why can't I do the same with his mid-life crisis?"

Andrew could see that one sink into Elaine's face. A long moment inflated before she turned away from Betty to face him.

"Andrew, thank you for the lovely meal. The favour is gladly returned."

Round Two — "Are you sure you're all right to drive?" — was dislodged
by the noisy arrival of the mover.

"Your fella there's going to have to give me a hand."

Andrew implored Elaine to stay, offering coffee or a walk while
changing his shoes en route to the door. By the time he was backing
up the porch steps with the first terrifyingly heavy wall-case, both
hands lost entirely to the weight, Elaine had started her car. Andrew
nodded his farewell just like Stan used to, dipping one eyebrow as if
stamping the air.

119

Rolling back into Ontario, he's ready to shed his stolen clothes. Tonight the sky's mixing bowl spoons out heat — damp, inescapable heat. Free from kaffiyeh and cape for nearly two days, he has also clocked nearly sixty kilometres tonight with the sweatshirt tied superfluously to the pannier rack. Finally, he is warm on his own pushed heat again.

As the countdown to Gananoque and Brockville lessens, he becomes certain he'll never need the sweatshirt again. A fungal pretzel, the filthy sweatshirt has drawn moisture in both directions, absorbing his sweat from one dark side and sucking humidity from the air with the other.

Just untie the knot. Let it slip into the night. Don't even look back. Given the rubber flak and the flung sacks of fast-food litter, what's one rag? Cotton, even. If he rolled back into the woods and left it beneath a tree, wouldn't some creature use it for a nest? No, this reek is pure human.

Neither justice nor paranoia prevents him from dropping the sweatshirt in a garbage bin at the next road stop. Utility, if not sentiment, endears him to the damp rag. If nothing else, it is a good pillow, an auxiliary bandage. And, should he have occasion to, it'd be something to show Betty, a tangible relic for his story. Look at it, try it on. It was tight to my chest. See where I cut the sleeves off? He'll have to wash it. Maybe he'll just keep it for a rag, not sacrament. He'll soon have plenty of painting to do.

Maybe she'll understand. Let her pull the sweatshirt over her head. Take her out riding and show her the hatred you have to inhale on the side of the road, how you see what a bully does with opportunity. Betty, I wore this for five days straight to get back to you.

Andrew, she would say, you never had to leave me.

120

My father fell. My father has died. My father is dead.

He had to first think the words and then consent to say them into the plastic rectangle of a telephone, then practise saying them, then press numbers and say them aloud. All with Stan's bloody body beside him in the hallway. He still doesn't know if he kneeled down to check Stan's vital signs or fell down. This sequence of memory is a slide show, not a movie. Rushing through the door. All the blood on the carpet. Then Andrew was at Stan's head, trying rudimentary first aid when Stan was so clearly beyond final aid. Neither his nose, nor mouth, nor his trache tube released air because of the pulpy dent in his head. Bald men can't hide a head wound. The finality of that wound was accepted just as the skin of Andrew's legs, already damp with sweat from riding, began to feel the wetness of Stan's blood seeping through his tights. He did not seem to stand up but was nonetheless running for the bathroom, puking and crying and puking.

When Betty finally heard Andrew describe this, she immediately understood why he then got blood all over the telephone. "You didn't wash your hands in the washroom after you were sick because, subconsciously, you knew that would have put you in front of the mirror."

Alone with Stan's body, Andrew had simply found himself on the phone, rational enough to try rehearsing his phrases first — *My father fell. My father has died. My father is dead.* — but not rational enough to understand that the blood on the telephone receiver had come off his hands. Maybe the paramedics would need to see this.

Pat would want to know, deserve to know, no matter the late hour. He could have called Larry, thought of calling Mark. No, no more phone calls, not yet. "Don't move the body," the emergency dispatcher had told him, unnecessarily.

He wouldn't move Stan's body, but he couldn't keep his still. What, should he have walked up the stairs? Had a shower while his father lay dead? Should he have watched TV while he waited for the ambulance? He had stepped back out the door, wanting fresh air. His bike still lay on the step where he had dropped it. He picked it up. He moved away from the doorway and Stan's body beyond it. He didn't lock the door. One leg climbed onto the bike. His cleats bit into the pedals. The crank arms still went around. He biked up and down the street, just like he'd done as a seven-year-old.

By the time the police arrived, he was rational enough to recognize they weren't using their sirens. When he rode up to the house and dismounted, the cruiser's window showed him he was still wearing his helmet. He took it off as he ushered two police officers inside. One tried to sit him down and ask him whom he could call, who might come over, to whom could he go?

In the morning, the phone started ringing. The funeral process felt like socially imposed denial. The errands, the paperwork and the shopping of death would keep him distracted. Pat had tried to catch him with one of these supposedly necessary questions before driving to see him.

"Did he ever talk to you about funeral arrangements or discuss what he wanted done with his body?"

No. Stan and Andrew had talked about oral sex, poor voter turnout in Canada, programmable thermostats, a bowel movement of Stan's that made him feel like he'd been splitting wood for an hour, mortgage paydowns versus RRSP contributions, seventeenth-century English poetry, short-suiting yourself on the deal in euchre, Churchill, engine braking, Tolkien and trench war, knee socks versus thigh-highs, trigonometry, the siege of Leningrad, curry, snow tires, chop saws and mitre boxes, Trudeau, Faulkner versus Hemingway and John versus Paul, customer service, desirable and undesirable assignments in the Second World War, how to shave up, Macbeth and Hamlet as opposites, loss and fear, Enigma machines, *connaître* and *savoir*, Switzerland, *The Waste Land*, nuclear winters, global warming, *The Black Stallion*, the importance of a woman's jaw, charcoal versus propane, Russian oligarchies, marine locks, pancreatic cancer, Louis Riel, affirmative action, asparagus and urine, CSIS, brown dress shoes, *Godfather I* versus *II*, plaster walls, Sir Wilfred Thesiger, gun control, the Arctic, fuel injection, atheism, Genghis Khan, porridge, Khrushchev's shoe,

Newfoundland, pulling the goalie, a deaf Beethoven weeping at the premiere of his *Ninth Symphony*, Interpol, Catherine Zeta-Jones, cherry tomatoes, early Jaguars, *Lucky Jim*, Modigliani not getting the tits right, bullfighting, Turgenev, seamless eavestroughing, poached eggs, Stan Rogers, how to use white bread when plumbing, Castro, seppuku, border collies, Boswell and Johnson, Israel, wool, the Euro, caribou, AIDS, Ella Fitzgerald in the day and Billie Holiday at night, the Halifax explosion, *The Lord of the Flies,* Bosnia, frozen yogurt, the marathon, Gretzky, the Pope, overpopulation, field goals versus running it in, Hitchcock, whether Kristin Scott Thomas really eroticizes intelligence, Paris, the full Windsor knot, provincial school exams, the burning of the White House, tipping, Salman Rushdie, fog, how to use your cheeks when smoking a cigar, hot-air balloons, *Cue for Treason,* zebra mussels, Pelé and speeding. But they'd never once talked about how Andrew should deal with Stan's death.

"Did he ever talk to you about funeral arrangements or discuss what he wanted done with his body?" Pat repeated.

"Not exactly, no."

But apparently he had talked to someone. Not twenty minutes after he was off the phone with Pat, a very polite and efficient member of the university's anatomy lab and museum called and addressed Andrew by name. He, too, wondered if Andrew knew of any plans for Stan's body.

"Is there a time we could meet? I see you're very close to campus. I'd be happy to walk over."

Typical of their ages and generations, Andrew had been more environmentally conscious than his father. He'd steered them away from fast food with equal arguments about health and waste. Stan had taken out the household trash for decades of his life, so he still thought of that job as something he should at least manage, if not do. Yet their recycling blue box came to the house long after Stan was still actually making trips to the curb. Andrew, not his dad, had clipped out the magazine article which showed that in the long run synthetic oil was cheaper, cleaner and better for the family car. But then in death, Stan had himself completely recycled. His kidneys and liver weren't affected by spinal disease, so out they went. Naturally, his bones were the big prize.

Unlike the funeral home staff, who used euphemisms one minute and invented new fees the next, the anatomy lab representative was honest, gratefully honest. "Andrew, we appreciate any offer of donation. But your dad came to us because he knew he was unique. Ours is the largest human anatomy museum in the country. I'm sure you already know how rare your father's condition is. His will be the first preserved syringomyelic skeleton in Canada."

"Where do I sign?" Andrew asked the lab rep, more himself than he'd been since he biked home the night before. This first string that Stan pulled from beyond the grave helped immediately.

"You don't. He already did."

The representative reached out to shake Andrew's hand.

121

The bike trip home was conceived in part as an antidote to school, however belated. He'd gone off to UNS thinking of the references he'd heard or read of September blues, that autumnal regret at not being back in school learning again, turning pages as the leaves fall. When he actually got to UNS, though, another consecutive degree felt more like homework than personal growth. Yes, he was learning; yes, he was challenged. The pace of the MA was harder, but in ways it was just more of the same. Biking, biking home, that would be the opposite of life in a library carrel.

Now here he is pulling another all-nighter to make a Kingston deadline. The deadline is his own, absolutely. Why sleep on the ground when he has a house seventy kilometres in the distance? Still, he's aware of how often he has pushed himself late into the night past mental and physical acuity with the Grant Hall clock tower pointing into the nearby night sky or Lake Ontario gurgling in the darkness.

Now that he has taken to sleeping in the open air, he's even more likely to sleep anywhere than he was when he still had a tent. After twenty more kilometres, this hyper-mobility of sleep begins to threaten his resolve to make it home tonight. Turning onto the lakeshore-hugging Thousand Islands Parkway renews his energy for another fifteen kilometres, though the road isn't called a parkway by chance. Mini parks hang off one roadside or the other, sometimes both. He could be asleep on a soft lawn in minutes. His new plan for the house can wait a few more hours. It's two in the morning. You'd really only be taking a nap. The sunlight will wake you up early.

A thousand kilometres behind him, before the cigarette mustang, before Rivière-du-Loup, when he had briefly chased the other touring cyclist, he'd stopped because he didn't want to be reduced to just racing. He had wanted more options than *leader* and *led*. That early trip, a ride but not a hunt, is barely memorable. Where was Nova Scotia?

Now he's finally sick of the limited role he has here as well. He hasn't changed his clothes in days. Yesterday he ate four submarine sandwiches. Life is either on the bike or waiting to get back on the bike. He needs a bath.

Because he is overtired and has biked into a nutritional red zone of low fuel and high energy expenditure, he's convinced that riding has become a state of fear. Originally, he biked and looked, rolled and saw. For the last three provinces, he's been checking his mirror constantly. His shoulders have been hunched for 850 kilometres.

He doesn't stop. Only home will get him off the bike.

122

Death makes you reconsider the telephone. As if extremely high or newly arrived from Mars, you marvel at the compact plastic rectangle in your hand. You press numbers, string a simple code, then slide into someone's mind. Later that same day, your past will begin calling you up, friends, relations, obligations. For the end of so much that you know, Press 1.

With Stan alive, the phone had been a palpable lifeline. There just in case, an ambulance just three digits away. Only in his year with Betty did the phone become something he learned to avoid. Let the machine get it. I prefer the company I have to the company which might be calling.

With Stan dead and the house suddenly empty, the phone brought him back to the world. Somewhere in the line of police, coroner, morgue, anatomy lab and funeral home, there had been a news leak. Neighbours told friends. Ex-colleagues told friends. Nurses told physiotherapists.

Just a few months later, living with Betty, he'd look back to answering those condolence calls of August as the last childish thing he did. Polite. Obedient. Trained. Thank you for your call. Thank you for your call. This is really happening. Finally, late in day two, he began doing more than just returning calls and used the phone for more than just making appointments or requesting forms. He reached Paul Tucker at his home in Ottawa.

"Paul, it's Andrew."

"Well, how are you, Andrew?" Paul asked. They had once shared those first dives of the morning, the lake as smooth as glass. The spill of mist.

"Breathing, apparently. I wonder if you'd like to do Dad's eulogy."

"I'm honoured. Of course I'll do it. This is big of you."

"Yeah, well, hatred is a burden," Andrew replied.

He turned the ringer off for the next two hours while he ripped up the stained entranceway carpet.

123

Just a year later, Betty and Andrew knew she was flying to Paris at the end of August, and he to Halifax a few days later, knew this rationally and financially, mentioned it at least once a week. But only after the start of August did it start to become physical: the anticipatory aches, a house they would miss, sex elegiac or admittedly exploitive. And her (reconciled) mother calling all the time.

"Now she couldn't be happier," Betty described. "She wants to meet me somewhere. Florence probably. What do you think?"

"A nice hotel in an expensive city. Warm food. I'd say do it despite a parent."

"I mean you too, asshole. You won't have bike school over Christmas."

"Probably not and I'll probably come. But I may need to do a little research jaunt at Christmas."

"I forgot. Riding in Utah is research."

"I'll probably come. I'd also like to drive you to the airport."

The night before her flight they did try to sleep before the four a.m. drive to Toronto, but where was sleep in laughter and tears, in your body and mine? Rosy-fingered dawn found them in the thick of the 401. They had lanes to watch, terminals to check.

Security regulations would have demanded her freshly purchased Swiss Army knife travel in checked baggage, not carry-on. Because Paris was the destination least likely to require screwdriver or knife blade, he knew as her bag was hoisted onto the check-in conveyor belt that she could be days before discovering he had switched her knife for a nearly identical one. When she had showered that last morning, he had unpacked her knife, wrapped its replacement in a paper note *(For cheese and bastards)*, then zipped her pack. A week earlier he'd had a shorter note engraved on the handle: *Again*. See *Again* every day you travel.

At the security check, he sewed this same word into each kiss. "I'll see you again, I will. Again. Again. Again."

Her speech wasn't much longer. Crying a little she pulled back, looked him in the eye and said, "Get it together." As she turned, her shoulders were starting to shake, but she marched them down a bright corridor into a crowded lineup without glancing back.

124

Even by car, let alone bike, the westward approach to Kingston is anticlimactic. A discrepancy between legal and actual borders significantly distorts the posted distance from empty highway into actual city. In its last zoning land grab, Kingston doubled or tripled its circumference, so the well-lit *Welcome to Kingston* signs only welcome you to more wooded highway. So known are these false claims of distance that he refuses to become excited. He keeps the necessary slog going with guarded skepticism for so long that his private landmarks finally catch him in near disbelief. Here was a parking-lot pee with Stan. Here the turnaround point on his one bike ride with Betty. Finally, the city's spill of light grows closer and closer. Then there are the familiar exits announcing the city's prisons, colleges and the military base. Home. Halfway home.

As the prison capital of Canada, Kingston has a density of halfway houses for the recently paroled that is disproportionate to its population. Re-immersion into society is there buffered with a few programs and rules, similar company and cheap living. An observable and proximate concentration of temptations (young flesh, house after house with inadequate protection and portable electronics, walking distance to rivers of alcohol) and absentee landlords unconcerned with neighbourhoods have placed several of these halfway houses in the city's student ghetto. *Halfway house.* Returning, Andrew is caught again by this phrase. *Halfway house.* Twelve kilometres away and he's still only halfway home.

125

We are each alone at funerals. Andrew's friends were there, the older ones slightly less awkward. More recent friends from campus hadn't even met Stan. Not yet knowing the death of parents (those ambassadors of death), these friends and classmates generally reverted into well-dressed silence. All fine by Andrew. Huddling with them he was spared too many *okays*. Are you okay? Is everything okay? Heather, an ex-girlfriend eclipsed by just a few years, was lovely and bright. Until meeting Betty, Andrew didn't yet know that he would have preferred a girl who called him on the extended length of his hug, who resisted his cheap press into her breasts. Mark was lithe and fit even in a suit.

Hushed drapes swallowed all the low funeral sounds. Just as Andrew realized where his internal voice was going — *Who's the chrome dome beside Dave Westfall? Do you need to go now before it starts?* — he saw Paul's calm briefly break. In seconds, his middle-aged face ran through the gamut of grief: disbelief, pleading, anger, then fear. Looking away, looking anywhere, Andrew met the prompting nod of the funeral director.

With quiet voices and light fingers, the staff directed Andrew and the efficient Pat into a side chamber. With friends nearby but now only half-visible, Andrew could partially feel Stan's legs inside the suit pants he was now wearing. In the past few years he had fully grown into the suits Stan himself would have now been swimming in. Perhaps there was a little vanity, not just altruism, in Stan's decision to leave his body to the anatomy museum. This way, his body wasn't tucked inelegantly into one of his old suits. The knee that started bobbing in the charcoal trousers wasn't sharply pointy like Stan's, yet in the jacket his shoulders filled out a worn stretch in the fabric. Even the suit had a memory.

A minister began to speak.

126

"Good afternoon, everyone," Paul Tucker began his eulogy. "We're here to honour and mourn our friend, Stan Day. To do so at all fairly, I'll need to be funny *and* incisive. Can everyone else hear him? Okay, Paul, he's saying, make it good. I'm honoured that Andrew has asked me to speak of Stan and hope that I can rise to the challenge.

"Stan was one of the funniest, most charming people I have ever met. Once at a steak dinner, which ended a conference we were at together, I witnessed Stan win over an entire table of strangers in ten seconds. 'Which one of you heartless bastards is going to cut this for me?' was his request for help, and we were powerless to refuse.

"Standing here, I know Stan wouldn't let me off by just saying he was funny. Dig deeper, he'd say, keep going. All right, his humour was the intersection of his intelligence and his generosity. We could never forget the mind lurking beneath that body. Here was a man never without a book, the friend who would call your answering machine to recommend novels, who would lend you his and never ask for them back, though don't for a second think he didn't know where each one was.

"It is both fitting and — I'm sure he knows — unfair that I begin today by speaking of challenge when challenge was so fundamental to every one of our thoughts about Stan. More on this later. Back to the laughs for now.

"I'm not quite sure, but I think Stan got funnier as he got — what do I say here? — more ill? That's not quite right. He'd been without pain for decades. His mind never had a cloudy day. I don't need to search for a word to describe his sense of humour; I just have to admit to one. (Stan chose to call a spade a spade, and I can't send him off with anything less than that kind of honesty.) Stan became funnier as he became more *dependent*. He wasn't desperately funny, although he certainly had his share of gallows humour. Nor was his the scheming humour of an aging or ailing man trying to salvage waning attention.

Stan was funny for two very Stanlike reasons: he was generous, and he was demanding. He'd make you laugh, even if you were a stranger, even at the expense of his own vanity, but he also didn't hide the fact that he'd appreciate the favour returned.

"Many of us here have had some experience with prison life. Everyone who's been inside a prison knows something that in polite life we often forget: our bodies make statements. The body language in prison may not be nice, but it's usually clear. Someone else in Stan's body might have walked around with a posture or a face that asked for help or scowled in bitterness. Not Stan. When he needed your help, he asked for it. The statement his body made was much more · demanding than *Help me. Amuse me*, his look liked to say.

"And, of course, he didn't just talk with his body. I'm not the only teacher or former teacher in the room. In honour of Stan, I'll share a trade secret. At workshops and conferences you'll see that many otherwise strict teachers suddenly become bad students: fidgety, disruptive and talkative. I once saw Stan interrupted repeatedly while he was trying to lead a workshop. He silenced his heckler with one choice word. 'You can be lippy on your time,' he told a guy half his age, 'not mine.' *Lippy*. What a word.

"Stan was usually too courteous to be lippy himself, but several of his comments have stuck with me over the years (and by years I mean decades). When we were undergraduates, Stan sought me out one day to tell me he had invented a Latin motto for himself. (Forgive us: we had beards; we smoked pipes.) *Tene nil*, he told me proudly, *Hold nothing*. We now know that all of this bravery was to be required.

"One more story. Just before he turned thirty, when his body showed a little, but not much, of the path it would take, he came knocking on my door late one night. His parents had died while he was still young, and he had carefully saved his inheritance, at least until that night. He knocked on my door saying, 'I've bet their wad, gambled it all.' He wouldn't explain, just hustled me into the car. Soon enough we were holding bottles of beer on the front lawn of what he already referred to as 'our house.' His speech was brief and totally unforgettable. 'I've never missed them so much,' he said of his parents, 'and yet the second most adult emotion I have ever felt is the recognition that I wouldn't be who I am without having lost them, lost them when I did. To want them back is to not want me.' There was Stan: 'second most adult emotion.' *Second-most.* I played my scripted part. 'And the first?' I asked. 'Fear of failure,' he replied. 'I didn't buy the house; we did. Pat and I. I proposed to her right here. Gambled it all. She said yes.'

"I hope everyone agrees that all of Stan is in that speech. It is my honour today to chart that gamble. No, it did not run as he planned, not as he then would have hoped. But I also know from my countless conversations with him that he would not have changed his fate for anything. He paid heavily for his satisfactions, but never unnecessarily. I am absolutely certain, certain because of the shine he could not keep from eye or voice, from a visible relaxation I saw enter that body we all snuck our worried glances at, that life had no joy greater, more sustained or more complete for him than the son we all admire.

"Andrew, your father had one word for you, one word that he used above all others, and certainly the one he used most naturally, most affectionately, and, I'll concur, the most accurately. Quite simply he called you his prince. How multiply right he was. Is.

"We all know that this father of a prince did not have an easy reign as king. Stan knew we want to be challenged in life, knew this and taught it. We want to be challenged and we think we'd like to be able to choose our challenges. And yet, as Stan knew, we must also be ready for those challenges forced upon us.

"In closing, I'll go back to that old brick house on Collingwood Street once more. I was there when the population of the house decreased. I finally knew that Stan had righted himself in a new life, had begun to meet a challenge he did not seek, when he took a little of Shakespeare's Richard the Second along with a glass of my Scotch. This, too, I shall never forget him saying: 'You may my kingdom and my state depose, / but not my grieves, still am I, king of those.' Although his kingdom would shrink and wane, he remained its king, never its prisoner."

127

He has been biking alongside the St. Lawrence River all night, more and more tempted to swim with every kilometre. When he lived in Kingston, he wouldn't have thought of swimming in the industrialized St. Lawrence or the lake it blossoms into. Bilge water. Pollution from both Kingston and across the water in upstate New York. Plus the usual cow shit E. coli. Unlike their parents, Andrew and Betty each grew up beside water they shouldn't have swum in. Not, at least, until this morning. After this trip, what's a little rumoured pollution?

With dawn breaking he's able to see the surface of the water, and even into a little of its depth, as he stands on the shoreline. Before undressing out in the open once again, before he has time to do anything else at the riverside, he reaches out with his right shoe and gently sets just the sole of it into the water. Twisting his ankle just a little, using the exact same movement that clips him in and out of his pedals, he rinses his Achilles cleat.

After his last week, the water isn't even that cold. He dives under to better scrub his limbs and the battlefield of his crotch. Floating on his back, he watches the sunrise spill into a familiar sky. His hair still feels dirty despite being wet.

Back on shore, dressed and chilly, he finds the bike a touch too heavy when he picks it up. The half-novel, part writing paper, part bandage, is lashed to his rear rack with a single skinny bungee cord. He frees the novel then mounts the bike. With his left foot clipped in and ready to go and his right resting briefly beneath him, he flings the damaged book out into the river. He knows how it will end.

128

Paul's closing words were not the final words of the funeral. When Andrew had invited Paul to deliver the eulogy, he neither anticipated nor disliked Paul's suggestion to "open comments up to the floor." Standing at the lectern, kings and princes freshly praised, Paul switched gears.

"And the man loved a chat," he said in closing. "The family has invited me to invite any of you to share your thoughts here today."

Pat did not go first. The first guest to rise was a short mustachioed man in an acrylic sweater whose darting eyes and column of visible tension running up his body gave him a weaselly appearance his speech would quickly belie.

"I'm Joe Buj. Stan Day taught me to read, as an adult, so you can probably guess where. I could stop right there. Stan Day taught me to read. That says enough, doesn't it? He changed my life. Or, as he kept insisting, he showed me how I could change my own life. But like this other guy here," Mr. Buj nodded his head at Paul, "I want to let Stan speak for himself. Most guys in prison are in prison their whole lives. Prisons here and here," he said, tapping temple then heart, "in prison by the time they're six years old, put in prison by fathers whose fathers put them in prison. I had a lot of walls around me. I didn't go to this man and ask him to teach me to read. He came to me. More than once. And I wasn't exactly church polite. I had a hunch his third offer would be his last. I understand impatience.

"Inside, with the teachers, you meet in rooms, never cells, and almost always in groups. He paid me the courtesy of dropping his voice for his final offer, but he kept his eyes on mine. He was standing, you know —" Joe Buj stretched out one hand to demonstrate Stan's crooked spine. "He looked me in the eye and said, 'How do you think I get out of here?' He shrugged those shoulders best he could.

"Thanks to Stan Day, I read every day now. I read every word I see."

After the funeral and its various speeches, as Andrew circulated among food offers from older women and fiercely strong handshakes from aging men, Joe Buj had just two private words for him. "Be careful," he said, jutting his chin.

129

Fittingly, mercifully, he gets to roll downhill into Kingston. More than anything else, the hill running from Fort Henry and Canadian Forces Base Kingston down to the La Salle Causeway welcomes him home. This is the hill he climbed a thousand times to start a trail ride. He made his legs and lungs climbing up what he's now screaming down. In the early morning light, as the Cataraqui River meets Lake Ontario, he can smell the fresh water of home. After nearly nine months of the salty tang of the Atlantic Ocean, the very air munching and corroding everything it can reach, fresh water seems so friendly.

Near the bottom of the hill, Royal Military College sits tucked on some of the best waterfront real estate in the country. From the outside, the national kill school looks like a yacht club decorated with cannons. Once again, Andrew's hunched back and buzzing bike roll on past the school's Memorial Arch. Over the years he has heard various rumours about RMC. Only cadets who volunteer for drug tests are allowed to leave the base out of uniform. Supposedly the torpedo monument on campus points in the direction of the shortest path to the United States. More lasting enmity has a sword-shaped weather vane atop one building pointed in the direction of Chown Hall, a female residence at Queen's. More probable are the drill stories about the Memorial Arch Andrew now rolls past. Apparently, incoming students are marched through that arch on arrival and then forbidden to do so again until they are paraded through at graduation.

The short metal causeway at the bottom of the hill feels like Andrew's own private Memorial Arch. Forts and trails fade behind him. Betty isn't here for his graduation parade, but he'll send her photos.

Past RMC, the Wolfe Island ferry awakens to its day.

130

At the funeral, when Pat rose to speak after Joe Buj, Andrew was flooded with relief. And trust, confident trust. However sad his parents' divorce was, it wasn't one of those theatrically vicious divorces in which any public microphone, even one at a funeral, was a chance to parade grievances and insults. More than just relieved, Andrew was keen to hear Pat. Yes, Mother, tell us what you can.

Her clothes were crisp and she kept her chin high. Gordon stared at her casually, but she didn't fixate on him or on Andrew.

"You two are hard acts to follow, but I guess we're all following a hard act. I'll be brief, and I too will let the man speak for himself.

"Falling in love and staying in love are two different" — she nodded at Paul — "*challenges*. In that ledger, Stan and I broke even. Fall, I once did, though, and he really got me with a book. When I agreed to marry Stan, he gave me an obligatory ring and understood when I returned it for something more to my liking. He always played to his limits. No, his real engagement gift was a new novel, Mordecai Richler's *St. Urbain's Horseman*. His inscription included the bravest statement I had ever seen: Test everything, especially my courage.

"Sadly, we did test everything, tested more than we knew we had, good and bad. I'm confident Stan grew to see that such is life.

"I relinquished his affection, but retained, I hope, some of his respect. Many of you in this room have felt that respect and know that we are rarely so flattered. Now we must shift our respect into memory. Memory, emotional memory, *is* respect. And Stan Day will always have mine."

131

Biking onto his Kingston street, the world is not too much with him. If he had thought at all practically of his return to the Kingston house, if he had not concentrated on the romantic living room of memory but rather on the stained and empty living room of fact — with its tenant's pizza boxes, torn paper and dead pens — he would have remembered sooner that the house is without electricity. He cancelled his contract with the power company before renting out the house and by now has long forgotten his original plan to re-establish service via email during a few urban days in Quebec City. All the distance he has covered compacts down into the single inch of travel in a disconnected light switch he now flicks up and down uselessly. Standing in the front hallway, flicking the idle switch, he snorts out of laughter for a change, not exertion.

Paper napkins and newspapers are strewn across the ground floor. Save for a three-legged chair abandoned in one corner, the bike instantly becomes the only furniture on the entire ground floor. Stale air hangs thickly in every room. In the kitchen, several cupboard doors yawn open. Only cold water runs. Upstairs, loose paper litters a palpably dirty floor. His shower curtain appears to have left with the tenants. Last August when he did a naive arithmetic in which the rent he would charge for this house significantly exceeded that of his Nova Scotia apartment, he had foolishly ignored how little he knew of his tenants. More than once, Betty had told Andrew Elaine's line that *love* means *need to live with*. Kicking aside what appear to be calculus notes, he agrees with this definition of love and would like to amend it by saying that to really know a person, you need to live with him or her. He didn't really know the students to whom he rented the house, so he'll now pay for it with days of cleaning.

In the bathroom, crumpled tissues litter one corner of the floor. A skin of grey scum is stretched across the bottom of the tub. As he wanders through the house opening windows and stirring up dust, he sees that several of the rooms he and Betty had painted already need to be redone. Numerous pockmarks and scrapes on the walls look like his tenants had attached spikes to all their furniture before moving out. In the second-storey stairwell, he recognizes a large black smear on the wall as the mark of a bike tire. Some dude felt he needed to store a bike up in his third-floor bedroom. What use was it in there?

He has never been so forgetful as to think he was biking home to a proper bed. From the packed third-floor room he had converted into a storage space, he's able to extract Betty's yoga mat and one sofa pillow from the dense cube of boxes, furniture and loose books. He heads to his old, old bedroom, its orange paint now scuffed, to stretch out and hope for sleep. Even the floor smells unclean.

At least the absence of furniture will make his cleaning and re-painting much faster. By the evening of his first day back, he once again wears sleeves of plaster dust and freckles of fresh paint.

His electricity gets restored on his second afternoon. Resumption of phone service isn't so quick, so he has to bike to a phone booth to call Pat. Already, the sound of her phone ringing is just the sound of her phone ringing, not a chime of relief. He's no longer phoning in the middle of the night, so he gets her answering machine, not her.

"Mom. I made it home. Big news. Give me a call tomorrow or the next day."

Once again he works from early each morning to past midnight each night trying to improve the look of the house. This time, the work is for a very different type of guest.

132

On her second last morning in Paris, Betty washes a thin shirt, reliable panties and worn socks in the dull sink of her dingy hostel room. She tries not to look at how the sink's once-white enamel has become porous with grime.

The hostel room came with Internet time she has purposefully saved until this morning. Descending dark stairs to check her email in what was once a broom closet, logging in to remind her mother for the fifth time when to pick her up, she sees a message from Andrew without quite admitting that glancing for his name in her inbox is still a kind of binary, Andrew or no-Andrew. The subject line is "tene nil" and there's an image attached.

The top of the email is one row of a picture she spends nearly two minutes watching arrive. A row of sky meets a roof. Eventually, the front of his house becomes recognizable brick by brick. Yes, okay, I haven't forgotten it. Finally, a new yellow-peaked something stands on the front lawn beside his smiling head. Peaked wood? Great, please send me more renovation pix of your house. Some kind of post. Boy is he smiling. And skinny. A yellow post. And holy fuck tanned. The yellow post holds a wooden For Sale sign that flies off its hinges, off the screen and straight into her. Anything he has typed must be below the image of him smiling beside a For Sale sign on his front lawn. The image arrives row by row like a horizontal, clothed striptease. Brick, body, For Sale sign. Brick, body, For Sale sign. For Sale, For Sale. What legs. The image ends at his bare feet on the tiny lawn, tan lines as stark as socks.

Healing is the admission price we pay for love, she had once written him. Beneath the bottom of the image, beneath his pale feet, he has written *Admission price paid* as if he were standing on it.

Acknowledgements

Some chapters have appeared in slightly different form in the following journals: *The Fiddlehead, Zygote* and *The Windsor Review.*

The installation described on p. 145 is by Jeff Koons.

The author acknowledges the financial support of the New Brunswick Department of Wellness, Culture and Sport.